Ex-Girlfriends United

Ex-Girlfriends United

MATT DUNN

LARGE PRINT
Oxford

First published in Great Britain 2008
by
Pocket Books
An imprint of Simon & Schuster UK Ltd.

01/16

Published in Large Print 2009 by ISIS Publishing Ltd.,
7 Centremead, Osney Mead, Oxford OX2 0ES
by arrangement with
Simon & Schuster UK Ltd.

British Library Cataloguing in Publication Data
Dunn, Matt, 1966–
    Ex-girlfriends united
    1. Single men - - Fiction.
    2. Dating (Social customs) - - Fiction.
    3. Large type books.
    I. Title
    823.9'2–dc22

        ISBN 978–0–7531–8414–1 (hb)
        ISBN 978–0–7531–8415–8 (pb)

1/16

Printed and bound in Great Britain by
T. J. International Ltd., Padstow, Cornwall

For Tony Heywood.
Thanks!

Acknowledgements

Thanks, again, to Patrick Walsh and the team at Conville & Walsh. To Kate Lyall Grant, Emma Harrow, and everyone at Simon & Schuster. To my parents, and Tina, for your continuing love and support. To Tony, Loz, Chris, and Stewart, without whom these books would be half as long. And of course, to the Board. You rule.

CHAPTER
ONE

When Dan rings on the doorbell, my first thought as I buzz him in is that my video entry-phone picture needs adjusting, because he's as white as a sheet, which for someone who spends as long on the sunbed at Tan-Fastic on the high street as Dan does is rather worrying. He's my best friend, and something of a minor celebrity here in Brighton, thanks mainly to *Where There's a Will*, the daytime antiques programme he presents on the TV.

"What's up with you?" I say, as he slams the door shut behind him. "Crowd of girls after more than an autograph chasing you down the street?" Unlike most normal people, success didn't go to Dan's head, but to his groin — something he's been only too happy to exploit occasionally. In fact, he woke up the day after he first appeared on television and thought "fuck me, I'm famous" — and then decided to adopt that as his mission statement.

"Chance would be a fine thing." Dan pushes past me, and walks into the front room, where I've been shredding some old bank statements from when Jane and I were together. "What on earth are you doing?"

"Shredding. You can't be too careful nowadays, what with this 'identity theft' lark."

"There are people that desperate?" Dan looks at me pityingly. "Anyone who steals your identity should be made to keep it. That'd teach them."

"Nice to see you too, Dan. And to what do I owe this 'pleasure'?"

"I need a drink."

"And the off-licence was shut, was it? Or did the guy behind the counter catch you flirting with his wife? Again."

Dan ignores me, walks into my kitchen, and heads straight for the fridge. "You seem to be out of beer," he says, poking around in the vegetable drawer at the bottom, which, and evidently to Dan's surprise, actually contains some vegetables.

"I don't drink beer any more. Remember?" I pat my stomach, which according to him, used to be on Wikipedia under the definition of "beer belly".

Dan shakes his head. "What's happened to you, Ed? It's not so long ago that you used to think a Terry's Chocolate Orange counted as one of your five portions of fruit and veg a day, and now . . ."

"There's some organic grape juice, if you'd like. Or I think we've got a bottle of sherry left over from last Christmas somewhere, if you'd prefer."

"Sherry?" Dan makes a face. "Do I look like an old woman to you?"

Normally, my answer to that question would be "yes", but given his apparent mood this evening, if I say

2

that, he might just burst into tears, or punch me in the face. Or both.

Dan walks through into the front room, where he collapses on the sofa and stares blankly at the television, so I bring the carton in from the kitchen and pour us both a glass of juice. But when he downs his in one, helps himself to a refill, and does the same again without saying a word, I start to get a little concerned.

"What's up?" I say, perching on the edge of the chair opposite.

Dan picks up the remote control and starts to flick uninterestedly through the channels. "Sam's not here, is she?"

Sam is my girlfriend. She's a personal trainer, and often works in the evening.

"Nope. She's got a late client. That's late as in after work, and not late as in dead, I mean."

Dan grins mirthlessly. "I wouldn't be too sure, remembering how knackered you used to look when she first started putting you through your paces."

"As a client, you mean?"

"Nope. As a boyfriend."

"Very funny, Dan. You were saying?"

"Oh, right." Dan sits up, and shifts uncomfortably in his seat, before picking the carton up again and emptying the remainder of the contents into his glass. "It's just that I, er . . . Are you sure you haven't got anything stronger?"

I nod towards his grape juice. "We could put some yeast in that."

Dan frowns. "Some *yeast*?"

"Yup. And some sugar. And then, if we wait for it to ferment . . ."

"Ha bloody ha, Edward."

"And anyway." I nod towards the television, where Dan seems to have settled on some episode of *The Bill*, which as far as I can make out, seems to be full of ex-*EastEnders* actors (I wonder whether they see that as a step up or a step down). "Stop trying to avoid the issue."

"Sorry." Dan clicks the TV off, then puts his glass back down on the coffee table, and stares at it for a few seconds. "I just, er, I mean, well . . ."

"What?"

He folds his arms. "You're going to make me say it, aren't you?"

"Well, that's normally how people find out something from someone else. Unless you'd like me to fetch you a pen and paper, so you can write it down?"

For a moment, it looks like Dan is actually wondering whether that might be the easier option. "Okay," he says eventually, before taking a deep breath. "It's just that, well, I seem to be having a little, you know, *problem*. Where women are concerned."

I don't quite know what to say. Normally, the only problem Dan has with women is which one to sleep with. "What sort of problem?"

"An embarrassing one."

Ah. How on earth do you console a friend with *that* kind of problem? "That's . . ." I search for the right word, although if he's talking about what I think he's

4

talking about, then I'm not sure there is one . . . "terrible."

"I know! And it's never happened to me be —"

At the sound of the doorbell, Dan suddenly stops talking, and leaps up off the sofa as if he's been electrocuted. I look at him strangely, then get up myself to buzz Sam in, and by the time she breezes into the lounge, he's standing in the far corner of the room.

"Hello, trouble," she says, walking over to where he's pretending to be interested in my collection of paperbacks on the bookshelf, before planting a kiss on his cheek. She's dressed in her trademark tight tracksuit, and is perspiring slightly from her jog home, meaning Dan is torn between pulling away from her slight sweatiness, and staying where he is to peer down her top. As usual, he chooses the latter option and then, again as usual, glances guiltily across at me to check whether I've noticed. "What brings you round here this evening?"

When Dan doesn't answer, Sam turns to me. "Edward?"

"He, er . . ."

"I came round to borrow this," says Dan, selecting a book at random from the shelf.

"A book?" says Sam. "Have you finally learned to read, then?"

Dan ignores her dig. "Just fancied a bit of bedtime reading."

"Which might come in handy at the moment," I say, before realizing that that's perhaps a little cruel, given Dan's recent admission.

"*The Da Vinci Code?*" says Sam, peering at the title. "I didn't know there was anyone left in the world who hadn't already read that. And didn't we all go and see the film together?"

"That's right," says Dan.

"And didn't you tell us, in a loud voice halfway through, that it was rubbish, and then get up and leave?"

"Er . . . That's right too."

"With some girl you'd met outside in the queue," I add.

"Much to the annoyance of her boyfriend," says Sam.

"Might have done," says Dan, guiltily. "I can't remember."

"So why the book?"

"I, um . . ." Dan looks helplessly across at me.

"Well . . . You've been wondering — ever since that night — just how it turned out, so you wanted to borrow the book to see how it ended. Isn't that right?"

There's the customary few seconds as Dan's not-so-speedy brain processes this particular piece of information, before he finally realizes it's actually not a bad excuse.

"Exactly."

Sam frowns. "Instead of just renting the film on DVD?"

"Yup." He nods. "Although now I think about it, your DVD idea is better."

"Or," I suggest, looking at my watch, "we could go out for a quick beer instead, and I could tell you what happens. Save you having to read it. Or rent it, for that matter."

Dan flicks quickly through a few of the chapters. "That might be better. It does have rather a lot of pages, after all."

"With a lot of big words," teases Sam.

I nod towards the door. "So, would you prefer to go out and talk about it?"

"Yes," says Dan, glancing furtively across at Sam. "Please."

Sam eyes us both suspiciously, and then just shrugs. "Don't mind me," she says, half-unzipping her tracksuit top. "I've got to go and take a shower anyway."

"Great." I pick up my wallet from the coffee table and slip it into my pocket. "Well, come on then, Dan. I'll buy you a beer, and you can tell me . . . I mean, I'll tell you all about it."

"All about what?" says Dan, momentarily confused.

"*The Da Vinci Code*, dummy."

Dan looks at the book in his hand as if it's the first time he's seen it, before putting it back on the shelf. "Oh, right. Of course. Well, you have a nice shower, Sam," he says, peering along the corridor towards the bathroom door, which is clearly visible from the sofa. "Or alternatively, we can stay here, Ed. If you'd prefer. I could get some beers in, and . . ."

I grab him by the arm and steer him towards the front door, stopping to kiss Sam on the way, feeling a little guilty that she's come round for one of our rare week-nights together and I'm abandoning her. But, equally, I don't feel I can quite tell her why — not until

Dan's gone, at least — although it's a conversation I know she'll enjoy. Dan never tires of boasting about his sexual prowess in front of her — or anyone, for that matter — so the more ammunition she has to get back at him, the better.

"I won't be late."

She takes one look at Dan's miserable expression and makes the "yeah, right" face. "Don't worry. I'm pretty tired, and I've got to be up early in the morning, so I'll probably just go straight to bed afterwards."

For a moment, given the prospect of an early night with Sam, I'm more tempted to stay in, but I can't abandon Dan in his hour of need, especially when he's looking so fed up. And, more important, because he was there for me a while back when Jane, my girlfriend of ten years, suddenly dumped me with the words *It's not me, it's you*, and headed off to Tibet to "find herself".

Back then, it was Dan who helped me through the worst of it, got me to sort myself out, lose some weight, smarten myself up, and eventually find *myself* again. And it was while I was finding myself that I found Sam.

"Where shall we go?" Dan says, as I shut the door behind me, and we walk out into the warm evening.

I shrug. "If only we knew somewhere nearby . . ."

Two minutes later, we're outside the Admiral Jim, our local, a regular watering hole as well as just around the corner from our respective flats. As Dan and I walk in through the swing doors, Wendy, the manageress, nods to me from the other end of the bar. She's about eight months pregnant, which she and boyfriend Andy are extremely chuffed about, and looks like she's eaten a beach ball.

"So," I say, once Dan's safely installed on a stool at the bar with a bottle of his favourite designer lager in his hand, "back to your little, ahem, problem. Unless you'd rather talk about *The Da Vinci Code*?"

Dan looks at me miserably. "To be honest, yes."

"Come on. The quicker you get it over and done with . . ." Oops. If that is, in fact, Dan's, er, difficulty, then that's perhaps not the most sensitive thing to say. "A problem shared, and all that."

"Well . . . It's women," says Dan, picking at the foil around the neck of his beer bottle, before pouring the contents slowly into his glass and taking a couple of sips. "I just can't seem to, you know . . ."

"No wonder you didn't want to discuss this in front of Sam." I cut him off, as much to spare my blushes as his, and put on my best concerned voice. "How long has this been happening? Or not happening, as the case may be?" I say, wondering whether I've got my initial diagnosis wrong. "I mean, maybe you're under a lot of stress at the moment. And, apparently, stress can make the body behave in all sorts of different ways. Or misbehave." I stop talking, conscious that I'm gabbling on — although that's probably because I seem to be more embarrassed about this than Dan is.

He stares at me for a second or two before realization dawns. "Not anything like *that*. God no." He takes a huge gulp of beer. "If that was the case, I'd have slit my wrists long before coming to talk to you about it."

"Oh. Right. Thanks. I think. So what exactly is the matter?"

"Like I've been trying to tell you. I can't seem to get . . ." He takes another mouthful of beer before continuing. "I mean, no one will go out with me any more."

"What?" I can't help but smile, relieved that it's nothing more serious — or too personal, to be honest. "The great Dan Davis? *TV's Dan Davis*, in fact, can't get a date?"

He shushes me anxiously, looking around to check that Wendy's out of earshot, as she's not his biggest fan. Although thinking about it, I'd struggle to name a woman who knows Dan who is, given his reputation. "All right. Don't rub it in. I'm going through a sexual crisis here."

"Sorry." I try to adopt a more sympathetic tone, but to be honest, I'm a little miffed at missing a night in with Sam for, well, *this*. "How long is it now?"

Dan narrows his eyes. "What's that got to do with it?"

"No, Dan. Not that. This celibacy of yours."

"Huh?"

"How long since you've, you know, *scored*?" I say, putting it into language he can understand.

"I don't know. About three weeks." Dan looks at his watch — the Omega Seamaster that he treated himself to after seeing one in a Bond film, then tried to take back when he found out there wasn't really a secret magnet in the case that you could use to unzip women's dresses — then leans across towards me.

10

"Three weeks, two days, and seven hours, to be precise," he says, lowering his voice.

I let out a short laugh. "Is that all? That's hardly a crisis. Jesus, Dan — you had me worried. I thought it was something serious."

"It *is* serious," insists Dan. "Three weeks is a long time for me. In fact, it's three weeks longer than, well, just take my word for it."

"Yes, but for any normal person, three weeks is hardly . . ."

Dan holds a hand up. "Let me stop you there. Remember, women are my thing. Just like yours is . . ." He frowns. "Remind me what you're good at, again?"

"Piss off."

"And I seem to have lost it," he continues, sitting up on his stool so he can inspect his reflection in the mirror behind the bar. "Though God knows how."

"You might just be going through a slump. It happens to us all."

Dan looks at me as if I've just made the most ridiculous of suggestions. "Not to me, it doesn't."

"Well, Brighton's a small town. Isn't it possible that perhaps you've gone out with most of the women here? And so you've forgotten that you've already dated the ones you're asking out, who of course are going to turn you down."

Dan perks up a little as he considers this, but his face quickly darkens again. "Nah. I think I'd remember. And besides, if I've already dumped them, then surely they'd leap at the chance to go out with me again?"

"Hold on a sec." I stand up, and move my stool back a bit, before sitting back down.

Dan looks at me strangely. "What are you doing?"

"Just making room for your ego."

"Very funny."

I take a sip of my wine. "Well, maybe you're just having an unlucky run. A bad spell."

Dan sighs. "Edward, a bad spell for me is having to spend two consecutive nights on my own. Three weeks?" He closes his eyes and shakes his head slowly. "This hasn't happened since I was fourteen."

I nearly spit my drink out in shock. "Fourteen? I didn't lose my virginity until I was . . . Well, that's not important. So, do you want to tell me exactly what happens?"

Dan looks around to check no one's nearby, but lowers his voice anyway. "Well, it starts off all normal. We make eye contact, they come over, we get chatting, maybe I buy them a drink, more often than not they buy me one . . ."

"It's tough being you, isn't it?"

He ignores me. ". . . and then they give me their number. So far, all pretty straightforward."

"So what's the problem?"

"It's just . . ." Dan waits as an older couple walk past us and sit down in the corner. "Well, I do the standard leave-it-a-day-and-then-call-them, and . . . Nothing."

"Nothing?"

"Nope. Whatever I suggest — a coffee, dinner, or just sex — they're suddenly not interested. You know what it's like."

I do, actually. Or at least did — until I met Sam. "Uh-huh."

"I mean, it happened again yesterday morning. Met this girl — Nicola, I think it was — at the gym, called to ask her out this evening, turned out she was washing her hair."

"Well, that happens. I mean, women do wash their hair. Apart from those dreadlocked crusties with all the dogs who live under the pier. And Britney Spears when she went a bit mental. But then that's because she'd shaved hers all off."

"Not every night. Which is what Nicola pretty much implied."

"Well, maybe you're leaving it too long. I mean, I'd call them as soon as possible."

"Which is why you've only had sex with two different women in the past ten years."

"That's not fair. True, but not fair."

Dan sighs, and stares into his glass. "I can't work it out. They're all over me when we meet. And then the next day . . . It's like I've done something. And I haven't even had the chance."

"Are you sure you're not misreading them? I mean, maybe they're just pretending to be interested."

Dan's mouth drops open, as if I've just made the most stupid suggestion in the history of the world. "Misreading them? I'm not some woman-dyslexic like you. And besides, if they weren't interested, they wouldn't give me their phone numbers in the first place, would they?"

"I suppose not." I take another mouthful of wine, and savour it thoughtfully, while trying to ignore my craving for a packet of crisps. "Although maybe they're just doing that to be polite?"

"Polite?" snaps Dan. "Don't be ridiculous."

"Why is that ridiculous?"

"Edward, when a woman's being polite, she doesn't give you her real number."

"She doesn't?"

"No," says Dan, as if he's explaining something to a five-year-old. "She gives you a made-up one. That way, you still walk away with a number, and it's not until you try and call it the next day that you realize what she's done. That's polite. This? Well, it's just downright rude. I mean, I just don't understand it."

And nor do I. Where women are concerned, if Dan doesn't understand what's going on, then I'm hardly likely to be able to throw any light on the subject.

We sit and sip our drinks, Dan sulking quietly, and me following the "when you don't have anything to say, don't say anything" rule, until a couple of attractive girls walk in and sit down at a table near the bar. Normally, Dan would be salivating like a dog in heat, but this evening, he hardly gives them a glance.

I nudge him. "Aren't you going to, you know . . ." — I nod towards their table, where the girls, having evidently recognized Dan, are whispering loudly to each other, while pointing at him in an unsubtle way — "give one of them a go?"

Dan just rolls his eyes. "What's the point?"

"They look pretty interested."

Dan sighs. "Edward, weren't you listening earlier? They all *look* interested. The 'looking interested' part isn't the problem. It's afterwards."

"Come on. I'll be your wingman."

He shakes his head slowly. "You've been watching your *Top Gun* DVD again, haven't you? Besides, I always fly solo."

"And flying won't be the only solo activity you'll be doing unless you keep trying. Remember what you told me when Jane dumped me?"

Dan frowns. "Er . . . That you'd brought it on yourself, you fat bastard? What's that got to do with anything?"

"No. 'Get straight back in the saddle', or something like that."

"I said that? Doesn't sound like me."

"At least go over and talk to them."

"What for?"

"Well, for one thing, I might be able to tell you whether you're doing anything wrong. Something that might be sending out some subconscious messages."

Dan scowls at me. "I'm sending out a subconscious one to you now. Can you guess what it is? I'll give you a clue. Two words. And the first one begins with an 'F'."

"Come on. It might be . . ."

"If you say the word 'fun', I'm going to punch you in the bollocks. Hard."

"I was going to say 'useful'."

"Nah." Dan gulps down the rest of his beer, then waves over towards where Wendy's sitting at the other end of the bar reading a copy of *What Baby?*, and points at our empty glasses. She waves back, indicates the half-full bottle of water she's been swigging from, and turns back to her magazine. "Forget it. I've had enough rejection for one day."

At a loss for anything encouraging to say, I decide to change the subject, and Dan's talk of rejection gives me the perfect opportunity. "Maybe you just need to start to think a bit more positively."

"Think positively?" repeats Dan, as negatively as possible.

"I mean, look on the bright side. At least you can concentrate on your big audition this weekend." Dan's up for a part in ITV 5's most popular daytime soap opera, set coincidentally here in Brighton, all about the lives and loves of the residents of a particular cul-de-sac. It's sort of a *Brookside*-on-sea, or *Seaside*, if you will, and called, imaginatively, *Close Encounters*.

"Yeah," says Dan, glumly. "I suppose. But I can't say I'm really in the right frame of mind for it."

"But it's *acting*, Dan. Not presenting any more. What you've always wanted."

"I know. But I'm having a bit of a crisis of confidence. And that's not exactly what you want when you're going for such a big part . . ."

"A big part?" interrupts Wendy, from behind the bar. "You can't be referring to your . . ."

"Dan's up for a role in *Close Encounters*," I say quickly. With the mood Dan's in, one of their normal verbal sparring matches could turn nasty quite quickly.

16

"*Close Encounters?*" says Wendy. "That crappy ITV 5 thing?"

"Do you watch it?" says Dan, bracing himself for one of Wendy's usual digs.

"I *love* it," she says, refilling my wine glass. "Dan, I never thought I'd say this about you, but I'm actually impressed."

Normally, Dan would be basking in the compliment, particularly given who it has come from, but this evening, there's not even the slightest flicker of smugness on his face.

"Yes, well, I haven't got it yet," he says, picking up the bottle of beer that Wendy's just placed in front of him and taking a large swig.

"What's the role?"

Dan shrugs. "Some love-them-and-leave-them type."

Wendy winks at me, then puts her hand on Dan's arm. "Well, you'll be just perfect."

I'm just settling up for our drinks — as usual, Dan's come out without his wallet — when the two girls who've been sitting nearby get up and walk over towards us. As Dan stares fixedly at his beer bottle, the shorter and prettier of the two taps him on the shoulder.

"Excuse me," says the girl. "But you're him, aren't you?"

"Who?" says Dan uninterestedly.

"You know? That Dan Davis. From the telly?"

With what seems like the greatest of effort, Dan swivels his head around, and looks her up and down slowly. His eyes linger briefly on her breasts, before he turns regretfully back to his beer.

"No," he says. "No, I'm not."

And from the way he's sitting, slumped miserably on his stool, I have to agree with him.

CHAPTER
TWO

Sam's asleep when I get home, which isn't surprising given that she's up at 6 a.m. most days with her clients who like to exercise before work, and despite me banging drunkenly around the bedroom in a not-so-subtle attempt to wake her, she doesn't stir. And the next morning, by the time I've finally regained consciousness, she's already long gone, so I don't get a chance to even exchange a few pleasantries with her. This is the one problem with our respective jobs — the timing. Sam's often free during the day, when I'm not, and then out working in the evening, when I'm hanging around at home, or has to go back to her flat to walk Ollie, her dog. It makes the odd night we spend together in the week a little more precious, which is why I feel bad about spending yesterday evening with Dan. Still, a friend in need, and all that.

Nursing a slight headache, and cursing last night's fifth glass of wine, I get halfway through my breakfast — a bowl of some sugar-free organic muesli that Sam's recommended, and which is about as tasty as a bowl of sawdust — before deciding that I'll pick up something a little less sugar-free on the way to my office, and head out of the front door, pausing to say a loud "hello" to

Mrs Barraclough, my very old, and very deaf, upstairs neighbour.

It's a short walk from my flat to work, in the centre of Brighton, although I take a slightly circuitous route this morning, avoiding the seafront in case Sam's there with a client, as I don't want her to see the Dunkin' Donuts bag I'm carrying. I'm a partner in a small IT recruitment consultancy, although when I say "partner", the only other person there is Natasha, who owns the business, which in reality makes it rather an unequal partnership — a bit like most relationships, I suppose. I do most of the work, and she lets me get on with it, while she gets it on with prospective clients. And while Natasha's reputation may have suffered as a result of her somewhat unique meet-with/sleep-with approach to customer satisfaction, business hasn't, so I'm certainly not going to complain.

When I eventually get to the office, to my surprise Natasha's already there, although given the fact that she's wearing the same outfit she had on yesterday, that's possibly because she's just been dropped off by whichever one of our clients she went home with last night.

"Fallen off the wagon?" she says, eyeing my choice of breakfast. Natasha saw me go through my transformation when Jane left me, and has been betting that it'll only be a matter of time before I lapse back to my old ways now that I'm "coupled up" again.

"Nope. And surely that's the whole point of this healthy lifestyle lark — that you can give yourself a treat every now and then? Besides, I've got a bit of a hangover this morning. Needed a bit of carbohydrate."

Natasha widens her eyes. "Really? Drinking on a school night as well? Celebrating something?" She's also convinced that it's only a matter of time before I make, to use her phrase, an honest woman out of Sam. Not that she's dishonest at the moment, of course.

"Nope," I say, blushing slightly. "Nothing like that. Out with Dan, actually."

I have to tread carefully whenever I mention Dan's name, as he and Natasha dated for a while, although when I use the word "dated", I mean it in the briefest — and purely sexual — sense. And while Natasha's probably as predatory as he is when it comes to the opposite sex, I can tell their parting wasn't as smooth as she'd maybe have liked.

"And how is Dan?" asks Natasha, although through slightly clenched teeth.

"Not too great, actually. In fact, he needed a bit of consoling."

"Consoling? Dan? What's happened — did he find a grey hair? On one of his girlfriends, I mean."

"Er, no. Not quite." I sit down at my desk and switch my PC on, wondering whether to share Dan's problem with Natasha, until it occurs to me that she might actually be able to shed a bit of light on it. And although he'll probably kill me if he finds out I've told her, by the way he was acting last night, if he doesn't get it sorted out — and soon — he's more likely to kill himself. "He's, um, going through a bit of a dry spell."

I've barely finished speaking when Natasha throws her head back and roars with laughter. For a good couple of minutes. So much so that I'm worried she's going to have a heart attack.

"Dan!" she says eventually, pulling a tissue from the box in her desk drawer and dabbing at the mascara running from her eyes. "A dry spell!"

"It's not funny, Natasha. He's really upset about it. It'd be like you losing your . . ." I stop talking, because Natasha's not known for her sense of humour. Particularly about herself. "He just can't understand why."

Natasha blows her nose, and tries hard to regain her composure. "Yes, well, he never was the sharpest pencil in the box, was he?"

This is true, unfortunately. In fact, Jane always used to compare Dan to one of those lava lamps — nice to look at, but not very bright. "How do you mean?"

"Well, has he considered that maybe the word's getting around that he's a complete and utter bastard?"

"Er, no." I have to concede on that one. "Maybe you're right."

"So what's he going to do?"

I shrug. "I don't know. But he's got this big audition coming up, and thinks maybe if he gets the part, it might help. You know how women are . . . I mean, some women can be. Impressed by that sort of thing, I mean."

"That's true," says Natasha. "Although, having slept with Dan, he's going to need a pretty big part if he wants to make up for . . ."

22

"Natasha, please."

She smiles wickedly. "So when is this audition of his?"

"Tomorrow. I'm going up to London with him."

"Ah, how sweet. And he wants you to hold his hand?"

"No, he, er, wants me to pretend to be his agent."

Natasha frowns. "I thought he already had an agent?"

"He did. But he had to sack her."

"Oh?" says Natasha. "Why?"

"The clue's in the word 'her', Natasha," I say, rolling my eyes. "Why do you think?"

For the rest of the day, I'm a little preoccupied with Dan's predicament. Try as she might, Natasha can't throw any further light on the subject, although that's possibly because she's right with her original "bastard" observation. I decide that maybe I need to talk to someone who hasn't actually suffered at Dan's hands — or any other part of his anatomy — but it's difficult to think of a woman I know who hasn't actually undergone the Dan Davis treatment. Eventually, I realize I don't have any choice, and even though I've promised Dan I won't mention it to her, Sam's probably my best bet. But it's not until the following morning, when Sam and I are out jogging along the seafront, that I try to bring it up — or rather, I'm just about to — when the noise of a car horn startles me. When I look up from where I've narrowly avoided tripping over the kerb and treading in some dog poo, there's a bright-orange Porsche 911 tailing us.

I speed up a little to tap Sam on the shoulder, and point towards the car.

"Someone you know?"

"Nope." She shakes her head and keeps on running. "Probably just some pervert in his penis-substitute Porsche. It happens sometimes."

I look at Sam's pert backside, covered by her tight tracksuit bottoms, and realize that it's a view that might make most men want to honk their horn.

"Do you want me to have a word with him?"

Sam stops jogging and smiles at me. "That's sweet of you, Edward, but don't worry. And besides, as fit as you are now, I think you'd have your work cut out to catch a Porsche."

I glare at the car, which is pulling up alongside us, and then have to do a double take. "Hold on," I say, peering through the windscreen. "That's not just some pervert. It's Dan."

The Porsche pulls over next to where we're standing on the pavement, and when the roof slowly folds itself back, the first thing we see is Dan's unmistakable grin, his teeth possibly bright enough to be seen from space given his recent pre-audition trip to The Tooth Hurts, his celebrity dentist in the North Laines.

"What do you think?" he says, proudly.

"What do you mean, what do I think? It's a Porsche. And if I'm not mistaken, a 911 Turbo S Cabriolet. Or something like that," I add, before Sam can call me an auto geek. "It's beautiful."

As I admire the car's sleek lines, Sam folds her arms and looks at me reproachfully. "You boys and your toys. It's only a car."

Dan unhooks his seat belt and smiles patronizingly up at her. "Sweetheart, that statement is so wrong on so many levels."

"Is it yours?" I say, not quite able to take in the stunning piece of machinery in front of me.

"Not yet," says Dan. "But I needed something to cheer myself up, and the guy at the dealership was only too happy to loan me this for a couple of weeks. Sort of an extended test drive."

"But you're considering buying it?"

"That's what I've told them," says Dan. "But thinking about it, my car is getting on a bit."

Dan currently drives a very flash Audi. "Oh yes. It must be at least, what, three years old?"

"Plus, like most men, I've always wanted one of these. And besides . . ." Dan presses a button on the dashboard, and the passenger seat reclines. "It won't do me any harm where the ladies are concerned." He winks at me surreptitiously. "If you know what I mean?"

I have to stop myself from agreeing with him. "What do you think, Sam? Would something like this ever make you want to go out with someone like Dan?"

"Maybe if he used it to run over every other man on earth." She regards the Porsche for a moment or two, and then looks at Dan. "It is nice, but I hardly think you turning up in a seven-eleven, or whatever it is, is going to make a difference to whether a woman fancies you or not."

"A *nine*-eleven," says Dan. "And you'd be surprised. You women are easily impressed. Which is lucky for you, Edward."

I give Sam a squeeze. "Thank goodness."

"And how much will this set you back?" she says, running her hand lightly over the bodywork.

Dan jumps out of the car. "About a hundred thousand," he says, using his sleeve to wipe off the nonexistent mark where Sam's just touched it.

"*Pounds?*" Sam whistles. "Are you mad? Either that or they're paying you way too much on *Where There's a Will*."

Dan shrugs. "Standard BBC rates. But it's sold around the world, and I get paid for all of those too." He nudges me. "I'm very big in the Balkans, apparently."

I nudge him back. "That's not what I've heard."

"Besides," he says. "It's practical, too."

"I've got to hear this," I say, looking at the rear seats, which are struggling to accommodate Dan's gym bag.

"Well, for one thing, it's a convertible. Which means I can work on my tan while driving, and therefore save money on sunbed sessions. Which, at ten pounds a time, will mean the car will eventually pay for itself."

I do a quick calculation in my head, then look at Dan's rather unnatural skin tone, remembering that his nickname in TV circles is apparently "Tan Davis". "In about a hundred years. Give or take."

Sam shakes her head in disbelief. "So that's where my TV licence fee goes. On buying you a posh car."

"Money well spent, as far as I'm concerned," I say, peering in at the black leather upholstery. "It's gorgeous."

"Couldn't agree more," says Dan. "And besides I thought it was in keeping with my persona."

"Bright orange and rather flash?" suggests Sam. "Well, you're not wrong there." She reaches over and pokes me in the stomach. "Anyway, Ed. We ought to get going. Don't want you to stiffen up."

"No, Edward. Mustn't get stiff," sniggers Dan. "Alternatively I could give you a lift? Well, one of you, unless Sam wants to sit on my lap? Although thinking about it, you're both rather sweaty."

Tempting as Dan's offer is, I know where my priorities lie. "Another time. And did you want something? Apart from to show off your Porsche, that is?"

Dan shrugs. "Not really. Oh, and don't forget, we've got my audition later."

"How could I? You've reminded me about a hundred times. And why do you think I'm out running with Sam at this ungodly hour when we could be at home in bed?"

Dan looks Sam up and down, and can't help licking his lips. "God only knows."

I nod towards the car. "And are we going in this, now, instead of on the train?"

"No can do, sadly," says Dan. "I've got my lines to learn. And I can't do that and control this baby at the same time."

"I could always drive," I suggest hopefully. "It can't be that different to my Mini."

"Yeah, right," says Dan, vaulting *Dukes of Hazzard* style over the side of the car and into the driver's seat. "See you at the station. Ten o'clock, don't forget."

"And what about you?" says Sam, as Dan roars off into the early morning traffic. "Do you want a Porsche?"

"I'm happy with my car, thanks," I say, jogging after her. "And, in fact, I think the Mini's a nicer car altogether. More compact. And practical. And economical . . ." I stop talking, wondering whether she's speaking metaphorically, and realizing if that's the case, then there is no good way out of this conversation. "Come on," I say. "Race you back."

When I eventually reach my flat, Sam's already sitting on the steps outside, doing her stretches. "What kept you?" she says, hardly out of breath.

"I, er, stopped for a paper," I pant.

"Well, where is it then?" she says, moving into another double-jointed position.

"Ah." I lean over and half-heartedly try to touch my toes. "I can't pull the wool over your eyes, can I?"

"And don't you ever try," says Sam, putting her hands on the small of my back and pressing downwards, causing my hamstrings to ping alarmingly.

"Ouch! Okay, okay."

When I eventually manage to stand up straight again, Sam's got a strange look on her face.

"Edward, don't be too influenced by Dan, will you?" she says. "I mean, I know he's your best friend and all

28

that, but sometimes . . . Well, he's just not very nice. Where women are concerned, I mean."

I put my arm around her shoulders. "Sam, if there's one thing that hanging around with Dan has taught me, it's how *not* to behave. Really. You've got nothing to worry about."

"Good." She stands up on her toes and kisses me. "Shower time?"

I look at my watch, pleased to see that I've still got an hour or so before I'm due to meet Dan. "You go first. I'm not that sweaty."

Sam takes me by the hand and leads me in through the front door, then peels off her T-shirt and throws it at me. "Well, we can always do something about that."

By the time I arrive at the station, Dan's pacing around anxiously outside Marks & Spencer's, chewing a piece of gum as if his life depended upon it. I wave hello, but when he catches sight of me, he just taps the face of his watch.

"What time do you call this?" he says, hurrying off towards the ticket barrier and motioning for me to follow him.

"Morning, Edward," I say, as sarcastically as I can. "Thanks for giving up your Saturday to come with me to my audition in London." I check the large station clock on the wall, just in case my old Timex has stopped. "Besides, it's only five to ten. What are you panicking for?"

"I don't want to miss the train, do I?"

"And you won't. Seeing as it goes at six minutes past. And you've already bought the tickets."

"Well, we've still got to get to the right platform."

"Which is . . ." I check the overhead noticeboard. "Platform two. Which happens to be all of fifty yards away. Calm down, will you? You're making me nervous."

"Sorry. Yes. Right. Calm." Dan takes a few deep breaths, before noticing my smug expression. "What are you looking so pleased with yourself about?"

"Nothing."

"Oh no!" Dan covers his face with his hands. "You've just had sex, haven't you?"

I can't stop myself from blushing. "Might have done."

"Great," says Dan. "I'm going through a drought of biblical proportions, and meanwhile you and Sam are at it like rabbits every chance you get. Talk about rubbing my nose in it."

I follow him through the barrier and along the platform, shaking my head to get rid of the image Dan's last sentence has just put in my mind, and then have to do a double take as he slips his sunglasses on.

"Er . . ."

"What?"

I point towards the train. "We're going on that, right?"

"So?"

"So, the light's hardly going to be dazzling in there. Or are you just trying to maintain a low profile?"

Dan shakes his head, and adjusts his Ray-Bans. "You still have so much to learn, Edward. Guys don't wear sunglasses to keep the sun out of their eyes. It's so they can perve at other men's girlfriends. And on a Saturday, on this train" — he presses the button to open the door — "there will be other men's girlfriends."

"But I thought you wanted to be caught?" I say, following him into the carriage. "Eye contact, and all that."

"Not by their boyfriends, I don't. And besides, at the moment, perving's my only pleasure."

The train's quite quiet, which is lucky, because even though the journey's less than an hour, I have to change seats due to the annoying nervous twitch Dan's left leg develops as soon as we leave Brighton. He doesn't say much, engrossed as he is in the script they've sent him to read from, which is fine by me, as quite frankly, I still don't know what to say to help him through his current dilemma — even if now was an appropriate time to bring it up. And when we finally arrive at Victoria, it's obviously not a moment too soon for Dan, as he's off through the doors like a greyhound out of a trap, sprinting down the platform before I've even got my jacket down from the luggage rack.

"What's the hurry?" I puff, when I've eventually caught him up at the ticket barrier. "I thought the audition didn't start till midday?"

"But we've got to get to Covent Garden. And you can never get a cab when you need one."

"A cab? What's wrong with the good old London Underground?" Dan normally loves any opportunity to travel on the Tube, following the poster campaign for a brand of breath freshener he did recently. "Get as close as you can" was the tagline, and Dan took this as literally as possible whenever he saw a girl he fancied, pointing to his face on the poster, and then inviting them to do as instructed. Amazingly, a surprisingly high number of them did.

"You're my agent, remember. And my agent's hardly going to take me to an audition on the Tube, is he?"

The cab fare for the ten-minute journey is more than the train tickets combined, but Dan doesn't seem to mind — especially since, once again, he's off almost before we've stopped, leaving me to pay the driver before following him out of the cab and into the throng of Saturday shoppers. The audition's taking place just off Long Acre, in a building next to a Mexican restaurant, and I manage the briefest of peeks at the menu before we're buzzed through into what appears to be some sort of dance studio. There's a huge mirror down one wall, and at first glance, what seem to be about twenty other Dans waiting around, all with identical teeth, tans, and clutching the same few script pages as if their lives depended on it.

Dan nods hello to a couple of them as we walk in, then strolls confidently over to the table at the far end, where a middle-aged, stern-looking woman is sitting, ticking names off against a list. He turns round and hisses at me to join him, so I hurry across to the table.

"Hi," he says, breezily, "I'm here for the audition."

The woman glances up from her clipboard, then looks Dan up and down dismissively. "Really?" she says, sarcastically. "Name?"

"Dan," he says, a little put out at not being recognized. "Dan Davis." I can tell he has to resist putting "TV's" first.

The woman raises one eyebrow, then turns her attention back to her list, scanning down with her finger to the Ds. "Oh yes. Mister Davis." She ticks him off. "We'll call you when we're ready for you. And you are?"

There's a couple of seconds before I realize that she's talking to me. "Ed. Ed Middleton."

The woman frowns at her piece of paper. "You're not on my list."

"He's not on many people's," says Dan, giving her the benefit of his trademark full-beam Davis smile.

"Oh. I'm not here to audition."

"No," says Dan. "They're not looking for retards."

I can't help but wince at Dan's non-PC comment, and worry that he's in danger of blowing his chance before he's even auditioned, but luckily the woman just ignores him, and instead looks up at me quizzically. "No? What are you then? His agent?"

"Er, yes, actually. That's right."

She frowns. "From which agency?"

"Er . . . Middleton Management," is the best I can think of, although the way I say it makes it sound more like a question.

"I haven't heard of them before."

"Well, we don't like to brag about our existence."

"Oh," says the woman dryly, "so you're sort of like a secret agent?"

"'Secret agent'!" Dan suddenly explodes in a fit of loud and somewhat overenthusiastic laughter. "Very good."

"No, nothing like that. But we're based down in Brighton, and . . ."

"You know," interrupts Dan, again. "Where *Close Encounters* is set?"

"Oh yes," says the woman, smiling humourlessly at Dan. "Brighton. Of course. I've only worked on the programme for two years, but thanks for reminding me."

As she goes back to studying her list, I quickly steer Dan off to one corner of the room before he can put his foot in it again.

"Good move," he whispers, elbowing me in the ribcage. "Mentioning Brighton. Stroke of genius."

"Thanks. Almost as good as your 'retard' comment."

"No," says Dan, without a trace of irony. "Yours was definitely better. I knew there was a reason I asked you along."

I grunt in response, then do a quick scan of the other auditionees. "No one else's agent seems to be here."

"Exactly," says Dan. "So who looks the most famous? Me."

Or the least mature, because he needs his agent here to hold his hand, I feel like saying. "So, what should I do now?"

Dan rolls his eyes. "Act like an agent, of course."

"Right. Which is how, exactly? We don't all move in your showbiz circles."

"I don't know." Dan glances furtively around the room, then nods towards the doorway. "Get me some coke, or something. And make sure people see you doing it."

"Jesus, Dan. Keep your voice down. Where on earth am I going to get you some of that? And what do you mean, make sure people see me? I might get arrested. That might have been what your last agent did for you, but . . ." I stop talking, because Dan's got a puzzled expression on his face.

"As in 'a can of', I meant," he says, pointing towards the drinks machine in the hallway.

"Oh. Sure. Of course. Have you got any money?"

"Yeah, right." Dan looks at me as if I'm stupid. "Like my agent's not going to be paying for my drink."

I stare back at him for a moment, but when it becomes clear he's not joking, I just shake my head and stroll across to the vending machine, realizing that, actually, his last agent was probably relieved to have been sacked. There's a selection of soft drinks, and for a moment I wonder whether I should call across and ask what he wants, but decide that'd only give him a chance to humiliate me in front of everyone. I drop a pound coin in the slot, and I'm just about to get him a Coke, but then remember hearing somewhere that you shouldn't give excitable children too much sugar, so decide on the "diet" version. My finger's hovering over the button, but when I look back over to where he's standing — either doing a set of breathing exercises or hyperventilating, depending on your point of view — I decide to err on the side of caution, so hit the "caffeine free" button.

With a sigh, I collect the can from the slot, and head back over. "Here."

Dan stares at my outstretched hand, but refuses to take the can. "What's this?" he says, a little over-loudly.

"It's, er, Coca-Cola."

"I wanted the leaded stuff. None of this diet rubbish."

"Well you didn't say . . ."

"I shouldn't have to," he barks, then turns to the guy next to him. "Agents, eh?" he says, rolling his eyes theatrically.

As he starts a series of voice warm-up exercises which, rather appropriately, seem to consist of him loudly repeating the word "me" several times, I stand there blankly for a second or two before heading obediently back towards the machine, then feed another pound coin into the slot, hit the "regular" button, and wait for the red and white can to clunk into the slot at the bottom. Dan's now performing a series of exaggerated stretches, causing a few of the other auditionees to start doing some of their own, so I pick it up and walk back over to where he's swinging his arms back and forth in front of the mirror.

"Here you go."

"Just put it somewhere. Can't you see I'm in the middle of something?"

He winks at me, obviously pleased with his "tough talent" act, then spins around and bounces down to touch his toes, pointing his backside towards me. For a moment, it occurs to me exactly where to put the can, but instead, and out of his line of sight, I give it a few vigorous shakes, then put it down on the table next to him.

"I'm just going to the toilet," I say, adding "if that's okay?" for effect.

"Go where you like," says Dan, from between his legs. "I can take it from here."

I suddenly remember the Mexican restaurant next door, and realize that I am in fact quite hungry, so wish him good luck, then turn and head out of the door. And as it shuts behind me, all I hear is the sound of a can being opened followed by an agonized shout, which proves that if Dan's voice wasn't warmed up before, it certainly is now.

CHAPTER
THREE

It's the following evening, and Sam and I are just sitting down to dinner when there's a frantic buzzing from the front door. When I hit the intercom button, I can just about make out what appears to be Dan's excited expression on the screen, although it's a little difficult to tell, given that he seems to be dancing around in the street outside. I buzz him in, and a second later, he bursts through the door with a large bottle of champagne in his hand.

"I've got it!" he shouts.

Sam kisses him hello. "Well, don't give it to us, whatever you do."

He gives her a huge smacker on the lips in return, and then advances in my direction, arms spread. Worried that he's going to do the same to me, I try and push him away, while holding out my other hand for him to shake, but instead he envelops me in a huge bear hug, which is unfortunate as my extended hand makes a rather firm contact with his groin.

"Can you believe it?" says Dan, breaking away from me and heading into the kitchen, where he helps himself to three of my five non-matching champagne glasses from the cupboard, and sits down at the kitchen table. "I literally just found out half an hour ago. Incredible!"

As he pulls the foil off his bottle of Moët, Sam pulls out a chair next to him. "This is your big audition, I take it?"

"Yup." Dan levers the cork out of the bottle with his thumbs and fires it upwards, causing a slight dent in my ceiling, before splashing some champagne into each of the glasses. "You're only looking at Wayne Kerr, new cat amongst the birds on *Close Encounters!*"

As he hands us both a glass, Sam scratches her head. "Er . . . *Close Encounters*? Wasn't that that film about aliens?"

I nod towards Dan. "That would make sense."

"It's also the name of ITV 5's biggest soap," he says, proudly.

"Daytime soap," I add.

"And is it . . . popular?" Her TV viewing habits don't quite extend to the satellite channels.

He nods. "It's got more viewers than *Where There's a Will.*"

"It couldn't have less," I whisper to Sam.

"Well, congratulations," she says, clinking her glass against his. "When do you start?"

"We begin filming in a fortnight or so," says Dan, downing the contents of his glass in one and filling it up again. "And then it airs a couple of weeks after that, apparently."

"Wow," I say. "And who are you playing again?"

"Some new character who's just moved into the close called Wayne Kerr. I don't know much about him yet, apart from the fact that he's very good-looking and a bit of a ladies' man." Dan grins. "It's the part I was born to play, really."

Sam takes a sip of her champagne, and makes eye contact with me over the top of her glass. "And you don't think the name's a little, well . . ."

"What's wrong with it?" Dan frowns. "I mean, I know Wayne isn't the coolest name in the world — unless you're Bruce Wayne. But then that's more about the car, probably."

"But . . . Wayne Kerr?"

"And?"

"It's just, well . . ." Sam hesitates. "It sounds a little like . . ."

"What?" Dan leans over and tops her glass up again, even though she's hardly touched it.

"Nothing, mate," I say, interrupting their conversation by putting an arm round his shoulders. "It's fantastic news, really it is. Congratulations."

"So — are you going to help me celebrate, or what?" Dan picks up the bottle of Moët again. "I've got another five of these in the car."

"Well, we were just about to have dinner . . ." I say, looking hungrily at the lasagne bubbling away in the oven.

"Great," says Dan. "I'm starving."

We're on to the third bottle of Moët, and Dan is scraping the lasagne dish so thoroughly that we're not going to have to wash it, when Sam perks up again.

"So, what was the clincher, then, that got you the part?"

He licks the last remnants of bechamel sauce off his knife, washing it down with a long swig of champagne. "What, apart from my obvious good looks and acting talent?"

"Yes, Dan," I say, patiently. "Apart from those."

"Well, it's a funny thing," he says. "For a start, I got a bit of an advantage when I had a little accident with a can of Coke, and had to take my shirt off in front of everybody. You could actually see a couple of the other guys wilt."

"From the smell of your armpits? Or was the permatan too much for them?"

Dan ignores me. "And then, apparently there were a couple of us who were neck and neck for it, but when it came down to making the final choice, they wanted someone who could really inhabit the role, you know? Someone who walked the walk and talked the talk."

"Someone who really *was* the love-them-and-leave-them type, you mean?" says Sam.

I smile. "A complete and utter . . ."

"So, anyway," interrupts Dan, "they checked my online rating, and after that it wasn't a two-horse race any more. In fact it was just a . . ." Dan struggles to find the appropriate phrase.

"One-horse race?" suggests Sam, after letting Dan struggle for a little longer.

"Exactly." Dan picks the champagne bottle up and tries to refill his glass, but only succeeds in splashing some on the table. "Result!"

"Hold on," I say, reaching over and taking the bottle away from him. "Back up a second. What online rating?"

Dan shrugs, and holds his glass out for me to fill up. "I dunno. There's some website, apparently."

I stop in mid-pour. "Website? What website?"

"Shag a slag . . . no, hang on, SlateYourDate, or something. It's like a review site. But for blokes." He stares at his empty plate. "Got any more of that lasagne?"

"Dan. Pay attention." I click my fingers twice in front of his face. "There's an online rating site? For blokes?"

He nods. "Apparently. Women go on there if they've had a bad time with their boyfriends, and they write reviews."

"About their exes?" asks Sam.

"I guess," says Dan. "So, anyway, they checked me out on there, and it seems I've got a reputation for being a bit of an old dog in real life, so they thought I'd be perfect for the part."

I lean across again, but this time rap on Dan's forehead with my knuckles. Twice. "Hello? Anyone at home?"

"Ouch!" Dan rubs his head, then picks up his spoon to check on his reflection in the back of it. "How many times have I told you? Never on the face. And what on earth did you do that for?"

I look exasperatedly across at Sam, who's staring at Dan like he's simple. "Daniel," she says, taking his hand. "Sweetheart. For the last few weeks, you've been wondering why you've not been able to get a date. Correct?"

Dan glares at me accusingly. "You told her?"

"No, Dan. She beat it out of me."

He looks at Sam's well-toned arms. "That I can believe."

"And then today," she continues, "you find out that there's a website where disgruntled women can rate their ex-boyfriends. Which you appear to be on."

"Yup," he says proudly.

"And does this website portray you in a particularly sympathetic light as far as these women are concerned?"

Dan shakes his head. "Apparently not. And a good job too, otherwise I wouldn't be such an amazing Wayne Kerr."

Sam and I try not to snigger. "And do you think that this site is a special one set up purely for casting directors," she asks, "or that most women will be able to have access to it? And in particular, the women who've been blowing you off recently?"

"Or not," I can't resist adding. "As it were."

Dan doesn't say anything for a good thirty seconds or so, and then his face goes through one of those slow metamorphoses like you see on bad science fiction films.

"You don't, er, have a computer handy," he says, suddenly sober, "do you?"

Five minutes later, I'm sitting on the sofa with Dan on my left, Sam on my right, and my laptop open on the coffee table in front of us. Like a concert pianist warming up, I crack the knuckles on both hands, then carefully type the words "slate", "your", and "date" into Google.

"You're sure you want to see this?"

Dan nods, and points at the search options. "Press 'I'm feeling lucky'."

"As opposed to 'getting lucky'," says Sam.

As Dan scowls at her, I click the mouse button, and the words *SlateYourDate. Let other women know what he's really like* load on the screen in front of us.

Dan nudges me. "Look," he says, pointing to a banner across the top of the page, which is currently scrolling the words *Get even with Steven, Get back at Jack* and *Have a go at Joe* in bright red. "I bet the next one's going to be 'Tell Ed he's no good in . . .'"

"Okay, Dan. We get the idea." I click on *Enter*. "And let's see how long you keep your sense of humour for."

Welcome to SlateYourDate says the introduction at the top of the screen. *Ever gone out with a complete bastard? Well, now's your chance to warn other women about him. Just click on the options below to file a review of your ex, or simply check out a potential partner.*

"Wow," says Sam, when we've finished reading it, then waited the customary few seconds for Dan to catch up. "I didn't know sites like this existed."

"Why not?" I say. "There are review sites for books, films, restaurants . . . I suppose it was only a matter of time. And all those social networking sites. I mean, look at Friends Reunited."

"True," says Sam. "Except this is more like ex-girlfriends united."

"If you two have finished your little debate, can we please get on with this?" interrupts Dan, who seems to be gripping the arm of the sofa tightly.

"Sorry, mate." I hurriedly click on *Enter Site*, and a new screen loads.

"'Please enter your log-in details,'" reads Sam. "'Or click "new account" to begin reviewing.'"

Dan stares in bewilderment at the screen. "What do we do now?"

"Do you have any log-in details?"

"No. Of course not."

"Well, we'd best go for 'new account' then, don't you think?"

Dan nods. "Good idea."

I click through to the next screen. "'SlateYourDate is a site for women only,'" I read. "'Please answer the following security questions to avoid fraudulent use.'"

"Fuck," says Dan. "We're screwed. How are we going to get in?"

Sam clears her throat. "Perhaps I can be of some assistance? I am a woman, after all."

"Oh. Yeah." Dan can't help staring at her breasts, as if to remind himself. "Sorry, Sam. Come on then, Ed. Get on with it."

I click on question one, and a multiple-choice box appears.

"Okay," I read. "'Which of the following is a shoe shop. Is it A) CK One. B) L.K. Bennett, or C) T.K.

Maxx'?" I swivel round to look at Sam, who just stares at the screen blankly. "Sam?"

"Er . . ."

I smile encouragingly at her. "Anything you'd like to contribute? As our resident woman?"

She folds her arms over her chest defensively. "Sorry, but I just don't know that kind of stuff. If they were asking about trainers, maybe . . ."

As I stare hopelessly back at the screen, Dan reaches across and taps the computer screen. "It's, um, 'B'."

"What?"

"The answer." He leans back on the couch. "'B'."

"You're sure?"

"Yup."

My hand hovers above the keyboard for a moment, and then I hit the letter B. There's a pause, and then the word "correct" appears on the screen.

"How on earth did you know that?"

Dan looks a little embarrassed. "Lucky guess."

"Really?"

"Well, that, and my subscription to *Cosmo*."

"You subscribe to *Cosmopolitan*?" says Sam incredulously.

Dan shrugs. "First rule of warfare. Know your enemy."

I turn back to the screen, where the second question has appeared: *How many romantic comedies have Tom Hanks and Meg Ryan starred in together? One, two, or three?*

"Sam?"

Sam adores these kinds of films, and her face scrunches up as she thinks about it, which is an expression I love. "Well, there's *Sleepless in Seattle*, obviously, and that other one about the bookshop where all the children go . . ."

"*Little Shop of Horrors?*"

"No!" She pokes me in the ribs. "*You've Got Mail*. And I'm pretty sure that it wasn't Tom Hanks in *When Harry Met Sally*. So that would be two."

"Two. You're sure?"

She nods. "I can't think of any since."

"Okay. Thanks." I'm just about to click on B when Dan reaches over and stops me. "Hang on. It's 'C'. Three."

"What?"

"It's 'C'. You've forgotten *Joe Versus the Volcano*."

"Forgotten?" Sam makes a face. "I've never even heard of *Joe Versus the Volcano*. What on earth is it about?"

"Well," says Dan. "There's this tropical island, and Tom Hanks and Meg Ryan go there to . . . Anyway, it doesn't matter. The answer's three. 'C'."

"Are you sure? Sam and I have never heard of it."

Dan nods. "Google it, if you don't believe me."

I type "Joe Versus the Volcano" into Google, and hit return. Surprisingly, Dan's right. "How would you know a thing like that?"

"I've seen it," says Dan. "In fact, there probably isn't a chick flick I haven't watched. Well, the first hour or so of it, anyway."

This doesn't make sense. I've seen Dan's DVD collection, and unless any of his X-rated imported Danish films count, there's not a chick flick, to use his totally unsexist phrase, in it. "What do you mean, the first hour or so? And since when have you been such a fan of chick flick . . . I mean, those kinds of films?"

Dan shrugs. "Easiest way to get sex early on in a relationship. She suggests the cinema, you say no, let's rent a DVD instead. Why? Because unless you're a fan of dogging, the cinema isn't the best venue for the first time you, you know, get intimate," he says, suddenly remembering there's a lady present. "If you see what I mean."

"I'm not sure I want to," says Sam.

"So you take her off to Blockbuster, and of course let her choose, and five minutes later, you're walking out with a copy of some god-awful romantic bollocks, because a woman's idea of televisual entertainment is something where the main characters spend the whole film trying to get together despite all the 'hilarious' obstacles in their path."

"As opposed to a nice film where they're just trying to shoot each other?" says Sam.

Dan ignores her. "Anyway. The downside of this is that you've got to sit through an hour or so of some sloppy rubbish. The upside is that you're at home, on the sofa, and you know it's only a matter of time before the stuff she's watching is going to make her all touchy-feely . . . As I said. I've seen them all."

"Although not quite all the way through to the end."

Dan grins. "What can I say? Apart from thank you, Tom and Meg, for some of the best sex of my life."

I hit C, and we work our way through the rest of the questions, Sam having a valiant stab at most of them first, and Dan correcting her when she gets them wrong, although when it comes to one about what size batteries something called a Rampant Rabbit takes, she doesn't even volunteer a guess, but heads off to get a glass of water from the kitchen instead.

"Double A," says Dan, blushing slightly. "And two of them. But it's best to buy rechargeable."

I close the window of my Google image search just in time as Sam comes back into the lounge. "I'm not going to ask you how you got that one," I whisper.

Dan grins. "Best not."

"Okay," I say. "Final question, and then we're in. 'Which of the following diagrams shows the correct way to wire a plug?'" But instead of the usual three multiple-choice answers, there are ten different diagrams, each with a check box next to it. "Huh? That's not very girly."

Sam reaches over and pinches me on the arm. "Don't be so sexist."

"I'm not." I rub my right bicep gingerly. "It's just that the rest have been rather more female-oriented, and this, well, isn't."

"They haven't all been that feminine," says Sam, possibly still a little disgruntled at getting so many of them wrong.

"Yeah, right," says Dan. "Chick flicks, handbags, shoes, and vib . . ."

"Let's just get on with this, shall we?" I interrupt, scanning quickly through the diagrams. "Number seven, I think. Dan?"

He peers at the screen. "Looks right to me."

"Aren't you going to ask my opinion?" says Sam.

"Seven it is then," I say.

I'm just about to click on the box underneath, when Dan stops me. "Hold on," he says. "Click on any of the others."

"What? Why?"

"It's a trick question," says Dan. "No woman would ever know the answer to that."

"I do, actually," says Sam, a little defensively. "And it *is* number seven."

"Doesn't matter," says Dan. "They're banking on you getting this wrong. And with this many options, any woman's bound to guess, and guess incorrectly. So that's what we're going to do."

He reaches across and clicks on one of the other diagrams. There's a pause, and then a new screen loads:

Congratulations, and welcome to SlateYourDate. Click on the button below to fill in your profile details, or alternatively, start browsing.

"We're in!"

"Back of the net!" says Dan, putting both hands on my shoulders and shaking me triumphantly.

As he and I jump up and high-five each other, Sam just looks at us disdainfully. "Shall we take a look, then, children?"

"Sorry."

"Yes," says Dan. "Sorry, Mum."

50

We sit back down on the sofa, and I turn my attention back to the screen, scrolling down to where there are a couple of buttons in the shape of hearts with either *Search Reviews* or *Post a Review*. When I roll the mouse pointer over either of them, the hearts break in two.

"Nice touch," says Sam.

I click on *Search Reviews*, and a new screen appears with a choice of either *Name Search*, or *Most Reviewed*. I glance across at Dan, who's gazing fixedly at the screen, and am just about to click on *Name Search* when his ego evidently gets the better of him, and he knocks my hand away, grabs the mouse, and clicks on *Most Reviewed*. There's a pause as the next page loads, and then a small diagram of the UK appears on the screen, divided into the usual geographic sections.

"What do I do now?" says Dan, evidently disappointed that he can't check out his score on a countrywide basis.

"Well, where do you live?"

He moves the mouse pointer down to the bottom right of the image. "Brighton, obviously. But I've gone out with women from all over the UK, so it's not really a fair sample . . ."

"Just get on with it."

With a sigh, he clicks on the *London and the South East* section, and stares at the screen, waiting for the page to load. Perhaps not surprisingly, when the list appears, the name *Dan Davis* is sitting at the number one position.

"Yes!" shouts Dan, leaping up again suddenly and punching the air with his free hand, causing Sam and I to jump. "Forty-six! Eat my dust, mister . . . Adam Bailey," he says, sticking two fingers up at the second-placed name on the list.

I shake my head slowly. "It's not something to be proud of, you know."

"Why not?" says Dan, doing that dance where you look like you're stirring a large pot of something, while rotating your hips in the opposite direction. "Top of the list. When was the last time you ever came first in anything? Apart from a pie-eating competition. And besides, they might not all be bad reviews."

Sam can't help but laugh. "Dan, the site's called 'SlateYourDate'. They're hardly going to be glowing testimonies, are they?"

He shrugs. "You never know. Anyway. I'm still number one. And it's always better to be talked about than not talked about, or something like that."

"Well, let's see, shall we?" I take the mouse back, and click on Dan's name. After the briefest of pauses, a chronological list appears next to it, causing Dan to snigger.

"What's so funny?" asks Sam.

Dan points to the top of the second column. "Date of entry! They've got good memories."

Sam rolls her eyes. "You're going to get a high score for 'maturity', I see."

I scroll down to the bottom of the list — which takes a while — and find the first "review", but when I see the date I have to do a double take. "Hold on. Forty-six entries — stop smirking, Dan — in thirteen months? That's nearly one a week."

Dan raises both eyebrows twice in quick succession, like a ventriloquist's dummy. "Well, there might have been some overlap at times."

"At most times, by the look of things," says Sam disapprovingly.

"Okay," I say, "where shall we start?"

"With Julie Smith," says Dan, pointing at the screen. "At the bottom. Which, funnily enough, is where Julie liked to be . . ."

"Dan, please." I click on Julie's review, which is titled, ominously, *Steer Clear*, and a dialogue box opens underneath, where Julie's added her comments.

"'Lost all interest once he'd got what he wanted'," I read. "'Bastard.'"

"Well, that's brief and to the point," says Sam.

Dan peers at the screen. "Is that all?" he says, sounding a little disappointed.

"What more did you want?" I click on *Back*, and select the next name on the list. It's a Sarah Smith.

"Aha," says Dan. "Julie's sister. She wouldn't go out with me until I managed to make her jealous by hinting that I really fancied Julie."

"What a lovely tactic that is," says Sam. "And you did more than hint about Julie, given the previous review."

"I know," agrees Dan, without a trace of irony. "Works every time."

"So shall we see what Sarah has to say about you?" Sam grabs the mouse, and clicks on Sarah's entry, which is just titled *Git*.

She stares at the screen, then swivels it round to face Dan. "'Went out with both me and my sister without telling either of us'," she reads. "'When we found out, she and I didn't speak for a month. And I never want to speak to him again.'"

"And she hasn't," admits Dan, sheepishly. "Although I can't say I've phoned her lately to check."

I take the mouse from Sam and click back to the main list. "'Sally Phelps'." Care to enlighten us, Dan?"

He frowns at the screen. "Er . . . Can't quite remember her."

I open the review box. "Well, can you remember the time you abandoned her in a restaurant after telling her you were just going to the toilet, because the girl you were two-timing her with had just walked in, leaving her to pay the bill, and then not even bothering to call her to apologize? Because obviously it made quite an impression on her."

"Oh, *that* Sally Phelps." Dan shifts uncomfortably in his seat. "Well, I assumed that she might not be so keen on me after that."

"I think that'd be a safe bet," says Sam.

I click back to the main page. "Shall we go on?"

Dan grimaces. "Do we have to?"

"Martina Evans. You slept with her once and never called her back."

"Right. I, er . . ."

"Susan Winters. You stood her up three times in succession, claiming that you were stuck on set, when actually you were making sure she was out so you could shag her flatmate."

54

"Yes, well, I . . ."

"Anna Peterson . . . I can't even read out what it was you did to her."

As I go through the list, Dan sits up suddenly. "How about that one? Lisa Roberts. She's given me four stars. That's good, surely?"

I look at where Dan's pointing anxiously at the screen. "That's not four stars, Dan. She's put 'He's a complete ★★★★'. It's a blanked-out rude word."

"And I can guess what it is," says Sam. "Although judging by some of the other reviews, it could be one of many."

"There's got to be some good news, surely?" says Dan, sounding a little desperate now. "I mean, here — Deborah Wells. We had a good sex life, Debs and I. She must have given me a decent rating."

I scroll further up the screen and click on Deborah's comments. It takes a second or two for the page to load, and by the look on Dan's face, it's the longest second or two of his life.

"Uh-oh."

"What does she say?"

"She says . . ." I speed-read Deborah's entry. "Well, she's given you one . . ."

"Well, if she's admitted that, then I can't have been that bad."

"Out of ten, Dan."

His face drops. "Ah. Anything else?"

I search the review box, hoping for something I can put a positive spin on. "She does say that you were very athletic in bed."

Dan brightens a little. "Athletic. Right. That's good, isn't it? I mean, athletes are fit. And with good stamina."

"Unless they're sprinters," says Sam.

"Thanks a lot," says Dan miserably. "But it doesn't really say much about my technique, does it?"

"Hang on." I look at the bottom of the screen, where the words *page two* have just appeared. "There's more."

As I click on the link, Dan covers his eyes with his fingers, like a five-year-old watching a particularly scary episode of *Dr Who* from behind the sofa. "I don't think I want to see this."

"*You* don't want to see it?"

"What does it say?"

"I thought you didn't want . . ."

"Just get on with it, Edward."

"Here." I swivel the screen round to face Dan before the page loads. "You look. There's some things you don't want to know about your best friend."

"Don't be such a prune, Ed."

"It's 'prude', Dan. And I'd say we're already way past that point, wouldn't you?"

With a sigh, Dan picks the laptop up and reads through the rest of Debbie's comments, his lips moving slightly with the effort, before putting it back on the coffee table.

"Well, she's obviously lost it."

"How so?" says Sam, glancing down at the screen.

"Well, under 'comments' she's put 'Dan always seemed to suffer from being a bit premature.' I mean, I like to be early. So what? It's better than being late, surely?"

Sam struggles not to laugh. "No, Dan. I think she means 'premature'. As in, well, you know, in bed?"

"Oh?" says Dan, followed by a much longer "Oh", but, strangely, he doesn't seem to be at all embarrassed.

"Oh?" says Sam. "Is that it?"

"Which is what Debbie used to think, apparently," I say.

Dan rolls his eyes. "Very funny, Ed. And why is it you women always see that as a problem?"

Sam stares back at him for a moment. "Where would you like me to start, exactly?"

"Yes, Dan?" I say, perversely interested in his take on this particular issue, in the same way that you can't help looking at a car accident whenever you're driving past on the other side of the road.

"Well, it's a compliment, isn't it?"

"I'm going to need you to explain this one."

"Think about it," says Dan. "The more sexy you think she is, the more turned on you're going to be, right?"

I shrug. "I suppose so . . ."

"And the most turned on you can be is when you, you know . . ."

I'm trying hard to think of anything but Dan mid-orgasm. "Please tell me that you're going somewhere with this."

"All I'm saying is that if I was, in fact, a bit 'premature', to use Debbie's phrase, then it wasn't my fault."

"But hers?" says Sam.

"Exactly."

"Because she was too sexy."

Dan nods. "You've got it."

Sam looks at me, a disbelieving expression on her face. "And this is the man who's taught you everything you know about women?"

"Not everything, I hope?" I say, blushing slightly.

"No. Not everything," replies Sam. "Thank goodness."

After a further half an hour reading through one ego-crushing review after another, I kill Internet Explorer — more of a mercy killing, really — shut the laptop, and stand up to stretch my legs. Dan, meanwhile, remains slumped on the sofa, staring helplessly at the ceiling.

"Come on, Dan." Sam puts a comforting hand on his knee. "It's not that bad, surely?"

"Not that bad?" He pulls himself wearily up on to his feet and starts pacing anxiously around the room. "How can you possibly describe that as 'not that bad'? It's a disaster. I'm going to be a bloody laughing stock. The minute I appear on *Close Encounters*, the tabloids are going to have a field day, and I don't want my face splashed across all the front pages for the wrong reasons."

I'm wondering what on earth the right reasons might be. "Well ..." I struggle to think of anything comforting to say, because quite frankly, he's right.

"Whatever happened to 'It's better to be talked about than not talked about'?"

"Yes, but . . ." Dan picks up the laptop, and for a moment I think he's going to throw it through the window. "Not like this. And besides, this is slander. Libel, even."

"It's only libel when it's not true, Dan," Sam points out.

"That's not the point," he says, waving the laptop in the air. "Jesus! Everyone's got access to the bloody Internet nowadays — even women. At home, at work. Even on their mobile phones."

I follow him round the room, and take the computer from him. "Surely they're not all going to check you out before they, you know, make their decision?"

"Well, they obviously have been, haven't they?" says Dan, getting more and more agitated. "When was the last time you went to see a film without reading a good review? Or bought a book? Or ate at a restaurant?"

"Well, last week, actually."

"I'm not talking about bloody Pizza Hut, Edward. I mean a top-end restaurant. Somewhere classy. This" — he jabs a finger accusingly at the laptop, which I've put back down on the coffee table — "is how places close down."

"But . . ." I look across at Sam for help, but she just makes the "don't bring me into this" face. "Well, maybe they'll spell your name wrong when they're looking you up."

"Yeah, right," says Dan, increasing the speed of his pacing so much that I'm worried he's going to wear a hole in the rug. "Because 'Dan Davis' is really tricky to spell, isn't it?"

I see a couple of straws and reach out to clutch at them. "They might spell it D-A-V-I-E-S. Or miss the page out altogether."

"Yes, but I'm top of the bloody list, aren't I? Even if they look at it just the once, they're going to know all about me." Dan starts to hyperventilate. "What on earth am I going to do? I'm stuffed."

Suddenly, Sam stands up and blocks his path. "Karma, Dan."

He stops pacing, puts both hands on the back of the sofa, and takes a few slow, deep breaths. "I'll try, Sam, but quite frankly, it's hard to remain cool when . . ."

"No, Dan. Not 'calmer'. Karma."

"Huh?"

"Listen." Sam takes Dan by the hand and leads him back to the sofa, where he sits down meekly. "For years, you've been treating these women badly. Now they're getting together to get their own back. To ensure no one else can get hurt the way you hurt them. As I say, it's karma. What's been around comes around, and all that."

"And you've certainly been around," I add.

Dan stares open-mouthed at Sam for a second, before turning to face me. "I didn't know your girlfriend was into all this New Age hippy bollocks."

Neither did I. "Well, whatever, Dan. But she might have a point. I mean, you have behaved pretty despicably."

Dan suddenly looks hurt. "When?"

60

"Er . . . All the time. With every single woman you've ever gone out with. And now I think about it, with the ones who weren't single as well."

"That's not true," says Dan defiantly.

"Yes it is. All of them. All except for Polly, that is."

As Dan winces, Sam looks up at me. "Polly?"

"She was Dan's first proper girlfriend. And last, if you define 'proper' as someone you're faithful to. For more than two weeks."

"Blimey, Dan," says Sam. "She must have been special."

"Yes, well," he says, evidently anxious to change the subject. "Getting back to the matter in hand, what on earth am I going to do?"

I sit back down next to him. "Join a monastery?"

"Change your name?" suggests Sam.

"Ha bloody ha. Haven't you got any sensible suggestions?"

I think about this for a moment, but realize that actually, even though it's now obvious why Dan's been going through this dry spell of his, I haven't. "You could always turn gay?"

"Yeah, right," says Dan. "Next you'll be telling me that I'm going to have to start being nice to them to cancel it all out, or something."

My eyes meet Sam's, and by the look on her face, she's obviously thinking the same thing as me. "That's a brilliant idea."

Dan looks up at me suspiciously. "What is?"

I stand back up and start pacing round the room myself. "What you just said. About being nice to them."

61

"I was *joking*." He puffs his cheeks out and exhales slowly. "And, anyway, chance would be a fine thing. I won't ever get near enough to anyone new to . . ."

"No. I mean your exes." I lean over and tap the top of the laptop. "The ones who've given you these bad reviews. Why don't you try calling a few of them up and apologizing? Seeing if you can't make it up to them?"

Dan frowns. "What good would that do?"

I put an arm round his shoulders. "Well, for one thing, it might get them to reconsider some of the harsh things they've said about you."

Dan considers this for a second or two. "You think?" he says, the look of hope on his face so pathetic I don't dare say no.

"Yup. *Karma*, remember? How long have you got before you, I mean Wayne, first appears on *Close Encounters*?"

Dan stares at his watch. "Four weeks," he says, a hint of panic in his voice.

"Well, you'd better get a move on."

He swallows hard. "And you really think it'll work?"

I nod. "Worth a try, at least."

"Sam?"

She smiles. "Absolutely."

"And after all," I say, "it was your idea."

"It was, wasn't it?" says Dan proudly.

"And a brilliant one at that," adds Sam.

Always a sucker for any kind of flattery, Dan gets purposefully to his feet, then grabs us both by the hand, as if he's swearing an oath.

"Well, that's what I'm going to do then."

CHAPTER
FOUR

Work's fairly quiet the following morning. There's no sign of Natasha, although that's not particularly unusual for a Monday given her typical weekend excesses, so I just get on with the pleasurable job of sending out a few invoices. By one o'clock I'm starving, so head out to the deli across the road to buy myself a bagel — with low-fat cream cheese, of course — and I'm just about to cross the road when Dan leaps out from behind the postbox on the corner.

"Jesus, Dan! You scared me."

He claps me heavily on the shoulder. "That was the idea, Eddy-boy. Normally when someone's hiding and they jump out at you, it's to give you a fright. Otherwise I'd just have called out 'Hey, loser' from across the street."

"Sorry, Dan. For a moment, I forgot you were five years old. What are you doing here? And why were you hiding? Apart from to scare the living daylights out of me, I mean."

He scans quickly up and down the street, then removes his sunglasses and cap and slips them into the man-bag slung around his shoulder. "Couldn't risk you-know-who coming out and catching me, could I?"

Since he dumped Natasha after their brief fling, Dan's been a little wary of coming in to meet me in the office, even though he reckons the two of them parted relatively amicably. Given what I've seen her do to some of her other exes, the fact that he's alive and still has his full set of genitalia means he's actually not that wrong.

"So, er, what do you want?"

"I've had an idea," he says, waiting for a car to pass, before following me across the road like an excited puppy.

"Another one? That's two in two days!" I stop on the opposite kerb and wait for him to catch me up. "This calls for a celebration."

Dan ignores my sarcasm and points to the Starbucks next to the deli. "Buy me a coffee and I'll tell you all about it."

As he grabs a table by the window, I join the queue and get us a couple of cappuccinos, wondering why it's me who's paying to listen to his idea, then walk over to where he's taking up most of a large brown leather sofa.

"So," I say, settling into the armchair opposite, "do I really want to hear this?"

"Well, the way I see it," says Dan, spooning the chocolate-encrusted foam off the top of his cappuccino and into his mouth, "is this. I'd love to start being nicer to women in the future. Really I would."

"Ri-ight . . ."

"But I obviously won't get a chance to do any of that korma stuff . . ."

"*Karma*, Dan."

"Karma. Sorry. Not until I've got myself into a position where I've apologized to anyone that I've, you know" — he makes the speech marks sign with his fingers — 'upset' first."

"Precisely. Apologize to the ones you've already offended, they change their ratings, you're free to go off and be nice to any new ones you meet," I say, wondering whether Dan's summarizing things for my benefit, or for his.

"Exactly."

I take a sip of my coffee, then almost have to spit it back into the mug it's so hot. "Okay. With you so far."

"But I'm not sure that calling them up and apologizing like you suggested is the best way of going about it."

"Why not?"

"Well, for one thing, because I don't have their numbers."

"What — any of them?"

He shrugs. "Well, to be honest, at the time I didn't see any point in keeping them. Plus the old phone memory gets full after a few weeks, so I just go through every month or so and hit *Delete*."

"And you can't just look them up in the phone book?"

He stirs his cappuccino absent-mindedly. "Nah. I wouldn't know where to start. And, anyway, it might be difficult over the phone."

"Because they might just put it down on you?"

"Something like that. So I thought I'd be better off going to see them instead. You know — use some of the old Dan Davis charm."

I think about reminding him that it was the "old Dan Davis charm" that got him into this mess in the first place. "Sounds like a plan."

"I'm glad you said that." Dan swallows a mouthful of coffee, before wiping his foam moustache off with a napkin. "Because that's where you come in."

"Me?" I get a sudden feeling of déjà vu, and not in a pleasant way. "How exactly am I involved in this?"

"Well, you being a headhunter, and everything. I thought you could help me track them down."

"Track them down? Can't you remember where they live?"

"Mate, I wouldn't even have remembered their names if they hadn't put them on that bloody website. Which is why I need your help."

"So, let me get this straight." I put my coffee mug down on the table and sit back in my chair. "You want me to find all these women who you've" — I try to find the most appropriate word — "*wronged*, so you can waltz in and convince them that they've been a bit harsh, and ask would they mind upping your rating a little."

He nods. "That's about the size of it."

"And how many of them were there again?"

"Er . . ." Dan retrieves his latest mobile phone from his pocket, and opens up the web browser where he's evidently bookmarked the SlateYourDate site. "Forty-seven, now," he says, still with a touch of pride. "Including the latest one."

"What do you mean, the latest one? I thought you hadn't met anyone new?"

"I haven't. Maybe there's some time delay on the reviews, or something."

I take the phone from him and peer at the screen. "Kate Griffiths?"

Dan cringes a little, evidently remembering how he and Kate parted. "She's as good a place to start as any, if I'm going to be cleaning up my act."

"Which you *are* going to be doing, right?"

"Sure," says Dan shiftily.

"And how do you expect me to go about this, exactly? And more importantly when? Unlike you, I do have a full-time job, you know."

Dan points through the window and across the street towards my office. "Yeah, but your boss is hardly there, is she? And besides, it won't take a man of your skills long to track a few women down, will it? Then all you need to do is take a few days off work, and . . ."

"Hold on. A few days off work? What on earth for?"

He grins. "To help me confront them. And convince them."

"Isn't that the sort of thing you can do yourself?"

"Well, ordinarily, yes. But I've a feeling I might need a bit of backup. A character reference. Someone to stick up for me. A wingman, remember?"

"Someone to call an ambulance when they deck you, you mean, or stab you with their nail files."

"Come on, mate," pleads Dan. "I don't have a lot of time here. And anyway . . ."

"Anyway what?"

"It'll be a chance for you to pay me back."

"For what?"

Dan leans forward on the sofa. "Sam? The whole Jane business? You wouldn't be in the smug loved-up position you are now if it wasn't for my help, don't forget."

"Well, when you put it that way . . ."

"Exactly."

I let out a long sigh, unable to see any way out of this. "Don't you keep in touch with *any* of your exes?"

"What's the point?" Dan shrugs. "There's always a new ex to meet. Easy come, easy go."

I don't like to point out to him that those last four words could be a description of both his dating strategy *and* his sexual technique — according to Deborah Wells, at least. "The point, Dan, is that women are people too. And they have feelings. And surely some of them could have become your friends?"

"I've got enough friends, thanks. And girls and boys aren't supposed to be friends. Girlfriends and boyfriends, yes. But friends . . . Didn't you ever see *When Harry Met Sally*?"

"Not as often as you, evidently. But what about everything else in the relationship? The companionship? Shared interests?"

He gesticulates towards me with his plastic stirrer, causing a few spots of coffee to drip on my shoe. "Ed, the only interest I really shared with any of them was, well, *me*. And to be honest, new relationships are only about one thing anyway."

"Which is?" I say, when Dan doesn't enlighten me.

"The sex," he says, licking the stirrer in a rather disconcerting way.

"That's not true."

"Yes, it is."

"No, it isn't."

"Says the man who's had how many new relationships in the last ten years?" smirks Dan. "Oh, that's right, one. And even then, you've got to admit it — when you and Sam first got together, you couldn't keep your hands off her could you?"

I don't like to tell him that I still can't, given his current dry spell. "Well, that's because it had been a while. What with Jane, and everything."

"Okay," he says. "But tell me it hasn't slowed down a bit a few months down the line."

"Well, that's not really any of your business," I say, trying to sidestep the issue. "And besides, it's not me that we're talking about, is it? It's you. And it sounds to me like all you're actually doing is using these women for sex."

Dan looks a little offended. "Nope. I'm just doing what everyone does in the early stage of any relationship. Trouble is, because my relationships never progress past that early stage, looking at them retrospectively it seems that sex is what they're all about."

I sit there, shaking my head at his "logic". "That's right, Dan. You're just doing what everyone else does. Apart from dumping all these girls after no more than a couple of weeks, not even giving them the chance to get any further with you. I mean, you're my best friend and all that, but I'm suspecting your motives here are a little . . . selfish?"

Dan makes a "so what?" face, before he sees that I'm serious. "All right. I admit I may not have acted quite as honourably in the past where women were concerned. But this has made me think about some stuff. Honestly. And I promise that when I manage to get this stupid ratings business sorted out . . ."

"*If* you manage to get it sorted out."

"When I do, I'll start treating them a little better. Be a bit more considerate. Think about their . . ." — Dan takes a deep breath — "feelings. Because I realize that I can't go on like this for much longer."

"Like what? Being such a bastard?"

His eyes drift over towards the adjacent table, where the pretty young barista is bending over to wipe it down. "No. Single. Anyway — I've got something for you."

He reaches into his man-bag, and produces what appears to be the kind of dossier that M always hands James Bond at the start of every mission — packed full of names, photographs, and the odd telephone number.

"What's this?"

"Just call it my ex-files," he says. "It's everything I've got. Thought it might be helpful when you're trying to track them down."

"Thanks, Dan," I say, as sarcastically as possible. "That's very considerate of you."

"Consideration has nothing to do with it. I don't have time to run around the whole park, wondering what tree the pussy's in. So you need to make sure I'm not barking up the wrong one."

"As opposed to just barking?"

I flick through the file that Dan's just handed me, realizing that I'd better get on with it, otherwise — to use his analogy — Dan might just have to find another park.

"So, you'll do it?"

"Have I got any choice?"

Dan folds his arms. "Not really."

"Okay. But on one condition."

"Name it."

"You do actually change your ways afterwards. Start treating women decently, and not just as more notches on your bedpost. Call them back when you say you will. Don't just sleep with them the once and then kick them out the next morning."

Dan looks at me as if I've just asked him to cut his own leg off, then grins that famous Dan Davis grin. "Done," he says, clinking his coffee mug against mine.

And as he stares longingly at a couple of girls walking past the window, I wonder if I have been.

I spend the rest of the afternoon trying to clear a window in my work schedule so I can concentrate on Dan's "project" for the next couple of weeks, before heading home to spend the evening with Sam, and I'm just cooking dinner — well, "heating" would be more appropriate, because everything's ready-made courtesy of those two famous chefs Marks & Spencer — when she deposits one of those multicoloured bags with string handles that's wrapping paper for people in a hurry on the kitchen counter next to me.

"What's this?"

She smiles. "I got you something."

I rapidly run through my mental calendar, checking I haven't forgotten any important dates. It can't be our anniversary, and even though I'd rather forget the fact that I'm past thirty now, I'm pretty sure it's not my birthday. "What for?"

"No reason," says Sam, sitting down at the kitchen table.

"Well . . . thanks."

"You don't know what it is yet."

I make a big play of carefully feeling the outline of whatever's in the bag, before reaching inside and removing a white, and rather weighty, cardboard box.

"What is it?"

"You'll find out in a moment." Sam shakes her head. "You men are always so impatient."

"Depends what we're unwrapping."

I carefully open the box and slide a grey leather case out of the white cardboard sleeve, eyeing Sam suspiciously as I do. "This looks rather . . . expensive."

She smiles guiltily. "Might be."

I flip the lid open, catching my breath at the sight of the TAG Heuer logo before carefully taking out the beautiful silver watch.

"Sam . . . I'm speechless."

"It was worth the money then."

"Well, you shouldn't have. I mean, I'm glad you did, but this must have cost a fortune." I take the old Timex off my wrist — the Timex that Jane bought me for my twenty-first birthday, slip the TAG on, and click the metal bracelet shut. It fits perfectly, and feels pleasantly heavy compared to my old watch. "How did you manage to get it the right size?"

Sam points to the Timex. "I just measured that when you were asleep."

I breathe a sigh of relief, realizing finally why Sam had the tape measure in the bedroom the other night. "But seriously, what's the occasion?"

"No reason. I just want you to know you're appreciated, that's all. I've seen you admiring Dan's, and seeing as I couldn't afford to get you a Porsche . . ."

"Sam, I don't want everything that Dan's got. Besides, I've got something better."

She leans over and kisses me on the cheek. "That's easy to say when he doesn't have anyone at all."

"I was talking about the Mini. But now you come to mention it . . ." I stop admiring my new watch, and turn the gas down underneath the pan. "Anyway, we'll hopefully get that sorted out soon."

Sam looks at me, a smile playing across her lips. "So, you're going to help him go through with it?"

"Go through with what?" I say, even though I know exactly what she's referring to.

"This wild-goose chase of his."

"It's not a wild-goose chase. He genuinely wants to track down his exes, and apologize. Explain to them why he behaved how he did. At the very least, it might give them some closure. And, anyway, I thought you were all for it?"

"I am." Sam retrieves a bowl of salad from the fridge, and peels the cling film from the top. "But I'm a little worried that the only closure is going to be their front doors slammed in his face, unless he really means what he says. Women don't want an explanation after the fact — they want it to not happen in the first place. These girls have probably been scarred by what he's done, and for some of them it's probably taken them ages to get over him. So the last thing they'll want is Dan suddenly turning up again."

"Maybe so. But this is something he feels he's got to do."

Sam sighs. "But why does he have to involve you?"

"Because he's my best friend. And because he's asked for my help. And more importantly, because I owe him."

"Owe him?" Sam puts the salad bowl down on the table and looks up at me. "What could you possibly owe Dan that's so great that you're prepared to run around after him like this?"

I walk over to her and take her by the hand. "You."

And, not surprisingly, she doesn't have an answer to that.

CHAPTER
FIVE

Kate's easy to track down, mainly because she works in Licensed to Grill, the café just around the corner from where Dan lives. The café we often used to go to for breakfast on a Saturday morning before Dan and Kate started "dating". The café that nowadays Dan has to cross the road to avoid, in case a stale bread roll comes hurtling out through the open doorway and towards his head. The café that even I don't go in on my own any more, especially since last time my cappuccino appeared to have a little more froth on top than normal.

When I meet Dan outside his flat, he's understandably a little edgy. What's more, he's dressed in what looks like his oldest workout gear.

"Preparing to make a run for it?"

Dan shakes his head. "Just don't want coffee stains over anything new."

I look down at my clean white T-shirt. "Ah. Good point. So she's working this morning?"

"Yup. Already checked through the window."

"And was the place busy?"

Dan shrugs. "A few people eating at the tables. No queue."

"Great. So are you all set?"

"I suppose so." He looks up and down the road nervously. "How should we play it? Wait until it's completely quiet in there, or do we just go in now? Safety in numbers, and all that."

"We? Tell me again why I'm coming in with you?"

"Because you're my wingman. My number two." Dan punches me playfully on the arm. "And I might be able to use you as a shield in case any hot liquids come flying my way. So come on — what's the plan?"

I pull out my notepad from my pocket, and consult the list that Dan and I made up the previous lunchtime. "Right. Kate Griffiths. Dated for approximately a week, slept with five times — impressive, I must say, Dan — and then decided you didn't want to see her any more. And why was that?"

He crinkles his forehead in concentration. "Because I didn't think it would work out."

"Obviously, Dan. But why did you think that was the case?"

"Because I'm a TV star, and she works in a café, and . . ."

"The real reason, please."

"Er . . . I can't quite seem to remember."

"Well, what did she write about you on SlateYourDate?"

He shifts guiltily from one foot to another. "Something about her wondering whether I just couldn't deal with the fact that she had a kid."

"That's terrible."

"I know. Why couldn't she have been more careful in the past? There are too many single mothers, and that little lad is going to grow up without . . ."

"No, Dan. It's terrible of you that you reacted like that, not that she has a child. How old is he?"

"Ten? Twelve maybe? Dan holds his hand out, palm down, at about waist height. "About this high." He shrugs. "To be honest, I don't know. I don't really do the whole children thing."

"So why did you go out with Kate in the first place?"

"Because she's got great tits. Which she'd rub against me whenever she put my cappuccino down on the table. I tell you, I've never drunk so much coffee in my life."

"But you knew she had a child before you asked her out, right?"

"Yup." Dan nods. "I'd seen them together in the street. From a distance, obviously. I'd followed her home one day when I was thinking of asking her out."

I decide not to ask Dan if he knows the meaning of the word "stalking". "And yet that didn't stop you sleeping with her in the first place?"

"Nope."

"Why not?"

"Because there's just something about young mothers," he admits sheepishly. "I mean, for a start, you know they've had sex a lot — because they've got a kid, obviously — so they're probably quite good at it. And they're also a lot more grateful, seeing as they probably don't have sex much any more — again, because of the kid. And enthusiastic, because it's probably the first time in ages that . . ."

I hold my hand up, unsure which of the holes in Dan's argument to point out first. "I'll just stop you there, Dan. Repeating any of that to Kate is hardly going to get you off the hook with her. In fact, you're more likely to get a hot sausage roll stuffed somewhere that even you wouldn't enjoy. What exactly did you tell her when you broke it off?"

"Er . . ."

"You did tell her something, didn't you? And not just avoid the café and stop taking her calls."

"I'd like to say 'yes' to that, Edward. Really I would."

"Dan!"

"Well, it was difficult, wasn't it? I mean, every time we went out, there was young Damian to think of, and . . ."

"Damian? Is that actually his name?"

"I dunno. Mark. Or Martin, or something." Dan shudders. "They're all Damian to me, Ed. Kids are scary. Haven't you seen *The Omen*? And then she started dropping hints that maybe I might like to meet him. You know, so we could do things together? And the idea of me becoming 'Uncle Dan' creeped me out, I don't mind telling you."

For some reason, the idea of him as "Uncle Dan" sounds rather creepy to me too, although possibly not for the same reasons. "So what you're telling me is that you purposely got a young mother to drop her guard and start sleeping with you, and then didn't give her any explanation when you dumped her, but let her think that it was because her having a child was something you couldn't deal with, even though you actually knew she had one in the first place?"

"Um . . ." When Dan doesn't answer, I begin to realize that this whole quest of his might not quite be as straightforward as I'd thought.

"Right. Well, you're going to have to give her one now."

"Hur hur."

"I'm serious, Dan."

"Okay, okay." He stuffs his hands into his pockets, and stares down at the pavement like a scolded child. "Such as?"

"Tell her . . . Tell her you were immature, and that you weren't ready for the commitment of taking on someone else's child. Oh, and say that you know you behaved despicably, but wanted to end it before you ended up hurting him as well as her."

Dan nods. "So lie, basically?"

"Dan, it's not a lie," I say, thinking *particularly the "immature" part*. "Because that's actually what might have happened. You have to realize that telling the truth sometimes is all that people want."

"Like Jane did with you?"

"Well, yes, to be honest. Okay, it might hurt their feelings from time to time, but at least they won't be forever wondering what they did wrong. Which in most of your girlfriends' cases, seems to be nothing, apart from agreeing to go out with you in the first place."

As Dan looks at me guiltily, I can only hope that some of this is sinking in. "Come on, then," he says eventually, before taking a deep breath. "Wish me luck."

We walk round the corner and on to Western Road, pausing outside Live and Let Fry, the chip shop next door to where Kate works — just so Dan can check his reflection in the window — before walking into the café. Kate's standing behind the till, but with her back to us, so I go and sit at a table in the corner while Dan makes his way hesitantly up to the counter. There are a few other customers sitting reading their papers or working their way through huge full English breakfasts, the smell of which immediately makes me salivate, and I'm just taking a sneaky peek at the laminated menu propped up against the tomato-shaped ketchup dispenser on the table in front of me when there's a loud shriek, followed immediately by a crashing sound from behind the counter.

I drop the menu and leap out of my chair, in time to see a worried-looking Dan helping Kate pick up the pieces of the plate she's just dropped.

She shoos him away angrily. "What are you doing here?"

"I came to, er . . . I wanted to . . ." He looks over towards me for support, and I nod encouragingly. "I needed to say something to you. To, um, you know, *apologize*."

This seems to take Kate by surprise, because she stops collecting the broken bits of crockery and stands up.

"Apologize? To me?"

"Yes," says Dan, nervously eyeing the jagged porcelain shards in Kate's hands. "For treating you so badly when we, I mean, after we, you know, went out."

"Slept together, you mean?" says Kate, a little too loudly for Dan's liking. "Because I don't think we ever actually left the house, did we? Or, more specifically, my bedroom."

"Keep your voice down," whispers Dan, as an old guy in the corner looks up momentarily from his copy of the *Sun*, although for the other diners their breakfast is too great a lure.

"Keep my voice down?" Kate throws the broken plate noisily into the bin beneath the till before raising the volume a notch or two further. "Why should I keep my voice down? And who's going to hear me, apart from . . ." She peers in my direction. "Edward? Is that you?"

"Er . . . Hi, Kate." I smile and wave, but given that she's just picked up a bread knife, I don't dare move from where I'm standing. Not surprisingly, Kate doesn't return either of my friendly gestures.

"So anyway," says Dan, leaning back slightly as Kate slams a breadboard down on the counter. "I wanted to say sorry, and that I, er, should have told you why we, um, split up."

"We didn't 'split up', Dan," says Kate, barely able to conceal the anger in her voice as she picks up a baguette from the breadbasket behind the till. "In fact, I could be forgiven for thinking that we're still together, seeing as the last time I saw you, you were tiptoeing out through my bedroom door, and I haven't seen or heard from you since."

"Yes, well, there was a reason for that."

"Which was what, exactly?" says Kate, as she starts to chop the baguette up roughly. Dan glances anxiously over at me, so I mouth the words "go on" at him.

"Because I, er, realized that I was too" — he clears his throat — "immature to be in a proper relationship. Particularly because of little Dam . . . I mean, Martin. Mark. Malcolm?"

"Michael!" says Kate tersely.

"You see? I can't even get that right. I'm no good with kids. I mean, once they get to sixteen I'm better, but then only if they're girls, and . . ." He coughs awkwardly. "Anyway, what I'm trying to say is that you've got every right to hate me, but when I saw the rating you gave me on that website, it was the first time I realized how much I'd hurt you, and, well, if there's anything I can do to make it up to you . . ."

As Dan assumes his best sorrowful expression, Kate finally puts down the bread knife and folds her arms. "So that's what this is all about. You're worried about your rating on SlateYourDate."

"No, not at all. I just hadn't realized that you felt so strongly about the way I dump . . . I mean, the way things ended between us."

"Rubbish," says Kate. "What's the matter? Struggling to get a girlfriend now because you're such a shit?"

"No," says Dan.

"Yes," I call from the other side of the café, as knowing Dan's defensiveness, he's in danger of undoing his relatively poor attempt at an apology. I walk over to the counter and put my hands on his shoulders. "Dan's really suffering, Kate. He's had a taste of his own medicine, and he's realized that he needs to change. Big time. And that's why he's keen to do anything he can to set the record straight. Isn't that right, Dan?"

When he doesn't answer immediately, I give him a quick shake. "Yes," he says, reluctantly. "Anything."

Kate looks at me for a moment, then at Dan, and a tight smile appears on her face. "Is that right?" she asks.

Five minutes later, we're walking back along Western Road, and Dan's in a foul mood.

"What were you thinking?" he shouts, shaking his head, then kicking an empty Fanta can angrily into the road, where it narrowly misses a passing police car.

"Karma, remember?"

"Yes, but . . . babysitting?"

"Don't think of it as babysitting, then. Think of it as community service."

"There's only one half of the community I want to service."

"Yes — and it's that that got you into trouble in the first place. Anyway, it might do you some good."

"How do you mean?"

"To spend time with someone of your own maturity level."

"But," he splutters, "I hate kids."

"Dan!"

"Well, not hate, exactly. But I wouldn't choose to hang around with a bunch of them."

"I should hope not."

Dan walks on in a moody silence until we reach the top of his road.

"Well, what on earth should I do with him, then?"

I nod towards Dan's Porsche, which is parked just around the corner. "Just take him for a spin in that. Hell, it'd be exciting enough for me, so imagine what a ten-year-old will think."

"But what if he's" — Dan makes a face — "sick in it?"

"Dan, he's ten years old, not ten months. And even your driving's not that bad."

"But . . . Friday night!"

"And you've got other plans, have you?"

Dan doesn't say a word, but just sulkily fishes around in his pocket for his keys. After all, we both know the answer to that question.

CHAPTER
SIX

I spend the rest of the week unsuccessfully working my way through Dan's "dossier", as many of his exes seem to have left the city, and in some cases, even the country, in an attempt to get over him. And while this hasn't stopped them trying to get one over on Dan — or at least their own back — via SlateYourDate, it makes my job a little harder.

By the Saturday, worried that time is ticking on and frustrated by the lack of progress, Dan has decided on a change of tactics, and so he and I are off to Eastbourne to find someone called Claire, whose surname he can't remember. She hasn't posted a review on SlateYourDate yet, but when Dan says that for safety's sake it's worthwhile trying to "head her off" just in case, I stop him before he can tell me what it was he actually did.

"That's a nice watch," he says, when I meet him beforehand for a quick drink in the Admiral Jim to discuss our strategy. "Is it real?"

"Yup," I say. "Unlike most of your girlfriends' breasts."

He clicks his fingers. "Hand it over."

Reluctantly, I unbuckle the clasp and slip the TAG off my wrist. "Be careful with it."

Dan takes the watch from me, and then of course makes a big play of pretending to drop it. "Waterproof to 30 metres," he says, examining the dial closely. "Well, that's good for you."

"Why?" I watch him anxiously, as he looks like he might want to test it out by dipping it in my glass of wine.

"You can only swim what, 25 metres max?"

"Very funny, Dan."

"Where'd you get it, then?" he asks, as I snatch it back from him and fasten it on my wrist.

"Sam."

"You traded her in for a watch?"

"No, idiot. She bought it for me."

"Uh-oh," says Dan, rolling his eyes.

"What do you mean, 'uh-oh'?"

"Well, it's not your birthday. Is it?" he adds, suddenly alarmed.

"No, it's not. And surely even you wouldn't forget that?"

"Of course not," says Dan, looking a little relieved, especially when I don't follow up by asking him when my birthday actually is. "So what are you going to get her?"

"When?"

"In return, dummy."

"In return? Why do I need to get her anything in return?"

Dan sighs, and then taps his beer bottle against my wine glass, as if ringing a school bell. "Are you sitting comfortably?"

"Huh?"

"Then I'll begin. There are a number of reasons that couples buy each other presents. The obvious ones, like birthdays and Christmases, the not-so-obvious ones, like anniversaries, or out of guilt."

"Well, I've got news for you, smart arse. This isn't any of those."

"Oh really?" says Dan, sceptically. "What then? Because there aren't any more."

"Sam just said that . . ." I can feel myself reddening. "That she wanted me to know that I was appreciated."

"Appreciated? You?" He starts to laugh. "That's a good one!"

I feel myself bristling slightly. Why shouldn't Sam appreciate me? In the face of Dan's reaction, I almost want to step over the line, and say that it's probably partly down to him — and *SlateYourDate* — that she did it. Seeing that many disgruntled women who have suffered at the hands of men — well, one man in particular — maybe just made her think that she might be on to a good thing with me. But of course I don't, because I'm not that nasty. And not that arrogant. And still suffering the effects of being dumped out of the blue by Jane too strongly to feel anything like that confident about Sam and me.

"Don't be such a cynic. Just because someone does something nice for you, you don't suddenly have to get all suspicious. Sam just decided to get me a present. Simple as that. End of story."

Dan folds his arms. "One that cost about five hundred quid, right?"

"I guess so." I know so, actually. Because I looked in the jeweller's window this morning.

"So, if you're ruling out any of the previously mentioned reasons for her getting it for you, and we dismiss your quite frankly ridiculous idea that she's done it because you're such a great boyfriend, that only leaves one thing."

"Which is?"

He sits back smugly in his chair. "She wants something back. And something of equal value."

"Don't be silly, Dan. That's not how it works."

"Yes it is. Remember the Christmas before last, when Jane wanted that really expensive Prada handbag?"

"What about it?"

"And you made some crack about how much it cost, and that she already had about ten handbags."

Which was an underestimation, as it turned out. "So?"

"And you remember she told you not to get her anything, and that she'd wait and see if it was any cheaper in the sales? So you didn't."

"Only because she wanted to choose it herself," I say a little defensively.

"And then, what did you wake up to on Christmas morning?"

"A set of golf clubs. And are you going somewhere with this?"

"Just hear me out. Were you expecting a gift like that?"

"Well, to be honest, no. They were top-of-the-range. Plus I didn't actually play golf then."

"So what did you do?"

"Well, I thought I'd better take some lessons, seeing as . . ."

Dan reaches over suddenly and cuffs me round the back of the head. "About her present, dummy."

I smooth my hair back down. "Well, I went out and bought her the handbag on Boxing Day."

"And there's my point."

I take an exaggerated look around the bar. "Where?"

"Don't you see? She wanted something expensive, couldn't justify just going out and getting it herself, so instead she bought you something to the same value just so you'd feel guilty enough to go out and do the same for her."

"Yes, well, I remember thinking at the time she'd been rather generous. But you're forgetting something."

Dan takes a gulp of his beer. "Which is?"

"Sam's not Jane."

Dan makes a face, and gestures towards me with his bottle. "She's still a woman, mate. Superior model, granted, but the same basic operating system."

"But she wouldn't be so . . ." I try to think of an adjective to describe Jane's behaviour that isn't rude. And it takes me a while. "Calculating."

"Mate, why do you think people use the word 'foxy' to describe women?"

"I thought it was to do with their looks?"

"Nah. It's because they're all so cunning. Even Sam. Besides, when was the last time you saw an actual fox you wanted to shag? Although thinking about it, given

89

my current status, if I could catch one of the red-coated little buggers behind the bins . . ."

I try to ignore the image Dan's just planted firmly in my mind. "I don't believe you."

"Okay," says Dan patiently. "Let's work this through. So she's just spent five hundred quid on you. Unprompted. What was your first reaction?"

"Well, I was flattered, obviously."

"And immediately after that?"

"Dan, please just tell me what you're going on about, rather than all these 'examples' of yours, which quite frankly are about as clear as mud."

"Okay. Sorry. Say I bought you a drink."

"Chance would be a fine thing," I say, looking at my empty glass.

"Yes, but say I did. What would your first reaction be?"

"What — after I'd picked myself up off the floor?"

"Yes," says Dan tersely. "After that."

"Well, I'd drink it, obviously."

"Obviously. And then?"

I know what he's driving at, although I hate to admit it. "I'd, er, probably buy you one back."

"Aha."

"Dan, sometimes people just do nice things. Generous things. Without expecting anything back."

"Not women, mate. And not in relationships. Otherwise you wouldn't be feeling so guilty that you didn't get her anything."

The annoying thing is, Dan's right. I do feel guilty. Guilty that Sam's spent what, for her, is an awful lot of money to buy me a present out of the blue. Guilty that I didn't think of buying her something first. And thanks to his little talking-to, I'm probably going to feel like this until I manage to get her something in return.

"And I suppose you've got some smug theory as to what it is she wants?"

"Yup," he says, picking up a discarded copy of the *Argus* from an adjacent table and flicking through it noisily. "But you won't want to hear it."

I sit there looking at him for a few moments, before snatching the paper away. "Just get on with it."

"Well, she's bought you a watch."

"Ye-es?"

"And a watch is?"

"Well, it's a clever wrist-borne way of telling the time, based on the fact that a quartz crystal vibrates exactly fifty times a second when electricity . . . Ow!"

"Sorry, mate," says Dan, as I rub my left nipple, where he's just done a painful tweak-and-twist. "Couldn't think of a quicker way to shut you up. Let's try a slightly different approach. Your watch came from where, exactly?"

"Er . . . Sam?"

"Nope. Try again."

I stare at the dial, looking for clues. "Switzerland?"

Dan rolls his eyes. "Think of where she bought it," he says encouragingly.

"Brighton?"

"For Christ's sake, Edward!"

"A jeweller's?"

"Finally. So, following this through logically, if I bought you a pint, what would you expect to buy me in return?"

"Well, a pint, obviously."

"Obviously. So if Sam's bought you this watch, then what do you think she wants?"

"A watch?"

He looks at me as if I'm simple. "Almost, but not quite. A watch is?"

I cover both nipples with my hands. "Er . . ."

"Remember where it came from."

"Jewellery?"

"Well done, Einstein. So she wants some jewellery that's not a watch but costs five hundred pounds. Which means she wants you to . . ."

As he beckons towards me in an attempt to draw my answer out, I think hard. Sam's not that big on jewellery. In fact, I don't even think she's got her ears pierced. And as far as I know, nothing else either. "Er . . ."

Dan eventually runs out of patience. "Give her a ring!" he almost shouts.

"What — and ask her?" I say, reaching for my mobile. "Isn't that a bit blatant?"

"Jesus. How you manage to get yourself up, dressed, and out of the house in the mornings is just beyond me," he sighs. "An engagement ring, dummy."

I nearly drop my phone in surprise. "Don't be ridiculous, Dan. We've known each other for, what, less than a year? So I hardly think she's going to be wanting me to get down on one knee."

Dan smirks. "You sure about that, are you? Sam's a pretty traditional type of girl. She'll want to do things in the proper way. And that starts with a trip to Tiffany's. Or Elizabeth Duke, in your case."

I'm wondering what to say in reply to Dan's quite frankly ridiculous theory when Wendy appears. She's had to undo the top two buttons on her jeans to accommodate her bump, and Dan can't help staring at the exposed flesh.

"Blimey, Wendy. You're looking . . . large," says Dan tactfully, before his eyes travel upwards. "Still, at least you've got some tits now."

"Are you sure you're not having twins?" I say, noting Wendy's expression suddenly darken.

She pulls out a chair and lowers herself into it gratefully. "I hope not."

"I had twins once," says Dan, gazing wistfully off into the distance. "Jackie and Julie. Or rather, Julie and Jackie. Anyway, didn't seem to matter. That was one crazy night, I can tell you."

Wendy gives Dan her usual disdainful look. "Congratulations, by the way."

"Thanks," says Dan. "I was rather proud of it myself. I mean, I was nervous when I suggested it to the two of them, but we'd all had a few drinks, and . . ."

"She means for getting the *Close Encounters* part, idiot."

"Oh. Yeah," says Dan. "Thanks."

"How are you doing?" I ask her.

Wendy smiles, and rests a hand on her stomach, although she could probably rest a pint glass on there if she tried. "Oh, not so bad. A bit tired."

Dan grins. "Which is just how I felt the morning after Jackie and Julie . . ."

"Listen, Edward," says Wendy, leaning towards me, which takes some effort. "There's something I have to tell you."

Dan points to her bump, and then jerks his thumb in my direction. "It's not his, is it? That'd be funny!"

Wendy looks at Dan for a moment, then leans forward, sticks her finger in his beer, and flicks it at him, causing him to nearly fall backwards off his stool. "Now *that's* funny."

"Thanks a lot, Wendy." Dan stares at the spots of beer on his Atari T-shirt. "This is vintage, you know?"

"Phew," she says. "Thanks goodness it wasn't a new one."

As Dan heads off to the toilet to inspect the damage, Wendy turns back to me. "Sorry about that."

"Don't worry about Dan," I say. "He failed his GCSE in tact and sensitivity. What was it you wanted to say?"

"It's just . . ." Wendy clears her throat. "Well, there's no easy way to say this. No point in dressing it up, I mean. So I'll just come right out with it. Tell it to you straight . . ."

"Wendy!"

"Sorry." She takes a deep breath. "I saw Jane the other day. In town."

94

"Jane? *My* Jane?" I suddenly feel a little weird, especially since I haven't spoken to her since she came back from her trip. "Oh. Right. How was she?"

Wendy shrugs. She and Jane used to be friends, although I don't think Wendy has quite forgiven her for flitting off to Tibet without telling her she was going. Or telling me, for that matter.

"She seemed fine. She was asking about you."

"Oh. That's nice."

"No, Edward. I mean, *asking* about you."

I'm still none the wiser. "Wendy, you're going to have to spell it out for me, I'm afraid."

"You know. Asking what you'd been up to."

"I've not been up to anything."

"No, Edward. Whether you had a girlfriend. That kind of thing."

"Oh. *Oh.* What did you tell her?"

Wendy just about manages to get her elbows on the table, then rests her chin on her hands. "Well, I kind of fudged it, to be honest. I mean, I didn't think it was my place to tell her anything, really. After what she did to you."

"A woman did something to you?" says Dan, sitting back down at the table. "When? And why do you look like you've seen a ghost? Or is that just from sitting next to the inflatable woman here?" he adds, moving his glass out of Wendy's reach.

"Wendy's just told me that she's seen Jane."

Dan takes a sip of his beer, frowning at me over the top of his glass. "Jane?"

"You know. *My* Jane."

He looks even more puzzled. "Who?"

"My ex-girlfriend Jane."

"Ah. *That* Jane. Sorry."

Wendy gives Dan a pitying look. "However do you remember any of your lines?"

"They don't give him that many. For that precise reason."

Dan ignores us both. "You threw me a bit with the 'my Jane' bit. I mean, it's just that she isn't any more, and . . ."

"What was she doing back here?" I say, cutting Dan off.

Wendy opens her mouth to answer, but Dan gets there first. "Well, it can't have been to see you, obviously."

"Why not?" I say, slightly offended.

"Because if that was the case, she'd have done that already. I mean, it's not as if she doesn't know where you live, or where you work."

He's got a point. "Was she . . . on her own?"

Dan raises one eyebrow. "Interested, are we?"

"Shut *up*, Dan." Wendy glares across the table at him. "Yes, she was, Edward. She said she was down visiting her mum for a few days. Death in the family, apparently."

"Shame it wasn't her," mumbles Dan, to no one in particular.

"Oh, no," I say, suddenly concerned, and wondering whether I should give Jane a call. "Did she say who?"

"Someone called Lucy," says Wendy. "Apparently her mum's distraught."

I can't help but laugh. "Lucy?"

"Edward," scolds Wendy. "That's not very nice — making fun of the deceased."

"Sorry, Wendy. But last time I saw Lucy, she bit my hand. Quite badly, actually."

It's Wendy's turn to look confused. "Who was she? A mad old aunt?"

"A dog. An old dog in fact."

Wendy raises both eyebrows. "I'm surprised you didn't know her then, Dan."

"No, I mean an actual dog. Lucy is, sorry, *was*, her mum's cocker spaniel. And a vicious one at that. So as far as I'm concerned, it's good riddance."

"Which is how I felt when Jane left," says Dan.

"Did she say anything else? About wanting to see me?"

For a moment, Wendy looks as if she's deciding whether to tell me something. "Not really. I mean, she asked about you, and all that, and I said you were fine, but then her mum appeared, so she didn't probe me too deeply, or anything."

"Hur hur," says Dan.

I'm slightly disappointed at this, although I'm not sure why, and, to be honest, a little hurt that Jane hasn't got in touch, even just to say hello. I mean, ten years is a long time. And surely I deserve at least that much?

"So, did she say if she was staying long?" I ask, trying to sound as uninterested as possible.

Wendy nods. "A few days. Until the funeral, at least."

Dan nearly spits out his beer. "They're having a funeral? For a dog?"

"Don't sound so surprised," says Wendy. "Pets mean a lot to some people."

"Hey," says Dan, holding his hands up. "I love animals."

"Dan, this isn't going to be another one of those stories we don't want to hear, is it?"

"No," he laughs. "Nothing like that. Although I do share certain animal characteristics. With the horse, for example."

"And with the cheetah," suggests Wendy. "Though not quite the same spelling. Did Jane's mum have Lucy for a long time, Edward?"

"I think she got her to keep her company when Jane left to go to college."

Dan grins. "That was a fair swap. Like for like, anyway."

"Dan!"

As I sit and listen to Dan insulting my ex-girlfriend, and Wendy half-heartedly defending her, I'm suddenly feeling nervous, wondering if Jane is going to turn up and surprise me, either here at the Admiral Jim or even at my flat. It seems weird, knowing that she's back in Brighton. That I could bump into her on the street. After all, it's not that big a city. And what am I going to say if I do? Have I forgiven her for running out on me like she did? Is it even me that needs to do the forgiving? I mean, it's been the best part of a year since she left, and I can't believe she hasn't been back before, so like Dan says, seeing me obviously hasn't been a priority for her. Which I do find a little hurtful.

But hey — I'm over her, aren't I? And happy with Sam. So why should I care? In fact, maybe I should be the bigger person, and make the first move. Call her up, or surprise her round at her mum's. Then again, maybe that's not such a great idea as, thinking about it, maybe her mum resents me for making Jane move away to wherever it is that she's been, and I don't want to get my head bitten off — although at least the same thing won't happen to my hand, thanks to Lucy's recent demise. But what good will seeing Jane actually do me? Do I actually need to close off that chapter once and for all, especially since — given what a great time I'm having with Sam — I didn't even suspect that it might still be open.

"Come on," says Dan, tapping his watch in front of my face, and disturbing me from my thoughts. "We've got to be somewhere, remember?"

"Oh. Yes. Sorry." I help Wendy up out of her chair, then follow Dan outside to where he's left the Porsche, having evidently driven it the hundred yards from his flat to the pub.

"Interesting development," he says, as I look up and down the street nervously just in case Jane's about. "Tell me something."

"What?"

"Isn't there just a small part of you that wonders if you could have won her back? If all that hell you put yourself through during those three months was worth it?"

"Won who back?" I say, knowing full well who he's referring to. "Besides, it *was* worth it. I got Sam out of it, don't forget."

"Yes, but even though you ended up with Sam, initially you did it all to get Jane back. Isn't that a bit like taking an exam and not ever finding out the result?" Dan whistles softly as he blips the Porsche open and climbs in. "I don't know about you, but it'd drive me mad. Crazy. I wouldn't be able to sleep at night after something like that."

"Shut up, Dan. I'm not interested."

"Course, the simple fact that you've got another girlfriend now might be enough to tip the balance. Nothing like a bit of competition to get a woman working overtime. So whatever you do, don't tell Jane about Sam when you see her. Otherwise it'll skew the results."

"There won't be any results to skew. Because I'm not even planning to meet up with Jane."

"But she might be planning to meet up with you. And then you'll be in trouble."

"Trouble? Why will *I* be in trouble? Dan, for the last time," I say, jumping into the passenger side and slamming the heavy door shut behind me, "I don't want to know."

"Well, you'd better make sure you steer completely clear then," he says enigmatically, before starting the engine. "Anyway, buckle your seat belt. Costa Geriatrica here we come."

As I reach over my shoulder and pull the seat belt out, I'm feeling more than a little confused — and not just because I can't seem to find the slot by the side of my seat to click it into. Because in spite of my denial about any interest in knowing whether I'd have managed to win Jane back, and despite my feelings for Sam, there's a part of me that says that maybe I *do* want to know. Jane's leaving *did* put me through hell — or rather, Sam put me through hell as a result of Jane leaving, although that was only because I paid her to do so. But before I can say anything about it to Dan, my head is slammed into the backrest of my seat as he stamps on the accelerator and guns the Porsche along the seafront.

"What do you think?" he says, patting the steering wheel affectionately. "Drives well, huh?"

I rub the back of my neck, wondering whether this is what whiplash feels like. "I take it you mean the car, rather than you? And, anyway, I thought you celebs were all supposed to own one of those new hybrid thingummys? Not something like this."

Dan's face falls. "What's wrong with it?"

"Well, for a start, it's not very green, is it?" I say, pointing to the electronic fuel gauge, which is showing a rather shocking twelve miles per gallon.

"Who cares?" says Dan. "Besides, given the amount I've reduced *my* emissions by over the last few weeks, I could almost single-handedly solve the global warming crisis. And I mean 'single-handedly'."

"Thank you for that image, Dan."

"Just listen to that sweet exhaust note!" He grins, braking hard for the speed camera by the Marina, then revving the engine excessively as he changes gear. "Sounds great, doesn't it?"

I finally manage to fight the G-forces and get my seat belt clicked in. "All apart from that knocking sound."

He eases off the accelerator slightly. "What knocking sound?" he asks worriedly.

"Oh hang on. That's my knees."

Dan gives me the briefest of sideways glances before overtaking a bus that's pulling out in front of us. As I shut my eyes, he speeds round the wrong side of a traffic island, then cuts back in at the last minute with a cry of "yes!"

"Er . . . Dan?"

"What?"

"I think what you did just then was illegal."

Dan smirks. "Which is why we're heading over to see Claire, funnily enough. She . . ."

"Please, Dan. I'm starting to think that the less I know about your escapades the better."

"Suit yourself," he says, tweaking the button for the electrically adjustable door mirrors, although I don't know why, given that he doesn't seem to be using them.

"So, how was the big night?" I say, keen to change the subject, and hoping that if I get him talking, given Dan's inability to multi-task, he might actually slow down a little.

He looks blankly across at me. "Big night?"

"Last night," I say, willing Dan to fix his eyes back on the road. "Your babysitting. What did you do?"

"Oh, *that*." He shrugs. "Spin in the car, trip to Burger King, then back to my flat to watch a DVD. Bit like one of my dates, really. Except I got to watch the whole film this time."

"What sort of film?" I have to ask, hoping it wasn't one of his, ahem, foreign ones.

"Some Disney thing he chose in Blockbusters. About some fish."

"Oh. Good. So, did you . . ." — I can't stop myself grinning at him — "enjoy it?"

Dan considers this for a moment. "It was quite good, really. The fish got separated from his dad, and . . ."

"No, Dan. The babysitting. Spending time with a small person."

"Fuck off," says Dan. "But let's just say it wasn't completely unbearable. And you know, I think I've got a way with kids."

"Well, having the same mental age undoubtedly helps. And Kate's agreed to delete your bad rating on Slate YourDate?"

"Yup." Dan makes to "high five" me, or rather, "high ten", which I don't dare do since he's taken both hands off the wheel, and we seem to be travelling at about ninety miles per hour.

"And you'll be spending time with him again?"

He looks at me as if I've just asked whether he enjoys cleaning toilets. "Ed, I looked after the kid for an evening. I didn't agree to adopt him."

"Fair point. And how do you feel? About righting your wrongs in that way?"

Dan slows down a little, although it's only because he wants to check out an attractive girl he's spotted waiting at a bus stop. "I don't know. It's strange, really.

Like a weight is slowly being lifted. As if I'm starting to see the light."

I'm impressed — if not a little surprised. "Really?"

"Of course not," splutters Dan. "Don't be ridiculous. It's just got to be done, hasn't it? Like going to the dentist. It's unpleasant, but you have to go through with it."

I exhale slowly. "And there's me thinking you were actually learning something. About how to treat women, I mean."

"Edward, I know everything about how to treat women. A lot of which I taught you, don't forget."

"But aren't you starting to worry that some of it might be, well, *wrong*?"

Dan looks at me open-mouthed. "Don't you think that it might be them?"

"What — all of them?" I ask, willing him to turn his attention back to the road.

He nods. "It's a possibility."

"All . . ." I try to remember how many bad ratings Dan had at the last count. ". . . forty-seven of them? With that many axes to grind, don't you think that they might have a point?"

Dan shakes his head. "Ed, what happens when you're headhunting someone for a job, and they tell you they're not interested? You go on to the next one. And then the next one. You don't accept that the job itself might be dodgy."

"I might if forty-seven of them turned me down."

He shrugs. "It's like my acting. I've been to hundreds of auditions. Hardly had even a sniff of a part.

Following your theory, I should have given up long before now. But here I am, with a new starring role in ITV 5's most popular soap . . ."

"Most popular afternoon soap," I correct. "Thursday afternoon, that is."

"Whatever," says Dan. "But you see my point. We're on this earth for a good time, not a long time, don't forget. So you've got to make the most of it."

"But this is *people* we're talking about. You shouldn't go through life hurting everyone you meet. Everyone female, that is."

Dan stamps on the brakes to avoid a brown Nissan Micra that's pulled out in front of us, and then accelerates past it, flipping the woman driver the finger as he does so. I cringe in my seat as we pass, as she's about eighty.

"Rubbish. It's a battle of the sexes. And in any battle, there are going to be casualties. You just have to make sure you're not one of them."

He reaches down and fiddles with the CD player, evidently satisfied that this conversation is over, while I try not to worry that he's straying dangerously close to the grass verge. As we veer between the lanes, I realize that my comment the other day about his driving being "not that bad" was perhaps a little hasty, and it's not until we reach the more sedate surroundings of Eastbourne that I'm finally able to prise my fingers off the dashboard in front of me, where I've been holding on so tightly that I'm almost expecting them to have left marks.

"Is it safe to open my eyes?"

"You big girl's blouse."

I suddenly remember why we're here. "Speaking of which, do you remember where Claire lives?"

"No need. She'll be at work."

"Oh," I say, when Dan doesn't enlighten me any further. "Right. Where's that?"

"Where I shagged her."

"Thanks for that, Dan. I meant what was she doing the last time you saw her?"

"Well, um . . ."

"What?"

"It's a little embarrassing."

"What was it?"

"Giving me a blow job."

"Jesus, Dan. You're a classy guy. I mean what was she doing for a job?"

"Exactly, a blow . . ."

"Dan, please. You do remember where she works, at least?"

"Yup."

I find a street map in the glove compartment. "Which is where, exactly?"

"Hold on. It's coming." Dan narrows his eyes. "Which funnily enough is the last thing I said to her."

I sigh and unfold the map, spreading it out on the dashboard. "What was the name of the street?"

"No need for that." Dan taps his forefinger against the side of his head. "All in here, Eddy-boy. When it comes to sex, I'm like an elephant. And I don't just mean that I've got a huge trunk."

Ten minutes later, we're driving down the same street for the third time. "I thought you said you could remember where she worked?"

He shushes me. "It's definitely somewhere around here. You've got to remember, things look different in the light."

"You're sure it was Eastbourne?"

"East something. Grinstead, maybe?" Dan suddenly hangs a sharp right, causing me to bang my head on the window. "Of course I'm sure. I was here doing panto. And that," he says, heading towards a large building with "Congress Theatre" written on the front of it, "is where I was."

"What were you in again?"

"*Babes in the Wood*."

"That's appropriate."

Dan grins. "Because of the babes?"

"No. The wood. Which just about sums up your acting ability."

"And my porn-star nickname."

"So, she's an actor?" I say, anxious to change the subject, or at the very least get the current image I have of Dan out of my head.

"Nope. She works in the pub around the corner. The Hussar. Which is where all the actors hang out. And which should be just about . . ." — Dan flicks the left indicator on the Porsche, then pulls noisily into a parking space that's got a "Disabled" sign beside it — "here."

I point through the windscreen at the blue sign with the wheelchair logo. "Should you be parking here?"

"Why?" says Dan, oblivious. "You think something might happen to the Porsche?"

"It's a disabled space."

"So? Disabled people can have nice cars too."

"Yes, but you're not . . ." I look at his blank expression and realize I'm wasting my time. "Never mind."

We get out of the car and peer up at the pub, which has a couple of rainbow-striped flags flying either side of the sign.

"She works in a gay pub?"

"A gay pub?" Dan frowns. "How can a building be . . .? Oh, you mean the clientele."

"Yes, Dan."

"How can you tell?"

I nod towards the "Hussar" sign. "The flags?"

"Nah, mate. That's just to show that it's an actors' hangout."

"Oh. Right. Like all those *actors'* pubs in Brighton."

"Exactly," says Dan. "Where I'll be welcomed with open arms once Wayne Kerr leaps on to the screen."

"More than you think."

Dan leans against the side of the car and gives me a little push. "So what are you waiting for, then? Off you go."

"What? Why do I have to go in?"

"Because I don't want to be recognized."

"By Claire? Or by anyone?"

"Just see if she's there, will you?" says Dan impatiently. "Then come out and get me."

"Well, what does she look like?"

"Er . . ." For a moment, Dan looks stumped, then pulls his mobile phone out of his pocket. "Hang on. I've got a photograph."

"Just make sure you censor it first."

I've seen some of Dan's phone photos of his girlfriends before. He's often in them at the same time — and I don't just mean the photos. But fortunately this one's just of Claire, and even though it might be hard to recognize her with her clothes on, I push my way in through the heavy wooden door and into the dimly lit pub. It's full of couples — same-sex couples, that is — and ignoring the heads that swivel in my direction, I make my way across to the bar.

Once my eyes have adapted to the gloomy interior, I spot someone who could be Claire behind the bar, and as she makes a "what can I get you?" face I start to say that I'm just looking for someone, but instead, feeling suddenly self-conscious, order myself a half of lager. I'm trying to force myself not to drink it down in one when another woman appears from a doorway behind the bar and walks over to where Claire's standing. They look a little similar, particularly in this light, and I'm just wondering how I'm going to tell which one of them is actually Claire, when something happens that makes it pointless. They kiss. And it's not just a "hello, nice to see you" kiss on the cheek, but a full — with tongues — kiss that almost makes me drop my glass.

I don't want to stare, but I don't want to miss it either. After all, it's the kind of thing I've only ever seen on video before — round at Dan's, I hasten to add. And when they eventually break apart from each other,

109

I hurriedly finish the rest of my lager and head back outside.

"So?" says Dan, turning the stereo down from its nightclub volume setting and sticking his head out through the car window.

"Start the engine."

"What?" Dan looks puzzled, and then suddenly nervous. "Why?"

"Because you're not going to be able to charm your way back into Claire's good books, I'm afraid."

Dan frowns at me. "Why not. Is she dead, or something? Or fat?"

I walk round the car and jump into the passenger side. "It's worse than that, actually. And I'm starting to wonder how you managed to charm your way into her pants as well."

"Worse?" Dan turns the key in the ignition, and the engine roars in response. "What could be worse than being dead? Or fat, come to think of it?"

"Well, she's, um . . . Let's just say her living arrangements have changed a little since you knew her."

"What has where she lives got to do with it?"

"Not where. How."

"Huh? She's not" — Dan shudders — "married, is she?"

"No. Well, I don't think so, I mean, nowadays, anything's possible. It's just . . ."

"Come on, Edward. Spit it out."

"Well, she's living with another woman."

"So?" Dan licks his lips, no doubt entertaining the possibility of a threesome.

"No, I mean 'living with'. In the biblical sense."

"She's found God? Mind you, she was fond of shouting his name when we were . . ."

"Dan!" I can see I'm going to have to spell it out to him. "Listen mate. I'm sorry, but . . . Claire doesn't seem to like men any more."

"Well, that's hardly my fault," splutters Dan. "I mean, I wasn't that bad to her."

"No. I mean she doesn't like men because, well, because she likes women now."

It takes a few seconds for this particular grain of information to process through the grey mush that Dan calls a brain, but when it finally does, instead of the shock I was expecting, Dan punches the air in celebration.

"Yes!"

I'm puzzled myself now. "What do you mean 'yes'?"

"She's a carpet muncher. A paid-up member of the dungaree-wearers' club. She's —"

"Gay, Dan. And what are you so happy about?"

"Isn't that obvious?" he says, dancing around in the car seat. "She slept with me, and now she's a les-be-friends. Result!"

"How on earth can that be a 'result', Dan? Surely even you'd think that the fact that someone's, er, *become* a lesbian shortly after sleeping with you might not speak too highly of your romantic prowess?"

Dan shakes his head, and steers the car out into the traffic. "Edward — only you could spin something like this into a negative."

I'm more than a little mystified. "How can it possibly be a good thing?"

"Think about it," he says. "She's had a taste of the old Dan DNA, and then obviously decided that no other man will ever match up, so in order to avoid living in a constant state of disappointment, she's decided to start drinking from the furry cup instead." He nods smugly. "Like I said — result."

I sit quietly for a moment, letting the wave of Dan's arrogance wash over me. "You don't think that maybe she was always . . ." — I struggle to come up with a description to match Dan's more colourful ones, but fail — "that way inclined, and just slept with you to see what it might be like with a bloke, and the experience merely reinforced her view that she was playing for the right team in the first place?"

"Why on earth would I?"

I've obviously momentarily forgotten the size of Dan's ego. "Well, maybe going on your recent ratings, for one thing. And, anyway, people don't just *turn* gay."

"Not in your experience, perhaps," says Dan, taking the opportunity of being stationary at some traffic lights to put the roof down. "Which we all know isn't that extensive. Anyway, you believe what you want to believe. The important thing is that now Claire obviously prefers a bit of tongue and groove action, there's no danger of her saying bad stuff about me. So we can go back to concentrating on the list."

"There it is again. That 'we' word."

Dan shrugs. "Just reminding you that you owe me."

"Bloody hell, Dan. Just keep saying it, won't you."

"Of course." He smiles. "No point beating around the bush. Which is the opposite of Claire's philosophy, of course."

Dan's ridiculously chirpy on the way home, so much so that it's a relief that it's impossible to hear him above the roar of the wind as we speed along the coast road. I'm not due to see Sam this evening, so I get him to drop me off at Tesco's, and I'm pushing my trolley round, going through a mental list of the "healthy" foods that Sam's recommended I stick to, while wondering whether I can sneak a packet of Jaffa Cakes in on the justification that there's at least a little bit of fruit in them, when I feel a tap on my shoulder. When I turn around, I nearly knock the display over in shock. It's Jane.

"Edward?"

I've thought about this moment: the time when I'd see her again — even before Wendy mentioned that she was back. Since the day she left me, in fact, I've wondered what I'd say to her. Some killer put-down, or snappy one-liner, to demonstrate that while she hurt me at the time, I'm over her now, and even though she was the one who did the dumping, it's me that's come out of it the better person. But this is a lot to put into a sentence, especially when feeling taken aback while holding a family-sized packet of Jaffa Cakes, so instead a croaky "Hello" is the best I can manage.

"I didn't recognize you at first," she says. "You look so diff . . . I mean, you look great. And your trolley's full of green things. If I hadn't seen you drooling by the biscuits . . ." Her voice tails off. "How are you?"

I manage to find my normal voice again, even though inside I'm reeling with shock, and I realize that it's hard to know what to say when you haven't seen someone for so long, especially after seeing them almost every day for ten years.

"Fine. I mean, good, thanks." In truth I should be angry with her for leaving me, and leaving me with just a note, and yet it's not anger that I'm feeling. So even though at the same time I can't work out whether it is actually nice to see her or not, I say it anyway.

"And you," she says, finally stepping forward and giving me a hug, as if my words have suddenly given her permission. She still smells the same, although I'd be hard pressed to remember the name of her perfume, and this suddenly strikes me as really strange — ten years of living with someone, and you can't even remember what scent they wear. I stand there awkwardly with my arms down by my sides, not daring to hug her back, until she lets me go, then squeezes my left bicep appreciatively. "Are those . . . muscles?"

I feel suddenly uncomfortable, as if she's seeing me naked for the first time, and I can't stop myself from blushing. "I've been spending a lot of time at the gym."

Jane looks puzzled. "As in 'Admiral'?"

"No, g-y-m. I've joined one. And I'm using it," I add, remembering the time she and I both signed up with an expensive fitness centre in Hove and I got so depressed after my initial "fitness" assessment that I never went back.

"So I see."

We stand there staring at each other for a second or two before it occurs to me to put the packet of Jaffa Cakes back on the shelf.

"So . . . How have you been? Where have you been, actually?"

Jane smiles, although I can't detect a trace of guilt. "Well, Tibet, obviously, which was amazing. There was this small village up in the mountains, and we all . . ."

"Not Tibet. After Tibet. Brighton's a small place. I thought I might have seen you around."

She shrugs dismissively. "I got a new job. In London. In the City. And it wouldn't have been practical to commute, so . . ." She catches herself. "You know I always fancied working in the 'big smoke'." She makes the speech marks sign, but whereas when Dan does it he just looks stupid, it makes Jane seem a little affected.

"And you got that job after you came back from Tibet, did you?" I say, a little more sure of myself now. "That was quick work. Even for someone whose boyfriend was a headhunter."

For the first time, there's a slight blush in Jane's cheeks, and I'm wondering whether mine are reddening too, from being so unusually direct with her. There's a pause as a teenager wearing his jeans almost around his knees pushes in between us and clears the shelf of the last five remaining packets of chocolate fingers, before Jane starts speaking again.

"No, I'd sort of been talking to them for a while."

"While you and I were still together, you mean?"

"Well, yes. And then the chance came up to take some time off in between . . ."

"So you really had no intention of coming back to me?" I say, cutting her off on purpose. "Despite what you said in your note?"

"My note?" Jane crinkles her forehead, then suddenly seems interested in something on her shoe. "Edward — we'd reached a point where, I mean, I just felt . . ." She looks around helplessly. "I'm sorry. This isn't really a conversation to be having in the confectionery aisle in Tesco's."

"Would you prefer to move to the fruit and veg section? Or perhaps next to the cold fish . . ."

Jane winces, but recovers quickly. "You know what I mean. Listen, I'm staying at my mum's for a few days. Why don't we have a coffee? Or a quick drink." She peers into my conspicuously alcohol-free trolley. "You do still drink, I take it?"

I'd like one right now, in fact. A large one. And maybe if we were in the wines and spirits section, I'd be twisting the top off the nearest bottle and taking a swig, such is the spot that Jane's just put me on. I don't want to go. In fact, I know I shouldn't go. I also know that I'm happy with Sam now. And even more important, I know that I'm much happier with Sam than I ever was with Jane. But as I stand there, I realize that there's still a part of me that needs an explanation. To hear exactly where — and when — we went wrong. And as much as I hate to admit it, Dan's right. Because I also want to know whether I'd have been able to win her back.

At the same time, it occurs to me that this is the perfect opportunity for a little revenge. A chance to reject her the same way she rejected me. To say "no

116

thanks" and just walk away with my head held high and a moral victory, if not a packet of Jaffa Cakes, in my trolley. And while I'd like to think I'm a bigger person than that, perhaps I'm not.

But whatever my motivation, surely saying no to her is the best way for me to achieve closure. So when I find myself doing the complete opposite, it comes as a complete surprise.

CHAPTER
SEVEN

Jane's mother lives in Hove, in one of the large houses near the park on the way out of town. I'm feeling uneasy as I drive up the familiar road, although that's probably as much from having not told Sam about where I'm going when I saw her last night — or again when I called her earlier today — as at my apprehension about seeing Jane. I'd had the chance to tell her, of course. Several chances, in fact. And I hadn't taken any of them. Because yesterday I was too scared of what Sam's reaction might be, and when I rang her this afternoon, I realized that the actual reason I was phoning her then was so she wouldn't call me later when I was out with Jane, and I was too ashamed. And it makes me feel so rotten — so sick even — that I find myself wondering how on earth Dan did this sort of thing, with all his different women, and still managed to sleep at night. Then again, actually *sleeping* was the last thing he wanted to do.

And while I tell myself that the reason for not telling Sam is to protect her, in actual fact, it's to protect me. Not that I'm planning to "do" anything, as far as Jane is concerned, of course. It's just that I don't feel good about any of this. And so the less I discuss it with anyone — Dan, and particularly Sam — the better.

I pull the Mini into the driveway and park it behind a small, sporty Peugeot that I'm guessing must be Jane's new company car, before walking slowly up to the front door and ringing the bell. The chimes sound strange not accompanied by Lucy's frantic yapping, and even though it's a stupid automatic reaction, when Jane opens the door and shows me into the house, I can't help but glance nervously down at her feet.

"Sorry," I say, the memory of my last vicious savaging still fresh in my mind. "Force of habit. Bloody Lucy. You'll excuse me not coming to the funeral, but I was worried I'd have wanted to dance on her grave."

"Mum, you remember Edward?" says Jane, in a loud voice.

Oops. I smile guiltily up at Jane's mum, who I hadn't seen standing behind Jane in the hallway, hoping she hasn't heard me insulting her recently deceased dog. Obviously she remembers me. I dated her daughter for ten years. Although from the expression of surprise on her face, she doesn't quite remember me like this.

"Of course. Hello, Edward. You're looking well."

Jane's mum and I never really got on. I suspect she thought I wasn't good enough for her daughter. And eventually her daughter came to realize that too.

"Hello, Mrs Scott." In all the years we knew each other, I never quite felt comfortable calling her by her first name. Come to think of it, I can't actually seem to remember what it is.

"We're just popping out for a drink," explains Jane, ushering me quickly back outside and towards my car before I can say anything else embarrassing. "See you later, Mum."

"Yes," I say, pleased to be out of the house. "See you later."

As Jane's mum watches us through the net-curtained window by the side of the front door, I walk Jane to the Mini and blip it open, noticing for the first time that she seems rather dressed up for a "quick" drink. In fact, she's wearing her black imitation-leather trousers — trousers which we used to refer to jokingly as her "pulling pants". Although after she had the affair, the joke wore rather thin. Like I'd mistakenly thought the trousers must have, seeing as she didn't wear them again.

"Nice car," she says, as I jump in and start the engine. "Whatever happened to the Volvo? Did it finally give up on you?"

"What, like you did?"

Great. I'd planned to ease into this. Maybe have a fun hour or so reminiscing about old times, before gradually steering the conversation round to what I really want to know. But instead I've leapt straight into it before we're even out of the driveway. And it hits home too, because Jane seems momentarily to lose her composure, maybe even seeing for the first time how much she hurt me.

As I accelerate up the street, my eyes fixed on the road ahead, she puts a hand on my arm. "Edward, I didn't give up on you. You gave up on yourself. What was I supposed to do?"

It's a good question, and in truth I don't have a good answer. If I was smart, I'd have worked this all out before. Prepared a series of telling responses and devastating put-downs. But even though I've had the best part of a year to come up with some, I'm still nowhere near Jane's level.

"I wanted to make a clean break," she continues. "A fresh start. And while that might not have seemed very fair to you, I thought it was best."

Best for you, perhaps, I'm close to saying. The Mini suddenly feels a bit claustrophobic, and I open the windows to get some air. "And you didn't think that just talking to me about it would have made a difference?"

"Edward, I'd tried talking to you until I was blue in the face. And it didn't have any effect. We'd fallen into a rut, it was getting boring, and I thought you were a lost cause. But looking at you now . . ." She sighs, exasperatedly. "Why did it take me leaving you for you to do something?"

Jane stops speaking and stares straight ahead, as a few drops of rain start to hit the windscreen. We drive on for a while, listening to the squeak of the wipers, until I break the uneasy silence.

"So are you seeing anybody now?"

I don't know why I'm asking that question. Maybe it's because I want her answer to be "no", so I can rub her nose in my current loved-up state. Or perhaps somewhere deep inside of me I want to know that she's found someone too, and that she's not feeling as lonely and terrible as I did in those few weeks after we split up. But equally it's perhaps because I'd prefer to know that she left me for someone else. Because that would make it a little more bearable. And less my fault that she went.

"No. No I'm not. I wanted to focus on work for a while, until I got my feet under the desk, so to speak."

"Oh. Right. Fair enough." And as I say those words, I suddenly hope that she's not going to turn the question round on me. Because I realize that, actually, I *do* want her to be happy. Like I am. And I also know that me admitting to seeing Sam might not actually be the sensitive thing to do, seeing as Jane hasn't found anybody yet. So when she inevitably asks, instead of lying, I take the usual male approach of trying to avoid the issue.

"And how about you? Anyone significant in your life?"

"Well, I still can't seem to shake Dan. Oh, and I got made a partner, you know? At work."

"Really?" Jane sounds more than a little surprised, although not as surprised as I am that my diversionary tactic seems to have worked. "Congratulations."

"Yes. Ever since you left, things have been going really well. Not that that's *because* you left. I mean it in a timing sense."

She laughs at my awkwardness. "Of course you did, Edward."

In truth, I'm finding it a little hard to concentrate on saying the right thing and drive at the same time, so it's a relief when I spot a pub I half-recognize on the next corner.

"How about this place?"

As I flick the indicator and park outside, Jane turns to me and smiles.

"That's sweet of you."

"What is?"

She stares fondly at the pub. "Remembering the place you took me on our first date."

I follow her gaze, suddenly realizing why the place seems familiar. Jane and I had come here to get away from the usual college watering holes. We'd even had our first kiss underneath the old wooden sign hanging over the door. And as we sit in the car, it doesn't occur to me that Jane might be reading something into this.

"Oh. Right. It doesn't seem to have changed much," I say, noting the same old peeling lettering.

Jane unfastens her seat belt and turns to face me. "No, but you have."

"Pardon?"

"The losing weight. The car. Even the haircut. And are those contact lenses?" She smiles, and puts her hand on my thigh. "And the muscles," she adds, giving my leg an appreciative squeeze. "Don't think I haven't noticed."

"Yes, well, after you left, I thought I'd better take a bit of your advice," I say, conscious that Jane hasn't removed her hand.

"So you did all this . . . for me?" she says, raising her voice slightly so I can hear her over the noise of the rain drumming on the car roof.

"Well, I kind of thought that we might have a chance. After what you said in your note. Stupid, I know."

She seems a little stunned. "It's not stupid, Edward. It's romantic. Possibly the most romantic thing I've ever heard. Especially from you."

As unaccustomed as I am at dealing with women and reading their signals — despite Dan's continued tutoring — I can tell that I'm in danger of getting into trouble here. Because Jane's got the same look on her face she used to get when she used to feel horny, or rather — especially towards the end of our relationship — when she'd had too much to drink, which sadly was the only time she'd feel horny. And we're sitting very close together in a very small car. And she's still got her hand on the inside of my thigh. And from what I can tell, she seems to be inching it upwards. I suddenly feel very uncomfortable, and it's the same dreadful sense of in-the-wrong-place discomfort you get when you're out shopping and you realize that you're accidentally browsing in the women's clothing section instead of the men's. Except I haven't just taken a wrong turn out of the changing rooms — this time it's completely my fault that I'm here.

Jane smiles. "Shall we?"

"Shall we what?" I say, more than a little nervously.

"Go inside. For a drink."

"Er . . . Let's just wait here for a moment? Let the rain ease off a bit."

In truth, it's not raining that much, but the real reason that I can't get out and walk to the pub is because I've got the beginnings of a hard-on. And while

124

it's more to do with Jane's simple physical proximity and the position of her hand on the top of my leg than any hidden feelings that are, ahem, arising, the last thing I want is for her to get the wrong idea. But what happens next shocks me even more.

"I'm getting wet," she says, shifting in her seat, causing her plastic trousers to make a rather unseemly noise on the leather upholstery.

Oh no. She must have seen. And what's she expecting? Us to reignite our relationship by having sex here, outside the pub, in broad daylight, on a busy street? And what's more, in a *Mini*?

"Pardon?"

"From the rain. How do you shut the window?" Jane finally removes her hand from my thigh, but it's only to start searching around on the door for the button.

"Oh. Right. Sorry." As I reach across to press the appropriate switch, all of a sudden, and to my complete surprise, Jane leans over and kisses me. On the lips. Which feels weird, because it seems comfortable and uncomfortable at the same time. And while I don't push her away, because that strikes me as being rude, I don't exactly respond either, and instead just hope that she'll eventually stop. But when she stays where she is and tries to push her tongue into my mouth, I clamp my lips together in a ridiculous turnaround of what used to happen whenever I tried to kiss the girls in my primary school class. And for a good few years afterwards, now I come to think of it.

Jane pulls away from me, a strange expression on her face. "What's wrong?"

"Nothing. I, er, that was just a bit unexpected, that's all."

"What did you want me to do? Say 'I'm going to kiss you now?'"

"No, I meant unexpected, as in against the run of play." I'm desperate to wipe my mouth, as there's a ring of Jane's saliva around it where her tongue was denied entry.

"Playing hard to get, eh?" she says, a look of mock hurt on her face.

"Not at all. I just don't think it'd be such a good idea."

"Why not? Come on, it'll be just like old times," she says, leaning across and putting one hand on my gear stick. But this time, I'm ready for her, grabbing her shoulders to stop her before she gets within tongue range.

"Old times weren't necessarily good times, if you remember."

"They could be," she says, pushing forwards against my hands. "Again."

That doesn't quite make sense to me — either grammatically, or given what I know about our relationship history. "Jane, I'm flattered. Really. But this just isn't right."

Her face suddenly darkens and she pulls away and stares moodily out of her window, giving me the vital couple of seconds I need to surreptitiously wipe my mouth on my sleeve. "Well, what are you doing here with me then?"

It's another good question. And to be honest, I'm not quite sure myself now. I think about telling her that maybe I'm just trying to end things on a slightly better note, rather than looking for the real reason that she left me so unexpectedly. I know now that revenge isn't what I'm after — not after seeing her lonely like this. Vulnerable, even. But then I stop myself. I don't owe her any explanation. After all, she's the one who dumped me, and then suggested we get together to talk about why. And now, as usual, she's making it sound like this misunderstanding is all my fault.

"I thought you wanted to . . ." I want to add the word "explain", but knowing Jane, she probably thinks that she already has. There's no way I'll ever get an apology from her — I know her too well for that — so in the end decide on what should be a fair compromise. "I mean, I just thought we could be friends."

"Friends?" Jane looks up in surprise. "Oh hang on. I know what this is about." She folds her arms, and a smile creeps across her lips. "Are you going to make me say it?"

Unfortunately, I am. And not because I want to try to force some confession or admission out of her, but because I don't really have a clue what she's talking about.

"Perhaps you'd better."

She takes a deep breath. "I want to give us another try, Edward. I don't want to be your friend. I want to be your girlfriend. Again." She takes my hand, and I don't have the heart to pull away. "Maybe I was a little bit hasty. I did a lot of thinking while I was away, and then when I came back I had to see you."

As the rain starts to ease off, along, thankfully, with my hard-on, this strikes me as not quite the case. As Dan said, if she'd really missed me, then she'd have come to see me the minute she'd arrived home, rather than leaving it so long. And even then she didn't make a special effort — in fact, we actually owe our meeting up again to her mum's dog dying. Even in death, Lucy manages to reach out and bite me. But this time, I'm determined she won't draw blood.

Because the more I think about it, the more I'm able to put two and two together. Jane hasn't missed me. She's missed anyone. She's tried this new life, and it hasn't worked out quite the way she planned, and she's been lonely. So then she sees me again, perhaps looking a little more attractive than when she left, and the prospect of something familiar, something comfortable, proved too hard to resist. It's like buying a posh new pair of shoes, but when you get them home, you find they're a little too painful to wear, so you go back to your old, comfortable pair instead. Especially when you see how well they clean up. To be honest, it seems a little fickle. In fact, it sounds like the sort of thing Dan would do. And I'm nobody's old shoes.

"And?"

Jane stares straight ahead at the condensation forming on the inside of the Mini's windscreen. "And when I did, I realized I'd made a mistake."

For a moment, I'm stunned — and not only because it's so rare for Jane to admit that she's been wrong about something. On the one hand, this is brilliant. I *would* have won. All those months of single-minded effort on my part, and it worked. But, as I said to Dan, it's not all about winning and losing. Or at least, it shouldn't be.

"But, Jane . . ."

"But what? You can't tell me that you haven't missed me."

"Of course I have. I mean, I did. But you left me, remember. What was I supposed to do? Just wait here for you to come back?"

Jane looks as if she's about to say "yes", then stops herself. "I see what this is all about. You're hurt. Angry with me. And rightly so. But that'll pass. And I know we can be good together again. Like before."

I frown at her. "Like when before?"

Jane swivels round in her seat to face me. "Pardon?"

"Like when before, exactly? When was the last time we were good together? Things weren't great for a long time before you left, Jane. And while I know that a lot of that was down to me, you have to accept some responsibility for that too."

"So it's my fault that you got fat and lazy?"

I want to say, well, in a way, yes. But that wouldn't be the most constructive thing to say at this point in time. "Jane, whoever's fault it was isn't important. But it happened. We drifted apart. And whatever the reasons for that, there'll always be the danger that it will happen again. And besides . . ."

"Besides what?"

And here it is. My chance to deliver the knock-out blow. And although I've been trying to avoid it for the past few minutes, I really haven't got any choice — especially if I want to stop her trying to kiss me again. And what's more, it really is the end of the argument.

"I'm with someone else now."

Jane sits bolt upright, as if the heated seat has suddenly switched itself on at the maximum setting. "You are?"

"Yes," I say, trying not to be hurt at the level of surprise in her voice. "And we're very happy."

"Who is she? Do I know her?"

"I don't think so. Her name's Sam." For some reason, I stop myself short of giving Sam's full name, then in the same instant realize I'm probably being a bit over-cautious. "Sam Smith."

Jane shakes her head in disbelief. "How long has this been going on?"

For some reason, the tone of her voice annoys me, as if she's accusing me of doing something immoral.

"For a few months," I say, deciding not to admit it was pretty much on the day that Jane came back from Tibet.

"Well, you didn't waste any time."

I don't know why I suddenly feel guilty. But then Jane always had that knack of making me feel like I was in the wrong. "I didn't know I was supposed to. Besides, aren't you forgetting one thing here?"

"What?"

"You'd dumped me. I was a free agent, remember."

"Yes, but . . . That's no excuse for jumping into bed with the first tart you meet."

"Sam's not a tart. She's a . . . personal trainer."

"And I suppose you were her client?" Jane lets out a short laugh. "Well, she certainly got personal with you, didn't she?"

"You don't have the faintest idea about her," I say, raising my voice slightly. "So please don't talk about her like that."

"I'm sorry, Edward. I'm just a little shocked."

"That I met someone else?"

"Well, yes. A little, to be honest. And so soon after I dumped, I mean, after we split up."

I didn't know there was a recommended time-frame, although if it's Dan, it's about ten minutes. And not necessarily post-dumping, either. "Anyway. You haven't got a leg to stand on."

Jane rolls her eyes. "Not this old chestnut again."

But I can't help myself. And besides, if you've got a valid argument, surely you can use it as much as you like? "You're the one who had the affair. Not me."

It wasn't strictly an affair, to be honest. Jane got off with someone when we were still together. A guy at work, who she snogged at some office do. And while it didn't go any further than that apparently, that was far enough for me.

Jane doesn't deny it, but instead, and in a way that's all too familiar, turns the whole argument around again. "Yes, well, that was your fault too."

"My fault? Next you're going to tell me it was a cry for help."

"Which it was, in a way. You don't think I really fancied Martin, do you?"

"Well, you managed to stick your tongue down his throat. And normally it's only people who fancy each other who do that sort of thing."

Jane blushes slightly, but quickly regains her composure. "But it didn't go any further than that."

"Oh. Well that's all right then. Phew."

Jane makes a face at my sudden childish outburst. "I did it to get your attention, Edward. Because you weren't paying me any."

Here we go again. All of a sudden, Jane has managed to make me feel that the break-up was all my fault. But surely, following her logic through, then I might have been behaving that way in the first place because of something she'd made me feel, or do? As I try — and fail — to come up with an effective counter-argument, ironically Dan's way of life suddenly seems the sensible, less complicated option.

I take a deep breath and exhale slowly. "Jane, there's no point trying to assign blame. What's in the past is in the past. And I think we both have to accept that whatever happened was down to both of us."

Jane looks at me from the corner of her eye, opens her mouth as if to speak, and then shuts it again. "I suppose so," she admits eventually, before wiping the condensation off the window with her hand. "It's stopped raining."

"Right."

"So . . . a farewell drink, at least?"

I consider this for a second or two, but on reflection I don't want to risk Jane having one too many farewell drinks and then trying to say "farewell" by attempting to stick her tongue down my throat again. "I don't think that would be such a good idea. Not here, anyway."

"Oh." Jane stares regretfully at the pub, and for some reason that makes me feel a little sad. I don't want to leave things like this — on an awkward note — not after so long together. Surely Dan is wrong about not being able to be friends with a girl, even when she's an ex-girlfriend? After all, he's wrong about so many other things. So even though I'm still feeling a little awkward about being here with her, the polite thing to do, I realize, is to let Jane take the lead now.

"So where do we go from here?"

She smiles, mischievously. "Well, how about back to my place?"

"Back to your place? Jane, I told you, I'm with someone."

"My mum's place, I mean. Just to drop me off. Unless you'd rather I walked?"

There's a part of me that would, actually, but of course I can't abandon her — after all, she might get rained on again. So instead I reach over and start the engine. "Sure."

We don't say much on the short drive back to her mum's, and I decline her offer of a coffee when we get there, which Jane seems to understand. As I'm dropping her off, she walks round to my side of the car and taps on the window, and I reach for the button and open it nervously.

"I'll be popping back down to Brighton from time to time," she says, leaning in and kissing me briefly on the cheek. "You know, for work, and to visit Mum, and stuff."

"Right. So . . ."

"So I'll see you around," she says, before striding off towards the house.

But it's not until I'm heading back home that I realize that wasn't a question, but more a statement of intent.

CHAPTER
EIGHT

I don't sleep very well that evening, and even the next morning find myself unable to concentrate at the office, thanks to Jane's somewhat out-of-the-blue appearance — and announcement. And after a lot of soul-searching when I should be searching for Dan's exes instead, I eventually work out that the problem I have with it is this: it takes a lot of effort to get out of a relationship — sometimes much more than it does just to keep going with one, and the longer the relationship the harder it gets — particularly if you've been living together. There are the practicalities, for example. You've got to find somewhere else to live. You have to separate all your financial affairs. You need to be prepared to deal with all the questions at work, or from your friends and family — people who knew, perhaps even liked, your other half — asking you why. And also, you've got to be prepared to break someone's heart.

And it's not just a snap decision. People don't wake up one morning and suddenly decide they'll leave after breakfast. It takes planning, resolve, sleepless nights lying next to the person you're going to desert — and awkward days lying *to* them as well. And all this has to be done covertly, if you want to avoid awkward scenes, or suspicious questions. I certainly had no idea it was coming. So Jane must have done an awful lot of that.

And it's not that I'm interested in getting back with her — imitation-leather pulling trousers or not. But I have to ask myself, why is she suddenly interested in me again? Surely my — admittedly dramatic — physical transformation hasn't been so impressive that it's made her forget, or even ignore, everything else that was wrong with our relationship? Because there was an awful lot wrong with it. I can see that now. And thinking about it, unless she's been stalking me over the past few weeks, she had no idea how much I'd changed until she saw me in Tesco's. So it's either genuinely because she thinks she's made a mistake, or because she's so unhappy with her single status that she's prepared to forget everything that was bad about us. And I don't really know how to deal with either of those two reasons.

It's a relief when I meet Dan for a coffee to discuss how we're doing on the SlateYourDate front, but as I take the opportunity to explain the events of the previous evening while we're in the queue at Starbucks, his expression moves from bewilderment to horror.

"You fucking idiot," he says, when I've finally finished. "Why on earth did you agree to meet up with her in the first place? Particularly after what you said the other day."

"I just wanted to make sure she was okay."

He takes his coffee from the barista, and follows me over to the condiments table. "After all the crap she put you through?"

"She did me a favour, don't forget. If she hadn't dumped me, I wouldn't have sorted myself out, met Sam . . ."

Dan reaches over unexpectedly and clips me round the top of my head, nearly causing me to drop the chocolate shaker. "That's like saying if you hadn't been mugged, you'd have only spent the money on something you might have liked. She put you through hell. And you certainly don't owe her any thanks for that."

"Yes, but we were happy for a long time."

"But together for a lot longer than that." He exhales loudly. "What are you going to tell Sam?"

"What?" I pause mid-shake. "Why should I tell her anything?"

Dan picks up a sachet of brown sugar and empties it into his mug. "Because otherwise, you'll be in twice as much trouble when she finds out."

"How's she going to find out?"

"Because they always do. Women are like blood-hounds. Give them the slightest hint you've been up to something, and they'll sniff the truth out sooner or later."

"But I haven't been up to anything."

"Then why are you worried about telling Sam?"

"I'm not worried about telling her."

"But you're not going to, right?"

"Er . . . No."

"Aha."

"Why is that 'aha'?"

"Because that means you're not quite sure about your feelings for Jane."

"No it doesn't." We carry our coffees over and hang around next to a table by the window, where a couple of students listening to their iPods at a higher volume than I'd play my car stereo look like they've nearly finished. "It means that I'm sure about my feelings for Sam. And I don't want anything to get in the way of those."

Dan scratches his head. "So, say for example you don't tell her, and then it comes up in conversation at a later date."

"How would that ever happen?"

"Well, through me and my big mouth for one thing. You know I'm not the most discreet of people."

"Why on earth would you want to go and do a thing like that?"

Dan puts a hand on my shoulder. "It's not that I'd want to. It's just that I might. Accidentally. And then what would you say?"

"Well . . ." I think for a moment or two. "I'd just be honest, and say that I met up with Jane the other day, and didn't tell Sam because I didn't want to worry her."

"Why should she be worried."

"She shouldn't."

"So why didn't you tell her, then?"

"What?"

"If she shouldn't be worried about it, then why on earth did you think that telling her would worry her?"

"Because . . . Well, that kind of thing worries women, doesn't it?"

"It does when you try and cover it up."

"I'm not trying to cover anything up."

"Yes, you are. By not telling her."

"Well, I'll just come out with it and tell her then."

Dan sucks air in through his teeth. "Best you don't."

"But you just said I ought to."

"No," he says. "I said you should have told her at the time. Not afterwards. The damage has already been done. You just have to hope she never finds out."

"But how can I do that, if you said she's bound to? Or if you blab?"

Dan puts a finger on his lips and winks conspiratorially. "Your secret's safe with me, Edward. Or let's hope so, anyway."

Fuck. Now I'm feeling really lousy. Why *didn't* I tell Sam about it? She'd have understood. And why did I agree to see Jane in the first place anyway? What did it really achieve, apart from possibly getting me in inevitable shit with my current girlfriend?

"But nothing happened. Or at least, nothing in the version that I'll tell her — if I ever tell her. So why is she going to be so upset about it?"

"About what?" says Dan. "The fact that you spent yesterday evening with your ex-girlfriend, or the fact that you didn't tell her about it?"

"Er . . . the first one. Which I suppose will inevitably mean the second one as well."

Dan taps the side of his nose. "The joys of ex."

"Pardon?"

"The ex factor."

"What?"

"Ex marks the spot."

"Dan, I'm going to have to slap you in a minute."

"Steady on, Rocky." He backs away, and does a little boxing feint, nearly spilling his coffee in the process. "Exes. The one thing absolutely guaranteed to get under a woman's skin and itch away at them. That's why that disease is called ex-ma, you know?"

"What *are* you talking about?"

"The fact that women never want you to be friends with your exes."

"Why ever not?"

"Because they want you to have gone through the most hideous break-up."

I blow on my coffee, causing a lump of chocolatey foam to fly off and land on Dan's trainer. "We did, don't forget."

"So why on earth do you want to have anything to do with her then?" he says, reaching down and wiping the foam off with a napkin. "That's what Sam'll be thinking. Trust me, women don't do that when the shoe's on the other foot, unless they're thinking about going back out with the person concerned. So that's obviously what she'll be assuming you're considering."

"But I'm not."

Dan holds his hands up. "Don't tell me that, mate. Tell Sam. And more important, tell Jane."

"But why should Sam care? I mean, she knows our history."

Dan smiles wistfully. "One little word. Insecurity."

That's actually quite a big word for Dan. "Please explain, Dan, before I lose the will to live."

"All women have it. Even supermodels. You look at old Claudia Schiffer and reckon she's a bit of all right. The perfect woman, even. But does old Claudia see it like that? No way. The first thing she thinks when she sees herself in the mirror is 'Aren't I ugly?' or 'My arse is looking huge today'."

"Yeah, right."

"It's true. I read it in *Heat*. And they're all like that: Naomi, Kate, the lot of them. And I'll tell you why. Woman are born insecure. It's in their genes. And even the fit ones have got body image issues. Why do you think they spend hours covering themselves in makeup every time they leave the house even for something as simple as getting a pint of milk from the garage? Because no matter how good they look, they're always worried about how they look. And sometimes it's worse the better-looking they are, because they know everyone else is snapping at their heels. I tell you, where women are concerned, it's dog eat dog. If you excuse the phrase."

As usual, I can't quite see the connection between what Dan's talking about and the real world. "So, what's this got to do with Sam and Jane?"

As the two students finally get up and leave, Dan wipes the nearest chair with a napkin and sits down at the table. "Because if there's one thing that women are more insecure about than their looks, it's their boyfriend's ex-girlfriends."

"But that's ridiculous," I say, sitting down next to him.

Dan sighs. "You know that, I know that, but women? No matter what you say, they always think that your ex was better than they were at everything, and so whenever one arrives back on the scene, cue lots of unreasonable behaviour."

I finally remember to start drinking my coffee, which is still hot enough to scald my tongue. "But . . . that's not fair. If you've been going out with someone for a long time, surely you can still be friends with them? Once you've split up, I mean."

"Course you can," says Dan. "As long as you don't tell your new girlfriend, or get found out."

"Rubbish. Surely it's better to be as open and honest as possible."

Dan lets out a short laugh. "Yeah, right. How do you think I'd get on if a current squeeze of mine thought I was still seeing any of my exes?"

"Well, some of them obviously did, if you study your feedback on SlateYourDate. And they were right to feel that way, in most cases. Which is probably why you don't actually have a current squeeze, I think you'll find."

"Just trust me on this," says Dan. "However understanding you think Sam is, and whatever she actually says to you about it, this is one issue I'm a hundred per cent right on. She'll never accept any reason for you wanting to spend any time at all with Jane."

"Or any of my exes?"

"Which includes, let me see . . . Jane, doesn't it?"

"But surely the fact I was with Jane for so long makes it . . ."

"Worse," interrupts Dan. "As a bloke, what's the most unpleasant thing about your girlfriend's sexual history?"

"Er . . ."

"The fact that she has one," says Dan, answering his own question. "And turning it around, women can't stand the fact that you've ever done anything at all with a woman before them. Sam knows that you've got ten years of history with Jane, and that's ten years of doing stuff that she'd rather not know about. Just try telling her that you and Jane used to eat at a particular restaurant, or listen to a particular CD, and I guarantee you that's the quickest way to never go there or play it ever again."

"But you can't deny history, surely?"

"I'm not asking you to deny it. I'm asking you not to admit to it. And believe me — there is a difference. So if you want to have anything to do with Jane ever again — and Christ knows why you would — then the last thing you should do is tell Sam."

"But I'd never want to go behind her back."

"Well, you can't have both." Dan regards me over the top of his mug. "And besides, I'd say it's a little late for that already. Wouldn't you?"

Great. Now I'm feeling really guilty. Like I've got something to hide. And thinking about what Dan's said, it is probably best kept hidden — which means I shouldn't feel guilty about hiding it, surely? Judging by the knot that's forming in my stomach, it doesn't seem to work that way, unfortunately.

"So what should I do?"

"Well, for one thing, don't see Jane again."

"Why not? Because I'd just be leading her on?"

Dan puts his coffee down on the table, and leans forward. "Remember, this is Jane we're talking about. And she's more likely to be doing the leading."

"Huh?"

"All I'm saying is, don't get suckered in by her 'I want you back' bollocks. I mean, she might, but I can't believe that she's launched into that within hours of seeing you again. It's more likely that she's just jealous that you've got yourself a hot bird."

"But she didn't even know I was seeing anyone. Until I told her, that is."

"Yeah, right," says Dan. "What's her specialist field again? At work, I mean."

"Marketing. Well, product positioning, based on market research, to be specific."

"All right. No need to run me through her CV. So bearing that in mind, you're telling me that she just came out with this big declaration without knowing all the facts first?"

"But why would she pretend to be . . ."

"Hurt? Surprised? Yes, well, it's obvious, isn't it?"

"Could you perhaps make it a little more obvious?"

Dan sighs. "She left you because she thought the grass was greener, right? Only now, she's realizing that the grass she left you for has turned out to be just a bare concrete patio, so she's come back to take a look at you, and found that your patchy lawn has been replaced with lush turf, ultra-modern landscaping, and even a bit of decking, and so naturally she's keen to check out your water feature . . ."

"Dan, in English, please."

"Sorry. Maybe she's not met anyone. And it's been a good few months, right — and God knows, a few days is bad enough. So maybe she just wants to be sure she's made the right decision. I mean, if you've managed to change so much physically, then maybe, just maybe, she might be thinking that you've changed all that other stuff too. The stuff she hated, like being such a slob, and crap in bed."

"Keep your voice down, please!"

"So she comes back, pretends to be all hurt, goes for the sympathy vote, whereas in reality, all she's feeling is a little bit jealous."

"Jealous? Why?"

He stirs his coffee thoughtfully. "Well, someone else is getting the benefit of her kicking you up the backside. And someone who's, well, without wanting to diss your ex, a lot fitter than she is. So Jane's obviously thinking 'What's she got that I haven't?' And you know how competitive she can get."

This is true. I've still got the scars from when we played on opposite sides in the Admiral Jim's Christmas non-contact rugby match. "So you're saying that her motivation might not be completely altruistic?"

"I would be," says Dan, "if I knew what 'altruistic' meant. All I'm trying to say is don't get your hopes up, because it might not be because she wants you back. She might just not want anyone else to have you."

And this is where I start to come unstuck. Because it's hard for me to accept that Jane would be so devious, or would want revenge. And for what? It's not as if I actually did anything to her, apart from maybe not be quite the kind of boyfriend she wanted me to be. So for her to suddenly want to spike my happiness with Sam would be just, well, mean.

"So what should I do about Jane? Just ignore her?"

"Works for me."

"Yes, but you do that to women even when you're going out with them."

Dan scratches his head. "Okay. Think of it this way. If you'd been in prison for ten years, and you finally got out, would you want to go back and visit?"

"No, but . . ."

"Well, there you go. Look at it that way."

"Dan, it's easy for you. You've had lots of practice at that sort of thing. I can't just cut her off completely. Not after ten years."

"Why not? That's exactly what she did to you."

He's got a point. "Because I'm not like that," I say, stopping myself at the last moment from ending my sentence with the word "you" instead.

"Do you still have" — Dan shudders theatrically — "feelings for her?"

I take another cautious sip of my cappuccino, which has finally reached a drinkable temperature. "I don't know. I mean, obviously I loved her once. I don't think that kind of thing ever just evaporates completely, does it?"

For a moment — just a moment — I think I catch a wistful look on Dan's face, although he might just be considering ordering another coffee. "Maybe not," he says. "But you do love Sam, right?"

I can't stop myself from blushing. "Er . . . I suppose so."

"More than you did Jane?"

"I don't know. There's not exactly a scale that you can refer to, is there?"

"And have you told her yet?"

"Not in so many words, no."

"Why not?"

"Well, it's not easy, is it?"

"Yes it is. You just open your mouth and say . . ."

"I mean, it's not that easy if you mean it."

Dan frowns. "Why on earth not? Surely that'd make it easier?"

"Because you're worried what the other person's going to say, aren't you? How they're going to react. There's only one thing you want to hear in response to 'I love you' and that's 'I love you too'. And I don't know whether Sam's quite there yet."

Dan looks at me for a second, then pretends to stick his fingers down his throat. "Only one way to find out, boyo. Assuming you want to find out, of course. But just remember how most women work."

"Which is?" I say, when Dan doesn't enlighten me.

"Well, they're after getting you to commit, right? So right up until they get that commitment from you, they're all extra-nice and lovey dovey and do-anything-for-you — particularly in bed, if you know what I mean. Then once you're hooked . . ." He sits back on his chair, then mimes reeling something in on a fishing rod. "So the longer you can leave them guessing, the better, in my book."

"A book that just happens to have a lot of blank pages at the moment."

"Yes, well, we're not talking about me, are we, smart arse?"

"So you're saying that even though I might love her, I shouldn't tell her?"

"Not first, no. Wait till she says it to you."

"But what if she doesn't?"

Dan shrugs. "Then she might not. But don't worry. All women do, at some point or another, even if it's only to get a reaction from you. But if you want my advice, concentrate on the future — your future with Sam, that is. And whatever you do, don't let Jane back into the picture. Particularly now, when you've got more important things to worry about."

"Such as?"

He smiles that famous Dan Davis smile, making me almost wish I had my sunglasses on. "Me."

When Natasha walks into the office that afternoon carrying her usual takeout coffee — and, unusually, one for me — I'm staring intently at my computer screen, trying to find some woman Dan chatted up over the phone when she called to try and sell him a broadband package. Trouble was, Dan was more interested in giving her a package of his own, and then never calling her back, which was why he ended up having to change his home number. Again.

"What're you doing?" she asks pleasantly, walking over and putting the paper cup on my desk.

I hurriedly conceal Dan's dossier under some papers on my desk, but it's too late for me to click the "minimize" button on my keyboard. "Just some, er, research."

"Into BT?" asks Natasha, peering at the screen over my shoulder. "Are we recruiting for them, now?"

"No, I'm, um, just trying to track someone down. For a friend."

Natasha's raises one eyebrow. "That friend wouldn't be Dan, would it?"

"Er . . ."

"Edward, we're a recruitment agency. Not a dating agency. Although now I think about it, the processes are about the same."

"It's not like that at all," I say. "Dan's in a bit of trouble. And I'm just trying to help him out of it."

"Oh yes?" asks Natasha. "Got someone pregnant, has he? Her father after him with a shotgun?"

"No, it's still the same stuff as before. I'm just trying to help him get back in touch with some of his exes."

Natasha laughs. "You could probably stop women at random on the street outside and you'd stand a pretty good chance of bumping into one of them. What's this for, then?"

"We thought, I mean Dan thought, that maybe it was time he changed his ways. Began treating women a little bit better. So he's starting by tracking his exes down so he can make things up to them."

"How is he going to do that?"

"Well, he's kind of doing reparations. Seeing whether he can cancel out the bad things he's done in the past."

Her eyes widen. "He's going to have his work cut out."

I swivel my chair round to face her. "Tell me something, Natasha. When you and Dan were, er, *together*, what was he like?"

She puts her coffee down and perches on the end of my desk. "What, in bed? Well, I've had better. And bigger, to be honest."

"No," I say hastily. "Not in bed. Generally. Did he seem totally, you know, into you? Sorry. Bad choice of phrase."

Natasha thinks about this for a moment. "Oh yes. At the start anyway. But then . . ." She smiles thoughtfully. "You know when you're at a party, and the person you're with seems to be constantly looking around, trying to find someone more interesting to talk to so they can get away from you?"

I do actually. It used to happen to me all the time. And sometimes still does, when I'm out with Dan. "I can imagine."

"Well, that's what your mate's like. It's like he suffers from that attention deficiency disorder where his girlfriends are concerned — or, at least, after the first week or so, anyway. We were in a restaurant once, and it got so bad that I had to poke him under the table with my fork."

This is true. Dan showed me the puncture marks on his leg. "And you didn't think it could be . . ." I check to see whether Natasha's got any coffee left to throw. "You?"

"Oh no. I've seen his type before. No matter what they've got, you know they're always on the lookout for something better." She jumps down from the end of my desk, and taps the top of my computer screen. "So if you want my opinion, you're wasting your time."

"How so?"

Natasha shrugs. "How many psychiatrists does it take to change a light bulb?"

"Is this a joke?"

"I'm worried that Dan's mission might be."

"Huh?"

Natasha picks her coffee up, and walks towards the door. "The answer's one, Edward," she says. "But the light bulb's got to want to change."

CHAPTER
NINE

For the next few days, in between the extra work I'm doing supplying Dan with contact details for his exes, and trying not to worry about whether I'm going to hear from Jane again, I'm determined that the last thing Sam and I will do is get into a rut like Jane and I did. I'm pretty sure that nothing we do is boring, but even so, I try to be as spontaneous as possible. In fact, I even plan to be spontaneous, if such a thing is possible. So when Sam comes round after work on the Wednesday, even though she's expecting to go out, I can tell she's a little tired, so I cook her a meal. And although it's only omelette and salad, I can tell she's impressed — or at least impressed that it's edible. And then on the Saturday, the weather's miserable, but instead of hanging around the flat watching a DVD like Jane and I used to, we head off to the afternoon showing at the cinema, and then take Ollie for a long, wet walk along the seafront. And the irony is, I start to enjoy myself more too, and realize that it's fun doing these different things. Exciting, even. And the more I realize this, the more I also recognize just how stale Jane and I got. It's a telling sign when the two of you spot an advert for a new film you'd both like to see, and at the same time you decide that you'll be happy to wait for the DVD to come out. And that was Jane and me. Always waiting until the DVD came out.

Sam seems to be enjoying it too, although I'm conscious of not wanting to tire her out, particularly given her early starts, and all the to-ing and fro-ing between my place and hers. And to be honest, keeping this pace up is pretty exhausting for me too, so when she suggests a night in on Sunday, I'm all too keen to agree. We need to find a balance, and fast, or I'm in danger of burning this relationship out or, even worse, scaring her off. But the trouble is, I'm still desperate. Desperate for Sam not to leave me like Jane did. Desperate to remain in happy coupledom. And desperate not to have to go through the whole single-guy-trying-to-meet-a-girl thing again — because that's no fun at all. And while I know that the secret to a successful relationship isn't just doing stuff on a whim, or remembering to go out to the cinema once in a while, these things all play their part.

And this, I think, is the problem. Because finding the right person to go out with, to be with, to spend the rest of your life with even, is possibly the most important thing anyone can do. And the most difficult thing to get right. And because it's the most important thing, that's why everyone spends the majority of their time trying to do it, or thinking about it. Our heart tells us we should do it. Our head tells us we should do it. Society tells us we're weird if we don't. Trouble is, it's made even harder by the fact that, for the most part, we're an incompatible species, in that while what we both want out of the relationship is fundamentally the same, it can seem so different.

It's further complicated by the fact that people change, too, as they get older — and at different rates. What we want, what we're like, and what we like in our twenties is different to what we want or like in our thirties and, I imagine, our forties, and so on. Yet here we are, expecting someone to make a commitment to stay with us throughout those times, and expecting them to change in the same way, and at the same time. Logically, statistically, the odds are against us. Which is why I need to be sure I'm placing the right bet.

Meanwhile, in between helping Dan out and trying not to get sacked by Natasha, I've still got the issue of what to buy Sam in return for my watch, but by the Friday, I think I've cracked it. After a quick trip to the shops, I'm walking back home, and I'm just crossing the road when there's a sudden flash of bright orange and Dan screeches the Porsche to a stop in front of me.

"Whatcha got there?" he calls, pointing to the Argos shopping bag I'm carrying.

"Present for Sam. And no, before you ask, it's not an engagement ring," I say, walking over and leaning into the car. As usual, despite the overcast sky, Dan's got the roof down.

"I should hope not, from bloody Argos." He peers into the bag. "What is it, then? Some kind of strange sex toy?"

"Nope." I reach inside and remove the admittedly rather phallic-shaped object from its box. "It's a combination screwdriver/drill. Cordless."

Dan looks up at me, an expression of disbelief on his face. "I'm sorry. You did say that this was for *Sam*?"

"What's wrong with it?" I say, somewhat taken aback by his reaction. "It's from Black & Decker's new women's range. And wasn't cheap."

"But you are."

"Pardon?"

Dan leans across the centre console and pushes the passenger door open. "Shut up and get in."

"What? Why?"

"Fuck it," says Dan. "I thought my work was done after I taught you how to get her. I didn't think I'd have to teach you how to hang on to her as well."

"I don't need your help," I say defensively, putting it back into the bag. "I can manage just fine, thank you."

Dan reaches over and snatches it from my hands. "So I can see," he says, pulling the door shut suddenly, then wheel-spinning off down the road, dangling the bag out of the car like bait as he disappears round the corner.

I think about giving chase, but I'm on foot, and besides, I've got a pretty good idea where he's headed. When I eventually spot the Porsche parked outside the Admiral Jim and push angrily through the door, Dan's sitting in the corner with the drill on the table in front of him.

"What was that all about?"

"Just trying to stop you making a huge mistake."

"What do you mean? Why is it a mistake?"

Dan exhales loudly. "Sam buys you a five-hundred-quid TAG-bloody-Heuer watch, and you buy her a *power tool*? I have to hear the reasoning behind this."

155

I pull out a chair and sit down opposite him. "Well, I'm just being thoughtful, aren't I?"

"Are you?"

I nod. "She's always saying she's got a lot of DIY jobs to do around her flat, and doesn't really have much in the way of tools" — I pause, while Dan sniggers at the word — "and so I thought . . ."

He holds his hand up. "Let me stop you there, Ed. Because you didn't think."

"Yes I did. I listened to what she said, and put some thought into getting her a present that'd be useful."

"And completely inappropriate."

"But she doesn't have one."

"Because she doesn't want one."

"But . . . It's pink."

Dan laughs. "Oh. Well, that makes it all right then."

I can see I'm not going to win this one. "Okay, smart arse, what's wrong with it?"

Dan picks the box up and examines it carefully before throwing it disdainfully back into its bag. "Out of interest, what was the last thing you bought Jane as a present? Before she dumped you, I mean?"

I wish he wouldn't keep mentioning the "D" word. "Well, there was the Prada handbag, obviously," I say proudly.

"Which we've already established she tricked you into buying for her. Next?"

"Er . . ." As I struggle to come up with an alternative, Dan flashes me his normal, annoying, know-it-all grin. "We'd kind of dispensed with the whole 'presents' thing."

156

"How do you mean?"

"Well, because we'd been together for so long, it just seemed a bit, you know, silly."

Dan does a double take. "Jesus, Edward. Have you forgotten the three nevers?"

"Huh?" I've never even heard of "the three nevers", whatever they are. "What are you talking about?"

Dan starts counting them off on his fingers. "Number one — never tell her she looks fat. Two — never get her name wrong in bed. And lastly — never, ever, stop buying her presents." He grins. "Oh, and never sleep with her mother. Or rather, never let her find out that you have. I've had to add that one recently. But, anyway, presents are a very important area to get right. I even buy women presents when I'm not intending to stay with them. Stupid little things, sometimes."

Knowing Dan, he could equally be referring to the presents *and* the women. "Why?"

"Simple. Tit for tat."

"Huh?"

He shrugs. "I buy them tat, and I get a bit of . . ."

"Dan, be serious, please."

"Listen, Ed. There are some things that are just the way they are, and you don't question them. I mean — I like sausages, but I don't want to know how they're made. And I certainly don't know why women put so much store by the fact you buy them stuff every now and again. They just do. Why on earth did you stop?"

"Well, Jane had a good job, and I had a good job, so if we needed something, we kind of just went out and bought it for ourselves."

"You mean, *you* did."

"No," I say defensively. "We both did. At least, that's what I assumed, the amount of time Jane spent shopping. Besides, she never seemed to like what I used to get her, so in the end I'd just give her the cash."

"Or 'let' her spend her own money on herself." He shakes his head slowly. "And they say romance is dead."

"But what's wrong with that?"

"What's right with it, you mean? Buying a present for a woman isn't about getting her what she needs. It's about getting her what she wants. Which is usually the complete opposite."

"Huh?"

"Well, what do women have the greatest number of, would you say?"

"In Sam's case, that'd be trainers, given her work and all that."

Dan rolls his eyes. "Okay. So that's shoes, right? And we know women love shoes. But open Sam's wardrobe, and you'd think they'd be the last thing she needed."

"Because she's got so many already?"

"Precisely. And yet buy her another pair, and you'd earn yourself no end of Brownie points. Whereas . . ." Dan retrieves the cordless screwdriver set and plonks it on the table. "Buy her one of these, which according to you she 'needs', and oh no."

"But why?"

"Because it's a DIY gift. And the only DIY gift a woman ever really wants is for you to come round and do it for her. Catch a woman with a box of spanners in her cupboard and you can be sure she'll bat for the other side. Give her one of these, and it'll be you who's doing it yourself before very long, if you know what I mean."

"But . . ." I scratch my head. "That doesn't make any sense."

"Welcome to the wonderful logic of women. Here." He beckons Wendy over from where she's wedged herself behind the bar. "I'll prove it to you."

Wendy puts down her copy of *Mother and Baby* and walks over. "Evening, Edward. Evening, Git-face."

Dan ignores her insult. "Wendy, tell us something. What do you want for your birthday?"

She rubs her stomach. "A lot of drugs and the world's quickest labour."

"Not birth day. Birthday. If we were going out together. What would you like me to give you?"

"Rohypnol?" She shrugs. "I don't know. A pair of Jimmy Choos, perhaps? They're shoes, Edward," she adds, noticing my expression.

"You see?" he smirks. "Proves my point."

"What point," says Wendy, menacingly.

"Only that when it comes to gifts, you women always want impractical things."

Wendy frowns. "Since when is a pair of shoes impractical?"

Dan nods towards her stomach. "Well, now, for example. Because for one thing, you won't be able to see them thanks to that huge bump of yours getting in the way, and for another, once you've actually sprogged, the chances of you putting on a pair of fancy shoes to go out anywhere nice is pretty remote."

Wendy opens her mouth to challenge Dan, but then realizes that, for once, she doesn't have a leg to stand on. "Fair point," she says. "But it's not my birthday for ages. What's brought all this on?"

Dan jerks his thumb towards me. "Sam bought Edward a present. Show her, Ed."

I pull the sleeve of my shirt up obediently to reveal my new watch, and Wendy whistles appreciatively. "So?"

He slides the bag towards her. "So he bought her this in return. And I was telling him how bad an idea it was."

Wendy picks the box up from the table, and examines the contents. "Much as I hate to admit it, Dan's right."

I look at the two of them helplessly. "Why is this so difficult? I mean, why should I feel pressurized into buying her something back anyway? Maybe I just won't bother."

Dan puts his hand on my shoulder. "Please, Edward. I'd like to be a best man one day. And seeing as you're the one friend whose girlfriend I haven't slept with, you're my only chance. So please don't fuck it up by making this one dump you as well."

I knock his hand off angrily. "She's not going to dump me just because I buy her something like this." I stuff the screwdriver back in its bag, and put it on the floor. "Is she?"

Wendy smiles sympathetically. "Maybe not, Ed. But equally, it's hardly going to convince her that she's the love of your life. Or vice versa."

160

"But you're suggesting it's some kind of game," I say, fumbling reluctantly through my wallet to check I've still got the receipt.

"It's all a game," says Dan patiently. "Life's a game. And you've got to know how to play it."

"But what are the rules?"

Dan shrugs. "That's the problem. They're different for everyone."

"So how am I supposed to know what they are?" I say, my voice sounding more than a little desperate.

"Trial and error, my friend. Trial and error. And trust me, this" — he picks up the bag from next to my chair, holding it between his thumb and forefinger as if it contains a dog turd — "is an error."

And this is my problem. Because just like I'm no good at dancing, or haven't got anything you'd call a singing voice, I'm starting to get more than a little worried that I'm no good at this relationship lark — especially if there are rules involved, and even more so if I don't have the faintest idea what they are, and particularly because I don't want to play by the rules. And I don't mean that in the way Dan does, doing everything to suit himself, and not worrying about hurting the other person. You should be able to do things because you *want* to do them, not because you should, like that guessing game you play as a child where the answer you give depends on what the other person says. I don't want that. Because I'm not a child any more.

The problem — and the reason that I'm doubting myself, is that it's just too confusing. Surely knowing what to do and how to behave with Sam should come naturally — after all, it's not as if I've never had a relationship before? And yet because of Jane's legacy, whenever I'm with Sam I find myself nervously thinking what the right thing to do is. It's like when you're driving and you accidentally hit the car in front. For the next few months, whenever you're behind the wheel, you make sure that you've given yourself enough extra space that, in the event of the car in front slamming its brakes on again, you've got enough time to stop yourself before you do any damage. Trouble is, I don't want to leave too much space in between Sam and me. In case she drives off.

And the irony of what I'm doing — asking Dan for advice on how to keep Sam happy — isn't lost on me either. Particularly because, in actual fact, it turns out that Dan's not so good at relationships after all. Here's someone who's longest relationship lasted ten minutes, whereas my longest one — my last one, in fact — lasted ten years. But as I sit here, staring at his smug face across the table, I suddenly have an idea: while I might not be able to learn from Slate YourDate — because I'm not on it, which I suppose is a good start — what I do have is my own ex-girlfriend back on the scene. So maybe what I *can* do is ask Jane exactly where I went wrong. Surely that's the best way of making sure I get things right with Sam. And while that means I do need to see her again, it's just to find out exactly from her how I stopped being a fun, exciting person to be with.

The more I think about it, the more it strikes me as such a brilliant plan that I can't help but blurt it out.

But by the looks on Wendy and Dan's faces, it's possibly not as brilliant as I've first thought.

"Edward," says Wendy. "That's a terrible idea."

"But I thought if I heard it directly. You know — from the horse's mouth."

"That's not a very flattering description of your ex-girlfriend," laughs Dan. "Although now you mention it, her nostrils were rather large. And when she used to wear those tight jeans, the view from behind was not dissimilar to . . ."

"Dan, do you mind?"

"Sorry, Ed. But Wendy's right. It's probably the worst idea you've ever had. Believe me, you don't want to go down that road, because at the end of that road there's a dead end, with a big dog, and that dog has very sharp teeth, and it's just about to slip its lead . . ."

"Okay, okay, I get your point. But . . ." I put my head in my hands, conscious that I'm using this next word an awful lot with Dan. "Why?"

"Why?" Dan leans across the table and flicks me painfully on the forehead. "Because you want to ask your ex-girlfriend — who quite possibly might want to split you up from your new girlfriend so she can have another crack at you — what it was you did wrong when you were together, in order to try and not make the same mistakes with your new girlfriend."

"But I've told Jane I'm happy with Sam."

I look across at Wendy, but she's nodding in agreement. "Of course you did, Edward. And that's why you shouldn't get her involved. Because there's nothing us girls hate more than seeing our former partner happily ensconced with someone new. Particularly when we haven't managed to couple up with someone ourselves."

"But . . . she dumped me."

"Which is even worse," says Wendy. "Because the very fact that you've managed to find someone else — and so soon — is making her think 'Hold on, maybe I was a little bit hasty. Maybe Edward wasn't such a . . .'"

"Loser?" suggests Dan.

"Well, I wouldn't quite put it like that. Bad bet at the time, maybe."

"I would," says Dan. "But Wendy's right. Particularly since your new girlfriend's so much hotter than Jane is."

"Do you really think so?"

"Sure. Sam knocks spots off Jane. Especially in the body department. She's got an arse you could crack walnuts with."

"Dan. Please. I meant whether you really thought that Jane might be thinking those things. Although thanks for the compliments about Sam."

He licks his lips. "Any time."

"Getting back to the matter in hand," says Wendy. "You need to get Jane out of the picture. And fast. For Sam's sake, if nothing else. No woman wants an ex hanging around."

"Especially an ex who's desperate to get back with you." Dan nudges me. "And she'd have to be desperate."

"It's no problem. If I see her again, and she tries anything, I'll just tell her that I'm not interested. End of story."

"And in the meantime, ask her if she'd be good enough to give you a few pointers about how to make sure you don't fuck it up with your new girlfriend like you did with her? That'll work," Dan says sarcastically. "This is Jane we're talking about, don't forget. She doesn't know the meaning of the word 'no'."

"Or 'goodbye', come to think of it," adds Wendy. "No, Ed, Dan's right. You need to leave her in no doubt that she's not welcome."

"Well, how can I put her off me?"

"You could try giving her one of these," says Dan, picking the Argos bag up off the floor. "Or if that doesn't work, start eating crap again. And smoking. And drinking beer. And give up the gym. Or alternatively, just run like the wind. At least you can now, thanks to Sam's influence."

"Sensible advice please, Dan."

He drops the bag next to his feet and nudges me. "Tell you what. Why don't I sleep with her? That'll put her off you. Make her realize what a real man's like."

"Retrospectively, you mean?" says Wendy. "Besides, that'd put her off all men. And I wouldn't wish that on anyone. Even Jane, after what she did to you, Ed."

Dan puffs his chest out. "Yeah right. There's only one way for a woman to go once she's slept with me, and that's down."

"To the STD clinic?" suggests Wendy.

"Or straight to her laptop," I say.

"Thanks a lot." Dan looks a little hurt. "But before you even think about anything else, just take that back."

"I'm sorry," I say, worried that for once I've crossed the line and offended him. "I didn't mean anything by it."

He kicks the Argos bag across the floor towards me. "I was referring to the screwdriver, numb-nuts."

When I finally get home, and after a long argument with the manageress at Argos due to the dent in the box from Dan's less-than-careful handling, I find Mrs Barraclough in the hallway. As usual, she doesn't seem to have her hearing aid turned on, and I don't want to give her a heart attack by tapping her on the shoulder, so instead I slam the front door shut, hoping she'll pick up the vibrations through her slippered feet. Unfortunately for Mrs Barraclough, this seems to have the same effect as a major earthquake, and it's all I can do to rush across in time to stop her from toppling over.

"Evening, Mrs B."

"Hello, Edward," she says, steadying herself against the gas-meter cupboard. "Where were you off to the other day in such a hurry?"

"The other day?"

"Yes," she says, reaching up to fiddle with the switch behind her ear. "In that loud car. With your friend off the television."

I think about telling her that we went to a gay bar in Eastbourne to meet Dan's lesbian ex-girlfriend, but worry that we might be here for a while. "Eastbourne," I say, having decided on the condensed version.

166

"Eastbourne?" Mrs Barraclough frowns, although given the usual number of wrinkles on her face, it's a little hard to tell. "Horrible place."

"What's wrong with it?"

Mrs Barraclough gives a short shudder, and for a moment I wonder whether she's having some sort of medical emergency. "Full of old people."

"Oh. Right." I peer at her face to try to detect a trace of irony, because she must be expecting a telegram from the Queen herself in the next year or so, but I can't spot any.

"And how is Stan?" Even though she always gets his name wrong — which amuses me as much as it irritates him — Mrs Barraclough loves Dan, and never misses anything that he's in. In fact, I never need to have the volume up on my TV when I'm watching *Where There's a Will*, thanks to the sounds coming from Mrs Barraclough's flat upstairs.

"He's fine," I say, conscious that there aren't enough hours in the day to explain his predicament to her.

"Such a nice-looking young man," she says. "I don't mind telling you, Edward, if I was fifty years younger . . ."

You'd still be old enough to be his gran, I think, before realizing that I've actually said it out loud.

"Pardon?"

"I said you must be his biggest fan."

"And how's that young lady of yours?"

Given our recent conversation, I wonder what exactly she means by "young". "She's fine, thanks."

"Lovely girl. Much nicer than your last one," says Mrs Barraclough. "What was her name again?"

"Jane."

Mrs Barraclough looks even more puzzled. Or, at least, several new lines appear on her forehead. "That's what your last one was called, too, wasn't it?"

"I thought you *meant* my last one."

"No." Mrs Barraclough gives me a look that seems to imply that I'm the deaf one. "The new girl."

"Oh." I'm just about to point out that Sam and I have actually been together for quite a while, so she's hardly "the new one", but then again, to someone of Mrs Barraclough's age, these things are all relative. "Her name's Sam."

"You didn't waste any time there, Edward. And good for you. That one's a keeper. Although I can't keep up with things nowadays. One day you're courting, the next you're moving in together." Mrs Barraclough winks at me — or at least, I think it's a wink, though it could be just some sort of facial tic. "Mind you," she adds, turning round and making for the stairs, "you're not getting any younger."

That gets a smile out of me, but as I head towards my own front door, I stop in my tracks. That's it. The perfect answer to my present dilemma with Sam. Forget power tools or engagement rings. I'll just ask her to move in with me.

Back when Jane and I first decided to live together, it just kind of seemed like the thing to do. There wasn't any romance involved. She was looking to move out of her mum's but didn't have a lot of money, and I'd recently bought the flat, so she ended up spending more and more time at mine, took over the majority of the wardrobe and the bathroom cabinet, until one day she just didn't leave. Up until she left *me*, that is.

The thing was, when I say we "decided" to live together, there wasn't much of a decision involved. I didn't actually ask her to move in — she just, well, did. And although it seemed like the natural thing to do, there was never any sense of excitement. No feeling that it was a major step we were taking, or that our relationship had suddenly notched up a level. We did it for practical reasons. And that's the problem with practicality. It's just not sexy.

And as I think about it, I realize that that's why I want it to be different with Sam. I want to make a big deal of asking her, and be nervous about what her answer will be. And while of course I want her to say yes, I also need her to know that it's a gesture from me, a statement that I care about her, and want us to spend more time together — and this is the ultimate way of doing that. I'm prepared to give away my freedom, my bachelor status, in a public display of our relationship, and surely that means something? Well, something more than a Black & Decker cordless drill/screwdriver set, anyway. Even a pink one.

I walk back over to Mrs Barraclough, who despite my protracted musings hasn't quite made it up the first flight of stairs yet, and plant a kiss on her forehead. "Thanks, Mrs B."

She stops mid-step, like a clockwork toy running out of spring. "What for?"

I smile down at her, and tap the face of my watch. "The answer."

Mrs Barraclough looks a little confused, and fiddles with her hearing aid again. "I didn't know you'd asked a question."

"I haven't, yet," I tell her. "But I'm going to."

Although when and how are things that I need to think very seriously about.

CHAPTER
TEN

Nothing much happens for the next couple of days. I don't hear anything from Jane, which on balance I'm relieved about, because it means I don't have to lie to Sam about it, or fend Jane off again. And equally, I don't see much of Sam, because she's too busy working when I'm not, and vice versa. But this is fine, because quite frankly I haven't quite plucked up the courage to ask her if she wants to move in with me. And even though I feel guilty every time I glance at my wrist, there's a part of me that's angry too. If Dan's right, then I can't help but resent her a little for trying to force an issue that surely should be up to me, a feeling that's made worse by the suspicion that my inability — or reluctance — to propose was possibly one of the things that contributed to Jane leaving me. And even if Dan's wrong, then I'm still a little narked with her — completely unreasonably, of course — for showing up more of my failings as a boyfriend for not knowing how to respond to what might simply have been a beautifully unselfish and wonderfully generous gesture.

I don't see much of Dan either, as he's supposed to be out scouring Brighton's many pubs and cafés trying to bump into some of the girls on his list, while I try to track the rest of them down through more advanced means. And between us, gradually, we're beginning to have some success: on the Friday lunchtime, I have to go with him to rent a dinner suit from Moss Bros on Church Road, as he's agreed to be Christine Harrison's personal waiter at the dinner party she's hosting at her house that evening. He of course ends up hiring the most expensive Hugo Boss outfit, and then finds out that Christine's "dinner party" is in fact her sister's hen night, so spends the majority of the evening waiting on them wearing little more than his Calvins and a bow tie. On the Saturday, he's at the Grand Hotel for afternoon tea with Alison Chambers and her mother, who's visiting from South Africa and is a massive fan of *Where There's a Will*. It's only just before he gets there that he finds out that Alison's mother thinks that he's still Alison's boyfriend, because Alison hasn't had the heart to tell her that they split up six months ago. So he ends up having to invent their life together over a plate of fairy cakes and a cup of Earl Grey. And then that evening, he's at a party at Melanie Long's house, where he's supposed to spend the evening flirting with Melanie to try to make her current boyfriend jealous so he'll pay her a bit more attention in future. Sam and I are invited too, because we both know Melanie anyway, and while we're looking forward to catching up with her, I actually end up spending most of the evening keeping Dan and Melanie's boyfriend apart, as the last thing Dan wants for his first day of filming *Close Encounters* is a black eye.

To his credit, Dan goes through with all of it without a single complaint, although as I drop him back at his flat later, even though Christine, Alison, and Melanie have agreed to rewrite his SlateYourDate rating, I can tell he's getting a little fed up with the whole process. So when I get a text from him on the Sunday morning announcing that he's had an idea, and asking me to meet him for a quick drink that afternoon, I'm a little suspicious.

"Uh-oh," I say, once we're ensconced at one of the Admiral Jim's corner tables.

"What do you mean, 'Uh-oh'?" he says, a little hurt.

I take a sip of my glass of wine. "Sorry, Dan, it's just that usually you having an idea either costs me money or embarrasses me."

"Rubbish," snorts Dan. "Like when?"

"Well, like now, for example, when I'm spending all my time tracking down your exes instead of doing any real work."

"That's hardly embarrassing."

"Okay. That day a couple of years ago when you suggested we went on that potholing weekend because you fancied the instructor."

"Always keen to force my way into tight passages," says Dan. "Oh — hang on. Wasn't that the time when you got stuck? And we had to pull you out? And when we did, your trousers came off in front of everyone?"

I shudder a little at the memory. "That's the one."

"Okay." Dan grins. "Fair point. But you'll like this one."

"Will I?"

He nods. "Sure. For one thing, it'll mean we don't have to traipse around on the trail of any more of my exes."

"Really?" I can't help feeling that I'm going to regret asking. "Come on, then. Let's hear it."

Dan leans forward and puts his elbows on the table. "Well, what we do is hire a venue that'll easily accommodate them all."

"Wembley Stadium, maybe?"

Dan ignores me, although he can't help looking smug at the inference. "Then what we do is send them all free tickets to a show there, and tell them it's going to be on TV, and that the audience will be involved in the filming too. They're bound to turn up, because everyone wants to be on TV."

"Ri-ight . . ."

"And then, when they're all sitting there waiting, I run out on stage — big surprise — and get them all to forgive me."

As Dan sits back in his chair, I give his great idea the consideration it deserves — about half a second. "That's great, Dan. And how would you suggest we — sorry, you — manage to convince these girls that they should offer you universal forgiveness?"

Dan shrugs. "I dunno. I just thought once we had them all in a room together, they wouldn't feel so hard done by. Might not think that they were alone. You know, that they shouldn't feel bad, because they weren't the only person that it happened to."

174

"Or, alternatively, they might decide to arrange a hanging. It's a stupid idea."

Dan looks crestfallen. "I just thought it might speed things up a bit."

"Why? Where have we got to?"

Dan pulls his mobile out of his pocket and consults his SlateYourDate page. "Well, we've done three this week, which leaves . . . Hold on." His face suddenly darkens. "There's some new ones on here."

I take the phone from him and scroll down the screen. Sure enough, there have been three more entries in the last few days. "How'd that happen? I thought you hadn't met anyone new?"

"I haven't," he protests. "More's the pity."

"Well, where have these come from, then?"

He rubs his temples. "I don't know. Maybe there are more of them coming out of the woodwork as they get to hear about the site."

"So we're actually back to square one?"

Dan puts his head in his hands. "Seems that way."

"It's just like painting the Forth Bridge."

"Not to mention the first three," sighs Dan. "There's got to be an easier way."

"'Fraid not, Dan." I pass the phone back to him and he scowls at the screen before putting the phone down on the table.

"It's just that, well, forty-seven to go." Dan furrows his brow. "At an average of, what, one and a half a week, that makes . . ." Maths was never his strongest point. Or English. Or science, come to think of it.

"About eight months, Dan. Give or take."

"Eight months! I can't be single for eight months. Forgetting the fact that there's less than three weeks to go before my ITV debut."

"ITV 5, Dan."

He puffs his cheeks out for a few moments and then turns back to me. "Well, what if we . . . I mean I, just did the last few, starting with the most recent?"

"What, do them backwards?"

"So to speak," sniggers Dan. "Although thinking about it, the wounds may be a little fresh that way. So start maybe with number forty, and work up to the present day. That way, hopefully any new woman might look at it and think maybe I'd been a bit of a bad boy in the past, but I'd kind of changed my ways recently."

"Well, that might work. But it's still going to take you at least a couple of months. Assuming any new ones don't suddenly appear."

"Well, if that's what it takes." Dan sighs. "I tell you, Ed, the sooner I get this over and done with and normal service is resumed, the better."

"Whoa!" I hold both hands out towards him, palms outwards. "Hold on a second."

"What?"

"What about our deal?"

"What deal?"

"You know. *Karma*. You changing your ways, and all that."

Dan looks over his left shoulder, and then his right. "Hang on. I thought Sam was here, for a moment."

"Tell me again why you're going through with all this? Because you genuinely want to change and make up for your past misdemeanours, or just because you're worried you'll never get laid again?"

"The first one," says Dan, although he phrases it more like a question.

"Because I'm not going to help you to lie to all these women, if that's all you're after. This should be a wake-up call for you. Make you realize that you can't just go through life being shitty to people once you've got bored of them. Have you never heard of ethics?"

"Well, I did go out with a girl from Southend once," says Dan hesitantly.

"Not Essex, Dan. Ethics. I'm serious. You need to start thinking of this like an AA meeting."

"The car breakdown people?"

I sometimes wonder if he's being deliberately thick. If so, he's a bloody good actor. "No. Alcoholics Anonymous. One of their basic ideas is that until you actually admit to yourself that you've got a problem, you can't begin the healing process."

"Ah, but I've been thinking about that."

"Oh yes?" I brace myself for one of Dan's pearls of wisdom. "And?"

"I mean, it's just that it's not really me we're trying to heal, is it? It's them. So they can stop being so bitter, get over it, and move on."

"What?" I've heard some things from Dan, but this one tops them all, and for a moment I don't know how to respond. "But don't you realize that it's you that's made them bitter? By the way you've treated them."

"Bollocks," says Dan. "They're bitter because they've lost out. They had me for a while, but weren't good enough to keep me."

"So you're saying it's their fault you behave like this?"

"Yup. And the reason they're so twisted is because it's a reflection on themselves."

I look at him incredulously. "How on earth do you work that one out?"

"Simple." Dan shrugs. "If they didn't have anything wrong with them, I might have worked that little bit harder to keep them."

"Pardon?"

"I'm serious," he says. "And you more than anyone should know what I'm talking about?"

"Me? How on earth . . ."

"Look what happened with you and Jane. She dumped you because you were such a loser, right?"

"Well, that's not exactly how I like to think of it . . ."

"And fair credit to you, mate, you realized she was right, and did something about it. Joined a gym, stopped smoking, changed yourself from dud into, well, not quite stud, but you see what I mean."

I'm not sure I do. "What's your point?"

"My point is that what you didn't do was moan about it by logging on to some stupid website to slag Jane off. And that's what annoys me about all these women. They're so bloody arrogant that they assume the fact they don't get treated like little princesses all the time can't possibly be their fault."

"It's hardly arrogance, Dan."

"Yes it is. Women always try to change us blokes. We never do the same to them. So why is that fair? I tell you, back when women knew their place, things were an awful lot simpler." He shakes his head, and takes a swig from his beer bottle. "Let them get away with stuff like this, and before you know it, they'll be wanting the vote."

I can't even begin to think where to start with this one. "So, you'd like a return to Neanderthal days? Knock her over the head with your club and drag her back to the cave by her hair?"

"The principle's still the same," says Dan. "Where do you think the word 'clubbing' comes from? It's just a different kind nowadays."

I'm a little taken aback by this. What I can't work out is whether Dan actually believes this rubbish, or it's all part of his big act. But although I wouldn't put it past him to actually believe it, if it is part of an act, then why is he putting an act on? I decide to try a different approach.

"Okay then. Let's analyse these women, one by one. What was wrong with Natasha, for instance?"

Dan mimes the *Psycho* shower scene, while making the accompanying screechy sounds. "What — apart from her mentalist tendencies?"

"Okay. Bad example to start with." I pick Dan's phone up, and choose names from the list at random. "Alex?"

"Wore too much perfume."

"Joanna?"

Dan waves his hand in front of his nose and scrunches up his face. "Didn't wear enough."

"Joy?"

"No Joy."

"Huh?"

"Didn't like sex."

"With you, or in general?"

"I won't even dignify that with an answer. Next?"

"Er . . . Vivienne?"

"Too far the other way. Suggested a bit of S&M to me, and I thought she meant she wanted to do it in M&S." He grins sheepishly. "That was one embarrassing shopping trip."

"Marie?"

"Too French."

"Too *French*? I thought the accent was supposed to be sexy?"

"You'd think so, wouldn't you? But I asked her what would make her life complete once, and she said 'happiness', but I heard 'a penis' . . ." He grimaces. "I was out of there like a shot."

"Debbie?"

"Too needy."

"Sue?"

"Too whiny."

"You've got an answer for all of them, haven't you?"

He nods. "I tell you, Ed, before this SlateYourDate stuff all happened, it was getting to the stage where almost as soon as I met a woman, I knew the reason I was going to leave her."

180

From what I can tell, it'd be because Dan's a commitment-phobic tart. And yet, thinking about it, there was one woman he was committed to. Or as committed as Dan gets, anyway.

"Okay. Let's try another tack. What was wrong with Polly?"

At the mention of her name, Dan stiffens slightly. "She's not on the list," he says, suddenly worried. "Is she?"

"No, but I'm just interested. What was wrong with her? You've said that there's been something wrong with every other girl you've gone out with, so what was wrong with Polly?"

Dan stares into his beer. "I don't know. It was a long time ago. I can't remember."

"Is it possible that you can't remember because there wasn't actually anything wrong with her?"

"Don't be stupid," says Dan. "She's a woman. Of course there must have been something wrong with her."

"Such as?"

Dan hesitates. "Just being a woman doesn't count?"

"No."

"Well . . ."

"Did she have fat ankles?"

"Nope."

"Did she smell funny?"

"No!"

"An annoying voice?"

"What — like yours is at the moment?"

"Was she rotten in bed?"

"None of your business," says Dan, being surprisingly coy about sex for the first time in his life.

"Did she dress like a tart?"

"Of course not."

"Did she not dress tartily enough?"

Dan sighs. "Where on earth are you going with this?"

"I'm just trying to work out what it was about Polly that made you dump her. And to see whether there's a pattern with the others. And you know what? There is."

"How do you mean?"

"There's one thing they all have in common with each other. And the reason you're dumping them so quickly."

"Which is, Einstein?"

"None of them are Polly."

"Don't be ridiculous."

"I'm not being ridiculous. They're not Polly. And if I was a psychiatrist, I'd say that the reason you haven't found anyone to replace her yet is simply because none of these other women measure up. And the reason that you move on so quickly is because you realize that pretty quickly. And yet, the reason that you can't actually move on is because you still haven't got over Polly."

"Yes, well, you're not a psychiatrist, are you," he snaps. "You're a bloody recruitment consultant. And what you know about women would fill a . . . well, a very small book. You know — with not many pages. So not a lot of space to write down what you know. Which isn't much."

"I get it, Dan."

He gestures angrily towards me with his beer bottle. "Okay, mister smart-arse relationship expert. If Polly was so special, then why on earth did I let her get away?"

"Well, that's obvious, isn't it?"

He stares at me for a second. "Is it?"

I nod. "Because you didn't realize it at the time. Because you were more focused on other things. Namely yourself."

"That's not true."

"Yes it is, Dan. Your TV career was just taking off, remember? You'd made it down to the last three for *Newsround*, and *Where There's a Will* was just around the corner."

"But . . . I . . ." Dan's mouth gapes open, then he just drains the rest of his bottle of beer silently. And the reason he can't say anything is because it's all true. I watched it all happen — well, Jane and I did. After being a bit of a tart at college, Dan met Polly soon after he left. A beautiful girl, but not one of those women who are aware of it. Genuinely nice, down to earth — God knows what she saw in Dan. But the two of them had hit it off, and started dating, and suddenly Dan was a different person. He didn't even look at other women — well, he looked, but didn't do anything more — because he seemed happy. Content, even. And although he got annoyed when we teased him that the two of them would be settled down in no time, I could tell that there was a part of him that thought maybe that wasn't such a bad idea.

And then his TV stuff all started — a little by accident, really. He and Polly had been having a bit of a rough patch. Nothing serious — just the sort of thing that all couples go through now and then. But then he and I are out at some charity auction, and Dan meets this girl in the bar and can't help but turn on the old flirt mode, and it turns out she's a producer for the BBC. Pretty soon, he's auditioning for *Newsround*, which he doesn't get when he says — on camera — he thinks global warming is a good thing because he'd actually like England to be a little hotter, but some other producer sees the audition tape, and before you know it, he's the new presenter for *Where There's a Will*.

So, anyway, he gets more and more seduced by the idea of being this big star — although presenting a daytime antiques programme on BBC 2 is hardly your-name-in-lights famous, but Dan acts as if it is. Polly can't deal with his new-found smugness, so the two of them end up splitting up. We all thought it was just a temporary thing, and that they'd get back together in no time, but the weeks turned into months, and that was it. And while, at the time, he pretended that it was no big deal, and consoled himself by trotting out his "plenty more fish in the sea" line at every opportunity, I could tell he was pretty upset. And still is, judging by the fact that he still won't talk about it.

"Listen, mate. Don't you think this is something you need to deal with? And before you waste any more time on this SlateYourDate stuff. Because it'll only get worse over time, you know."

"Rubbish," says Dan. "Already dealt with, as far as I'm concerned. And besides, why will it get worse? I thought things were always supposed to get better after a while. 'Time, the great healer' and all that."

"The reason they'll get worse is because every woman you meet who isn't Polly makes you realize just how great things were with the two of you. Reinforces it, in fact. So every relationship you have after her lasts a shorter time because you know sooner that they're not going to be the one. Because you already know who the one is."

Dan shakes his head. "I'm sorry, Ed, but you know I don't believe in this 'the one' bollocks. After all, you thought Jane was the one until she dumped you. And now it's Sam. Who'll it be if you and Sam ever split up? Which you will if you don't get this 'present' lark sorted out."

I resist his attempt to turn the conversation back to me. "But that's where you're wrong. Just like I was wrong about Jane being the one. Because 'the one' is reciprocal, isn't it?"

"Is it?" says Dan, although possibly because he doesn't know what the word "reciprocal" means.

"Of course it is. I thought Jane was the one, but she obviously didn't feel the same about me, therefore she wasn't. But I know it about Sam, because everything with Sam is better, and I hope to anything that she feels the same. But you and Polly are the complete opposite. No one's ever compared to her, as far as you're concerned. In fact, forget stupid theatre ideas — I've

185

got an idea for how you can put an end to this whole karma business in one go."

Dan suddenly looks interested. "Which is?"

"Well, you told me something once, and it was good advice."

"It was?" Dan looks a little surprised.

"Yup. You said that in any relationship, the person who cares the least has the most power. And while at the time I thought it was a little, well, harsh, I've realized since then that you were absolutely right."

"I was?" Dan looks pleased with himself. "But what's that got to do with me and Polly, exactly?"

"Well, if you extrapolate . . ."

"Extrapolate? Is that something rude?"

". . . then, supposing Polly is the one. Suppose you track her down, instead of these other forty-odd women. See if you feel anything. You see her and either realize there's nothing there any more, in which case I'm afraid it's back to the drawing board, but if the opposite is true — which I suspect it might be — and the two of you get back together, then you won't have to worry about all this SlateYourDate stuff. Result."

Dan doesn't say anything for a while, and then looks at me levelly. "I'm not sure, Ed."

"Why not?"

"Because what if I do see her and, you know, feel something, and . . ." Dan swallows hard. "She doesn't want me back? Or if she won't see me in the first place?"

"Come on, Dan," I say, reassuringly. "Surely everyone deserves a second chance?" But while I stop myself adding the words 'even you' to the end of that sentence, I can't help wondering whether that's actually true. And if it is, then is that what Jane's banking on me giving her?

When I go round to Sam's later, she doesn't answer her doorbell, despite Ollie's frantic barking, and there's no reply when I ring her mobile either. I'm just starting to get worried, and contemplating whether to break in to see if she's all right, when she opens the door, still dripping wet from the shower.

"Sorry," she says, giving me a soggy kiss, while trying to keep the towel she's wrapped around herself from slipping down. "I'm running a little late."

"That's okay." I follow her inside, pushing Ollie's nose away from my crotch while wondering how I can get him to run off with Sam's towel instead. "What happened? I thought you'd finished work ages ago."

Sam clicks her fingers, and Ollie retreats obediently into his basket. "Some potential new client called me earlier to arrange a meeting, and then stood me up. I wouldn't have minded, but they were so insistent it had to be today — a Sunday, of all days — and then . . ." She smiles, ruefully. "Anyway, so I've just wasted the best part of an hour hanging around in the café at the end of the pier, approaching strange women. Sounds like the kind of thing you've had Dan doing all week."

At the revelation that this potential new client was female, my stomach lurches, and I'm about to ask if they had a name, but stop myself, convinced that I'm being too suspicious. And besides, Jane wouldn't have been stupid enough to use her real one.

"Didn't she leave you a number?" I say hesitantly.

"Oh yes," says Sam. "But then when I called it, it didn't seem to work. I must have written it down wrong."

"Does that happen a lot? Clients standing you up, I mean?"

"Never. Well, sometimes they chicken out, but never without at least letting me know." Sam shrugs, causing her towel to flap open tantalizingly. "Oh well. If she really wants to see me, she'll phone back."

Sam undoes the towel, then uses it to dry her hair unselfconsciously in front of me — a sight that would normally leave me unable to think about anything else. And yet, I can't help but feel more alarmed than aroused.

Of course, there could be a hundred and one explanations for what happened to her today — none of them involving Jane. There are a thousand women who might need a personal trainer in Brighton — some of them perhaps following my example after Jane dumped me, maybe even a few of them doing it as a result of being dumped by Dan. And even though Jane used to come home from work sometimes and shock me with stories about some of the things she'd had to do in order to gain a competitive advantage over some competitor's product, and I'd feel that sometimes there was a fine line between market research and stalking, Jane's hardly the stalker type. Besides, what good would it do her to meet Sam? Unless, of course, she hadn't been planning actually to meet her but, to borrow Sam's phrase, just wanted to "see" her.

But what can I do about it? Convince myself that I'm wrong, and just put it down to coincidence? Or call Jane up and tell her I know what she's up to? Not a smart move if I'm wrong, particularly since I'm trying to avoid any further contact with her. As Sam disappears off to her bedroom to get dressed, I look over at Ollie, who seems to have dozed off in his usual leg-twitching way, and I decide, perhaps wrongly, that my best course of action is to let sleeping dogs lie.

CHAPTER
ELEVEN

Today is Dan's first day of filming on *Close Encounters*, and as his "agent" I've called round on my way to work to wish him good luck. To be honest, I'm more interested in getting his advice on how to ask Sam to move in, having bottled out again last night, although that was partly due to my fears over the identity of Sam's mystery client. When he answers his front door, I'm quite pleased to see that he's back to his usual chirpy self. Or so his cheery greeting of "morning, loser" would indicate, anyway.

"Not nervous, then?"

"Nah." Dan follows me into his kitchen. "Let me tell you, when you've done live TV, this kind of thing's a doddle."

"Yes, but, this is *acting*, isn't it? And you've not done much of that, have you?"

He shrugs. "Maybe not. But I don't know what the big deal is. These actors, they get revered and all that, but all they're really good at is kids' games."

"Kids' games?"

"Yup. Every kid loves to dress up and play pretend. That's all acting is. Piece of piss." Dan pauses to check

190

his reflection in the side of the stainless-steel kettle. "Remember, I was in *Casualty* once."

"So you keep reminding me. As 'corpse number two'. Which meant all you had to do was lie still for five minutes."

"So? It's hard to play dead." He grins. "Just ask Sam."

"What's it got to do with her?"

"She does it every time you're in bed together."

I pick up what I guess must be the script from Dan's kitchen table. "So, have you learnt your lines?"

"Hands off," he says, snatching it from me. "That's highly confidential, that is. Leak it to the press and I'll be off the show before you can say 'and the BAFTA for best-looking soap actor goes to . . .'"

"Dan," I say, grabbing it back from him and flicking through the pages, where he's helpfully marked his bits in yellow highlighter pen. "I'm hardly going to leak it to the press. Besides, I don't watch *Close Encounters* anyway, so I'm hardly going to be interested in . . . You get to sleep with *twins*?"

I can't believe it. For some people, life imitates art. For Dan, it's the other way round. If *Close Encounters* counts as art, that is.

He grins. "Yup. Although not both together, sadly. And then I tell each of them that I thought I was sleeping with her when I was sleeping with the other one — which is a pretty good excuse, if you think about it — when secretly I knew all along."

"This kind of stuff isn't exactly going to show you in the best light, you know."

Dan sticks his lower lip out and shakes his head. "At five grand a week, and all the actresses I can eat — on screen, at least — who gives a damn?"

"And you're not worried that it might influence what you're trying to do? Making amends with all these ex-girlfriends of yours?"

"Nah," he says. "In fact, the way I see it, it might actually be a good thing. Make them realize that however badly I treated them, I wasn't as bad as Wayne. Sorted."

"And what about Polly."

Dan looks a little annoyed. "What about her?"

"Have you thought any more about tracking her down?"

"Er . . . No."

"Because?"

He rolls his eyes. "Because I haven't, all right?"

"And at the risk of asking the obvious question, why not?"

"I don't know. I've been busy."

I walk over to Dan's expensive state-of-the-art fridge and remove a bottle of freshly squeezed orange juice from inside the door, surreptitiously checking the sell-by date as I unscrew the cap. "Doing what? Apart from avoiding the issue."

"Stop giving me a hard time, Edward. Besides, she knows where I am. It takes two to tap dance, don't forget."

"Tango, Dan."

"No thanks. But I'll have a Coke, if there's one in there."

192

I look at him for a second, not sure if he's joking, then hand him the can of Pepsi that I find on the shelf. "Except she doesn't, does she? Because you've moved house and changed your telephone number what, three times since the two of you split up. And she's the injured party. She's hardly likely to come chasing after you so you can break her heart again, is she?"

"I didn't break her heart before."

"No?"

"No."

"And how's she going to feel?" I say, when Dan doesn't elaborate.

"When?"

"Well, when she sees you on TV. And it reminds her why the two of you split up."

He shrugs. "I don't know. And I'm never going to find out, am I?"

"But she's the key to all of this," I say, pouring my juice into a glass, then adding some ice from the ice maker in the fridge door. "You're running around trying to make things good with all these other girls, when in actual fact you're completely ignoring the one you really need to sort things out with."

Dan sighs and leans against the kitchen counter. "Edward . . . I just can't. Not with her. It'd be too . . ."

"Painful?"

"Complicated. And I just don't need any more complications in my life right now."

I look at him incredulously. "What do you mean, any more complications? Right now, the hardest decision you have to make each day is what to spend your money on. Some people dream of having your life."

"They do, don't they?" beams Dan, opening the Pepsi carefully to avoid another audition accident. "But don't you get it? That's why I can't even think about Polly. Because three years ago, I had to choose between my career and her. And whatever you might think, that was a tough decision for me to make. And I chose my career, which I don't need to remind you is on the verge of that big break that every single person who works in this business dreams of. So why would I want to risk chucking it all away to chase after what might have been, particularly if there's a massive chance that it was never meant to be in the first place?"

I sip my juice quietly, as I don't really have an answer for that. Because the funny thing is, as much as I'm convinced he's wrong, I can see that he's got a point. Things have always been easy for Dan, based on a combination of his good looks and blasé attitude. The only thing he's ever had to work at in his life has been his career, and although it hasn't been "work" in the sense that most normal people know it, I can see that now, more than ever, he needs to follow it through. And yet I can't help thinking — because I'm so happy with Sam, and because I know it's a happiness that Dan's not experienced since his Polly days — he's missing out on what's really important.

"Anyway," continues Dan. "Did you come round to wish me good luck, or was the real reason to try and convince me that Polly's the answer to all my problems?"

194

"The first one. And because I wanted to run something by you."

He glances at his watch, and then the digital clock on the front of the oven, just to double-check he's not going to be late. "Okay. Shoot."

I drain my glass of juice, and then launch into my — or rather, Mrs Barraclough's — great idea. But when I've finished explaining it to Dan, his reaction isn't quite what I was expecting.

"You want to ask Sam to live with you?" he says. "What on earth are you thinking about? Don't you like sex any more?"

I feel myself blushing slightly. "What do you mean?"

Dan shakes his head slowly. "Want to know how to stop having sex with a woman? Ask her to move in. It's why pub landlords never drink. When anything's available twenty-four-seven, it just kind of loses its appeal."

"That's rubbish, Dan."

"It's not rubbish." He swallows a mouthful of Pepsi, and then burps loudly. "It happened to a mate of mine."

"Who?"

"You, dummy. With Jane, remember?"

I don't like to remind him that was probably because she stopped wanting to have sex with me, and not the other way around. "Yes, well, it won't happen with me and Sam. Besides, I wanted to make some sort of declaration, you know?"

"Well, you're certainly making one of those," he says. "And it's saying 'Please walk all over me.'"

"But I don't like living on my own. I lived with Jane for nearly ten years, don't forget. And you before that."

"So you just want some company? Well, get a dog, then."

"No, it's not like that at all, Dan. I like being part of a couple. Things are more fun when there's two of you."

"Sex, for instance," he says longingly. "Not that you'll be finding that out if you move her in."

"Not just sex. There's other stuff too."

"Such as?" Dan looks genuinely interested.

"Well, for example, I like coming home and having someone say to me, 'How was your day?'"

"Let me show you something." He reaches into his pocket and retrieves his mobile. "This is called a 'telephone', and any time you want to have that particular conversation with someone, all you have to do is press these little buttons and there'll be someone to speak to on the other end. Easy."

He holds out the phone, and for some reason I take it from him. "Yes, but it's not the same as having someone actually there, is it?"

"You've obviously never tried phone sex." He points to his mobile. "All you have to do is set it on 'vibrate', and . . ."

"Dan, please," I say, handing it back to him hurriedly before wiping my hands on a tea towel. "It's not all about sex."

"Yes it is. You're letting someone invade your personal space, just so you can invade hers whenever you like. And, believe me, it doesn't actually work like that. I'm serious, mate. Women should be fragrant things, who have spent hours getting themselves ready, doing whatever they have to do like shaving their legs — and other bits — in private. The last thing you want is to see them actually doing it — and with your razor." He taps the side of his head with his index finger. "Think long and hard about this, Ed. Because what might seem to you like a great romantic gesture is actually a recipe for disaster."

"I don't care. I'm going to ask her."

"Don't you think it's a bit early?"

I look at my watch. "No. She's been up for hours."

"No, I mean in your relationship, dummy. You've been together, what, less than a year?"

"It won't be if she's feeling the same way."

"Aha," says Dan, in his usual annoying way. "But there's a big chance she might not be."

"Thanks very much. You're the one who talked about engagement rings."

"Yes, but *you're* the one who suggested she might not be ready for the 'L' word. Just the other day, in fact. And, besides, she might not be ready to move in with anyone. After all, she's obviously been living on her own for a while. What with the dog and everything."

"Yes, but she lived with her previous boyfriend for a while. And she likes me better than him. Or at least I think she does, or she'd still be with him, wouldn't she?"

Dan finishes the rest of his Pepsi, then scrunches the can up and drops it in the bin. "Okay, say you ask her, and she says no. What do you do then?"

"Er . . . I dunno. Keep things the way they are, I suppose."

"Except they won't be, will they?"

"Why not?"

"Because you'll have made this big gesture to her, which she's shoved straight back in your face. And you'll know it, and she'll know it, and so everything you do from then onwards will have the knowledge in the background that she turned you down."

"Don't be ridiculous."

Dan sits down at the kitchen table, and motions for me to do the same. "I'm serious. She'll think twice about staying over at yours, because in the back of her mind, she knows you'll be thinking that she's quite prepared to stay for a night but doesn't want to stay full-time. And because of that, her visits will get less and less. Honest, Edward, you want to think long and hard about whether this is what you really want, because nothing ruins a relationship more quickly than a mismatch in expectations. And I should know. I've ruined hundreds for that very reason."

"But Sam's not like that."

"How do you know?"

And I don't, in truth. I'd be guessing. Which, given my previous success with women, might not be the safest bet in the world. Because what does "moving in" actually mean? I don't mean on a practical basis, more what does it signify? It's a halfway step towards marriage, surely? A trial period, where we can see if we can occupy the same four walls without actually killing each other, before deciding whether to take that next step.

Dan is right about one thing, though. Because the trouble is, what happens if it doesn't work out — for whatever reason? What happens if you decide that, actually, you preferred just seeing this person a few times a week, rather than every morning sat on the toilet while you're brushing your teeth? Because then you're stuck, aren't you? You can hardly say 'I'm sorry, it's not working out like this, let's just go back to how it was', can you? Not without taking a bigger step backwards than the one you thought you were taking forwards.

But surely if you do want to be so close to someone — maybe even to marry them eventually, it's important that you see them in all their grainy reality — and they see you the same way. Because that's what life really is. One big lump of grainy reality. And although it's up to you how grainy that reality actually is, it's certainly not all one long honeymoon. As Jane and I proved.

Do I want to see more of Sam? Of course I do. But do I want to see her every day, and risk repeating what happened with Jane and me? Well, surely that's up to me now. And besides, I think it's a risk worth taking, given the potential prize.

"So you're saying that if I do decide to ask her, I shouldn't make a big deal of it?"

Dan nods. "Exactly. In this kind of situation, stealth is your friend. Suggest that she moves some of her stuff in gradually, perhaps. Get her to spend a few extra nights. See how that goes first."

"But that was what happened with me and Jane. It wasn't a big deal. And with something like this, I kind of think it should be. Because it does mean something to me. And I'd hope it will to her."

Dan makes a face. "Well, why not just go the whole hog, then?"

"What do you mean?"

"Like I said before — ask her to marry you. Instead of this namby-pamby halfway-house 'Let's move in together and see how it goes' grand gesture that you're thinking of doing, why not be a man? Put your money where your house is, so to speak."

"But . . . it's way too early for anything like that."

"Why? You've already said you're prepared to share your life and your flat with her. What've you got to lose? Apart from your girlfriend, and half of your worldly goods, that is."

"Jesus, Dan. Talk about taking the romance out of it."

"Aha," he says triumphantly, and I get the sudden urge to punch him. "So you do have doubts?"

"I didn't. But I do now, thanks."

And it's true that I do. But not about my feelings for Sam. They're stronger than the ones I had for Jane, and I'm sure about that now. But after what happened with Jane, and the way she dumped me out of the blue, my doubts are all about how much Sam actually feels for me, and whether any major declaration of feelings on my part is going to scare her off, or suggest neediness, or that I'm still on the rebound — or even all of those things. Does she still think I'm damaged? Not over

Jane? And how long, officially, does the rebound period last? A month? Three months? Six? Or is it over as soon as you meet someone else? I'd ask Dan, but his only concept of "rebound" is how firm his mattress is.

And as I help myself to some more juice, I realize that I don't, actually, know that much about Sam. I've never even met her parents, although that's because they live abroad — Spain, apparently — rather than the fact that she's too ashamed of me to introduce us. But I'm assuming they're happy, because they're still together, and therefore I'm hopeful that Sam's view of marriage is a healthy one. But what about kids? Does Sam want them? I mean, that was possibly one of the reasons that Jane and I split up — not because one of us wanted them and one of us didn't, but because we didn't ever talk about it. I know Sam likes children, but then she's already got the dog, and she used to have a cat, too, until it got run over. Were they children substitutes? Did she get them because she's been desperate to have kids for ages, and the pets have had to do for now?

But even as I understand how little I know about her, something else becomes clear to me too. If that isn't a good enough reason for asking her to move in with me, then I don't know what is.

"You know what you need to do?" says Dan.

I sigh. "If I did, I wouldn't be in this mess."

"Poker."

"Is sex your answer to everything?"

"No — *poker*. The card game."

I'm even more confused. "What?"

"You know — keep your cards close to your chest. Don't show your hand too early. And it's best to stick between eighteen and twenty-one." He smiles. "Well, that last one's pontoon. But the principle's still the same, whether you're talking about cards or women."

"Huh? How does that help with me and Sam, exactly?"

"Simple. It's time to start bluffing. And see if she calls you."

"But I'm no good at that sort of thing."

"And that's why this plan's so brilliant. Because you don't need to be. All you need to do is get her to think you're going to ask her the big question, and then see what her reaction will be."

I frown across the top of my glass at him. "But isn't that a little . . . dishonest?"

He shrugs. "All's fair in love and war. And sometimes, there's very little difference between those two states."

"But why do I need to call her bluff?"

"Simple," he says, folding his arms. "In life, there are several questions you only want to ask if you're already sure what the answer's going to be. 'Will you marry me?' for example. 'Is it mine?' Or 'Have you ever thought about a threesome?'"

"Dan!"

He grins. "And this is one of those. Because think of the alternative. You ask her to move in, she says no, and even though she might have a valid reason, you'll always think that it's actually because she just doesn't like you enough. And like I said, that'll hang over your relationship like a bad smell, meaning you'll be afraid to ever ask her again."

"So you think she'll say no?"

"That's not what I said. But just remember — there's no going back from this."

I stare into my glass in desperation, as if I'm going to find the answer in the swirl of orange bits. "So, how on earth do I" — I try and match Dan's analogy — "lay my cards on the table, without actually . . ."

"Laying anything? S'easy." Dan leans back in his chair and stretches, although it's actually so he can covertly check his watch. "Go on holiday."

"What — to get some thinking space, you mean?"

Dan reaches over and cuffs me around the back of the head. "No, you fool!" he says, in his best Mister T voice. "With Sam. Take her away somewhere nice for a few days. And go self-catering. It'll be like you're living together, without *actually* living together, and sometime during the week — assuming things are going well — you can just slip into the conversation something about how lovely it would be if the two of you could do this all the time. If she reacts all funny, you can say that you just meant going on holiday. If not . . . She's on the phone to Pickfords the minute you get back."

I stare at Dan for a second or two while I consider what he's just said. On the one hand, it's not a bad plan. It'll give us both a taster of what it might be like living under the same roof. And the downside? Well, I get to spend a whole uninterrupted week with Sam. Brilliant.

"You're smarter than you look, you know."

"Thanks!" says Dan, before frowning, as he tries to work out whether that's an insult or not. "Just remember, sound her out as much as possible beforehand. Start from the opposite point of view, even. Don't get yourself into a position you can't easily come back from, or dismiss as a misunderstanding, if it starts going somewhere you don't want it to."

"Right," I say, not having the faintest idea what he's talking about. "And you'll be all right on your own? I mean, with all this Slate YourDate stuff going on?"

"I think I'll manage," says Dan, although possibly more because it means it'll give him a break from my nagging about going to see Polly. "Besides," he adds, pointing to the script on the table. "It's showtime!"

"And so, where do I take her? I mean . . ." — I change the sentence, as Dan starts to leer at my unfortunate choice of phrase — "any suggestions as to a good holiday destination?"

He shrugs as he stands up, then picks up his car keys off the table, which is obviously my signal to leave too. "Somewhere hot, obviously. You'll get to see her in a bikini all day, and then at night you'll get to rub after-sun lotion all over her." He grins. "Even where the sun don't shine, if you know what I mean?"

"And that'll help me convince her to move in with me?"

"Nope," says Dan. "But at least you'll get a shag out of it."

And as I follow him out through his front door, I realize that that last exchange probably illustrates the fundamental difference in our philosophies.

204

CHAPTER
TWELVE

The problem I have with these talking-tos that Dan feels duty-bound to give me on a regular basis is that sometimes they're more confusing than helpful. And while I know he's convinced he's got some uncanny perceptive ability when it comes to understanding women — like the Dustin Hoffman character in *Rain Man* had with maths — I'm not so sure any more. *Rain Man* was an idiot savant, and at times I reckon that Dan's actually more like the first half of that description.

And so for the next few days, even though I see quite a bit of Sam, I've now built it up into such a big deal thanks to Dan's "advice" that I'm too anxious to say anything, about either the holiday or any of the other issues on my mind. And the more worried about it I get, the more my behaviour seems to go in the opposite direction, so maybe it's time away from her I need at the moment, to get my head straight.

By Wednesday evening, and with Sam asleep in front of some rubbish film round at my flat, I realize that it's probably now or never, and to be honest, I'm verging towards the "never" option. I need to think carefully how I'm going to play it. and I'm so desperate that I decide a session at the gym might help me to work out what I'm going to say.

I manage to extricate myself from underneath her legs without waking her, half-shut the window blind, and walk quietly into the bedroom to get changed. When I emerge a few minutes later dressed in my workout gear, Sam opens one sleepy eye.

"What's up with you? Normal clothes in the wash?"

"No, I'm, er, off to the gym."

"Oh." She sits up and yawns. "Right. That's keen. Well, give me a couple of minutes to get changed and I'll come with you."

"No, that's OK. You're enjoying your film," I say, nodding at the TV, where the end credits have just started rolling. "I won't be long. Besides, you must be tired."

"Never too tired to put you through your paces," says Sam, stretching flirtatiously. "Here or in the gym."

"No, don't worry. You stay here. I just fancied a quick session." I don't add the words "on my own", but Sam immediately understands that's what I mean.

"Oh." Her smile fades.

"I mean, it's just, you've already had two clients this evening, and I thought . . ."

"Right. And you don't you want me to come," she says, suddenly wide awake. And this time, I know she's left the words "with you" off on purpose.

I suddenly feel extremely guilty, as well as incredibly useless at this relationship lark. How can a simple idea of going for a workout in order to work out how to ask your girlfriend if she wants to go on holiday with you with a view to moving in, plus trying to give her a bit of rest time as well, suddenly escalate into a misunderstanding like this?

"Yes. I mean, no, it's not that. It's just . . ." I walk over and sit down next to her on the sofa, thinking that if I'm going to sound her out about stuff, then now's as good a time as any. "You're not worried that we see too much of each other? No — not too much," I add quickly, when I see her face fall even further. "I mean, a lot. No. That doesn't sound right either."

"What are you trying to say?"

Oh shit. I'm in danger of starting one of *those* conversations. And I'm no good at them — particularly when I don't mean to start one in the first place. So much for my effortless, casual "holiday" suggestion.

"It's just that, well, we spend a fair bit of time together — which is lovely — but don't you sometimes think it'd be good to do some things on our own?"

"Why?"

"Why?" That's a good question. "Er . . . So we've got something to talk about when we do see each other."

As soon as I say this, I realize how lame it sounds, given that my life seems to revolve mainly around Sam, Dan, work, and the Admiral Jim — and not necessarily in that order. Because while in principle if I was maybe a polar explorer, or a heart surgeon, coming back from my latest expedition or difficult transplant operation might give me something interesting to tell Sam all about, a trip to the gym, however, might not be the best starting point. And the idea of needing "something to talk about"? Well that just suggests we've got nothing to discuss as it is. It suddenly occurs to me why Jane and I never had this kind of conversation, and I wonder — because I'm so rubbish at them — whether maybe she'd have dumped me even sooner if we did. Then again, that might be another reason Jane and I split up — because we *didn't* have enough of them. Aargh.

"Right," says Sam, standing up quickly. "I'll be off home then."

"What?" I glance at my watch, which by now, quite frankly, I'm starting to resent a little. "But it's still early."

Sam shrugs. "So? A good time for you to go to the gym, apparently. And then I'll look forward to you telling me all about it sometime."

"Sam, I didn't mean it like that."

She folds her arms, and stares down at me. "Well, how did you mean it, exactly?"

"It's just . . . Do you ever think about what's going to happen in the future?"

"What, cars that fly, or holidays on the moon? That sort of thing?"

"No. I mean us. Our future."

Sam's starting to look a little concerned. "What's brought this on?"

"Nothing. I mean, everything. I just wondered, you know, whether we needed to talk about . . . stuff."

"Do we have 'stuff' to talk about, Edward?" she asks, her voice sounding a little strained.

I look back up at her, feeling slightly awkward given that I'm still sitting on the sofa and she's standing over me, but I worry that if I stand up, then I'll be too close to her, and I don't want to do that and then have to take a step backwards. "Don't we? Doesn't everyone? I don't know. I mean, we get on okay, don't we?"

"That's the most romantic thing I've ever heard."

Ah. This isn't quite going to plan — not that I had much of a plan in the first place. There's nothing for it. I'm just going to have to come straight out and ask her — otherwise I'm going to get myself into even more trouble. And surely now's as good a time as any — after all, she's already mentioned holidays. Although I'm not sure the moon is such a great destination. Particularly given my fear of heights.

"I just think we could do with a short break."

"What?" Sam walks over towards the window, and yanks the blind open suddenly, causing us both to blink in the yellow glare from the street lamp outside. "But I thought things were going so well between us?"

It takes a few seconds before realization dawns. "No. I mean a holiday. You and I. Together. Not *that* kind of break."

"Oh," she says, visibly relieved. "A holiday. Right."

"It's just that, well, I don't have a lot on at work at the moment, so it's probably as good a time as any for me to take some time off, and you said a few of your clients were away too, so . . ."

"A holiday?" Sam seems to be a few sentences behind me. "Really?"

"Really."

"Natasha won't mind? You going away at such short notice, I mean."

"Nope. Besides, I'm a partner now. I can just take time off whenever I want it." This isn't strictly true, though given the amount of time Natasha's been spending in the office recently, I could probably just go and she wouldn't even know.

"And Dan?"

"Well, we could ask him to come too, but he might feel like a bit of a gooseberry."

"No, I meant will he be okay? Without you?"

"He'll be fine. I'll leave him with a list of names and addresses to work through while I'm away. Or, alternatively, we could always check him into the kennels with Ollie."

Sam walks over and gives me a hug. "Well, in that case, yes. I'd love to."

"Great," I say, warming to the idea more and more myself, particularly because the thought of seeing Sam in a bikini for a week is particularly appealing. "I'll pop out tomorrow and pick up some brochures if you like."

"No need," says Sam. "I already know the perfect place."

"Fantastic. Where?"

"In Majorca. It's a really nice villa, quite close to the beach. So maybe we could just go there? If you fancy it, that is."

A villa? That means self-catering. This is falling into place rather nicely. "Majorca sounds great. So does a villa. Is there a pool?"

"Oh yes."

"Fantastic," I say, picturing her in the water. Without her bikini.

"Brilliant," she continues. "And my parents have been dying to meet you, so . . ."

My excitement suddenly wilts, as if it's had a bucket of cold water thrown over it. "I'm sorry — they're, er, coming too?"

"Oh no. They live out there, remember? I thought that we could go and stay with them. At their villa. What do you think?"

"Er . . ." Majorca is part of Spain. Where her parents live, of course. This wasn't quite in my plan. Bang goes my idea of the two of us cosying up together at some little romantic retreat. But on reflection, it's a positive sign, surely, this "meeting the parents" thing? And because I can't think of a decent enough excuse or a single viable alternative I agree.

"Great," says Sam excitedly. "That's settled then. I'll call them tomorrow. They'll be so pleased."

"Great," I say, not quite sharing their predicted pleasure. "Well, that's better than us splitting up, I suppose."

Sam pokes me in the stomach. "Just a bit."

I put my arm round her shoulders, and sit her back down on the sofa. "I'm sorry, Sam. I'm not very good at this relationship stuff. I love spending time with you. Really I do. But my last girlfriend dumped me — out of the blue. And I don't want it to happen again. Especially with you. Not that there's anyone else it could happen with . . ."

Sam smiles at me, and squeezes my hand. "That's sweet, Edward — I think. But the reason I like going out with you is because we have fun. Together. And

211

when we do things, it's nice to be able to talk about them as a shared experience, rather than 'well, I did this', and 'you did that'. And don't worry. I'm not going to do a Jane on you." She grabs me round the waist. "Unless you get fat again, of course."

"Really?"

"Really. Don't forget, I used to live with someone who always wanted to do his own thing. And you know what? We ended up with nothing in common. And that's even worse."

As Sam rests her head on my shoulder, I sit there, stunned, for a moment or two, that I seem to have escaped. If I'd started this conversation with Jane, we'd be in the middle of a full-blown argument by now, and yet Sam and I seem to have cleared it up immediately. And I don't know if it's because I'm relieved at heading off a potential argument, or pleased that she's agreed to come on holiday with me, but I can't stop myself from saying it.

"I do love you, you know."

Sam doesn't say anything, but squeezes me even harder, and then kisses me for a long, long time. Not surprisingly, I don't quite make it to the gym.

CHAPTER
THIRTEEN

"You moron," says Dan, when I meet him in the Admiral Jim the next evening, where he's been sat for the previous hour signing and stuffing into envelopes a series of "apology" letters. "What did you want to go and say a thing like that for?"

I rub the top of my head where he's just cuffed me. "It just kind of slipped out. I was so relieved, and . . ."

Dan rolls his eyes. "Have I taught you nothing? All your good work undone by one stupid four-letter word."

"What do you mean, undone? Sam seemed pretty chuffed when I said it."

He ignores me. "What are you going to do now?"

I frown at him. "What do you mean, 'What am I going to do?' I don't have to 'do' anything."

"No, you're right," says Dan. "You don't. At least, not if you want the balance of power in this relationship to slip completely in her favour."

"Dan, what are you talking about? It's not all about a balance of power. It's not even a struggle."

He shakes his head. "Yes it is. Relationships work on a simple reward system where women are concerned.

You do things for them, they have sex with you in return, all because they're hoping you'll say those three little words."

"Huh?"

"It's the endgame they're after. Which is why you never, ever tell them that until you have to. Talk about playing your trump card too early."

"What do you mean, 'have to'? When would you ever 'have to'?"

"You'd be surprised." He makes a face, and it's the kind of face that makes me not want to know any more. "And how was the sex afterwards?"

I grin back at him. "Fantastic."

"Aha." Dan waves his beer bottle in front of me. "You see? It's all a negotiation — even when you don't know there's anything to negotiate for. So how did she respond, exactly?"

"Well, I'm not going to go into details . . ."

I don't know whether Dan looks disappointed or relieved. "Not that. I mean, she said it back, right?"

"Er, no, actually," I say, suddenly panicking. "Maybe she thinks it's too early on. Maybe I've scared her."

"But she'd already agreed to the holiday?"

"Oh yes. Like a shot, actually. We're going to stay with her parents in their villa and . . ."

"Her parents?" Dan puts his beer bottle down on the bar. "She certainly tricked you into that one."

"What do you mean?"

"The old disguised meet-the-parents trick. Pretty impressive, though, using the holiday lure."

I'm still amazed that Dan seems to identify with all of these like they're tried-and-tested strategies. "I'm sure it wasn't a trick. Sam's not like that."

He shakes his head. "When are you going to learn, Edward? They're *all* like that."

"All like what?" says Wendy, who's just appeared behind the handpumps. She's wearing a tight white three-quarter-length T-shirt, revealing a belly button you could hang a coat off, and holding an empty Malibu bottle by its neck.

"Lovely, and fragrant, and always right," says Dan quickly. He waits until she's thrown the bottle away and made her way back to the other end of the bar before continuing. "I mean, the decent thing for Sam to have done was offer you a way out. Let you go and get some brochures first before mentioning that her parents have a place in Majorca. Then suggested the two of you head out there for your holiday, unless you had somewhere else in mind, thus giving you a chance to back out with some other location excuse. Not to have presented it as one of those 'village fête' things."

"Fait accompli, you mean?" I see his point, but don't really mind that much, even if she did it on purpose. "Still, it might be fun. And there's not a lot I can do about it now, so I might as well just grit my teeth and enjoy it."

"I think you'll be doing more of the first one."

"What are you talking about now?"

"Well, for one thing, her dad's going to be watching you like a hawk."

"What? Why?"

Dan sticks a stamp on the last of the envelopes, sorts them into a pile, then takes a long pull on his beer. "Okay. Every dad hates the fact that his little girl . . ."

"Sam's twenty-nine."

"But she's still his little girl. And always will be. Now will you stop interrupting?"

"Sorry."

"His little girl has grown up. And now has boyfriends who want to sleep with her. He was once a young bloke, right, so he knows exactly what we're like. And so the thought of someone treating his little princess the way he used to treat women at your age . . ." Dan stops talking, and draws his finger across his throat in a cutting motion.

"But . . ." I want to say: "I'm not you," but that's a little cruel. "He'll see how I am with Sam. And that I always treat her well."

"That's not my point. Meet the parents in any normal circumstances — out for dinner, say — and the dad's going to be at least civil. Because the only way for him to get through the evening without castrating you with the blunt end of his dessert spoon is to convince himself that after the meal, you'll be driving his daughter home and dropping her off with no more than a peck on the cheek. But you're staying with them — and for a whole week. So every time they wish you goodnight, he's going to be quietly seething at the fact that the two of you are going to be at it like rabbits under his roof the moment his back is turned. And in the morning? That small talk over breakfast, when he knows you've spent the last eight hours rogering his daughter?" Dan laughs. "It'll be the least shagging you ever do on holiday. Which is good, come to think of it, because it'll prepare you for when she moves in."

I'm starting to feel depressed now. "So, you're telling me that I shouldn't go?"

Dan shakes his head. "Too late for that now, sonny-boy. But just think of it as a week-long interview, because her parents are going to be interviewing you as a potential son-in-law, and at the same time you're interviewing Sam as a potential flatmate."

"That doesn't sound like much of a holiday."

Dan shrugs. "Yes, well, that was never the point of the exercise, was it? And at least you're a recruitment consultant, so you should be good at it. As long as you remember what your motivation is."

"Right." I look at him, waiting for a further explanation. "Meaning?"

"Getting her to move in with you, dummy. Everything you do on the holiday should be with that aim in mind." He helps himself to a Kettle Chip from the packet on the bar that I've been eyeing hungrily for the last ten minutes. "It's like my acting. Every time I do a scene, I say to the director, 'What's my motivation?'"

I don't want to imagine what his motivation was in the scene with the twins yesterday. "And that helps, does it?" I say glumly.

"Of course it does."

"Give me an example."

"Well, when I did *Casualty* . . ."

"As a corpse under a sheet, for the hundredth time!"

217

"It's still acting," sniffs Dan. "Anyway, I said to the director 'What's my motivation?' and he explained that I was a young man, in the prime of life, who'd been knocked down and killed by a runaway ice-cream van . . .'"

"Hence the ninety-nine takes it took you to get it right?"

Dan ignores me. "Seriously, Ed, that kind of thing really makes you think. I knew what my character's motivation was for lying on that slab, and thanks to that, I gave the performance of a lifetime. Well, the end of a lifetime, if you think about it."

I look at him in disbelief. "It's a wonder that Hollywood didn't come calling. And, anyway, how does that help me?"

"Simple. Just apply the same technique to every situation you find yourself in."

"How on earth is that going to work."

"It already has," says Dan. "Remember when Jane left you, everything you did was aimed towards getting her back. The exercise, the embarrassing situations you put yourself through . . . You couldn't have done any of it if you didn't have the motivation, right? Even though you decided you didn't want her in the end. And now, it seems that it worked."

"I suppose."

"So now, say you were thinking about maybe asking Sam to do something else, like trying anal sex for the first time."

"Dan!"

"Sorry, but you get my point. Or rather, she'll get yours. But only if you think about what your motivation is, and keep that in mind throughout every stage of the process." He sits back on his chair. "Trust me. It's foolproof."

"It'd have to be, if it works for you."

"I'm not kidding. Say I meet a girl and I want to get her into bed, everything I do, and everything I say, is with that goal in mind. That way, my body language, the tone of my voice, how I treat her, are all geared towards that too. And they pick that stuff up, women. All those subliminal messages. Remember, ninety per cent of communication is non-verbal." He looks along the bar, where Wendy is flicking through a copy of *Epidural Weekly*, raises his eyebrows, and puffs out his cheeks in a 'hey, fatso' kind of way. Wendy just smiles, before giving him the finger. "See?"

"I'm not so sure. I mean, isn't it just a little bit . . . mercenary? I mean, I'm not trying to coerce her into anything she doesn't want to do."

"Apart from the anal sex bit, obviously."

"Dan, please."

"Sorry, Ed. But it's not coercion. You're just trying to influence her decision. And the more she picks up on how much you want something, the more likely she is to go along with it."

"And you really think that'll work?"

"No, Edward. I told you all of that for absolutely no reason at all," he says, getting up and heading towards the toilets. "Of course it'll work," he calls over his shoulder. "There have been studies on it, and everything."

As I can't help but smile at the idea of Dan ever reading anything like a "study", something occurs to me about how he lives his life, and how in particular — at least where women are concerned — he makes everything into a battle. And thinking about it, Natasha's the same with all of her men. It's not just about scoring, but more about scoring points. And that can't be the way to run a healthy relationship, can it? What about partnership? What about cooperation? What about wanting to do something for the other person because they'll appreciate it, rather than for what it'll ultimately do for you?

And although it's probably not the best reference point, I can't help thinking back to my relationship with Jane, and wondering exactly when it was that we stopped doing things like that for each other or, more important, *why* we stopped. Because once you get to that stage, then surely there's no point in being with that person any more? And I suppose the real skill is recognizing when you're there. Which Jane obviously did.

And it occurs to me that that's why Dan's destined to fail in every relationship he has — and probably why he ended up making a mess of things with Polly. Because he's always starting from a position of inequality. Imbalance. And constantly trying to push the balance even further in his favour. And while even I understand you have to make some concessions as you go along, you shouldn't be making sacrifices. Especially not human ones.

I'm wondering how to explain this to him when Wendy waddles over.

"How's it going with Mister Bastard?" she says, hauling herself awkwardly up on to Dan's still-warm bar stool.

"I'm not sure," I say. "I think he's still got a long way to go. And he doesn't seem to realize that maybe he's picking the wrong kind of women."

"What — ones with a brain?"

"The opposite, actually. I think that Dan thinks he wants a female version of himself."

Wendy shudders. "What a thought!"

"Exactly. But in actual fact, there's hardly enough room in any relationship for one ego the size of Dan's, let alone two of them." I take a sip of my wine, which seems to taste a bit funny, although that could be from all the envelopes I've been licking. "It'd be a disaster."

"So what does he need then? A doormat type?"

"No. Not exactly. Because he would, literally, walk all over them. He just needs someone who's content to let him be Dan. Who's independent. Who's firm, but not too demanding. And who doesn't get frustrated whatever he does. Oh, and who's tolerant in the face of all his, er, behavioural issues . . ."

"But Mother Theresa's dead, right?" says Wendy.

I laugh. "Unfortunately, yes. But Dan would probably even find fault with her. No, what he needs is someone . . . like Polly."

"Polly?" Wendy looks a little puzzled. "His ex-girlfriend Polly?"

"Yup."

"That's not a bad suggestion. Have you tried telling him that?"

I nod. "But he thinks he can still go on using and abusing these girls, ultimately leaving him feeling unsatisfied . . ."

"And them, apparently," grins Wendy.

". . . whereas if he'd just meet up with Polly again, he'd at least see what he's been missing. Trouble is, he just won't listen."

"Yes, well, they do say that love is blind — and deaf as well." Wendy thinks for a moment or two. "Why don't you fix it up for him?"

"How do you mean?"

"Set up a surprise meeting between the two of them."

"Nah. Dan's thick, but he'd never fall for anything like that. Besides, I've got to make him *want* to see her."

Wendy rests her chin on her hands, and her elbows on her stomach. "What about Facebook?"

"What about it?"

"Why not start a dialogue between the two of them on there? Set up a false profile for each of them. Get in touch with Polly, and make her think she's talking to Dan, when in fact she'd be talking to you, and vice versa. Sort of a 'Fakebook', if you like."

"And then maybe suggest a meeting?"

"Exactly," says Wendy. "Each would think it's the other one who's suggested it, so they're more likely to want to go."

This is brilliant. And what's more, in the absence of any other ideas, it might just work. Because I'm convinced that if I can just get them together in the same room, then Dan will see what he's been missing, and Polly . . . Well, I don't know what Polly's reaction will be. But at least it might be enough to shock him into some sort of change in his behaviour. And I'm getting to the stage where I don't mind what I have to do to achieve that.

"Wendy, you're a genius."

"I know."

"Assuming Polly's on Facebook, of course."

Wendy looks at me like I'm from the Middle Ages. "Edward, *everyone's* on Facebook."

"Of course they are, Wendy. I'm just winding you up," I say, making a mental note to join — or whatever it is you do — myself.

"Let me know if you want a hand," she says, easing herself carefully down off the stool.

"That's very generous of you. I thought you weren't too keen on Dan."

"I'm not." She nods towards where Dan is finally emerging from the toilets. "But if there's ever a chance to play a joke on him, then count me in."

"Come on, Wendy. Admit it. There's a part of you that feels sorry for him."

"Nope," she says, making her way back towards the bar. "But I do want to stop him treating women as badly as he does. And if I can give him a helping hand . . ."

Dan looks at her suspiciously. "What did the Michelin Woman want?"

"Don't be rude, Dan. She was actually offering to give you a helping hand."

"I'm not that desperate," he says. "But I tell you, if I don't get some action soon, I'm going to go mad. Or blind."

"So that's why you were so long in there," calls Wendy from behind the bar, having obviously overheard our last exchange. "I hope you washed your hands?"

"Nothing like that," says Dan, blushing slightly. He leans across to me and lowers his voice. "Actually, I was just confirming this evening's torture session."

"In the toilets?"

"The joys of modern technology." He removes his mobile phone from his pocket, and points to the screen, where someone called Rachel has sent him a text.

I scan through it quickly, and then have to read it again. "She wants you to *what*?"

"Go out for a beer with her current boyfriend, tell him about the shitty way I treated her, and show him my scar. So he knows not to do the same."

"What scar?"

"You know. The one on my arse." Dan has a small scar just above his left buttock which he likes to tell girls he got in a knife fight, whereas in actual fact he was trying to get a view of his backside in a mirror one

224

day, but ended up slipping over and sitting on the metal comb he always used to carry in his back pocket.

"But Rachel didn't do that to you."

"He's not going to know that, is he?"

"That's ingenious — although I'd be careful where you are when you show him. And, dare I ask, what was the 'shitty way' you treated her."

Dan shifts uncomfortably on his stool. "We just didn't see eye-to-eye on stuff."

I find Rachel's entry on Slate YourDate. "Well, that seems a little bit harsh. I mean, just because the two of you didn't agree from time to time, that's no reason to give you such a bad rating."

"My thoughts exactly," says Dan, sniffing his lager suspiciously, as if he suspects Wendy of tampering with it.

"So, what sort of stuff?"

"What sort of stuff what?"

"Didn't you see eye-to-eye on, exactly?"

Dan shrugs. "Just . . . Stuff."

"Such as?"

"I dunno. Lots of stuff."

"Like?"

"You know — the usual. What restaurants to eat at. What DVDs to rent. How often we'd see each other." He helps himself to another Kettle Chip. "My infidelity."

"Whoa. Your *infidelity*?"

Dan nods. "Yup. Seems she had a big problem with the fact that I slept with someone else just before we broke up. Said she couldn't trust me ever again after that. Even though I did it for us." He pops the crisp into his mouth and crunches it noisily. "Me and Rachel, I mean, rather than me and you."

"Hang on, Dan. You were unfaithful to Rachel, and then you tried to explain it away to her by saying that you did it for the, and I use the word advisedly, *good* of your relationship. Which she found a little tough to take."

"I know," says Dan. "Unbelievable."

"Well, I'm having a problem believing it, and I'm your best friend, so I can see how she might have too."

"Why?" Dan picks up the packet of Kettle Chips and, after tugging on one of the corners to make a spout, tips his head back and empties the crumbs into his mouth, before washing them down with a mouthful of beer. "All I was trying to do was work out how I felt about her."

"By sleeping with someone else?"

"Yup. It's like you and Jane."

I can't wait to hear this. "How is it like me and Jane, exactly?"

"Well," explains Dan. "You say that you're over Jane, right?"

"Right. Most definitely, in fact."

"And one of the reasons you're sure of that is because when you're with Sam, you know that it's better than how things were with you and Jane."

I'm not quite following this. "And?"

"And so one way to tell what you felt about Jane is by how much more you feel about Sam. Am I right?"

"Well, partly . . ."

226

"So obviously, if you're in a relationship, and you're wondering what you feel about the person you're going out with, then the best thing to do is to start seeing someone else. To give you a yardstick, if you like. Sleep with them and you feel nothing, then the relationship's sound. But if you think you like the new one more, well . . ." He finishes his beer, and tries to attract Wendy's attention for another. "Anyway, Rachel should have been flattered."

"Flattered?" Dan's logic is so twisted it's in danger of doing itself an injury. "How?"

"That I thought enough of her to, you know . . ."

"Cheat on her?" I shake my head. "Dan, you never cease to amaze me."

"Thanks."

"I didn't mean it in a good way. And how did she find out?"

"I told her, obviously."

"Obviously. Why?"

"To see what her reaction would be."

"And don't tell me." I try hard to follow Dan's line of thought — or rather, thoughtlessness. "If she'd been mad about it, then you'd have known she had feelings for you, but if she was cool with you cheating on her, then you'd know it was time to move on. Although, of course, the fact that she *was* mad about it meant that you thought she was the jealous type, so you dumped her anyway."

Dan leans across and claps me on the shoulder. "I do believe you're beginning to get it," he says, grinning like a proud father on sports day.

"So you're telling me that you're quite prepared to throw out things like trust and commitment —" I roll my eyes at Dan when he grimaces at the mention of that particular word — "just to follow your hare-brained theories?"

Dan shrugs. "They're not hare-brained. They work for me."

"But they quite obviously don't, Dan. This is what I've been trying to tell you for the past couple of weeks. These women *don't like* the way you treat them. That's why you're in this mess."

Dan takes my onslaught without flinching. And when I finally pause for breath, he swivels round on his stool and leans in towards me.

"Ed. Let me explain something to you. When was the last time you hired a car?"

"Hired a car? What's that got to do with anything?"

"Just humour me, will you?"

"Okay. It was when Jane and I went on holiday to Italy. One of those Fiat Cinqui . . . Chinky . . . Those small Fiat cars. We could hardly get our suitcases in the boot. And Jane said . . ."

Dan holds his hand up. "Okay, okay. I get the idea. No need to run me through your holiday snaps. And what did you think of it? Apart from the, ahem, size issues, of course."

I make a face. "It was fine. Cheap. Didn't break down. Got us from A to B."

"And did you keep it nice and clean? Check it had oil in it every morning? Top up the windscreen washer bottle at night?"

"Er . . . No. I just, you know, drove it."

"And now that you've got the Mini. How is that different?"

"Huh?"

"Well, you take good care of it, don't you? Even wash it by hand."

"So? Why does that make a difference?"

"Because the Mini's for keeps. It's yours. You've got a lot invested in it. And you love it. Whereas the hire car, well, you know you're going to give it back at some point, aren't you? And up until that point, all you want is something cheap to get you from A to B."

I see his point. And while I can't fault his logic for once, his basic premise is wrong.

"Except you don't, do you?"

"Huh?"

"You don't want something cheap."

Dan shrugs. "Well, I wouldn't mind. Particularly at the moment."

And as he leans over the bar and helps himself to another bottle of lager, I stop short of reminding him that he already had his Mini. In fact, he had his Rolls Royce. Which is why it's such a shame that he traded it in.

CHAPTER
FOURTEEN

I spend Friday morning sorting things out at work, while Sam finalizes the holiday arrangements with her parents, who apparently are "really looking forward" to us coming to stay. To be honest, I'm really looking forward to going, despite Dan's accusations of trickery on Sam's part. The highlight of my last holiday abroad with Jane was a row about the hotel I'd booked having paper-thin walls, and her annoyance at being kept awake night after night by the honeymooning couple in the room next door. This of course was my fault, and when she'd escalated the argument and complained that I never made her moan that noisily when we were in bed, I'd said that was because she moaned loudly enough the rest of the time. Cue stony silence for the rest of the trip.

By midday, I'm sitting at my desk actually doing some work for a change, while wondering what to have for lunch, when there's a knock on the door. Expecting to see Dan playing one of his tricks, I look up warily, but instead of his idiotic grin, there's a young woman holding a bouquet of flowers almost as big as she is.

"Delivery for you."

"Ah. Natasha's out, I'm afraid. And I don't know when she'll be back. I can give you her home address, if you like?"

The woman walks in through the doorway. "They're for an Edward Middleton, actually," she says, an amused expression on her face. "That you, by any chance?"

"Er . . ." For a moment, I'm so shocked, I forget my own name. "Yes. Yes, that's me. I mean, I'm he. Him."

"You sure about that, are you?"

I pick up one of my business cards to show her. "Yes. Sorry."

"No need to apologize," says the woman. "And no need for ID. Here." She hands over the large bunch of — well, I'm not sure what they are. "Someone thinks a lot of you."

As she walks out of the office, I stare suspiciously at the bouquet in my hands, holding it like I would a baby with a soiled nappy, while wondering who they're from. I've already discounted Sam, because she hasn't ever before, plus it'd be a little silly to send me some so close to us going away on holiday. It can't be Natasha either, as in all the years I've known her, the occasional gift of a cup of coffee from Starbucks across the road is the most she's ever managed — maybe with a flapjack on my birthday if she remembers. It certainly wouldn't be Dan, as a thank-you for my help with this Slate YourDate stuff — he'd think men giving flowers to each other was way too gay. And try as I might, I can't think of anyone I've found a job for recently who'd be grateful enough to send me something like this. Which only leaves one person that it could be. And I'm so taken aback by this that I don't even think to look in the most obvious place to check.

I'm still standing there five minutes later, wondering whether I should put them in some water, or in the bin — when there's another knock on the door. I'm hoping it's the woman from the florist's, having realized she's made a mistake, but it turns out to be worse than that. It's Sam.

"What are you doing here?"

She puts on a hurt face. "It's nice to see you too."

"No, I didn't mean it like that. I thought you'd be working. Or getting ready for the holiday."

She smiles. "It doesn't take that long to pack a bikini. So I thought I'd surprise you. See if you were free for lunch."

"Oh. Right."

"So . . . are you?"

"Um, yes. Let me just . . ." I stand there helplessly, holding the flowers, until Sam walks over and takes the bouquet from me. "They're beautiful," she says, inhaling the scent deeply. "Are they for Natasha?"

"Er . . ." And even though I realize later that if I'd have just said "yes" at this point, then I'd be able to head off any awkwardness, I find myself saying the exact opposite. And then inwardly kicking myself so hard that it's a wonder Sam can't see me wince.

"No?"

"No, they're from . . ." I can't do it. I want to be honest, and tell her that I think they must be from Jane, but actually, I've got no proof of that. And if it is the

232

case, and I say so, then I'm going to have to tell Sam about the other night too, and that's not going to make for the most pleasant of lunches, let alone holidays. I have to think on my feet, although not necessarily, as it turns out, with my brain. "I mean, they're for you. From me. Kind of a 'happy holidays' thing."

"Oh, Edward, they're lovely." She leans over and kisses me. "And there's a card," she says, reaching in between the stems and retrieving a small white envelope.

Fuck. There's a card. Fuck fuck fuck.

"You weren't supposed to see that."

"Why not?"

Because I didn't, I want to say. "I mean, you weren't supposed to read it. With me here." I try and take it from her hand, but she's too quick for me.

"Don't be embarrassed, Edward."

"But . . ."

Quick I think, as Sam slits the envelope open and pulls out the small white rectangle. *Do something.* Only trouble is — what? I could hit the fire alarm button on the wall, or maybe pretend to have a heart attack, although the way my chest is thumping at the moment, I might not need to pretend. I stand there rooted to the spot, looking for any change in Sam's expression as she silently reads the words on the card, and then hold my breath as her eyes meet mine.

"That's sweet, Edward."

"It is?" Surely Sam isn't that understanding. If Jane's written anything about us seeing each other the other night then "sweet" is probably the last word I'd expect Sam to use.

"Yes. 'For all the good times, and the ones to come.'" She smiles up at me. "We do have a good time, don't we?"

"We do," I say, almost shaking with relief, while at the same time feeling a flash of anger towards Jane. "Now, you mentioned something about lunch?"

"Yes," says Sam, slipping the card back into its envelope. "I'm starving."

I suddenly remember that I was, too. And yet funnily enough, as I steer Sam towards the door, my appetite seems to have vanished completely.

Almost as soon as I've waved goodbye to Sam and Jane's/my/her bunch of flowers after lunch, I take out my mobile and give Jane a call.

"It's me."

"I'm sorry," says Jane. "Who is this?"

"It's Edw . . . You know full well who it is."

"To what do I owe this pleasure?"

"Let's see if you can guess."

"Oh," she says, innocently. "You got the flowers, then?"

"Yes, I got the flowers."

There's a pause, and then Jane's voice comes back on the line. "You're welcome."

"I didn't say thank you."

"I know. I was being sarcastic. Didn't you like them?"

234

"Yes. No. I mean, *flowers*. Flowers are for, well, romance."

"And how would you know, Edward? You hadn't sent me any for ages. Which was one of the reasons we split up."

There she goes again, and within, what, fifteen seconds? Turning everything into a barb. A dig at me. Her tone immediately transports me back towards the last days of our relationship — although I didn't know they were the last days at the time, of course. And while stuff like me not buying Jane flowers wasn't why we split up — the *reason* I didn't buy them was — surely not even Jane would send me flowers just to remind me I never used to send her any?

"Well, it was very kind of you, Jane. But inappropriate."

"Inappropriate? Why?"

"Because we're not together any more. And you don't go around sending flowers to people when they're in a relationship with someone else."

"Why not?"

"Because it just makes things . . . awkward."

"Oh, I'm sorry, Edward," she says, sounding the complete opposite. "Did something happen? That wasn't my intention."

Yeah, right, I'm thinking. Jane rarely does anything without knowing exactly what the potential outcome might be. That's why she's so good at her job. "No. Nothing happened."

"Oh." There's a trace of something in her voice, and it might just be disappointment. "Good."

"And what was that note all about?"

"Well," she says. "I thought we got off on the wrong foot the other night, that's all. So I was wondering whether you wanted to meet up. For a coffee. As friends. Next week? I'll be back down in Brighton, so . . ."

"I can't."

Jane hesitates. "Can't? Or won't?"

"I'm going away next week. On holiday. So I can't."

There's another pause, even longer this time. "On holiday?"

"Yes, on holiday. That's allowed, isn't it?"

"With her?"

"With Sam." I emphasize her name, even though I'm sure Jane hasn't forgotten it, and it's maybe a little cruel, but I add the following words anyway: "My girlfriend."

But Jane doesn't miss a beat. "Okay. Well, have a nice time," she says sweetly. "Perhaps I'll see you when you get back."

"Perhaps," I say, although I'm already talking to a dead tone.

As I slip the phone back into my pocket, I remember that the last time Jane said something similar to me — in the note she left me when she, well, left me — I didn't see her for the best part of a year. This time, however, I've got an uneasy feeling that it might be different.

When I meet Dan in the Admiral Jim later, I have to stifle a laugh, as he's wearing a gorilla suit. Or at least I assume it's a gorilla suit, and not just that he's missed a couple of appointments with his waxer.

"Dare I ask?"

"Wipe that smile off your face," he says crossly, picking the rather realistic headpiece up from the chair next to him so I can sit down. "This is all your bloody fault."

"My fault? How come?"

"Karma," says Dan, in as sarcastic a voice as he can manage, wiggling his head from side to side at the same time for effect. "Well, that and bloody Emma Andrews."

"Emma Andrews?" I run through my mental list of the most recent Slate YourDate names, which are so well etched on my memory now that I don't need to consult the website any more. "Wasn't she the one you dumped in front of all her friends, because you said you could never love a girl with fat ankles?"

"Yup," says Dan. "So now she wants to get her revenge by getting me to plead with her to take me back in front of them too, just so she can turn me down. And it just so happens that the ideal time to do that is at a party she's going to this evening."

"Which is a fancy dress party, I take it?"

"No. But all my other clothes are in the wash." He looks at me as if I'm stupid. "Of course it's bloody fancy dress. And this is all the BBC props department had at short notice. One of Attenborough's old ones, apparently."

"Well, it's very realistic. And at least no one will know who you are."

"Not until I do the big reveal, and take this off," says Dan, patting the head. "And that's if I don't collapse from heat exhaustion first. It's bloody sweltering in here."

I take the hint that Dan's evidently dropping, and walk over to the bar, where Wendy's struggling to keep a straight face.

"My usual please, barmaid. And a banana daiquiri for Kong over there."

"Don't," sniggers Wendy, handing me the drinks she's already poured for us with one hand, while grabbing her stomach protectively with the other. "I laughed so much when he walked in that I thought I was going to go into labour."

"Speaking of which, shouldn't you be off on maternity leave soon?"

"What," says Wendy, smirking as Dan tries — and fails — to make himself look inconspicuous in the corner. "And miss all this fun at his expense? No chance."

I carry the drinks back over to the table, where Dan is trying valiantly to ignore the amused stares from the other drinkers, and put his beer down in front of him, then have to go back to the bar to get him a straw, gorilla hands evidently not designed to pick up pint glasses. After a couple of noisy slurps, Dan checks his watch, which he's fastened around the outside of the gorilla suit's arm, adding to the outfit's slightly surreal quality.

"Did you want to come? I'm sure Emma wouldn't mind."

"I thought it was fancy dress?"

"It is," says Dan, nodding towards my black Paul Smith suit, which he always jokes makes me look like one of the Blues Brothers. "You won't even have to get changed."

"No thanks. I've got some packing to do."

He stands up and wedges the gorilla head under one arm. "Well, at least give us a lift, then. It's a long old walk."

"And don't tell me — your knuckles aren't up to it?"

Five minutes later, I'm dropping him off outside Emma's house on the outskirts of Hove.

"There she is," says Dan, pointing to where Emma's waiting for him on the doorstep dressed like some Amazonian warrior. I can't quite make out what she's got in her hands, although worryingly for Dan it looks like a bag for a video camera.

"Uh-oh. Have you seen what's she carrying?"

"Yeah," he says, grimacing. "About a stone and a half extra. This is going to be so embarrassing."

As he gets out of the car, slips the gorilla head on, and begins to trudge reluctantly towards the front door, I wind the window down.

"Have a nice time," I call after him, having to raise my voice above the noise of the music that's thumping out from inside the house. "And remember — no monkey business."

CHAPTER
FIFTEEN

It's Sunday evening, and in stark contrast to the pale, listless bunch getting off the plane, the crowd waiting by the arrivals gate in Palma airport is made up of brown-skinned, healthy-looking people. As I catch sight of my pasty-faced reflection in the glass double doors, I realize just how long it's been since I've had a holiday, and even though we're due to come back the following Saturday, I'm looking forward to the next six days with Sam as much as I would a whole month off. Admittedly, I'm a little nervous about meeting her parents, but the flight's been fun — thanks partly to the four small bottles of champagne and the tiny packet of overpriced Pringles I've treated us to in celebration of our first trip abroad together — and when our bags appear at almost the same time as we do, I take it as a good omen for the rest of the trip.

As I follow Sam out through customs and past the assorted hire car desks and timeshare salesmen, she suddenly lets out a squeal of delight, abandons her luggage, and sprints over to a tanned, well-dressed woman waiting by the barrier.

240

"And this", she says, turning round and smiling encouragingly at me as I come puffing into view with the suitcases, "is Edward."

To my surprise, Sam's mother grabs me in a huge hug and plants a rather sloppy kiss on my cheek, which I have to fight the urge not to wipe off. "Hello, Edward," she says, not quite letting me go, then taking a pace backwards to look me up and down. She's an older version of Sam, really; similar height, and only a slightly larger build, and I find myself thinking that if girls do really turn out like their mothers, I'm not in for a bad ride. "We've heard so much about you."

"Likewise," I say. "Hello, Mrs Smith."

"Please call me Veronica."

This is great. Ten seconds in, and I'm already on friendlier terms with Sam's mum than I was with Jane's after ten years. "Okay, Mrs Smi . . . I mean, Veronica."

"Come on," she says, grabbing Sam around the waist. "Your dad's waiting in the car."

We stroll out of the airport building and across to the pick-up area, which is a concept that Dan would probably want to take literally if he were here, and I'm just starting to wilt in the heat — despite it being mid-evening — when Sam does the squealing thing again, and runs over to where a large Mercedes off-roader is parked half up on the pavement.

As Sam's mum and I follow her across the road, the driver's door opens and a man emerges, sweeping Sam off her feet in a massive bear hug. I swallow hard — Sam's dad is huge — and as he extends a dinnerplate-sized hand towards me, I almost forget myself, and end up nearly giving him my suitcase instead.

"Mister Smith," I say, rather formally, recovering just in time to shake his hand.

"Edward," he booms, as I try not to wince at his vice-like grip. He's got one arm protectively around Sam's shoulders, and while he's certainly not unfriendly towards me, something about his body language makes Dan's words come leaping back to mind.

Sam and her mother get into the back of the car, while I go to load the suitcases into the Merc's cavernous boot, which Sam's dad has just blipped open. "Leave these to me, Edward," he says, picking them both up as if they weigh nothing. "You jump in," he says. "Up front with me. Let's let the girls catch up."

"Sure," I say, aware my voice is at least two octaves higher than his.

I'm already beginning to perspire, though that's more from the aptly named sweatshirt I'm wearing, so it's a relief to get into the air-conditioned car. But when I climb into what I assume is the passenger side and click my seat belt into place, I'm a little surprised to find a steering wheel in front of me. I'm just trying to work out what's going on when there's a tap on the window, and I look up to see Sam's dad peering in. Sheepishly I unhook my seat belt and climb over the gear stick and into the actual passenger side. "Sorry."

"Not a problem." Sam's dad shuts the door behind him. "Easy mistake to make."

242

Ah. Not so great. I know how possessive men are about their cars — just look at Dan and the Porsche, which he's still not let me drive — and as if sleeping with his daughter wasn't bad enough, within five minutes of meeting Sam's dad I've already tried to drive his Merc.

It's a short trip from the airport to Sam's parents' place, made even shorter by the fact that Sam's dad drives the huge off-roader like it's a racing car, and when we eventually pull in through the electronically operated gates and park in front of the kind of villa that you normally see on the news owned by retired criminals, I'm more than a little relieved. Until, of course, it occurs to me that Sam's dad might actually be a retired criminal — or not even a retired one. And I'm dating his little girl.

"It's not much," says Sam's dad, as I can't help but whistle appreciatively as we get out of the car. "But it's home."

As Sam and her mum lead the way, her dad and I grab the suitcases out of the back of the car and carry them through the heavy wooden front door and into the cavernous hallway.

"Come on," says Sam, as her parents make their way into the kitchen. "I'll show you to your room."

"My room?" I whisper. "Don't you mean *our* room?"

Sam makes the 'What can you do?' face. "Sorry, Edward. I should have said. My mum and dad are a bit funny about this kind of thing."

"But . . . we're adults."

243

"Maybe." She glances back down the corridor, where Sam's dad has just pinched her mum's bottom, causing her to blush furiously. "But I sometimes doubt that they are."

We reach the end of the hallway, which takes a while, and Sam opens the door to my room. There's a single bed down at one end, and a couple of pictures of bull-fighting scenes on the wall.

"This looks . . . cosy."

She smiles. "It won't be so bad. It's just for appearances really. I'm just along the hall, and it's not as if my dad will be guarding my door with his shotgun, or anything."

I swallow even harder, conscious that Sam's just said "his shotgun". Not "a shotgun". Because by the looks of Sam's dad, he might actually own a shotgun. And a sawn-off one at that.

Trying to hide my disappointment, I dump my suitcase in the bedroom, locate the bottle of wine I've bought as a present from duty-free, and walk back up the corridor to Sam's room. It's positively palatial compared with mine, with huge bay windows opening on to the garden, and a slightly worrying collection of soft toys on the windowsill above the bed.

"I think they still think I'm twelve years old," says Sam, nodding towards the windowsill.

"Can't you get rid of them?"

Sam shrugs. "They're not that bad. Besides, they're the only parents I've got."

"No — I mean the cuddly . . . Very funny."

"Anyway, what's wrong with them?" says Sam, picking up a vivid pink bear and giving it a fond squeeze.

"I think I'd feel like I was being watched. And not just by your dad."

Sam takes my hand and leads me reluctantly out of the bedroom and into the lounge, where her dad is standing in the corner behind a small, white-tiled bar, which appears to be stocked with every imaginable variety of alcohol. And given the colour of the liquid in some of the bottles, some unimaginable ones too.

"So, who'd like a drink?"

"That'd be great," I say, perhaps a little too quickly, but I'm in need of something to calm my nerves. "Why don't we open this?"

I hand over my bottle of red wine, and Sam's dad examines it suspiciously. "Thanks, Edward. But perhaps this needs to breathe a little?" he says with a smile, although the tone of his voice suggests he feels it's more in need of resuscitation. Instead, he opens a bottle of cava, and pours us each a glass.

"A toast," announces Sam's mum. "To Edward."

"To Edward." Sam beams at me.

"Yes," says Sam's dad, a little cautiously, before clinking his glass against mine. "Edward."

"Oh. Right. To, er, me," I say, more than a little embarrassed.

"Shall we go and sit on the terrace?" suggests Sam's mum — I mean, Veronica — sliding open the large glass doors. "It's a lovely evening."

"Good idea." Sam's dad picks up the bottle of cava. "After you, Edward."

I follow Veronica through the door and up on to the terrace, where the unexpected sight of the nearby Mediterranean literally takes my breath away. But not as much as what happens next.

"What a view," I say, at the exact moment that a gust of wind lifts Veronica's skirt up around her waist.

"That's why I married her," says Sam's dad.

"Oh no," I say, suddenly embarrassed, edging away from him. "I didn't . . . I mean, not that your wife isn't . . ."

"Edward. Mind the . . ." And I don't hear the next word Sam shouts, because it's drowned out — literally — by the rush of water in my ears as I step off the edge of the tiles and fall straight into the swimming pool.

Fortunately — although I realize these things are all relative — it's the shallow end, and as Sam and her parents rush to the side of the pool, I try to wade as non-chalantly as I can over towards the steps, and climb out.

"Glad to see you've got your priorities right," says Sam's dad, nodding towards where I've managed to hang on to my champagne glass, although its contents are somewhat watered down now.

"That's quite a sight," I say, trying not to drip on Sam's dad's shoes as he takes my glass from me and examines the contents to see if they're still drinkable. "The view from the terrace, I mean. A little, er, distracting. I bet loads of people have done that?"

"No, actually," says Sam's dad, obviously trying not to laugh. "You're the first."

"I'll get you a refill," says Sam, looking a little less concerned now she knows I'm okay. "Unless you'd like some more water?"

"Come on," says Veronica, grabbing my arm and walking me back into the villa. "Let's get you out of those wet things."

She leads me back into the villa, stopping at a cupboard in the hallway to find me a large towel, although I'm relieved when she lets me squelch the rest of the way by myself. Great. What's the point in making a good first impression, if your second one is going to be so crap?

By the time I get changed into some dry clothes and emerge back on the patio, Sam and her parents are sitting around the table next to the pool. I carefully take the chair furthest away from the water and sit down, gratefully taking the glass of cava Sam offers me.

We chat for a while — catch-up stuff between Sam and her parents, mostly, with the odd question about me and what I do for a living thrown in. And as we talk, basking in the evening sunshine, which I'm more than grateful for after my unplanned dip, the mistake I make is trying to match Sam's dad glass for glass, because I start to feel very, very drunk. I don't know whether it's just me trying to be polite, or whether there's something more primeval at stake and I'm trying to prove that I'm "man enough" for his daughter, but I can't seem to slow down the rate at which I'm finishing every glass. And it's not that I can't take a drink either, because I've never had a problem with that. It's just that I can't take as many drinks as I used to, partly because I'm out of practice, but equally because I'm not quite the same bodyweight as I was when I used to drink regularly. Also it's more of a problem this evening, because all I've had to eat is twelve — I counted — Pringles on the plane. Too late I begin to realize that I can't take as many drinks as Sam's dad — and doubt that anyone can. In fact, I'm starting to wonder whether he's featured in *The Guinness Book of World Records* under alcohol consumption.

When, an hour or two later, Sam and her mum move inside, Sam's dad shows no sign of joining them, and instead just fetches another bottle of wine. And by the time he's opened the bottle of Scotch that seems to have miraculously appeared on the table, I'm having trouble saying anything coherent. But this is okay, as Sam's dad likes to talk. And talk. And fortunately it's the kind of talk that only requires a nod, or a grunt, or even the occasional drool from me. In fact, he loves the sound of his own voice — although I don't, because his low rumbling tones, combined with the amount I've had to drink, are in danger of lulling me to sleep.

Thankfully, by the time I've nearly slipped off my sunlounger — twice — Sam appears to save me. Or at least I assume it's Sam. And her twin sister, as at the moment there seem to be two of her.

"Hello, sweetheart," says Sam's dad, without the slightest trace of a slur. "You still up?"

She rests a hand on my shoulder. "Thought I'd come and rescue Edward."

Sam's dad laughs. "He doesn't need rescuing. We're having a good old chat, aren't we, Eddy?"

Through my drunken haze, I'm actually quite pleased with myself. After all, despite my earlier dunking, he's just called me "Eddy", which has to be a good sign. And we *are* having a good old chat — even though it's a bit one-sided. I smile and nod, which is about all I'm capable of.

"Besides," continues Sam's dad. "He can look after himself. Can't you?"

It takes a few seconds for me to realize that that was a question directed at me. And one that requires an answer. With the greatest of efforts, I look up at Sam and nod again, although my eyes are saying "help me".

"Well, if you're sure . . ." says Sam reproachfully. "Although it is past midnight."

I try and smile back at her, but end up producing what's little more than a leer. Maybe I can't, actually, look after myself. Maybe if I even try and stand up and walk back towards the villa I'll be unable to avoid falling in the pool again. Maybe I'll just sleep out here this evening. After all, it's warm enough. And certainly very comfortable.

"Okay," says Sam's dad, mercifully. "Point taken." I watch with relief as he screws the top back on the bottle of whisky, and stands up. "Well, goodnight then," he says, ruffling the hair on the top of my head with one enormous hand, before kissing Sam on the cheek.

"G'night Samzdad" is the best I can manage in response. And I'm proud of myself for even that.

"Come on, you," says Sam, hauling me up out of my chair as her dad disappears inside. "Bedtime."

"Perfect," I say, although it comes out more like "pervert". "Your place or mine?"

"I think we'd better do mine, don't you?" says Sam. "Unless you'd feel more comfortable in a single bed?"

"No thanks," I say, turning to kiss her, which takes all my powers of coordination. "I don't want to do anything single ever again."

We make our way back into the villa, where Sam disappears off into the bathroom, so I stumble into her room and flop down on her bed, then gaze past the slightly sinister collection of stuffed animals and through the window up at the clear night sky, thinking to myself that it doesn't get any better than this.

And I'm right. Unfortunately.

When I eventually wake up the next morning, my first thought is whether Sam and her parents are all right, because from the way I'm feeling the roof of the villa has obviously collapsed during the night, and is now resting entirely on my head. I gingerly open my eyes, the effort of which is harder than anything I've ever done in the gym, to see Sam leaning over me, the look on her face halfway between amusement and compassion.

"Good morning!" she says brightly, bending down to kiss me lightly on the forehead. Even that hurts.

"No it isn't," I croak.

"A little bit hungover, are we?"

"Well, I certainly seem to be. Did you drink a lot too?"

Sam rolls her eyes. "There are six empty wine bottles in the kitchen. And my dad's supply of Scotch seems to have a severe dent in it."

At the mention of the word "Scotch", my stomach does a half-flip. "Please, Sam. I'm a little bit delicate."

She puts a cool hand against my cheek. "So you won't be wanting that fry-up my mum's making you downstairs?"

By the time I've had a shower — and fought off the desire to spend the morning retching into the toilet — I'm feeling marginally better, although it's the kind of margin that you'd struggle to write a lot of notes in. It takes me three goes to get my shorts on the right way round, and deciding that shoelaces are a step too far, I eventually arrive in the kitchen barefoot, where Sam's mum and dad are sitting drinking tea and looking decidedly chipper.

"Morning, Mrs Smith. I mean, Veronica."

"Morning," says Sam's mum. "Sleep well?"

"Yes, thanks. It was the waking up that was the problem."

"So I see," says Sam's dad, tapping his watch, but with a smile on his face, although it's an effort to keep the smile on mine when I realize I can't remember his name. Or if he actually told me what it was during our "chat" last night.

"Never mind what time it is," says Veronica. "You're on holiday, after all. What can I get you for breakfast? Eggs? A bacon sandwich?"

My stomach lurches again. "Just some coffee, thanks. Black."

As she pours me a cup from the plunge pot on the table, I glance across at Sam's dad, wondering whether I said anything last night that might embarrass me this morning. Worse than that, I don't have any memory of what happened after Sam and I went to bed, so I'm hoping that he's not going to make some comment about the sleeping arrangements, but fortunately he's more engrossed in the small transistor radio he seems to be trying to fix. Eventually, he puts it down on the table and presses a button on the side.

"Ta-da," he says proudly, as some tinny flamencotype music leaps out from the speaker.

"Well done, love." Veronica walks over and puts an arm round his shoulders. "He's very good with his hands, is Martin."

Martin. Of course. I nod towards the radio. "So I see."

"It's important for a man to be good with his hands," she says, kissing Sam's dad on the top of his head. "Are you, Edward?"

"You'd better ask Sam. I mean I've fixed a couple of things round at her flat," I say, backtracking slightly when Sam's dad looks up sharply and I see how that might have a double meaning. "DIY stuff, I mean."

"Well, that IKEA cupboard is still just about standing, if that's what you're referring to," laughs Sam. "So I suppose so."

I lean against the kitchen counter and sip my coffee, watching the interaction between Sam and her parents.

They're obviously a loving, close family, and it amazes me how Sam's mum and dad are still so happy, so obviously satisfied with each other's company and, let's face it, still so tactile, after so many years together. There's none of the staleness, or the constant digs at each other in front of other people that Jane and I seemed to get into — although more Jane than me, it has to be said — and they've been together for a lot longer than she and I were. And I find myself thinking that this is surely what relationships *should* be like. Taking a real delight in the person you're with, rather than taking issue with what they do, how they behave, or even how they look. And for the first time, I start to think that this is the kind of future I want. Like Sam's parents. Not in Majorca, necessarily, although to be honest, as long as I'm with Sam, I kind of don't care where it is.

Veronica refills my coffee mug, then loads the rest of the breakfast things into the dishwasher. "We're off into town," she says. "Do you two want to come along for the ride?"

Ah. A car journey is perhaps the last thing I feel like this morning. Fortunately, Sam twigs.

"No thanks," says Sam. "I think we'll just stay here and kick back by the pool."

"Kick back?" says Sam's dad, nudging me. "That's not something rude, is it?"

I can't help but blush. "Er, no. It means . . ."

"He knows full well what it means. Leave them alone, Martin," says Veronica. "Well, in that case, we'll probably take our time. Maybe stay out for lunch as well. Give you kids a few hours on your own to settle in. Anything we can get you?"

Some paracetamol, I want to say. *Strong ones.* "No, thanks."

"I'll get some more whisky in," says Martin, winking at me conspiratorially.

"Great," I say, clamping my mouth shut in an attempt to stop my stomach from appearing.

"Come on," says Veronica, grabbing the car keys from a hook by the kitchen door, then pulling Martin up from his chair — no mean feat — and marching him out along the hallway. "You two have a nice time."

"Don't do anything we wouldn't do," calls Sam's dad, slapping his wife's backside playfully as they head out through the front door. By the looks of things so far, that gives me pretty much carte blanche.

As soon as I'm sure the coast is clear, I walk out on the terrace — giving the pool a wide berth this time — and collapse on to the nearest lounger.

"Alone at last," says Sam, stretching out on the one next to me. "I'm sorry about my parents, Edward. They can be a bit . . . full on."

"No, they're great. Really. I like them. Your dad's certainly an . . ."

"Alcoholic?"

"I was going to say 'interesting character'. But now you mention it."

Sam smiles. "He's harmless, really. And he likes you. He was saying this morning how he feels the two of you really bonded last night."

"Yes, I'm sorry about that. I thought it was important to, you know, make an effort."

She looks at me levelly. "Shame it didn't last all evening."

I put my hand over my eyes to shield them from the sun, which is poking over the top of a large palm tree in the corner of the garden. "What do you mean?"

"Last night. On the way to the room, you couldn't keep your hands off me. I thought I was in for a good night. And then when I got back from the bathroom . . ."

"What?"

"You were fast asleep. And snoring. Loudly. And no matter what I did, I couldn't wake you up. And I certainly tried."

"Ah. Sorry about that. That'll have been the whisky."

Sam reaches over and takes my hand. "Well, just make sure you don't have any this evening. I'm going for a walk to the beach," she says, standing up. "And I'm assuming you won't want to come along?"

I sit up briefly, and then flop back down again. "Just give me a couple of hours to sleep off this headache, and then I'm all yours."

She pokes me in the stomach. "That's what you said last night. I'll see you later, then. And make sure you don't get burnt."

Sam kisses me goodbye, and I peel my T-shirt off, position my lounger so the palm tree is shading it, and gratefully shut my eyes. Almost instantaneously — although when I catch sight of my watch, it's actually a couple of hours later — I feel someone shaking me awake.

"Edward. Edward!"

"Whassup?" I say, still half asleep. "Where's the fire?"

"All over you, by the look of things," says Sam. "And red's not your colour. Quick. Inside."

I follow her gaze to where I'm evidently in direct sunshine now, the sun having long ago moved from behind the palm tree, and what's more, judging by the bright-pink colour of my torso and legs, I've been in it for quite a while. Bright pink, that is, apart from where I've been sleeping with my arm resting across my chest, where there's now, outlined in red, a perfect imprint of my hand over my left nipple, as if someone's been fondling me.

"Ah," I say, followed by "Ow!" as my skin starts to crackle the second I move.

We hurry into the villa, Sam pausing to grab a bottle of after-sun from the bathroom, and into my bedroom, where she draws the curtains, and then starts to rub the lotion all over my front. Any other time, I'd find this quite sexy — if I didn't look and feel like a pork scratching.

"Ouch! Gently, please."

"Don't be such a baby."

"But it's *cold*."

"Which is a feeling you're going to be grateful for in a few hours."

Once she's finished, I gingerly pull my T-shirt back on, where it promptly sticks to me, causing Sam to snigger.

256

"What's so funny?"

"You look like some bad wet T-shirt competition."

"You want to see wet T-shirts, I'll show you wet T-shirts," I say, grabbing her playfully round the waist. "Which way's the pool?"

"Well, you didn't have any trouble finding it last night."

I pick her up to put her over my shoulder, and as she starts to struggle, causing my shirt to chafe painfully on my chest, my mobile suddenly bleeps. "I ought to get that," I say, putting Sam back down and retrieving it from the bedside table. "It might be . . ."

"Work?" protests Sam. "But you're on holiday."

"I was going to say Dan, actually. I told him he could message me if he had any problems."

Sam laughs. "Dan has a lot of problems. And you don't want him texting you every time, or you'll never get off the phone."

I grin back at her, and flick through the phone menu. It's not from Dan. Or even Natasha. But from Jane. Asking if I'm free for a coffee *next* week. I stare at the phone, wondering how she got this number, and then realize that it's my fault — having called her from it the other day, when I was so incensed after the flowers incident.

"Anything exciting?" asks Sam. "Or has Dan just broken a fingernail?"

My first response is to say that it's a wrong number, or just a marketing text, but I've already lied to Sam about seeing Jane the other night, and about the flowers. And maybe it's my hangover, or even that I'm suffering from sunstroke, but it suddenly occurs to me that if I lie to her about this as well, who knows where I'll stop?

"It's, er, from Jane."

"Jane?" Sam stares at the phone in my hand. "*Your* Jane?"

"Well, technically, she's not any . . ."

Sam cuts me off with a look. "What does she want?"

"Nothing."

"Really? Why is she texting you, then?"

I try to lighten the situation by pretending to read out her message. "'Dear Ed. I want you back. Please ditch your new girlfriend, even though she's much fitter than me, in all senses of the word.' How should I reply?"

A smile starts to creep across Sam's face. "Well, you better tell her 'yes' then. Poor girl."

"Well, if you're sure . . ."

Relieved, I lean over to kiss Sam on the cheek, while slipping the phone into my trouser pocket, but Sam pulls away before I can make lip contact. "Seriously, Ed. What's she doing texting you? After all this time."

"Seriously. Nothing. Look." I get the phone back out of my pocket a little too quickly and drop it on the tiled floor, causing the battery, along with part of the plastic casing and a couple of the buttons, to fly off. "Shit." I bend down and retrieve the various parts, wincing a little as the skin on my stomach protests against being moved, and try to reassemble the phone, but I can't seem to get the battery to click back in.

"That was convenient," says Sam suspiciously.

"Sam, you don't think that I . . ." I stop myself, because actually I have. "She's back in Brighton and was just wondering whether I wanted to meet up. For a coffee."

"Why?"

I shrug. "I don't know. Maybe she's going through what Dan's going through. You know — feeling guilty about how she treated me, and wants us to be friends again." There. That didn't sound so bad, did it? And it's nearly the truth, although Jane's idea of what "friends again" means is perhaps a little stronger than I've let on.

We stare at each other in stalemated silence for a while, before Sam turns and looks out of the window. "And do you want to be friends with Jane again, Ed?"

Ah. This is one of *those* questions, isn't it? "I don't know. I mean, I kind of thought that she was off my Christmas card list after what she did, but . . ."

At the word "but", Sam spins round and looks me straight in the eye. "Have you still got feelings for her?"

"Who?" I say, knowing full well that she's talking about Jane, but hoping to buy myself a little extra time to think of something to say.

"You know who," says Sam. "Jane."

"Of course," I say, before the change in Sam's expression makes me realize that that's completely the wrong thing to say. "I mean, yes, I still care about her . . . But I don't care *for* her."

"What's the difference?"

Good question. What *is* the difference? "Well, I mean, you don't just stop caring about someone after ten years together," I say, making a mental note to never say anything again unless I can explain it. "I mean, when I saw her again I knew that I didn't feel anything *that* way."

"When you *saw* her?"

"Er . . . Yes."

"Which was where, exactly? From a distance, I hope?"

"No. We, er . . . She was back in town for a funeral, and I bumped into her, so we ended up going for a drink. Well, I say a drink, but we didn't even get as far as the pub. It's a funny story . . ." I stop talking, because judging by Sam's expression, she's not going to find it the slightest bit amusing.

"You went for a drink? With Jane?"

"Well, technically, no, but . . ."

"And when were you going to tell me this?"

"Well, I wasn't."

"Why not?"

"Because it didn't mean anything."

"How can going for a drink with your ex-girlfriend behind my back not mean anything? Why didn't you mention it before?"

Sam's voice is getting louder, and Dan's words aren't so much as coming back to haunt me as leaping out from behind the door and shouting "boo!"

"It just didn't seem important at the time, that's all."

"But it's important enough to tell me about it now?"

"No . . . I mean, yes . . . But only because she texted, and you asked." Aargh. Bloody Dan. Why did he have to be right about this, of all things? "I just don't want

260

us to have any secrets, that's all. And I didn't mention it because I didn't know how to, because it was obviously awkward, given that you know our history, and all that, and I didn't want to hurt you."

Sam hesitates. "Did she tell you she wants you back."

"No. Well, not in so many words."

"Not in so many words? What do you mean by that?"

"Well, I mean, she said she thought she might have been a little hasty."

"But you told her about us?"

"Not at first."

There's a pause, and it's considerably longer than before. "Why not?"

"Because . . . Because I didn't want to upset her."

"And why would she have been upset to have found out that you've moved on? She dumped you, Edward. So surely that means you can go out with whoever you like without worrying about whether your ex-girlfriend gets upset?"

"I suppose. It's just that I didn't want to hurt her feelings. And then, when she tried to kiss me, and I told her about you . . ."

"She . . . kissed you?"

"Well, yes. Tried to. But I didn't kiss her back, or anything."

"Oh," says Sam sarcastically. "Well, that makes it all right, then."

"Sam, let me explain. It's not how it sounds. I mean, it just started to get too complicated. And then, when she sent me those flowers, and you came in just after they'd arrived . . ." I stop talking, because from the look on Sam's face, my position has just got considerably worse.

"She sent you those flowers?"

"Er . . . Yes."

"Which you then tried to pass off as being from you to me?"

Sam's sounding angry now, so I don't say anything. Because what is the right thing to say? Even if Dan were here, I'd challenge him to talk his way out of this situation. And this is why I hate arguing — not just because I'm bad at it generally, but because I've come to realize that all men are genetically programmed not to be able to argue with women.

Because when women argue, they use tricks to catch you out and make you feel bad, like kids used to at school when they'd say "What hand do you wipe your bum with?" and you'd reply "The left one", and they'd say "Yuk — don't you use toilet paper?" — and there's no comeback from that. And while I could probably win those kinds of arguments with a kid now, where women are concerned I'm just not smart enough to see them coming. I don't necessarily lose because I'm wrong. I lose because I'm not good at arguing their way. And that's not fair.

It's not that I always think that I'm right, either — and why does there have to be a right and wrong anyway? I have my opinion, she has hers, and in actual fact both can be right. So what it boils down to is that one of us — and it's usually the man — has to compromise his beliefs. And surely that's even worse?

262

What I've tried to do, by admitting that Jane tried to kiss me, and that I rejected her by telling her about Sam, is prove to Sam that — because I didn't kiss Jane back — I'm not interested in her. But instead, my admission that there was kissing, albeit completely one-sided, seems to have had precisely the opposite effect.

I know how this usually works, from here on in, because this used to happen a lot with Jane. She'd say something harsh, and I'd finally snap and say something back that was nowhere near as harsh, but I felt I had to get a dig in because I was being unjustly accused, and then she'd start crying — on purpose, rather than because I'd upset her. And then I'd feel lousy, of course, and end up apologizing. And losing.

But Sam doesn't say anything harsh. There's not even anything illogical or irrational to her argument. She's obviously upset and hurt, and as she storms out of my bedroom and along the corridor into her room, the worrying thing is, I can fully understand why.

When I catch up with her, my face burning as much with shame as sunburn, she just looks at me, any trace of compassion she might have had replaced with what appears to be steely determination.

"Sam . . ."

"Get out, Edward."

"But . . ."

"Just leave, will you?"

"Sam, I . . ." There are tears starting to form in her eyes, and I reach out for her, but she shoves me away, pushing so hard that I actually slide a couple of yards backwards on the tiled floor, and out into the corridor.

"Just *go!*"

And given the unmistakable tone of her voice, plus the fact that she's just slammed her bedroom door in my face, I don't seem to have much choice.

The taxi journey to the airport is pretty miserable, but not as miserable as the seven hours I sit nursing my scorched body on the world's most uncomfortable plastic chair in the airport lounge, while waiting for the next available flight. It's cost me just over three hundred pounds to get a ticket at short notice, but the money's the least of my worries. I'm more concerned I've lost something much more precious.

There's a part of me that wants to go back to the villa and explain. Tell Sam it's all been a misunderstanding. But I'm scared. What if I do, and even after all that she still rejects me? And what if her father does actually have a shotgun? The way I'm feeling, the last thing I want to be is shot in the Balearics.

I desperately want a drink, but I'm driving the Mini back from Gatwick later so I don't dare, and for the first time in a long while I'm craving a cigarette. I get up and wander round the airport shops, looking enviously at the huge duty-free cartons, with their cheery "smoking kills" messages. Well, dead might be a little bit better than the way I'm feeling at the moment.

Have I been stupid? Ignorant? Naive? At least I'm sure of my feelings for Jane at the moment — and they're all murderous. Everything she ever did was always planned to the last detail — I remember that now, from the way she was at work, to that bloody Prada handbag episode — and I've got no reason to suspect that any of this — the flowers, the timing of the text — are in any way different. I think about phoning Dan, but of course my mobile's broken, and besides I don't really want to add to his problems. Anyway, he's probably in the middle of filming that scene with the twins — doing take after take, knowing him — that he's been banging on about all week. Instead of banging all week in real life, like he used to.

The flight's pretty full, but I'm relieved to see that I've got a window seat, and I sink into it gratefully, staring out at the Spanish sunshine while trying to ignore the crackling soreness of my sunburn. I'm just congratulating myself on the fact that at least the seat next to me seems to be empty when a grotesquely fat man squeezes his way along the aisle and stops at the end of my row. Now I've got nothing against fat people — I used to be one myself, after all — and I nod hello to him as he edges into the space next to me. But what I'm not prepared for is the sudden, violent shove against the window I get as he sits down, and his flabby torso squeezes over and under the armrest and into my side. He's already sweating from the effort of making it to the middle seat, and I think to myself that surely he can't be a regular traveller, but when he produces his own personal seat-belt extender from his inside pocket I realize that this obviously isn't the first time he's flown.

For a moment, I feel like complaining to the stewardess, but decide against making a scene. Although I've paid for a seat, and I'm only getting to use about two-thirds of it, knowing what airlines are like the chances of me getting a hundred-pound proportional refund are, unlike my neighbour, rather slim. And I feel sorry for him too — I'm a shade under six foot tall, and I'm finding the plane cramped, so I can't imagine the discomfort he must be in, even though, judging by how the woman on the other side of him seems to have been forced halfway into the aisle, he's got more space than either of us.

As the plane starts to taxi down the runway, I say a silent prayer, hoping we'll manage to get off the ground with the extra weight on board, then spend the rest of the uncomfortable flight trying hard not to think about what's happened between me and Sam. I try to sleep, but it's impossible given the way my mind is racing, and especially with any chances of using my left armrest having disappeared — along with the armrest itself — into my fellow passenger's folds of fat. I'm stuck, squashed, oppressed, and quite frankly having difficulty breathing. Even reaching the inflight magazine from the seat pocket in front of me is an impossible manoeuvre, and when the stewardess asks if she can get me anything, I'm tempted to reply "a crowbar".

It's a relief when we finally land, just after midnight, at a rainy Gatwick. I've got a crick in my neck from where I've been forced awkwardly against the window, and I'm so keen to get off the plane that I have to resist the temptation to help my neighbour out of the row of

266

seats by planting my foot against his backside and pushing.

As I wait the usual forty-five minutes for my suitcase, which eventually turns up missing one of its castors, I can't help reflecting on how it's a mirror of my current situation — you spend ages waiting for your one to arrive and then when it finally appears, the wheels fall off. I make my way towards the car park, feeling childishly resentful towards Gatwick Airport, as for the second time in a year it's been partly responsible for my single status. At least the Mini starts first time, although for such a small car it feels surprisingly empty on the way home.

Though not, I realize miserably, as empty as I do.

CHAPTER
SIXTEEN

I'm woken the next morning by an insistent buzzing from the front doorbell. Thinking — *hoping* — that Sam's got an early flight home, and has come straight round to see me, I leap out of bed and rush towards the intercom, but no such luck. It's Dan.

"What the hell are you doing back?" he asks, as I let him in. "And, er, nice tan."

Ah. I remember I'm wearing nothing but my boxer shorts, and look down to see my skin is still the same vivid pink colour — except for the hand print, which I'd hoped might have faded overnight. "Dan, it's much too early for your insults. What do you want?"

"Nothing, really," he says, peering over my shoulder to where my suitcase is lying abandoned in the hall. "Just saw the car and thought it was a bit weird. On your own?"

"Yup."

"No Sam?"

"That's what 'on my own' would indicate, yes."

He pushes past me and walks into the kitchen. "Holiday went well, then?" he says, helping himself to a carton of orange juice from the fridge.

"What do you think?"

He nods towards my chest. "I warned you that you were playing with fire. And people who play with fire always get burned — although usually not quite as literally as you."

"Yes, Dan. Very funny."

He takes a swig of juice directly from the carton, then offers me some, but I wave him away. "So I guess you won't be needing to get that extra set of keys cut after all?"

I pull out a chair and sit down at the kitchen table. "Dan, have you ever heard of the word 'consideration'?"

"Yeah. It's just before the word 'contraception' in my dictionary of things I hate to use." He takes a seat opposite me. "What happened, exactly?"

"Exactly?"

As I explain the circumstances to Dan, he makes the "I told you so" face. "Didn't I say you should never go back. Even for a peek."

"But it wasn't my fault."

"It never is, my son. Where women are concerned, 'fault' doesn't come into it. Because the one thing they're sure of is that it's never theirs."

I put my head in my hands, and stare miserably down at the table. "So what on earth do I do about it?"

"Explain. Tell her the truth."

"I tried that. Which is why I'm sitting here without her."

"Okay, well lie to her then. Tell her Jane's dying of some incurable disease, and . . ."

"Dan, be serious. I made a mistake. Although I didn't know it was one at the time."

He sighs. "That's the thing with women. It's all a learning curve — but in reverse. You have to get stuff wrong to find out what works and what doesn't. I mean, you can't just say 'I'll do so-and-so with new woman, because that worked with my previous girlfriend'. And at the end of the day, they're all different. And you're going to have to realize one thing."

"Which is?"

"Whatever you do, it's never going to be enough. These storms are going to happen every now and again. And all you can do is weather them."

"So where does that leave me with Sam, then?"

Dan swallows the final mouthful from the juice carton and puts it down on the table. "What exactly did she say?"

"Not much. She just told me to go."

Dan looks at me strangely. "That's it?"

"Yup — 'just leave', or something like that."

"And you did?"

"I'm here, aren't I?"

"And it didn't occur to you that she might have just meant the room, and not, actually, the island?"

Fuck. I put my head in my hands in disbelief. "Er . . ." *Fuck fuck fuck. Fuck shit bollocks fuck*, in fact.

Dan watches me as I beat myself up for a few moments. "So, just to clarify, she didn't say 'It's over', or 'You're dumped', or anything like that?"

"I didn't exactly take notes, but I don't think so."

"No tears?"

"Well, I was pretty miserable on the plane, but I managed to hold it together."

"Not you, dummy. Her. What was her emotional state?"

"Er, angry, I'd guess."

Dan breathes a sigh of relief, then puts a hand on my shoulder reassuringly, removing it when I wince from my sunburn. "Well, there you go."

"Huh? Have I missed something?"

"Only about ten years of dating. Angry is different to emotional. Angry passes. Angry can be dealt with after a suitable calming-down period. Emotions? Well, that's a different ballgame — as you found out with Jane."

I stand up and walk over to the sink, then fill up the kettle and switch it on. "I'm sorry, Dan. I must be jet-lagged or something, because you're not making any sense."

"Two sugars in mine," he says, nodding towards the coffee pot. "Well, think of it this way. Jane had made up her mind over a period of time to leave you, because she'd fallen out of love with you — again, over a period of time. But luckily for you, Sam's not distraught because of some gradual change in her emotional state. She's angry because of something you did that she didn't like, and that you didn't tell her about."

"How is that lucky for me, exactly?"

"Okay." He picks up the empty juice carton again. "Say Sam likes a particular brand of juice, and it's Saturday afternoon, and she's run out of this juice, so she asks you to go to the shops and buy some. You're a man, right, so unless it's football teams, beer, or

271

condoms, you don't particularly care about what brand of thing it is you're buying."

"Because juice is juice," I say, deciding that it's too early in the morning to question him about the third item on his list.

"Exactly. But women have spent their entire lives trying to find out what kind of juice it is they really like, because that kind of stuff — like face cream, washing powder, and so on — is really important to them. So she says to you, 'Can you go and get me some more *brand* X juice when you've finished watching the football?' and you agree, because you're nice like that, so come half-time you go off in your good-natured way and buy some more juice, which isn't her brand, because you were watching the game, so all you actually heard her say was 'blah-blah-blah juice blah-blah-blah football' . . . And she goes ballistic. You think you've done a good thing, buying her some more juice, but oh no. You've committed one of the cardinal sins."

And this is obviously what I still don't get. "But why does she get so worked up over me buying the wrong juice?"

Dan sighs. "Because she doesn't just see it as you buying the wrong juice. She sees it as a reflection of your whole relationship. She thinks that the reason that you've gone out and bought the wrong juice is either because you're thoughtless, and just haven't been paying attention every time she's bought that particular brand, or even worse, that you don't care that she likes that particular one, and so you simply got the first one you saw."

"But . . . it's just juice."

Dan picks the juice carton up and examines it carefully. "It is to you and me, Edward, but to a woman? They make whole relationship appraisals from this kind of thing."

"So you're saying what I did with Jane is like buying the wrong juice? From Sam's point of view, I mean."

"Sadly, no. But fortunately for you it's closer on the overall scale of women's narky things to that than sleeping with her mother might be. And trust me," he adds, "when that happens, that's not pretty. What was it that she seemed most upset about? The fact that you'd actually been in contact with Jane, or the fact that you didn't tell her about it?"

"Er . . ."

"Bet I can guess."

I think back to our conversation, which was only yesterday, but already seems like a hundred years ago. "The not telling her. I think the phrase 'going behind my back' was used."

Dan nods slowly, like a doctor considering his diagnosis. "And what did you say when she accused you of that."

"I said that I hadn't wanted to hurt her."

"Ding!" shouts Dan, miming ringing an imaginary bell. "Rookie mistake."

I look at him helplessly. "Why is that a mistake?"

"Because telling a woman you didn't want to hurt her is the same as admitting you did something hurtful, and didn't want her to find out about it."

"But it wasn't like that."

"Not to you it wasn't. And not to me either. But they're a different species, remember."

I scratch my head. "So what should I have said?"

"Well, nothing would have been a good start."

"Yes, well, that would have been lying."

Dan gives me a "so?" look. "You needed to convince her that what happened with you and Jane was nothing. Didn't mean a thing. And you don't do that by admitting there was something emotional about it."

"But there *was* something emotional about it."

"Not as far as you tell Sam, dummy. Whenever you're caught out like that, always play it down. If she sees you're not bothered by the whole thing, then that gives her no reason to be either. Tell her it had some emotional importance, however, and she's bound to be concerned. Because in her eyes, you're trying to hide something."

"So what do I do about it?"

Dan folds his arms, rests them on the table, and leans forward in the manner of a police interrogator. "You tell me."

I stare up at the kitchen ceiling for inspiration. Sadly, all it tells me is that one of the spotlight bulbs needs replacing. "Er . . ."

He reaches over suddenly, and raps me sharply on the forehead with his knuckles. "Buy her some more juice, dummy. Only this time, make sure it's the right brand."

"That's all?"

As I rub my head, Dan picks up the empty carton and lobs it into the bin in the corner. "Pretty much. But give it a bit of time, for a start. Wait until she comes back, then apologize. And make sure you don't do it again."

"I shouldn't call her now? Rather than waiting to speak to her at the weekend?"

"As opposed to the strong end?" Dan laughs at his own joke. "Nah. No point rushing into any huge declarations of love, or anything. Give her a chance to miss you, which might help soothe her anger a little. Remember, woman are like elephants. And not just physically, some of them. Mentally. As in they never forget. So even after a week, it'll still be as fresh to her as the day it happened."

"Thanks for clarifying that for me, Dan. Which is why you're having the trouble you're having, I suppose."

Dan grins guiltily. "Maybe. But Sam is bound to calm down. Eventually."

"I don't know. She seemed pretty angry."

"And there wasn't anything else contributing to her mood? She didn't have the decorators in, or anything like that?"

It takes a few seconds for me to see what he's talking about. "Dan, you can't blame everything on time of the month."

As the kettle clicks off and I make us both a coffee, I think about what Dan's said. Perhaps he's right and I was an idiot for leaving. But maybe in time Sam will calm down and I'll get a chance to apologize, and she'll forgive me, and it'll all be okay. I've got to hope so, at least, because the last thing I want to do is go through this whole process again.

But at the same time I spot the fundamental flaw in his argument. If it is that simple, then why on earth hasn't he tried that with Polly? And judging by his reaction when I confront him with this, he doesn't like his own logic turned back on him.

"So you've never been tempted? After all this time? Just to look her up and say hello?" I ask, once he's recovered from the obvious shock of my question.

"Why the hell do you think I've kept my distance from her?" he says, taking a sip of his coffee, grimacing, and then spooning in the sugar I've evidently forgotten to add. "I don't want to know if she's sad. More important, I don't want to know if she's happy. I just don't want to know what she's up to, full stop. That way, I don't have to think about it." He stirs his coffee thoughtfully. "You know that phrase 'ignorance is bliss'? Well, that's my philosophy, and I'm sticking to it."

"But surely that proves why you need to see her. To work out how you feel about her. I mean, fair enough, if you're saying you don't care about what she's doing now, then that means you're obviously over her, but . . ."

"I never said I didn't care about her. I just said I didn't want to know. There's a difference, Edward."

"But don't you *need* to know?"

"Why? So I can 'move on'?" Dan shakes his head. "I've already moved on. Several times. And it's the reason I don't see her, or any of them, and don't even respond to their messages or calls afterwards. Because if

I can't see that I've hurt them, then I don't think that I have."

"That's pretty callous, don't you think?"

Dan shrugs. "Maybe. But it works for me. Or at least it did, before Slate YourDate reared up and bit me on the backside. And I'm sorry if I can't be all New Age and touchy-feely like you seem to have become where this relationship stuff is concerned, but that's just the way I am."

We sit there in silence for a while, me drinking my coffee slowly, Dan just staring into his, before I have an idea.

"Do you want me to speak to her? On your behalf, I mean. See what she's up to. Sound her out. That sort of thing?"

Dan looks up at me. "Please, Edward. Just drop it."

"What, you'd rather let sleeping dogs lie? Not that I'm suggesting she's a dog, of course . . ."

Dan makes a strange expression, as if he's testing the flavour of a boiled sweet. "Hang on," he says. "Something's just occurring to me."

"Steady on, mate. Take it easy. Do you need to lie down, or something?"

"What you said. Few days ago. About how you know if you're over someone when you don't give a shit."

"Well, they weren't my exact words."

He finishes the last of his coffee, making a face as he swallows the dregs. "So if that's the case, and you're happy with Sam . . ."

I can't quite see where this is going. Which is usually the case with one of Dan's 'revelations'. "Ye-es?"

"Well then, why do you care so much about Jane?"

"What?"

"Why do you give a shit about whether she's okay or not? Whether she's happy? She dumped you, don't forget, so you don't owe her anything. And yet here you are, sneaking around behind Sam's back and getting yourself into trouble, just to see that your ex is all right." He angles his head and raises one eyebrow. "Sounds a bit fishy to me."

"It's not fishy," I splutter. "And it's just that I don't want to see anyone hurt. Especially when they've been special to me for so long."

"Even though you might end up hurting Sam in the process — and have already, by the sound of things." Dan shakes his head. "Look to the future, Ed. Not at the past. Sam's the future. So if you don't want to fuck it up, tell Jane to fuck off."

"I can't just tell her to f . . . I mean, treat her like that. It's not in my nature."

"After what she did to you?"

"Which was partly my fault, remember. And she's not all bad."

Dan stares at me for a moment, as if he's deciding whether to say something, and then obviously makes that decision. "Listen, Edward. It's great that you're so concerned about Jane. Really it is. Shows what a nice guy you are, how caring you can be, blah blah blah."

I shrug, ignoring Dan's sarcastic attempt at a compliment. "We were together for a long time. I at least want her to be happy."

"Well, that's very noble of you," says Dan. "It's just . . ."

"What?"

He takes a deep breath. "Well, Jane's not this perfect woman that you seem to be intent on looking out for."

"What do you mean."

"Nothing," says Dan, noticing my face suddenly darken. "Let's just change the subject."

He stands up and makes for the sink to rinse his mug out, but I grab him tightly by the arm as he walks past.

"No, let's not. What did you mean?"

"Just that . . ." He looks down at my hand strangely, and I relax my grip a little. "Listen, I never told you this, but do you remember that party at the Admiral Jim?"

"Which party?"

"I dunno. The one where you'd drunk so much you nodded off in the corner."

"And you drew that Hitler moustache on my face while I was asleep."

He grins. "Oh yeah. That was a laugh."

"With permanent marker. That I couldn't get off for a week." And so had to cancel all my meetings until I'd grown a real moustache to cover it up, which looked even more ridiculous, and Jane of course hated, so wouldn't let me anywhere near her. Not that she'd needed an excuse for that by then.

"Ah," says Dan sheepishly. "Sorry, mate. Anyway, Jane was pretty drunk too — as we all were — and she and I got chatting . . ."

"What about?"

"Well, she was telling me how she didn't know where you and her were going, and that she wasn't happy the way things were between the two of you. That kind of stuff."

"Jesus, Dan. Why on earth didn't you tell me?"

He shrugs. "Er, to be honest, I forgot. And then when I did remember, there just didn't seem to be a time when I could bring it up. Either Jane was there, or . . . To be honest, maybe I thought it was just her rambling on. You know how women get when they're drunk. Bringing up all sorts of emotional bollocks."

"Dan — anything with the word 'emotional' in it isn't necessarily always bollocks, you know?"

"Whatever. Anyway, so we were up having a dance while you're still snoring away, and the slow records came on, so I of course make to go and get a drink but Jane grabs hold of me and pulls me back on to the dance floor."

The hairs on the back of my neck start to rise. "And?"

"Well, we're lurching around to some crap by the Commodores, and she starts talking about how the two of you don't sleep together much any more, and how even women need a good shag every now and again."

I can't believe what I'm hearing. What's more, I'm not sure I want to hear any more. But I know I have to ask, even though I have to force my next words out. "And what did you say?"

"What — after I'd shagged her?"

My expression obviously causes Dan some worry, so he hurriedly changes tack. "Only kidding, Edward.

What do you think I said? You're my best friend. I'm hardly going to shag your girlfriend, am I?"

I pause just long enough to sow a seed of doubt in his mind, which I suppose is a bit cruel, but then so was him withholding this kind of information. "I suppose not."

"And then . . ."

I bristle again. "Then what?"

"Well, she told me she thought she could do better. Than you, I mean."

"And . . . And what did you say?"

Dan puts an arm around my shoulders and gives me a matey squeeze. "I told her that she couldn't, of course."

Even though I realize later that it's possible to take his comment two ways, this is why Dan's my best friend. Because despite him shafting just about every woman he's ever laid eyes on, he'd never, ever, do the same to me. And there's not a lot of people you can say that about.

CHAPTER
SEVENTEEN

It's official — I'm pathetic. And the reason I'm so pathetic is that I've possibly misread the situation with Sam so badly that for the second time in as many years, my ignorance about how to behave in a relationship has contributed to me being single again. And it's worse this time, because even though it's only been a day, I really, really miss Sam — much more than I ever did Jane, tellingly. And although Dan's pretty sure that what's happened between her and me is only a temporary "blip", to me it feels like the end of the world.

While I've never been one to run away from my problems, right now a run seems like a good idea, as it's possibly the only way I can do something that'll make me feel worse than the pain that's thudding away inside of me.

It's late afternoon, and as I head along the seafront, the traders are just taking down their stands by the West Pier, cramming assorted tie-dye T-shirts, toe rings, incense, and other hippie paraphernalia into boxes, ready to be taken out again in the morning. I run on past the beachfront bars, where traditional fish-and-chip shops mingle with loud theme pubs, up the slope in front of the arches housing the art galleries, and along the pier, towards the dodgems and helter-skelter at the end, then back past the assorted shooting booths with their crooked rifles and dodgy superglued-on coconut shies that put the "unfair" into "funfair", trying to forget about what's happened. But no matter how colourful the surroundings, I can't stop thinking about Sam.

As I run, acutely conscious that it's the first time I've run on my own for a while, I think about how far I've come from my Jane days. For a start, when I jog past the first-aid station on the beachfront nowadays, the St John Ambulance crew don't look concerned any more. A couple of drunk women even wolf whistle me as I sprint past the shelter where they're consuming a bottle of something brightly coloured. Kids in passing cars no longer point at me and laugh as I jog on the spot, waiting for the green man at the crossing — in fact, it wasn't so long since I *was* the green man at the crossing, looking for a nearby bin to be sick in. And while in the beginning it may have all been because of Jane, nowadays it's all thanks to Sam.

There are a couple of surfers out on the relatively calm water, paddling frantically every time something more than a ripple comes their way, and as I jog past, I understand how this is Dan's philosophy too. To ride every wave, however short that ride may be. And I also realize just how different we are. I'm not after a short ride. And I'm too weary to keep up this frantic paddling.

I keep running until I get as far as the evocatively named Hove Lagoon, which in reality is a shallow concrete basin of cloudy water on the promenade where windsurfers and sailors can practise the basics, without fear of stormy seas or getting out of their depth, and the irony's not lost on me. All of a sudden I feel sick, and I lean over the metal railing in case I have to throw up on the beach, but pull back at the last minute due to the drunk guy sleeping on the pebbles beneath me. And while I'm worried that he might not have appreciated my particular surprise gift of a hot meal, I'm even more concerned about how I'm feeling. And not that I've overdone it, but from the idea that I might be about to lose an awful lot more than just my lunch.

Once the feeling of nausea finally passes, I jog back along the seafront, picking up the pace as I get near my flat, but no matter how fast I run I can't seem to shake off the feeling that something awful's happened. I cut back up through Brunswick Square, and sprint through the mews next to the Admiral Jim and along my street, where I eventually collapse against the railing outside my flat, panting loudly. And as I gasp for breath, I'm pleased that I'm dressed in my running gear and sweating heavily, otherwise anyone seeing me might have confused my heaving chest and the water running down my face for something else.

"Edward," says Wendy when we're sitting in the Admiral Jim later, and I've explained the previous day's events to her too. "See it from Sam's point of view."

"I was trying to. But that's the thing about us blokes. The thing that gets us into trouble all the time. We're actually incapable of doing that."

"Okay." Wendy pulls her T-shirt down in an unsuccessful attempt to cover her bump. "The way Sam's probably looking at things, Jane dumped you, remember. That means you didn't dump her."

"Right."

"So Jane had obviously fallen out of love with you."

"Okay."

"But you hadn't necessarily fallen out of love with her."

"I have now."

"But Sam doesn't know that, does she?"

"Doesn't she?"

Wendy rolls her eyes. "No. As far as she's concerned, there was no change in the way you felt about Jane."

"Because it wasn't me who did the dumping?"

"Exactly."

"What are you two talking about?" says Dan, jumping up on to a bar stool next to me.

Wendy narrows her eyes at him. "Love, Dan. Something you wouldn't know anything about."

"I've been in love," protests Dan.

"With someone other than yourself?" asks Wendy archly.

"I fall in love all the time," protests Dan. "At the shops. In the gym. Just this morning, in fact, with a girl I saw at the petrol station. I even asked if I could fill her up, but . . ."

"That's not love, Dan" says Wendy, cutting him off. "That's lust."

"And there's very little difference between those two things," he says. "Both four-letter words beginning with 'L', both make you do crazy things, and neither lasts very long."

I nudge him. "So I've heard."

"That's rubbish," says Wendy. "Guys like you are incapable of love."

"That's not very fair," says Dan. "True, but not very fair."

Even though I'm pretty wrapped up in my misery, I'm not too teary-eyed to miss an opportunity like this. "What about Polly?"

Dan just about manages not to flinch. "Maybe I thought so at the time. But now I realize that it wasn't real love. Well, not in the true sense of the word."

"And what is the true sense of the word, exactly?" asks Wendy, intrigued now. "Come on — let's see if the great lover Dan Davis can actually explain what love is."

"Aha," says Dan. "That's the whole point. It's one of those things that you can't explain. Because it doesn't make any sense."

She frowns. "How does love not make any sense?"

"Well, we men are designed to go around and sow our seed, right? To ensure the survival of the species. And yet, love means we're supposed to stay with one woman only, which to us men doesn't quite fit in with what we know our biological programming to be. So as a guy, you just have to accept that it's there, however illogical it seems." He shrugs. "It's just one of those things. Like nipples on men."

"And sausages," I add, keen to show I've been paying attention.

"Exactly."

Wendy does a double take. "Sausages?"

"It's a long story," I tell her. "But that's not right, Dan, surely. About love, I mean. How can you just let something like that take you over, without knowing what it is?"

Dan shrugs. "You don't really have the choice, do you? In fact, the only thing you can do is stop yourself from getting into a situation where it's going to get you. So, if you don't want to fall in love, don't go to the butchers."

"Thanks for clearing that up," says Wendy sarcastically. "But getting back to the matter in hand, Sam obviously worries that there's a part of you that hasn't moved on."

"But I have moved on, obviously. To her."

Wendy pats my hand sympathetically. "But she doesn't really know that, does she? And neither, I suspect, do you."

"I'm pretty sure I have."

"But how do you know?"

"Well, by the fact that . . . I mean, because . . ."

"You've already admitted you care about Jane," says Wendy. "And to Sam."

"Not the smartest move, Eddy-boy," agrees Dan.

"But you women are always going on about how we never express our feelings," I protest. "How we never say what we really mean. All I did was answer Sam's question honestly. It's not as if I was lying."

"Ah, but maybe you should have," says Dan.

"How so?"

"Well . . ." He thinks for a moment. "Remember the classic 'Do these jeans make me look fat?' question. If a girl ever asks you that, even if she *is* fat, what's the answer?"

"Well, 'no', obviously."

Wendy nods encouragingly. "And how do you know that?"

I glance across at Dan. "Because Dan told me."

She rolls her eyes. "Even though it's a lie, you realize why it's the correct answer?"

"I think so," I say. "Because there are some questions that only have one answer."

"Precisely," says Wendy. "And that's why, when Sam asked you if you still had feelings for Jane, you should have said no. End of story."

"But I didn't say I had feelings for her. I said I cared about her."

Dan exhales loudly, and mimes ringing a bell above his head. Twice. "Ding-dong. Rookie mistake number two. That'll get Sam's jealousometer working overtime. I can tell you."

"But . . . why?"

Wendy smiles. "It's simple, Edward. As far as we're concerned, you only have room in your hearts for one woman. Except for your mum, of course."

"Why?" says Dan. "Is she fit?"

288

As Wendy looks at Dan disdainfully, I'm a little puzzled. "But I thought it was a good thing to be caring? To show you had a sensitive underbelly."

"Nah," says Dan. "Show a woman anything sensitive, and she'll kick you in it."

Wendy shakes her head. "Anyone ever tell you you were a little bit cynical, Dan?"

"I'm serious. Look at poor old Edward. He's tried to be honest — stupidly, maybe — with his girlfriend, and all it's achieved is to get him in trouble."

Wendy sighs. "It's not what he said, Dan, so much as when he said it. I mean, there's a time and a place."

I'm really confused now. "But when's a better time than when someone's just asked you a question? I mean, this was part of the trouble with Jane and me. We let so much stuff go unsaid that it built up and led ultimately to us splitting up."

Dan nods. "Well, that and you stuffing your face with pies every evening."

"I'm serious. This is how it should be."

"Maybe it should," says Wendy. "But it's just not the case. And I'm not saying that honesty's wrong, Edward. Just that you need to think about the consequences of what it is you're actually being honest about. And find a good time to say it."

"Exactly," agrees Dan. "That way, it's not lying, but delaying the truth. Which isn't the same thing at all."

I scratch my head. "So let me get this straight. Every time Sam asks me a question, I've got to stop and think what the right answer should be, as opposed to just telling her how I really feel about it?"

"Sounds like a sensible policy," says Dan.

"Exactly," agrees Wendy. "Imagine you're at a dinner party. And say the host has served up something you don't like. What would you do?"

"Well, eat it, of course."

"And would you tell her, when she asked if you were enjoying it, that actually you weren't?"

"No, of course not."

"And why not?"

"Because there isn't any food that Edward doesn't like," snorts Dan.

I ignore him. "Because I wouldn't want to hurt her feelings."

"Aha!" says Wendy, obviously having picked the phrase up from Dan. "And there's your rule of thumb."

"Where, exactly?"

"If she asks you about your feelings . . ." says Wendy.

". . . then think of hers before you answer," says Dan.

"So you're saying that most of the time, when women ask us a question you don't want to hear the truthful answer?"

"Nope. We just want to hear the right answer."

"But why?"

"Simple," says Dan. "Because what they're actually looking for is reassurance."

"Huh?"

"Let me turn it around," says Wendy. "If I was in bed with Dan . . ."

"Fat chance," interrupts Dan. "Especially now."

". . . and he asked me whether I thought his penis was big enough, even though I'd probably be wanting to get on to *The Guinness Book of Records* to add him to the 'World's Shortest' section, the correct answer would not of course be 'no'. It also wouldn't be 'I've had bigger, but yours is fine.' What he wants to hear is that his is the biggest, and no other one could possibly compare."

"Which would be true," says Dan, pushing his tongue against the inside of his cheek.

"So my point is, sometimes it's better to reassure than tell the truth. The trick is recognizing when those times are, and what those questions might be."

"And more important," says Dan, "what the answers are."

"But . . ." I puff my cheeks out in frustration. "You're both talking as though this is just one big game."

"It is," says Dan. "As is most of life."

"But surely not when you're talking about someone's emotions?"

"Even more so," he says. "As you well know."

I look across at Wendy but she, for once, finds herself nodding in agreement with Dan.

"Anyway," continues Dan, "in the meantime, look on the bright side."

"Bright side?" My mind goes back to when Dan said exactly the same thing to me after Jane had dumped me. "How can there possibly be a bright side?"

"I'm serious," says Dan. "You can never truly know someone — or, more important, how you feel about someone — until you've split up from them. So this is a great chance to find out what Sam's really like. And whether *you* really like Sam."

And as I think about this later, I realize that perhaps Dan's right. If, by the end of the week, I still really, really miss Sam, then it'll prove to me what I feel about her. And if she's prepared to forgive me something like this, then anything in the future — leaving the toilet seat up, or forgetting our anniversary — should be easy to deal with. So while I might not be feeling much brighter in myself, at least I can see there might, conceivably, be a bright side. And that's something, I suppose.

CHAPTER
EIGHTEEN

The next few days are the longest of my life. It's hard to resist the temptation to give Sam a call, but I suppose Dan's right, and I ought to give her some time to calm down. When I eventually get round to picking up my new phone, the old one seemingly beyond repair despite my best efforts with a tube of super-glue, there are three messages on it — none of them from Sam, sadly, but all of them from Jane, wondering whether I've thought any more about her "offer". I'm assuming she means her offer of a coffee, rather than the two of us getting back together, but I decide to play it safe and — despite Dan's helpful suggestion of a two-word reply — don't respond to any of them. After all, it was a text that got me into this mess in the first place, so the less I have to do with that particular form of communication the better.

My sunburn's calming down a bit — although it's being replaced by a not very fetching peeling all over the front of my body, making my chest hair look like it's got dandruff, and from the front my legs look like I'm wearing a pair of pink stockings. At least I'm still on holiday, so I don't have to mope around the office. But by the Wednesday, I'm a little tired of moping around at home, so it's a relief when Dan calls up and suggests a round of golf. He's actually bought his "practical" Porsche now, and although he insists on driving it the short distance from his flat to mine, we still have to go to the golf course in my car, as his doesn't have enough room for the two of us as well as our golf bags.

The sun's shining brightly as we tee off, although my expression suggests otherwise, and despite Dan's best attempts at lightening the mood, I can't stop worrying about what's going to happen when Sam comes back. By the time we're halfway down the third fairway, Dan's starting to get fed up.

"For Christ's sake, Edward, cheer up will you? You're putting me off my swing."

"Well, excuse me. But some of us have got more important things to think about than getting a stupid white ball into a hole a quarter of a mile away."

"Not at the moment you haven't. Because there's nothing you can do about it until she comes back. And it's going to be all right. Trust me."

"Dan, it was trusting you that got me into this mess in the first place."

Dan stops, mid-address, and looks at me with his mouth open. "Rubbish. If you'd have asked me whether you should have met up with Jane in the first place, I'd have said absolutely not. So what do you do? You go behind my back — as well as Sam's — meet up with your ex, and then get caught out. I hardly think any of that's my fault."

Ah. When he puts it like that, I suppose he's right. "Still, at least it gives me some time to help you sort out this Polly business."

Dan stiffens slightly, and silently draws his five-iron back before shanking the ball off into the bunker next to the green. Mine's in there already, but it's taken me a couple of extra shots to get there. Which again is the story of my and Dan's lives, it seems.

"Thanks," he says, scowling at me over his shoulder, before throwing the club noisily back into his golf bag and marching off to find his ball. "And for the millionth time, there is no 'Polly business'."

"But Dan," I say, hurrying after him. "Polly was the love of your life. How can you not want to at least see if you've got another chance with her?"

"Will you please stop going on about this 'love of your life' bollocks?"

"It's true though, isn't it?" I say. "She was. I mean, is."

Dan stops abruptly, causing me to bump my left shin painfully against the bottom of his golf trolley, then wheels round to face me.

"But how do you know? How does anyone know? Surely that's the sort of thing you can only truly admit on your deathbed? I mean, sure, we were 'in love'," he says, making the speech marks sign. "But as to whether she was the love of my life?" He shrugs. "Ask me again in fifty years' time."

"When it'll be too late."

Dan pretends not to hear me and starts walking again. Despite the heavy bag on my shoulder, I manage to keep up, although I make sure I keep a little more distance this time.

"Okay, smart arse," he says, once he reaches the lip of the bunker, where his ball is plugged halfway into the sand. "Say you go out for dinner this evening and eat a pizza, and it's the best pizza you've ever had. Are you never going to eat another pizza anywhere else again?"

"Well, no, of course not."

"And why not? Surely if you think it's the best pizza in the world, then there's no point going anywhere else?"

"No. Because it's only a pizza. And there's lots of other pizza restaurants in the world. And I can always go back to that particular pizza restaurant any time I want."

"Aha!" says Dan, looking up from where he's sizing up his next shot. "And that's my point. Polly's pizza was good. Perhaps the best I've ever tasted, admittedly. But there are lots more pizza restaurants in the world, so who knows — I might find a better one? And anyway, I really, really, *really* like trying different pizzas." He pokes me in the stomach with the end of his golf club. "Although, not as much as you used to."

"But that kind of pizza — I mean *love* — the love of your life, only comes round the once. That's why you're wrong. And I know you don't like to admit it, but there's a strong possibility that Polly was yours. And you could search your whole life trying to find someone who matches up to her, and end up having to compromise when you can't. And that's how divorces happen."

296

"Aha again." Dan looks back down at his ball, settles his feet into the bunker, and takes a swing. There's a huge explosion of sand as the ball pops out of the bunker and rolls to within a foot of the hole. "But it *doesn't* only come around once. That's my point. There can't be only one person for everyone out there. Otherwise, statistically, you'd never meet them. Therefore there has to be more than one, or else everyone would end up divorced. That's the reason why playing the numbers game works. You're increasing your chances. And, besides, you can always go back to that first great pizza restaurant once you've tried all the others."

"Aha yourself! Because most people *do* end up divorced nowadays. And besides, *you* can't actually go back to any of these restaurants whenever you want, can you? Because they're either closed, or you're banned."

"Well, that's just the risk I have to take, isn't it?" he says, shaking the sand off his shoes. "And unlike you I'm an optimist. There was a reason for Polly and I splitting up, don't forget. So I've got every reason to believe that there's still a possibility that out there somewhere is a better Polly. With a tastier topping, or a crispier crust . . ."

"Enough of the pizza analogy, please, Dan. You're making me hungry."

"Sorry, mate." He removes his putter from his golf bag and strides up on to the green. "But you get my point."

"No, actually." I walk over to where my ball is nestling under the front lip of the bunker and, checking Dan's not watching, pick it up and toss it towards the flag, before climbing out nonchalantly and strolling over to where it's stopped, a couple of feet further away from the hole than Dan's. "Because all I see you doing is subconsciously comparing everyone else you go out with, or rather sleep with, because 'go out with' would suggest some sort of relationship that lasted more than a week, to Polly. And so of course you're never going to find the new Polly. Because the moment you meet them, you're already convinced they can't possible compare, so of course they don't."

As Dan stares at me, I line my putt up, then hit the ball firmly towards the hole. It runs about a foot wide, and goes approximately the same distance past on the other side as from where I've just hit it.

"Great shot," he says sarcastically, standing over his ball and casually knocking it into the cup. "That's another hole to me."

"Which I'm worried is how you see this dating lark."

Dan lets out a short laugh. "Not at all. Well, perhaps. But the truth is . . . Maybe I met Polly too early. Maybe I wasn't ready at the time to settle down. Maybe she wasn't either. And although that's . . . unfortunate, I'm not going to lose any sleep over it. Because that's life, isn't it?" He leans down and retrieves his ball from the hole, before wiping it and putting it into his pocket. "And there'll be plenty more opportunities."

298

I walk over to the other side of the green and pick my ball up, then follow Dan back to where we've left our golf bags. "Except, there won't be, will there?"

"Huh?"

"There won't be. More opportunities. Not as long as you've got this Slate YourDate stuff hanging over you."

"Which we're trying to fix," says Dan. "Remember?"

"And it's proving more than a little difficult, need I remind you? You've done, what, five in the last few weeks, and the total number is still rising? And, may I remind you, there's not an awful lot of time left until *Close Encounters* airs."

"So what's your point?" he asks as we walk over to the next hole, where a fat man is struggling to bend over and put his ball on the tee.

"My point is this, and I've made it before, why spend all your time trying to fix forty-plus problems, when you could achieve the same result by just fixing one?"

"Which one?"

"Polly, you moron. Just give it another go with her. Then you might not have to fix things with all the rest — which I know you're not enjoying, and, quite frankly, not having much success with."

Dan looks at me for a moment, and then turns to stare at the fat man on the tee, who's lining up to hit his drive. Given the size of his belly, which would give Wendy's a run for the money, it's a wonder he can even see the ball, and given that he only manages to hit it about fifty yards, perhaps he can't.

"Okay then, Casanova," says Dan as we watch the fat man huff and puff off down the fairway. "Tell me something. I know you think Sam's 'the one', but is she also the love of your life?"

I think about this for a moment. "Well, I don't know yet. I mean, I guess she could be — assuming she takes me back after everything that's happened. We get on great, and I really fancy her, and so far I haven't found that much to find fault with, but it's early days, isn't it?"

Dan inspects his golf ball thoughtfully. "And yet if I'd asked you the same question a few years ago, what would you have said then?"

"I didn't know Sam then, obviously, so I can't really . . ."

Dan suddenly bounces his golf ball off the top of my head. "Stop trying to avoid the question. You know what I mean."

I rub the spot where the ball's just hit me. "I don't actually."

"You'd have said Jane, wouldn't you?"

Ah. He's got me there. "Er . . ."

"Admit it. You'd have said Jane. And so you'd have been quite happy — if Jane hadn't walked out on you, that is — to stay with her for the rest of your days in that nightmare you mistakenly thought was domestic bliss."

"That's because I didn't have any idea that it could be so much better with someone else."

Dan smiles. "And it is better, isn't it? In every way."

"I suppose," I say, reluctant to disrespect Jane.

"And that's *my* point. That's why I'm not desperate to get Polly back. Because there's a part of me that believes there's probably someone better out there for me. Or at least someone as good."

"But there hasn't been, has there?"

"Pardon?"

"Since Polly. And it's not as though you haven't been looking. And how else do you explain the fact that you move from one to the other so quickly?"

Dan grins. "It's like the old joke — Why do dogs lick their balls?"

"Pardon?"

"Because they can!"

Given what I'm beginning to understand about Dan's basic urges, if he could do that, he might not be in this mess. "Think back to when this all started."

"When what all started?"

"This womanizing of yours?"

He shrugs. "I'd hardly describe it as 'womanizing'. I'm more of a serial dater."

"And parallel, at times," I remind him. "But I think you'll find it pretty much started at the same time as your TV career. Just after you and Polly split up."

Dan sighs. "Edward, I can see where you're going with this. And you're wrong. Because the real reason is that I get . . . bored."

"What do you mean, bored?"

"With the stuff that you like." Dan sighs. "You know. Begins with a 'D'."

He can't mean doughnuts, surely? I suddenly feel hungry again. "What are you talking about?"

"Domesticity."

"How would you know? You haven't lived with anyone, except for Jane and me for a while. And that was only because you couldn't take the hint and find a place of your own."

"But that's because I like my own space. And the last thing I want is some girl clogging it up with her shoes and handbags, or — even worse — feminine toiletries."

"Dan, it's not like that. You don't suddenly get a bathroom cabinet stuffed with Tampax the minute they move in."

"Yes, you do. Women always leave stuff at your gaff, because it gives them an excuse to come and visit to check up on you. Even when you've split up from them."

"Jane didn't leave anything."

Dan opens his mouth to reply, but then thinks better of it. Instead, he just watches the fat man line up his next shot, which he slices into the trees to the side of the green. "Yeah, but what about all the boring domestic stuff? Or when you just want to be yourself? You know, walk about in your underpants, or eat last night's cold takeaway for breakfast?"

"You can still do that. There's no rule that says you've got to be on your best behaviour twenty-four-seven. And that's what's fun — to truly feel relaxed with someone. Living together is like buying one of those compilation CDs. You have to listen to some of the okay tracks along with the ones you really like — but it's the ones you really like that you buy the album for."

302

"Very profound, Ed. But have you never thought of just downloading the tracks you want?"

"Sure," I say, wondering whether I should remind Dan that he seems to have reached his download limit. "But then you never actually own the CD, do you?"

He shrugs. "Which she'll only steal from you when she goes."

I'm beginning to worry that Dan's a little bit too cynical for me to get my point across. "Just don't see it as losing half of your space, or half of your independence. Because you're gaining something too."

"Yeah. Eight stone of extra weight that it's impossible to shift. And someone suddenly getting their expensively manicured hands on half your stuff."

"That's rubbish, Dan. It's called 'sharing'. And remember — it's better to give than to receive, and all that?"

"Yeah right," he snorts. "Whoever said that has never had oral sex."

I fold my arms. "Is everything always about shagging with you?"

"Yup," says Dan. "And that's a philosophy that I'm happy to stand by."

"But look where it's got you."

"Hmm. A fantastic flat, a Porsche, and a starring role in a prime-time soap opera. So what's your point?"

I'm not sure I've got one now. "Just that, well, at the end of the day, sex is just, you know, sex."

Dan looks as if I've just insulted his mother. "Anyone who uses the words 'just' and 'sex' in the same sentence isn't doing it right. I tell you, I'd give my right arm for a shag at the moment. Well, maybe not my right one."

"All I'm saying is, there's more to life than this materialistic, superficial stuff."

"I know there is, Edward. And I'm going to focus more on it, I promise. When I can't do this any more."

"But don't you see? You can't do it *now*. Thanks to Slate YourDate, your reputation's in tatters. We live in the digital information world. It's a global village. You're never more than a click away from . . ."

Dan holds up his hand to stop me. "Ed, you lost me at the word 'digital'."

"Okay, okay. Say you do manage to put things right on Slate YourDate, what happens when you do meet her?"

"Who?"

"The perfect woman. The female Dan."

He makes a face. "For some reason, I'm strangely turned on by that idea."

"I'm serious," I say. "Imagine you meet a girl who you're really attracted to, but she turns out to be shallow, self-obsessed, and only after one thing?"

Dan grins. "You're right. It does sound like my perfect woman."

"But imagine if you want more. What if she doesn't want to know? How are you going to feel then, if she's everything you want?"

"Yes, well, you can't find everything you want in one person, can you?"

"Why not?" I say, almost shouting now, convinced that Dan's wrong. Because surely if you think that you can't, then you must be looking for too much, or even the wrong thing. Yet again, I'm sure that it's because he's comparing them all with what he sees as his ideal. And finally and for the first time, Dan decides to admit it.

"You just don't get it, do you?" he says quietly.

"Get what?"

"If you've had someone who you thought was the real deal. Almost . . . perfect. But you decided to walk out on them because at the time you wanted something else more, then, well, you've got no choice but to keep pursuing that other thing, haven't you? Because you've made a decision. Made your choice. Made your bed, and you've got to lie in it."

"With a series of women who'll never compare."

Dan shrugs, although without a lot of conviction. "They might. You never know. Like I say, it's a numbers game, isn't it?"

"Yes, but you're playing it wrong, aren't you?"

"What are you now? Some dating expert?"

"No. All I'm saying is this. At work, when we're interviewing for someone for a specific job, we make sure we have a list of criteria, and only invite people in to see us who match that list. That way, we're more likely to get someone we want. Who fits the profile. Who'll be compatible. What you're doing, however, is giving the job to anyone you like the look of on a temporary basis, irrespective of their, er, qualifications, and then sacking them when they — not surprisingly — turn out not to be good enough for the position in question. It's no wonder you're struggling to find the ideal candidate."

"Yes, but what if the ideal candidate doesn't exist?"

"But she does, doesn't she?"

"Really?"

"Yes. Polly."

Dan looks as if he wants to wrap his golf club around my head. "For the two millionth time, Ed, that's over. Finished. Done."

"How do you know?"

"Because there's something you don't know about Polly and me. Our relationship, I mean."

"What now? Don't tell me there's another skeleton in the Davis cupboard, and that she's actually your cousin?"

Normally, Dan would make some kinky comment at that, but this time he just stares off down the fairway. "You remember when Polly and I split up. And I said it was because I wanted to focus on my career."

"Yup."

"And you gave me a big lecture because you said she was the best thing to ever happen to me, and I was being selfish and short-sighted for behaving like that."

"I'm not sure I was quite that harsh, Dan."

"You were, Ed. I remember it as if it was yesterday. But the fact is, I wasn't quite truthful about what actually occurred."

"How so?"

Dan suddenly seems a little pale. "Jesus. You're going to make me say it, aren't you?"

"Uh-huh."

"She. Dumped. Me," he says, wincing, as if every word is painful.

"What?"

"She dumped me."

"No, Dan. I heard you. It was rhetorical."

"You're telling me!"

There's a pause, as I try and work out whether Dan actually knows what "rhetorical" means, and then I can't help but repeat myself, just to make sure.

"So. Polly dumped you?"

"Keep your voice down," hisses Dan, even though there's not another person within a hundred yards of us.

"I'm sorry," I say, "but the great Dan Davis. Dumped. By a woman. I mean, who'd have thought?"

"All right," he snaps. "Don't make such a big deal of it."

"So, what actually happened?"

Dan sighs. "We were in my flat one night, and it all started over some silly thing about *Where There's a Will*, and me having to film on her birthday, and I said that it was unfair of her to ask me to choose between my career and our relationship, and she said that only I would see it as a choice, and we ended up arguing . . . Anyway, I threatened to walk out, and she told me that if I walked out of that door then I might as well never come back."

"Which was a bit unfair, seeing as it was your flat."

"Quite. So you know me. I can be a little pig-headed at times. And so I walked. And just kept on going. And then discovered I'd forgotten my wallet, so had to walk all the way back. By the time I got home, she'd gone."

"And you've not even spoken since?"

"Not unless the words 'Piss off, Dan' when I dialled her number by accident one night when I was drunk count as a conversation. Besides, what for? She obviously didn't understand me."

While that may have been true, for the first time I think that I'm beginning to. "So win her back."

"How?"

"Like I did. With Jane."

"Only you didn't, did you?"

"Yes, but I could have. I did everything she asked me to, and it worked. And you can do it too. You can change."

Dan looks me up and down. "Edward, if I lost the amount of weight that you did, they'd be checking me into the Priory faster than you could say 'substance abuse'. Besides, you're applying logic to an emotional problem. Jane didn't just mean for you to change your underpants and then she'd go out with you again. She meant *change*. Be someone else. Or, at least, the old Edward. The Edward she used to know."

"So what would Polly want you to do?"

Dan thinks for a moment. "Give up on my TV career, for one thing. Get a proper job. Stop looking at other women."

"How do you know that? *She* might have changed, you know."

"So?" says Dan. "I haven't."

"Yes, but . . . She might be a bit more accepting now. Maybe she's realized that it was unfair of her to try and restrict your career back then. Perhaps she's seen what a success you've made of it, and is actually proud of you. But she's also too proud to make the first move."

Dan looks along the fairway, where the fat man has disappeared to find his ball in the trees. "Listen, Ed," he says, bending down and placing his ball on the tee, before adjusting his golf glove. "We're different, you and me. You love this 'comfort' lark. This domesticity. But that's when it gets boring for me. I'm a hunter-gatherer. It's the thrill of the chase, and all that."

Aha. "Except it isn't really, is it?"

Dan stops what he's doing and peers at me strangely. "What do you mean? Isn't what?"

"A chase."

"What are you talking about?"

"When was the last time you actually chased someone?"

"Are you being kinky?"

"I'm serious, Dan. I've seen how it goes. It's never a chase. In fact, it's kind of the reverse."

He looks puzzled. "The reverse?"

"Yup. Remember when you took me to that nightclub last year?"

"Dragged you kicking and screaming, you mean."

"Whatever. Anyway. You had women throwing themselves at you. And all you had to do was stand there."

Anyone normal would blush at this point. But not Dan. "What can I say? You've either got it . . . Or you don't get it." He holds his hand up in the "high-five" position, then looks hurt when I don't respond.

"But that's my point. It's like the lions who only go for the wounded wildebeest. The easy targets. You just do that, but in reverse. And let's face it — a lot of your girlfriends have been, well, easy. In fact, I reckon that's what you're scared of."

"Don't be ridiculous. I'm not scared of anything."

"You're scared of spiders."

Dan shudders, and scans the grass around his feet anxiously. "Yeah, well, they're not natural, are they? I mean, eight legs. Who needs eight legs? And their little beady eyes. And the way they sit there in the bath, just waiting to crawl up your . . ."

"Dan, stop avoiding the issue, and just admit it, will you?"

"Admit what?"

"That you're just a big girl, for one thing."

"Well, you are what you eat," he says feebly.

I suddenly get the feeling that I'm on to something. That now's my chance to push Dan over the edge. To make him finally confront Polly. And if I can wrap this all up in the next couple of days, then that leaves me free to concentrate on Sam when she gets back. "That's it, isn't it? You're scared of having to do the chasing for once in your life. Especially if there's a good chance you'll get rejected."

"That's not true. I . . ."

"Yes it is. In fact, you're probably right. You couldn't get her back if you tried. And, quite frankly, I'm surprised that you managed to hang on to her for as long as you did."

Dan stares at me for a second or two, then grips his golf club rather firmly and does a couple of practice swings dangerously near my head.

"It's all right for you, Edward. You've only ever swum in the shallow end of the dating pool. Polly was — is — something special. And while, yes, my heart might be telling me one thing, my head is saying something different. And I don't know which one to listen to."

"I'm impressed, Dan. I always thought it was a different body part you used as a guide."

"Very funny." Dan walks over to his ball, takes a few seconds to adjust his stance, and then rips it straight down the middle of the fairway.

"Maybe you just need to listen to the loudest voice."

"Which is yours, at the moment," he says, plucking his tee out of the ground and striding purposefully up the fairway before I've even had a chance to hit my drive.

"You can walk away from people, Dan," I call after him, "but you can't walk away from how they make you feel."

Dan stops abruptly and swivels round to face me, ripping a hole in the fairway grass with his spikes. "You're talking about Polly, right? Not you."

"Right, Dan."

"Well, I've got better things to do than waste my time on someone who might not want me."

"Actually, Dan, the way things are going, I don't think you have."

And judging by the way he doesn't even flinch when my drive goes whistling past his ear, Dan might just be starting to believe that too.

CHAPTER
NINETEEN

"What's up with him?" asks Wendy, as I follow a scowling Dan into the Admiral Jim for lunch.

"Long story, Wendy. But I've nearly convinced him to try and track down the love of his life."

"He just needs to look in the mirror," says Wendy.

Dan smiles sarcastically. "For Christ's sake, both of you. Why do you have to keep going on about this 'love of your life' bollocks?"

"Because it's so important," I say, grabbing a bar stool.

"Especially if you don't want to turn into a weird, lonely old man who buys himself a sports car and tries to pick up young girls. And you're pretty much there already," says Wendy, pointing to Dan's Porsche key ring, which as ever he's chosen to throw "casually" on the bar rather than keep in his pocket like the rest of us do.

Dan takes the stool next to me. "And what about you, Wendy? Is Andy the love of your life? I mean, this was all a little bit fast, don't you think?"

"It doesn't feel like it," says Wendy, rubbing her stomach, which looks like it's being stretched to bursting point. "Which I guess is how you know.

Besides, he'd better be. You don't think I'd let just anyone do this to me, do you?"

Dan opens his mouth to answer, before thinking better of it, and instead slowly pours half of the bottle of beer that Wendy puts down in front of him into his glass.

"So isn't it just worth a go?" I say. "Just to make sure?"

Dan shrugs. "Okay. Supposing, just supposing, she might be. What if I'm not ready for it right now? What if I still want to have a bit more fun before settling down with her? Or anyone."

"But can you really afford to let her get away? Polly's lovely. And if you're not careful, she'll be snapped up by someone else — if she hasn't been already. Besides, is it really fun? All this running around with these different women? Not forming any solid relationships? Everything based around sex?"

I can tell by the grin spreading across Dan's face that I've asked the wrong question.

"Edward's right, Dan. It's actually more fun when you're in something longer-term. Committed," says Wendy.

Dan makes a face. "Like he had towards the end with Jane? That seemed like a barrel of laughs."

I gesture towards him with my glass. "Ah, but I know better now. Since I've met Sam. And just like *you* know Polly was the one."

Dan raises both eyebrows. "And how do I know that, exactly?"

314

"Weren't you listening earlier? Because none of the others have been. Any of them. It's not as if you haven't been looking."

Dan shakes his head in disbelief. "But that's just it. I *haven't* been looking. I've just been having fun."

"Yes you *have*. You just won't admit it. And besides that fun would seem to be over now."

"Maybe . . ." admits Dan grudgingly.

"There's no maybe about it," I say. "As it stands, no woman will go out with you. Or at least, no new one, anyway. And I'd guess that most of your old ones won't either, given the feedback they've given you."

Wendy puts a hand on his arm. "At least see her, Dan. And see how you feel about her. And, more important, how she feels about you. At least you'll be able to move forward then."

Dan brushes her hand off. "Okay, okay," he says resignedly. "And it might have the added benefit of shutting the two of you up, I suppose."

"Great," says Wendy. "I haven't been to a good wedding for ages."

Dan ignores her. "But what makes you think she'll want to see me? I mean, we hardly parted on the best of terms. And it's been a while since we split up."

I think for a second. "Well, for one thing, she hasn't given you a bad rating on Slate YourDate. And let's face it, most of your other exes couldn't wait to put the knife in."

His face brightens a little. "That's something, I suppose."

"And she's got to be curious as to how you're doing now you're this big television star."

"Maybe," says Dan. "Although to be honest, Polly never quite understood why I did what I did. She'd have much rather I got a proper job."

"Such as?" asks Wendy.

"Good question," says Dan. "I'm not sure exactly what else I'm qualified for. Apart from sperm donor obviously. Particularly at the moment."

Wendy grimaces. "That's a little too much information, thanks, Dan."

He helps himself to a cashew from the bowl on the bar. "And how should I play it, exactly? I mean, what do I wear?"

"What do you wear?" I shake my head. "I'd say that's the least of your worries."

"Although a stab-proof vest might be an idea," suggests Wendy.

"And what about the venue? We'd need neutral ground, obviously."

"Dan, this isn't about the handover of a prisoner of war. It's two old flames meeting up to see if there's still a spark."

He laughs. "You've been reading too many of those Mills and Boon novels, Ed. Besides, you're forgetting one important thing. How do I get her to agree to meet? I mean, I can't just phone her up and talk to her, can I?"

"You're right," says Wendy sarcastically. "Dan Davis can't possibly do what most normal people would do.

Well, what about an email? Or sending her a text. Or a bunch of flowers. Or even writing her a letter?"

"Nah," says Dan. "Not my style."

"Well, why don't you just surprise her? Turn up at her house?"

Dan shakes his head. "What if she's living with someone? That's hardly going to go down well. Besides, I don't know where she lives."

I suddenly have an idea. "Okay. Turn up at her work then. At lunchtime. As if you've bumped into her" — I make the speech marks sign with my fingers, then realize it's a habit I've picked up from Dan — "'accidentally'. Ask her if she's got time for a quick coffee. Tell her you've got something important you'd like to discuss with her."

"Er . . . Which is what, exactly?"

"Her future happiness."

"Or unhappiness," teases Wendy. "If the two of you do get back together, that is."

"I don't know," says Dan, staring into his half-empty — in both senses of the phrase — glass.

"And you never will. Unless you at least talk to her."

"That's easy for you to say. I'm no good at this 'talking' bollocks. Actions speak louder than words, and all that. And I'm a man of action."

"Well, do a mime in front of her, then," I say exasperatedly. "Stop making excuses, or trying to turn this into something more complicated than it needs to be."

"You're the one putting the pressure on me," wails Dan. "All of a sudden, it's become the most important meeting of my life. And I don't want to fluff my lines."

317

"But you won't," I say. "Especially if you treat it like an audition. God knows, you've had enough of them. And this time, you know your part inside out."

At the mention of the word "part", Dan inevitably sniggers. "But all this is assuming that we can actually find her in the first place."

I tap the side of my nose. "Aha. They don't call me Sherlock for nothing."

"Who does?" asks Wendy.

"I certainly don't," says Dan. "I mean, I've called Edward a lot of things in his time, but never Sherlock. Lard-arse, for one. Or Porky. But never . . ."

"Do you want my help or not?"

Dan grins. "To be honest, no, actually."

"Well, tough, because you're getting it."

"Fine."

"Fine."

"So that's agreed, then? I find her, you go and see her?"

Dan looks at me sulkily. "S'pose so."

"Promise?"

"Cross my heart," says Dan mockingly.

"I didn't think you had one," says Wendy. "Along with a brain, now I think about it. Or any other vital organs."

"There's only one organ that's vital in my life," smirks Dan.

And as he and Wendy bicker across the bar, I sit back on my stool, gingerly fingering the bump on the top of my head where Dan hit me with his golf ball. I'm slightly amazed that my reverse psychology seems to have done the trick, and just hope I'll have as much success convincing Sam to see my point of view when she gets back at the weekend. Although, hopefully, it won't be quite as painful.

"So how on earth *do* we track her down?" says Dan, once Wendy's waddled off to serve some other customers.

"Well, what was she doing the last time you saw her? Work-wise, I mean."

"Oh," says Dan. "Right. Um . . ."

"Jesus. You really were self-obsessed back then, weren't you?"

He scratches his head. "Hang on. I'm just thinking. I don't want to get it wrong now."

Five minutes later, I'm still waiting. "It'd be quicker for me to phone Jane and ask her."

"Would you?" says Dan, reaching into his pocket for his mobile phone.

"Don't be ridiculous. Think."

"I've got it," says Dan eventually. "She worked for the council."

"Brighton Council? Well, that should be pretty straightforward."

"Er . . ."

"Great, Dan. Do you have any idea how many councils there are in this part of the world. Have you ever tried Googling her?"

Dan sniggers. "That always sounds rude to me."

"What about Friends Reunited?"

Dan shakes his head, so I pick his mobile phone up from where he's left it on the bar, open the web browser, and search on several combinations of Polly's name and the word "council", but apart from some strange reference to the national parrot owners' club, there's nothing. Next, I log into Friends Reunited, and MySpace, but there's no sign of her on there either.

"What about Facebook?" suggests Dan.

"Worth a go," I say, not wanting to tell him I've already looked, and thankful that I didn't act on Wendy's "Fakebook" idea — although only because I couldn't work out how to do it.

Dan reaches over and types his email address into the log-in box, followed by what looks to me like the word "shagger" as his password.

"Is that your mother's maiden name, or your first pet?"

"Very funny."

I log into his account, and have to do a double take. He's got three hundred and fifty-seven friends, and apart from a couple of exceptions, they're all women. Since joining up the other week, I've got about five, and three of them are Dan, Wendy and Sam.

"Blimey, Dan. That's impressive. And what's the deal with this bunch on the right?" I say, indicating a collection of photos of some rather attractive women.

"They're my 'Top Friends'," he says proudly. "Although sadly the feeling isn't mutual."

"And why aren't I in there? Aren't I one of your top friends?" I ask, a little hurt.

"Yes, well, I haven't slept with you, have I?"

"So this is actually a list of the women you've had sex with?"

320

"Yup." Dan grins. "A sort of a Sit-on-My-Facebook."

I type Polly's name into the search box, but even though there are a couple of new Polly Martins on there, there's no one who looks like it could be her. With a sigh, I realize that I'm just going to have to resort to Plan A, which is to phone around later, and hope I can find her the old-fashioned way.

CHAPTER
TWENTY

When I ring on Dan's doorbell, he answers almost immediately, although it's hard to hear his voice on the intercom, due to the strange buzzing noise in the background.

"What are you doing in there?" I have to shout, which alarms a rather large man walking past, but not as much as when Dan's "Morning, fuck-face" booms loudly out into the street.

"Sorry, mate," says Dan, opening his door and jerking a thumb over his shoulder towards the front room, where the noise is coming from. "Just doing the cleaning."

"That was 'cleaning' and not 'cleaner', I take it?"

Dan grins. "Yup. Learned my lesson there."

"So you've hired another one?"

"What. Cleaner? No, no one seems to want to work for me any more."

"Yes, well, word must have got around about how messy things with you can get. So who's that I can hear doing the hoovering?"

"Aha," says Dan. "That's Marc."

"You've employed a man? I suppose that's one way to guarantee you won't be tempted to sleep with them."

"Nope," says Dan, waving me into the front room. "Even better than that."

I follow him into the lounge where, although I can hear the noise of the vacuuming, there's no sign of anyone there. That is, until a small round metallic object bangs painfully into my right ankle.

"Jesus!" I jump up in shock.

"No," says Dan. "Mitsubishi, actually." He reaches down and picks the small whirring object up, before clicking the off switch on the side and handing it to me.

"What on earth is this?"

"The latest in household gadgetry. Meet Marc — Mitsubishi's Automated Robot Cleaner. Just switch him on, put him down, and off he goes. Leaving you to get on with the more important things in life."

"Which in your case would be what, exactly?"

Dan smiles. "I dunno. But I'm sure I'll think of something."

"And how much did this little technological wonder set you back?"

He creases his forehead. "I can't remember. A grand, or something."

"A thousand pounds? For a *vacuum cleaner?*" I hand it back to him, careful not to drop it.

"Why not?" says Dan. "At ten pounds an hour for a cleaner, that's an awful lot of cleaning."

"And is he . . . I mean it, any good?"

"It will be. Once it learns its way around and stops taking chunks out of my skirting board. And your ankles, obviously." He switches the sleek little device on again and places it back on the floor, where it scurries off in search of dust in his otherwise spotless apartment. "Small, quiet, and with a lot of suck. A bit like my ideal woman, really."

"But . . . a thousand pounds?" I say, watching warily as it disappears under the sofa.

Dan shrugs. "It's nothing, really."

"It might not be to you."

"It isn't. You know how much they're paying me for this new series?"

I do, actually. Dan's mentioned it at least five times a day ever since he got the job. "You're paying them to let you be in it, aren't you?"

"Nope. Five thousand an episode. And I'm contracted to do thirty-eight episodes a year. That's . . ." Dan stops talking, and looks at me helplessly.

"An awful lot of vacuum cleaners. Anyway — are you ready?"

"I was born ready," says Dan. "Er . . . what for?"

"We've got a date. Remember?"

"Eurgh." Dan shudders. "Steady on, mate. I mean, I know it's been a while, but I'm not that desperate."

"No, dummy. Not you and me. You and Polly. Remember?"

"Ah, yes." Dan walks over to the fridge and helps himself to a bottle of some designer fizzy water, although the design seems to be all about the shape of the bottle. "I've been thinking about that."

"And?" I say, when Dan declines to elaborate.

"Yes. I think we need a change of tactics."

"What kind of change of tactics?" I ask suspiciously.

"Well . . ." Dan twists the top off the bottle and takes a large swig, then tries unsuccessfully to stifle a burp. "Instead of just going there, surprising her, and forcing her into a confrontation, I thought we could, you know, *not* go."

"And?"

He steps back hurriedly as Marc whizzes by. "That's about as far as I'd got, really."

"Come on, Dan. Don't chicken out on me now. We have to go."

"Give me one good reason why I should."

"Well, the fact that I'm giving up my day to drive you there?"

"I said one *good* reason."

"I could be at work, you know."

"Pah," says Dan. "Last time I looked, you were supposed to be on holiday. And, anyway, you can take a day off work when you feel like it. Besides, what you do is hardly work, is it? I mean, phoning someone up, asking them if they want to change jobs . . ."

"Oh, and dressing up and pretending to be someone else is better, is it?"

Dan shrugs. "At least I'm an artist. I bring pleasure to millions of people."

I'm conscious that Dan is playing for time — and that's something he doesn't have a lot of. "But mainly yourself, at the moment. Which is why you're going to go through with this."

Dan stares at me while he finishes the rest of his water. "Okay," he says finally as if he's doing me a favour. "You win. Just let me go and get changed."

"Fine. I'll wait here."

"Fine."

As Dan disappears off into his bedroom, I sit down on his huge leather couch, nearly sliding off the edge each time I have to lift my feet when Marc buzzes past. There's a pile of magazines on his coffee table, so I flick through a couple of them as I wait for him, but when after ten minutes he still hasn't appeared, I start to get a little concerned.

"Dan?" I knock on his bedroom door and walk in, to find him staring vacantly into his walk-in wardrobe.

"What?"

"You're going to meet your ex-girlfriend. Not to some film premiere."

"Which is why it's so difficult for me to find the right outfit. I mean, I've never had to dress up to impress women. In fact, normally I just take off my clothes."

"What's wrong with what you were wearing?" I point to the Armani jeans and sweatshirt he's discarded on the bed.

"Don't be ridiculous," says Dan. "They're my cleaning clothes."

I try hard to stifle a laugh, seeing as Dan's efforts at cleaning seem to involve little more than bending over and flicking a switch. "Well, do you want me to pick something out for you?"

Dan makes a face. "Yeah, right. And I'll be asking you if you know any good chat-up lines next."

"Just get a move on, will you? We're supposed to be 'bumping' into her for lunch. And at this rate, she'll have left for the day."

"But ..." Dan crumples up his sweatshirt and throws it into the wardrobe, and for a minute I think he's going to collapse on the floor and have a tantrum. "I don't want to go!"

"Well, you have to. It's something you need to do."

He puts on a sulky face, then sits down on the edge of the bed. "But why?"

I think about sitting down next to him and putting an arm around his shoulders but stop myself, knowing what his reaction would be. "Have you completely forgotten the whole point of this? Irrespective of these other women, you need to decide what you feel about Polly. And the only way you can do that is by actually, physically, seeing her, and finding out whether there's a strong emotional response."

"Right. So this is how it's going to play. I see Polly again, I don't give a shit, prove to you I'm over her. Sorted."

"Yup," I say, although judging by his reaction this morning that's looking more and more doubtful.

"And you'll stop bleating on at me?"

"Exactly. So pull yourself together, and get a move on."

"Right. Fine." Dan takes a couple of deep breaths. "I'm an actor. I can pull this off."

"Dan, you're not trying to pull anything off. This is the one time for you to be honest with yourself. And her. Show Polly the real Dan."

Dan looks up at me for a second, and then flops down on his back and stares up at his bedroom ceiling, which I'm pleased to see doesn't have a mirror on it. "Well, maybe that's what I'm worried about."

"How do you mean?"

"You know. Like pubs? The smoking ban?"

"Huh?"

"People love pubs, right? Despite the crappy decor, naff ornaments, and surly bar staff . . ."

"Leave Wendy out of this."

Normally Dan would find that funny, but evidently not today. "But despite all that, you used to go in and sit there quite happily, peering through that foggy atmosphere, inhaling someone else's second-hand smoke, and walking out smelling like, well, you used to when you were a twenty-a-day man, because that was what a pub was like. What you expected. What people loved."

I'm struggling to see where this is going. "And?"

"And now, there's a smoking ban, pubs don't have that cloaking smokiness any more. And so they smell of, well, pubs. Stale, beer-soaked carpets. Sweaty staff. And people don't want to go there any more. Because they realize what they really smell like, under all that. And they don't like it."

"So you're worried that Polly's not going to like the way you smell? Metaphorically, I mean."

"Yeah," says Dan. "Metaphorically. Remember, Polly knew me before I was 'Dan Davis'."

For once, he doesn't make the speech marks sign, but even so, I know what he means. "But what if she does? What if, actually, she prefers the real Dan. The one who's not hiding behind all these veneers?" I stop myself, worried that Dan's going to think I'm talking about his recent cosmetic dentistry. "I mean, what if she's really grateful, because finally she gets to see the real you? And don't forget, I think she knew you a little better than that back then."

"Yeah, but then there's another problem."

"Which is?"

"If for some reason I'm not, actually, over her, what do I do then?"

"Well, you deal with that if it happens."

"How?"

"Er . . . By deciding if you want her back, of course."

"Brilliant. Only one slight flaw in that plan, as far as I can see it."

"Which is?"

"Like I said the other day." Dan sighs. "What if she doesn't want *me* back? What then? Say I go there, and realize that she's the love of my life, and I can't live without her, and I" — he swallows hard — "tell her that, and then she, you know, rejects me. What do I do then?"

Ah. For a moment, I'm tempted to say that he'll have learned a valuable lesson. He'll finally get to feel what the rest of us guys have felt through the years, and probably what all of his ex-girlfriends have experienced at his hands — which is why they've been writing what they've been writing on Slate YourDate. But I can't. Because if I do, there's a real chance that he won't go through with seeing her in the first place.

Throwing caution to the wind, I walk over and sit down next to him. "Remember when you had to go to the STD clinic when you got that rash, you know, *down there*, after sleeping with that girl you met on the beach. What was her name?"

"Samantha," says Dan immediately. "I'd hardly forget her. What about it?"

"Well, you didn't want to go, because you were scared of hearing something that you didn't want to hear, but you needed to find out the answer. Because if you didn't, then your whole relationship future might have been put in jeopardy."

"So?"

"Well, this is just like that. And hopefully, like that time, you're going to find out that what you were worried would be something serious is no worse than . . . What was it, exactly?"

Dan reddens slightly. "I was allergic to Samantha's lipstick."

"Exactly. And this time, like then, I'll be there to hold your hand."

"Metabolically."

"Metaphorically."

"Well, that's a great comfort."

I can tell he's being sarcastic, but by the change in his body language, the message has got through to him. Eventually he looks up at me, the expression on his face like a faithful old pet on his way to the vet's for the last time.

"I suppose I'd better get ready then."

"Great. That's the spirit."

Dan stands up, then walks purposefully over to the doorway, and grabs hold of the door handle. "So fuck off out of my bedroom, will you?"

It's nearly one o'clock, and we're just along the coast in Worthing — which is the *actual* council Polly works for — sitting in the Mini, just round the corner from her office, and near a parade of shops and cafés which, assuming she hasn't brought a packed lunch with her, she'll have to visit at some point this lunchtime. I'm starting to get hungry myself, and hoping she'll be out soon, as Dan's constant edgy fidgeting is starting to get on my nerves. He's eventually decided on his standard uniform of new-but-made-to-look-old jeans and a fitted shirt, but topped off today, even though it's cloudy, with sunglasses and a cap.

"What?" he says, as I glance at my watch for about the twentieth time.

"You are sure she's actually in the office today?"

He tugs the peak of his cap even lower and peers at me over the top of his Ray Bans. "I guess so."

"What do you mean, you 'guess so'? Didn't you check this morning like I asked you to?"

"How on earth would I have checked? Gone into reception and asked for her?"

"Well, that would have been one way." I stare at him for a second or two, before removing my mobile from my inside pocket and dialling her office number.

"What are you doing?" says Dan, suddenly alarmed.

"Just making sure we haven't wasted the last two hours."

The phone rings a couple of times, before the receptionist answers with a bored-sounding "Worthing Council."

"Oh, hi," I say. "Is Polly Martin in today?"

There's a pause, and then: "Yes she is. I'll just put you through."

As the receptionist transfers the call, I hit the "end" button, but make sure Dan can't see me doing it.

"Oh, hi, Polly," I say to no one. "Edward here. Dan's friend?"

"What are you doing?" he mouths nervously.

I ignore him. "Yes, that's right. It has been a long time. Well, I'm just waiting in a car outside with Dan, and we were wondering . . . Yes, that's right. Would you like to speak to him?" I hold my phone out, but Dan just shakes his head, staring at it like it's radioactive — until he notices the "call ended" message.

"Bastard!" He retreats further under the peak of his cap. "But she is there, right?"

"Yup. Which means she'll have to come out at some time, won't she?"

Half an hour later, when the rumbling from my stomach is in danger of drowning out the radio, I'm starting to doubt whether Polly eats at all, and I'm just about to suggest we go and get a sandwich ourselves from the café on the corner when Polly appears from inside the glass door. She looks quickly up at the sky to check the weather, buttons her jacket up, then strides off down the road.

"Quick," says Dan, sitting up suddenly.

"Quick what?"

"There she is."

"So I see, Dan."

He bangs on the dashboard impatiently. "Come on then."

"Do you want me to follow her in the car?"

"We can hardly do it on foot, can we?"

"We can even more hardly do it in the car, unless you want me to drive on the pavement, and don't you think that'll look a little suspicious?"

"Just hurry up, will you?" He reaches across and tries to twist the key in the ignition. "We'll lose her."

As I'm fighting him off, out of the corner of my eye I see Polly disappear into the café. "Get off, Dan. She's gone in there. Happy now?"

"Ecstatic," he says, his voice suggesting the opposite. "Right. What are you waiting for?"

"What do you mean, what am *I* waiting for?"

He nods towards the café. "Go in and talk to her."

I frown at him. "Me? What am I possibly going to say to her that wouldn't be better coming from you?"

"I'm serious," pleads Dan. "Go and explain. Or at least go in and convince her to see me."

"But surely if you go in and see her, I won't need to? Because she'll already be seeing you."

"Tell you what . . . Why don't you pretend to be me? Tell her you've been in a terrible accident, and had a skin graft, or face transplant, or something. Which is why you look like this."

I'm not quite sure how to take that. "And what about the increase in height? Not to mention the decrease in ego."

"I don't know, Edward," says Dan, panicking slightly. "You're smart. You'll figure it out. Besides, you do this all the time at work."

"Not speak to your ex-girlfriends, I don't," I say, although admittedly I have been doing some of that recently.

"No. Pretend to be someone else."

"I think you'll find that that's your job."

"No," says Dan impatiently. "You know, when you have to say that you're not a headhunter to get past the receptionist. And then convince people who don't want to speak to a company that it's in their interests to at least hear what they've got to say. That's all I'm asking you to do for me now. At least get her to hear me out."

"How?"

"I don't know. Tell her I'm dying of cancer, or something, and my last mission in life is to make peace with all my exes. Yes. That might just work." Dan takes his cap off and rubs the top of his head, quite clearly thinking this is a brilliant idea.

"But that would be a lie."

Dan looks at me as if I'm stupid. "So?"

"So the last thing you want to do is start lying to her. At least, not straight away," I say, remembering our conversation of the other day.

"But I wouldn't be lying to her. You would."

"Yes, but this is about you. Not me."

334

"Fine," says Dan, almost shouting. "Have it your way."

"Fine."

Reluctantly, he takes his glasses off, spends thirty seconds adjusting his hairstyle in the mirror on the back of the sun visor, then takes a deep breath. "Right. Wish me luck."

"Good luck!" I say, rolling my eyes. "Now get on with it, or you'll miss her."

He opens the car door, then shuts it again before getting out. "What am I going to tell her? About why I'm here, I mean."

"The truth, Dan."

"Right. The truth." He grabs the door handle again, then turns back to face me. "Which is?"

"Jesus, Dan," I say, looking anxiously towards the café, not wanting to have to come here again tomorrow and waste another day staking her out. "Shouldn't you have thought about this a little beforehand?"

"I just thought I'd, you know, wing it. But now I'm here that doesn't seem such a good idea."

"Just tell her . . . Tell her you've missed her, and you wanted to apologize for the way you treated her, and you'd like to think the two of you could be friends."

He shudders. "There you go again with that 'friends with a girl' business."

I lean across him, open the passenger door, and give him a firm shove. "Just get going."

Dan climbs grudgingly out of the car and starts to shuffle towards the café like a five-year-old being sent to his room, before stopping by the window and peering back helplessly towards where I'm sitting. I stare at him for a second, then just mouth "go on" and give him the thumbs up.

As he smiles nervously and pushes through the door, I shake my head and switch the car radio on, preparing myself for a long wait. Two minutes later, the sound of the door being flung open startles me, but not as much as the sight of a dripping wet Dan jumping into the passenger seat.

"Don't say a word. And just drive, will you?"

I try to ignore what I hope is just water dripping down on to my leather upholstery.

"Well, that went well, I see?"

Dan peels his shirt off. "Couldn't have gone better," he says, drying his face on it. "Come on. Let's get out of here."

I start the engine and indicate to pull out of the parking space, then change my mind. "No," I say, switching the ignition off, before rummaging around in the glove compartment. "Let's not."

"Come on, Ed. Stop messing about."

"Just one second . . ."

"What are you doing?"

"Trying to find my umbrella. Just in case she's got herself another drink."

Polly looks exactly as I remember. Dan always used to describe her as the "girl-next-door" type — which would be true, if you lived in a street full of amazingly attractive models, I suppose. She's still stunningly pretty, with the same blonde curly hair, and the most incredible green eyes — eyes that look as though they've been crying. I brace myself, then walk over to her table.

"Mind if I sit down?" I say, resting my hand on the back of the spare chair opposite her.

Polly looks up, and for a moment it's clear she doesn't recognize me. "Yes, actually," she sniffs. "I'd rather be on my . . . Edward?"

"Hi. Polly," I say, checking that she's out of drink. Thankfully her water glass is empty, probably because Dan's wearing most of it, although rather worryingly the waitress chooses that moment to walk over and place a large cappuccino on the table.

"What are you doing here? I've just seen . . . Oh, hang on. This can't be a coincidence."

I pull the chair half out from under the table, and when Polly doesn't protest, pull it out the rest of the way, and sit down.

"Just think of me as the United Nations. Here on a bit of a peacekeeping thing."

She smiles, although it's a rather tight-lipped one. "Where's your blue helmet?"

If Dan was here, he'd be sniggering at that. "I'm undercover."

Polly dabs at her eyes with her napkin. "So. What did *he* want? Surprising me like that."

"To see you, of course. To explain a few things."

"That's rich." She leans back in her seat. "And sneaky."

"Well, he thought you might not have wanted to see him."

"He was right."

"Ah." I catch the waitress's eye, and order a cappuccino for myself. "So, how have you been?"

"Fine. Up until now," she says, blowing her nose, before crumpling up the napkin and placing it carefully on her saucer. "You look well. How's Jane?"

"Okay, I guess. She left me."

"Oh, Edward. How rotten. I'm sorry."

"Don't be. It was a while ago. And although it was quite messy at the time, I've forgiven her. We're still in touch, in fact."

Polly looks at me for a moment, then picks up her cappuccino and takes a sip. "Very clever, Edward. But I'm with someone else now. And the last thing I need is for Dan to come back on the scene and complicate things."

"He doesn't want to complicate things, Polly."

"Of course he does," she says. "I saw the look on his face. And even if he didn't, he's going to. I mean . . . I was in love with him. And it took me a long time to get over the fact that he was obviously in love with someone else."

This comes as a shock to me. As far as I'd been aware, and particularly given Dan's recent shocking admission, he hadn't left Polly *for* anyone. "Really? Who?"

"Himself, Edward. Or, at least, his bloody career. Whatever that's turned out to be."

"But he was different then, Polly. A lot more immature. He didn't really know what he wanted."

"And he does now, I suppose?"

"Yes. And that's why he wants to see you."

"What for? So he can make some huge declaration of love, and ask me to forgive him and take him back, only for him to break my heart again?"

The way she says this makes me realize that saying "yes" probably isn't the smartest move at this moment. "Not exactly. But like I said — he needs to explain why he did what he did. He feels he owes you that."

"I know why he did what he did, Edward. Because he's a selfish, egocentric . . ."

Polly, perhaps fortunately, doesn't finish the sentence, given that the waitress chooses that moment to arrive back at the table with my coffee. But as I pick up my spoon and start to eat the frothy chocolate-flaked topping, Polly just stares at hers.

"He was like that, Polly," I say, desperate to break the awkward silence. "But now he's mellowed. Matured."

"Ha!"

"No, honestly. Something's happened to him that's made him realize that perhaps he hasn't behaved in the best way in the past. And he doesn't have a lot of time to put things right."

She looks up at me, suddenly concerned. "He's not sick, is he?"

Only in the head, perhaps. "No, nothing like that. Unfortunately." I smile across the table at her, and she half returns it. "He's just . . . Listen, it's no good coming from me. Why don't you give him a chance to explain?"

"Why should I?"

"Five minutes. That's all it will take."

"I don't know, Edward. This is all a bit of a shock. I mean, nothing for three years, and then out of the blue he just appears." She sighs. "What would you do?"

And fortunately, I've got an answer for that.

When I get back to the car, I have to stifle a laugh. Dan's got the climate control turned up to its hottest setting, and is using the jets of air from the dashboard vents to dry himself off. Given the amount of product he evidently uses in it, his hair has set horizontally, making him look like a dog with its head poking out of a moving car window.

"Bloody hell." I shut the door behind me, and immediately have to open a window. "It's like a sauna in here."

"What did she say?" Dan flicks the heater switch off anxiously. "Will she see me?"

"Not today. But she'll think about it."

He stares at me for a second or two. "She'll think about it?"

"Yup."

"Was that the best you could do?"

"At least I didn't get anything thrown over me."

Dan nods slowly. "Fair point. I suppose that is something."

"So she's going to call me. And let me know."

"When?"

I start the car, and pull out into the traffic. "When she's had a chance to think about it."

"Right." Dan flicks the heating back on full. "Which will be when, exactly?"

"I don't know." I open the rest of the windows to let some cool air in before the dashboard melts. "A day. A week. It's hard to say."

"But it looks promising?"

"I'd say so."

"How promising, exactly?" says Dan, when we've driven about fifty yards further up the road.

"I dunno. A six, maybe?"

"Six. Great." Dan fiddles with the temperature control, then pulls down the sun visor to check his hairstyle in the mirror. "Out of?" he asks, trying unsuccessfully to smooth his hair down, before giving up and putting his cap on instead.

"Christ, Dan. Drop it, will you? Some things you can't control. If she calls, she calls. If she doesn't, well, at least you tried."

"Right." Dan slips his sunglasses back on, and then clears his throat noisily. "But you know that thing you said earlier?"

"What thing?"

"That thing that you said I said?"

"Er . . ."

"Well, you were right. Or rather, I was."

"What about?"

"You know," says Dan exasperatedly. "That 'strong emotional response' stuff. It doesn't get much stronger than that."

"What? Throwing a glass of water over you? I suppose not. Just think yourself lucky she didn't stab you in the eye with her fork!"

"Not hers," says Dan, turning to stare out of the window so I can't see his face. "I meant mine."

CHAPTER
TWENTY-ONE

I make sure I arrive at Gatwick in plenty of time, so I can get a position by the barriers right in front of the arrivals doors. On Dan's advice, I haven't let Sam know I'm coming — to be honest, I was scared that she'd have told me not to bother — so I'm banking on surprise working in my favour, and at least giving me a few vital moments to apologize. And while I still don't feel that I've actually done anything wrong, apart from maybe not being completely upfront with her, it's clear to me that what I did wasn't right, either. I only hope that Sam sees it that way too.

The one thing she's sure to see is the large cardboard sign I'm holding. I've written "I'm an idiot" in large black marker pen letters — large enough so she can't miss it — and I can certainly read it in the reflection of the glass doors, as, evidently, can the people who are standing either side of me, smirking slightly whenever I make eye contact.

I look up at the arrivals screen anxiously. In truth, there was no way I'd have missed her flight landing, as I've been here for ages — I'd checked my diary in a panic last night and had misread "Sam — airport" as "5 a.m. — airport", and got here just before sunrise.

Still, there hadn't been that much traffic at that time in the morning, and at least it meant that I could have a leisurely breakfast, although I hadn't felt like much more than a strong cup of coffee. Or three.

I look at my watch, and I'm wondering whether I've got time to go to the toilet — again — when my mobile rings, and Dan's number flashes up on the screen.

"What do you want?"

"Listen, mate," he says. "And I have to say this as a friend. Before Sam comes home."

"What?"

"Are you not in the slightest bit tempted? The thought of having Jane back. On your terms."

"No, Dan. And anyway, it wouldn't be my terms, would it? Jane doesn't do other people's terms. Besides, if there's one thing you taught me, it was to be independent. Stand on my own two feet. Live my own life."

He laughs. "And so what did you do? Rush straight into a serious relationship with someone else not five minutes after you've finished your last one. What happened to your 'me' time?"

"I had that in the three months after Jane left me. And I didn't like it." I check the arrivals board again. "Dan, some of us like being half of a couple. I've done single, and I've done couple, and I can tell you which one I prefer."

Dan hesitates. "Er . . . Couple, right?"

"Yes, Dan. Stephen Hawking must be so relieved that you decided to go into TV and not physics."

He ignores me. "All I'm saying is, there are ways to do the 'couple' thing."

"And there are ways not to do it. As you quite clearly demonstrate."

"Just don't give your independence away too easily. You don't want to get yourself into another Jane situation, do you?"

I bristle slightly. "How do you mean, 'another Jane situation'?"

"You know — letting her walk all over you. Ask her to move in, and the danger is she's suddenly as clingy as a wet shower curtain."

"Yes, well, I'm not going to let that happen, am I?"

"Aren't you? Are you sure about that?"

I am sure about it. Because unlike Dan, I'm determined to learn from my mistakes — especially since I can look back now and recognize all the mistakes I made with Jane. And while, at the time, my motivation for making them might have been the subconscious knowledge that the relationship wasn't right, with Sam things are different.

And while maybe that's a problem too, I don't want to be scared to be spontaneous any more. Worried that there's more meaning attached to any little gesture I make, or anything I say. Afraid that Sam's going to read more into it than there really is.

Because surely that's not the way to conduct a relationship? Maybe, in one way, it is better to be like Dan and just go through it blindly doing your own thing, and pleasing yourself, expecting the other person to just take you as they find you. Otherwise, how can you be true to yourself, if you're always trying to do the right thing by someone else?

For example, I don't eat pizza as much as I used to. And I love pizza. And it's not that Sam's told me that I can't. It's just that what pizza represents is my old lifestyle or, more important, my old life with Jane. I know that Sam knows that too, so to eat one would be saying a lot of things, including that I consider my new life with her to be just like my old life with Jane. And although I know it wouldn't really, I'm scared that she might see it that way. While I'm sure Sam wouldn't say a thing, I'd worry about what she was thinking, which would make every mouthful taste rubbery, rather than lovely. And that can't be right, can it?

Because you can't live your life doing everything for other people. You've got to do stuff for yourself, and those people closest to you have to understand that and accept the way you are. Which is why Dan has to understand that there's probably a part of Polly that understood why he was the way he was. That knew his desire to be famous was an intrinsic part of him. And while it was perhaps his fault that he wasn't able to include her in his overall grand plan, she's partly to blame too. Because she knows that it's what makes Dan, well, Dan. And real love means allowing someone to be who they have to be. Not trying to change them.

And this is the one thing that I can't quite work out. Have I been behaving towards Sam the way I'm behaving because I want to, or because I feel I ought to? Is the way my relationship with Jane went affecting things between Sam and I, even on a subconscious level, and if so is that a bad thing? Am I compromising too much of how I want to be, simply so I can be with her? If that's confusing for me, no wonder it's hard for her to grasp.

When I share this with Dan over the phone, he clears his throat impatiently.

"Edward — has anyone ever told you that you have a habit of making things too complicated? Stop over-analysing everything."

"What are you talking about?"

"Simple. For most major purchases or decisions in life, you can break things down into two questions. Do you like how it looks, and do you like how it sounds."

"Have you been sniffing those marker pens again?"

"I'm serious. You want to buy a car? How does it look and how does it sound. A TV? Perhaps reverse the order of those two questions."

"But we're talking about women here."

He laughs. "Same thing applies, only even more so. Just go on your gut reaction. For example, what happened the night you first met Sam? Were there fireworks?"

"I don't think so. I mean, we were in a café, and I couldn't really see what was going on outside."

"No, you muppet. How did you feel?"

"Well, you have to understand, when I met her, I was still with Jane. So I couldn't really feel anything. Apart from sick, after that first run she made me go on."

Dan sighs. "Aren't you forgetting that you'd just been dumped? So, technically, you weren't with her."

"Well, okay, maybe I wasn't *actually* still with her. But in my mind I was. I wanted to be. And that was the only reason I was with Sam. So she could train me to get Jane back."

"All right. When did you first think that you and Sam might, you know, be an item?"

"I dunno. Just before Jane was due back from Tibet, I suppose."

"While you were still with her?"

"Well, as you so helpfully pointed out, she had just dumped me."

"Aha," says Dan. "But to all intents and purposes, you wanted Jane back. And yet you still asked Sam out."

"That's not exactly how it . . ."

"So how is that any different to what I do, mister Pot Kettle?"

"Because," I have to think for a moment, "because in my case, one of us had actually been dumped. You don't always tell people. You just adopt the 'don't call us, we'll call you' scenario, and assume that they'll realize it's over, while you're merrily pursuing the next one. Plus, even if I did do that, I only did it the once."

"Fair enough. So, back to my original question — were there any fireworks? Because don't forget, what you had with Jane you thought was love. But it was really just routine, wasn't it?"

"Dan, all this 'fireworks' stuff. Love at first sight. It doesn't really happen, you know. Love is something that grows. Over time."

"Yeah, but you've got to agree it's not as much fun poking the bonfire if there aren't fireworks going off overhead. All I'm saying, Edward, is be careful. Don't go leaping in if you're not sure. But if you are, and if you really like Sam, don't run your relationship like the one you had with Jane."

"Dan, you're missing the point. Jane and I were great for a good few years before it went wrong. And besides I think I know enough now to see the signs, and to stop Sam and I going the way that Jane and I went."

"Yeah, right," says Dan. "Which is why you've been feeling so miserable for the last few days, and why you're waiting at the airport to apologize. Me? I don't really like any of them. So I never go into it thinking it's going to last. Or be 'the one'. That way, when it isn't — and it never is — I never get disappointed. But you go in with this starry-eyed expectation . . ." He sighs. "Listen, mate — all I really wanted to say was that if you're so sure you want to do this, then best of luck to you. And don't fuck it up."

"I won't. As long as I bear in mind what it is she wants."

"No, Ed. Bear in mind what *you* want. Because at the end of the day, that's the most important thing."

He's right, of course. But as Dan ends the call, I realize that what he's failing to see is this: right now, Sam is what I want. And if that means me having to compromise on some other, quite frankly less important stuff, well, that's a price I'm happy to pay.

I slip my phone back in my pocket and check the arrivals board for the millionth time. Sam's flight landed forty-five minutes ago, so allowing for what always feels like the three-mile walk from the plane to the baggage reclaim, and then the interminable wait for her luggage, she should be coming through any minute. I hold my sign up a little higher, and hope.

Eventually I spot her through the doors, and I'm so relieved she's actually here that I get a lump in my throat. And when she catches sight of me, any worries I had about what her reaction might be are dispelled the second her face breaks into a smile. She drops her case, runs over, and gives me a huge hug over the top of the barrier, crushing the cardboard notice against my stomach.

"Ow ow ow."

Sam lets go of me and steps back abruptly. "What's the matter?"

I peel my shirt off my still-raw stomach, which is sticky with after-sun. "Sunburn. Not quite gone yet."

"Yes, well," Sam grins. "Serves you right."

"For not telling you that I met up with Jane?"

"No. For trying to out-drink my dad. But now you mention it . . ."

"I'm so sorry about that, Sam. I didn't say anything about it because it just didn't seem important. And to tell the truth, I was embarrassed about the reason I agreed to meet her in the first place."

"Which was?"

"Jane walked out on me because of something I did. Or rather, lots of things I didn't do. And I needed to find out what they were."

350

"To see if you could win her back?" she says uncertainly.

"No. To make sure I didn't lose you the same way. Which was stupid, because I ended up losing you anyway."

Sam smiles up at me. "You haven't lost me, Edward. And I'm the one who's sorry. I overreacted. It's just that I knew how hard you'd worked to get Jane back. And then, when you didn't, I guess I thought I was some sort of on-the-rebound consolation prize."

Hang on. This can't be right. Sam's apologizing to *me*. If there is a God up there, then He must feel that he owes me a favour. "On the rebound? God no."

"And then, when you left, I thought it was because you wanted to be with her." There are tears in her eyes, and I'm not far off myself.

"God, Sam, no. Not at all. I just thought you were telling me to, well, maybe I misunderstood what you said, and . . ."

"I know." She puts a finger on my lips, then grabs my arm tightly, and it feels good. "Dan phoned me, and explained everything."

"Huh?" Suddenly I don't know what I'm more confused about. The fact that Sam seems to think that she's in the wrong, or that Dan actually did something selfless. And for me. "I beg your pardon. Dan phoned you?"

"That's right," says Sam. "Yesterday. He asked me not to tell you. At first I thought you might have put him up to it, but then I realized you'd never do something like that. And when he explained that you were only trying to do the right thing — by both of us — and that he was the one who'd told you not to say anything about Jane, I realized that I owed *you* an apology." She leans across the barrier and gives me a kiss, which I return gratefully. "If you'll have me back, that is?"

"Sam, I don't know what to say."

She smiles. "'Yes' would be a good start."

"Well, in that case, yes."

Sam walks back over and picks her suitcase up, then we make our way, hand in hand, towards the car park. "I'm sorry I ruined your holiday," she says, as we stop in front of the lift.

"You didn't ruin it." I press the "call" button. "Jane ruined it. And it was only after the flight back from Majorca that I understood something about her. Or, rather, about you and me."

"Which was?"

I start to explain about my flight, sat next to the hugely obese guy, but as I get deeper into the story, Sam stops me. "So, what you're saying is that going out with me is like having a really fat person sat next to you on an aeroplane?"

"No. Completely the opposite. But that's how it felt with Jane."

Sam frowns. "But I've seen a photo of her. She's not in the least bit fat. I mean, she could do with a bit of toning up around the thighs, but then . . ." Sam stops talking. "That wasn't what you meant, was it?"

"No. Although now you mention it . . ." I smile mischievously. "It's just that going out with her made me feel like I felt on that flight. Suffocated. Smothered. Crushed. Like I couldn't move. Couldn't breathe, even. Except I didn't realize it at the time. And I'd been sitting there for so long that I couldn't do anything about it."

"Until she got up and gave you some space, you mean?"

"Exactly." I follow her into the lift, and press the button for our floor. "Or more important until we both got off the plane."

Because it only occurred to me this morning — on the way here, in fact — that this is the way it should be. You pay the same fare, after all, so you should expect to get the same ride as everyone else. But some people just don't let you have what you're entitled to. Some of them even eat your in-flight meal-on-a-tray. Even though they might not be doing it on purpose, they can't help it. It's just in their nature.

"And," Sam swallows hard, "you don't think that about me?"

"Not at all. With you, I feel like I've got my own, comfortable window seat. In first class. And someone nice to sit next to. And I hope it's a long-haul ticket, because I'm looking forward to the in-flight entertainment."

I stop talking, because I've run out of plane journey analogies, and also because I think Sam's got it.

"I'm sorry we fell out, Edward," she says, once she's sure I've finished. "If it's any consolation, I've had a rotten few days."

"Me too. What did you tell your parents? They must think I'm rather rude."

"On the contrary. I said that you had to rush off for an important meeting at work. They think you're quite the businessman now. And can't wait to have you back again. I think my dad thinks he's found himself a new drinking buddy."

"So . . . we're okay?"

Sam leans across and kisses me again. "We're more than okay, Edward. Now take me home, please."

"Home? Oh yes. That reminds me. I've got something for you." I reach into my pocket and remove the small presentation box I bought from the jeweller's yesterday, but as I'm doing so I accidentally pull out a couple of pounds in small change that I'd been saving for the car-park machine and drop it on the lift floor. I kneel down to pick the coins up, while handing Sam the box at the same time. "Here."

"What's this?" she asks, not quite taking it.

"It's just that we've been together for a while now, and we get on really well, but I didn't think it was really working out as it was, because of all the time we were spending apart . . ."

I stop talking, because Sam's looking a little pale. "What are you trying to say, exactly?" she says, pulling her hand away.

"Well, I just think we've reached that point where we can't go on like we have been. You've got to admit, it's been a little tricky."

For a moment, I can't work out why Sam's face has suddenly taken on a strange expression.

"Hold on," she says, "we just said we were okay, and now here you are down on one knee, but it sounds like you're breaking up with me instead."

The lift doors open and I look to my left, where an older couple have spotted us, and seem to be watching with amusement. The woman's nudging her husband and pointing in our direction, and it doesn't occur to me what they're finding so interesting until I catch sight of our reflection in the lift's mirrored back wall, where I'm quite clearly kneeling down while handing Sam what looks like a jewellery box. I almost jump to my feet.

"No, you don't understand. It's not a ring. I mean, it is, but it's for keys. A key ring."

Sam takes the box and opens it slowly, peering at the contents before breaking into a grin.

"With your front door key?"

I nod. "I thought you might want one. Of your own, that is. I mean, I know you had one a while ago when you were my trainer, but I thought that now we'd make things a bit more official."

"So . . . You're asking me to move in with you?"

Ah. I suddenly spot the fundamental flaw in my plan. What was supposed to be a symbolic, romantic gesture has run the gauntlet from Sam suspecting I'm dumping her, straight through to me virtually getting down on one knee, all the way to me asking her to move in. And instead of being a funny misunderstanding, it's in danger of becoming awkward. And although, in actual fact, I wasn't, suddenly it seems like the best idea in the world.

"Well, er . . . Would you like to?"

"What about the dog?"

That's not the answer I was hoping for. I hurriedly try to lighten the mood. "Dan won't mind. He'll just have to find someone else's fridge to steal food from."

"No, *my* dog. Ollie."

Ah. In truth, I'd forgotten about Sam's collie, especially since he navigates my flat's polished wooden floors as if he's wearing ice skates. "Er . . ."

The older couple clear their throats, and I realize they're actually waiting for the lift we're in, so I quickly pick up Sam's suitcase and lead her out.

"Why don't we move into mine?" she suggests, as we walk towards the car.

I look at Sam as if it's the silliest idea ever. "Because my flat is . . ." I start to say, and then shut up, because the last thing I want to imply is that my flat is bigger, or nicer, or in a better location. And equally, I realize that "because I asked first" isn't the most mature of arguments.

"It's just", continues Sam, "that I've got a garden, and what with Ollie, and everything."

"But what would we do with mine?"

Sam shrugs. "We could always sell it. And spend the money on a boat, or something."

"A boat? But I'm not the best swimmer in the world."

Sam grins. "I was joking, Edward. Rent it out. We could do with the money. Especially now I'm going to be giving up work to start a family."

"Er . . ."

356

It takes Sam nearly a minute to stop laughing. "Your face!" she says, gasping for breath.

"Yes, Sam. Good one."

"Sorry, Ed. I couldn't resist it. But . . ."

"But?"

Sam takes me by the hand. "It's just . . . I've kind of always thought of your flat as your and Jane's place. And I know it's silly, but I'd feel a bit funny about moving in to where she's been."

"Oh. Right."

"So you'll think about it?"

I nod. "I'll think about it." Although, if the truth be told, after how I've been feeling for the last few days at the prospect of losing her, I don't have to.

CHAPTER
TWENTY-TWO

It's Sunday lunchtime, and we're at the Admiral Jim having a celebratory reunion drink, and even though I'm not supposed to know about Dan phoning Sam, I've invited him along to join us. Sam's quizzing him about his first day on *Close Encounters*, and Dan's obviously enjoying talking about his specialist subject — himself — but when he suddenly stops speaking and peers over my shoulder, it's clear he doesn't know how to react to what he's just seen. Assuming it's one of his exes, and possibly with a gun, I turn around apprehensively and follow his gaze to the doorway, just in time to catch sight of Jane walking towards the bar.

For a moment, I think we'll be okay. We're sitting in one of the darker corners, after all, and Jane never likes to wear her glasses in the daytime — she used to say they gave her a headache, but I know it's because she thinks they make her look too "bookish", whatever that means — so she might not see us. But as Wendy's pouring her a glass of wine, she can't stop herself from glancing nervously in our direction — a movement that Jane can't help but pick up on. Immediately, I swivel back round, just in time to catch Dan's look of horror.

"Quick," he says. "Hide."

Sam glances at him, then at me, a puzzled expression on her face, before the penny drops.

"Oh, how lovely," she says, giving my leg a quick squeeze under the table.

For a second, Dan's suggestion almost seems like a sensible plan, although the three of us crammed under one of the Jim's smallish tables might not quite do the trick, glasses or no glasses. I'm just eyeing the fire exit behind the pool table when there's a hand on my shoulder.

"Edward," says Jane. "What a pleasant surprise. And Dan. How's the best-looking man in Brighton?"

"Fine, Jane." As usual, Dan can't resist the onslaught of flattery, although, unusually, he doesn't get up from his chair. "Thanks."

Jane looks down at Sam, her mouth taking on a shape similar to a smile. "I'm Jane, Edward's ex-girlfriend. I'm sure he's told you about me."

At that moment, I'm sure that Jane was Sam's mystery client. After all, why would she assume that this is Sam and not just some girl who's here with Dan instead?

To her credit, Sam doesn't flinch. "Yes — you're the one that upped and left him. I'm Sam. Edward's current girlfriend. And I know he's told you about me."

I have to admire Sam's quick thinking. In one sentence, she's managed to cut off any chance Jane had of scoring any points. And Jane knows it too, because she can't quite work out what to say next.

"Well, it's nice to see you," says Dan, eventually breaking the awkward silence.

"And you," says Jane, eyeing an empty chair at the next-door table. "It's been a long time."

As she stands there with her glass of wine, Dan shifts awkwardly on his stool. I'm willing him not to say it, and I'm sure that Sam is thinking the same, but with Jane showing no sign of going anywhere, Dan's resolve finally crumbles.

"Do you, you know, want to join us?"

It's the polite thing to say. Of course it is. And the equally polite response on Jane's part would be to acknowledge this, and say something like "Thanks, but another time, maybe" before heading back to the bar — from where Wendy's watching uneasily — or even just finishing her drink and leaving. But instead she puts her glass purposefully down on the table and grabs a nearby chair.

"That would be nice," she says, sitting down right in between Sam and me, so much so that Sam has to move round to accommodate her.

No, it wouldn't be nice, I'm thinking. In fact, it would be the direct opposite of nice. And I'm just about to say something when Jane beats me to it.

"Finally, Edward, we get to have that drink."

I smart a little at the inference she puts behind the word "that", and am just wondering how I can reply to her without being rude, when Dan clears his throat.

"So, you're here for a while?"

Jane shrugs. "Oh no. I just came down for the funeral, really."

"Oh yeah," smirks Dan. "Your dog."

Jane glares at him across the table. "It's not funny, Dan. My mum was devastated when she died. I mean, she'd had her for ten years, and then when she went so suddenly . . ." Jane stops talking and can't meet anyone's eyes, conscious of the irony in what she's just said.

Dan, however, remains blissfully unaware. "So what are you still doing here?"

"Pardon?"

"What are you still doing in Brighton? If the funeral was, what, three weeks ago, I mean. Have you moved back down?"

Jane takes a large mouthful of wine. "Oh, no. I just had to come back to, you know, for work."

"For work?" Dan raises one eyebrow. "And how is the new job going?"

"Fine, thanks." Jane puts her glass down. "In fact, we're thinking of taking over a company here in Brighton, so I thought I'd stay down for a while and check them out."

"Ah," says Dan. "You're here to see what the competition's like."

"That's right," says Jane, fighting to keep her eyes from flicking across to where Sam's sitting next to her. "It's always good to know what you're up against."

I know what she's referring to, and it's not work. Finally, after ten years, and although it's taken an absence of quite some time, I'm starting to understand her and her devious ways.

"Oh, I see," says Dan. "And there's me thinking that the new job wasn't going so well. And that you'd come back down to see whether your old position was still available."

"Oh no," says Jane, looking at him strangely. "Nothing like that."

Dan frowns. "So, you're not interested? In your old job, I mean."

Jane laughs, but there's not much humour in the sound. "No, Dan," she says slowly, as if explaining it to a backward child. "I'm not."

"Well, that's a relief," says Dan. "Although I'm a little surprised to hear it."

It's at this point that I realize what Dan's doing. Trying to provoke a reaction. And if I can see this, then Sam must do too, and so, surely, does Jane. And it's funny, because even though Jane probably knows she shouldn't, she can't help but ask.

"Why?"

"Because I thought you'd already applied for it," says Dan. "And been turned down."

There's a pause — and it's a pause that's even more pregnant than Wendy, before Jane swivels round to face me. "What have you been telling people?"

As all eyes focus on me, I'm conscious that I haven't said a word since Jane's arrival. Even now, and even though she might deserve it, I don't want to hurt her, and certainly not in front of everybody. And it's not misplaced loyalty, but just that I can't actually come up with anything to say that will show her in a good light. And the funny thing is, I think that I'd have to go a long way back in our relationship — years before we split up, possibly — to find anything good to say at all.

"The truth, Jane," I say, my words puncturing the awkward silence. "Unlike you."

Jane stares at me, the accusation of betrayal clear from her expression, and yet for once I don't feel the slightest bit guilty. After all, if there is anyone here who's been betrayed, it's certainly not her.

"You're pathetic, Edward," she says, suddenly getting to her feet. "A pathetic loser. I don't know what I ever saw in you."

I try to think quickly of something to say to defend myself, but how on earth does anyone respond to a comment like that? Fortunately, what happens next means that I don't have to.

"Jane," says Sam, evenly but firmly. "I think it might be time for you to leave."

As she gets up out of her chair, Jane whirls round to face her. She's at least six inches taller than Sam — ten if you include the hair — but Sam doesn't flinch in the slightest.

"Don't you tell me what to do," spits Jane.

"Okay. But just tell me something," says Sam calmly. "What?"

"If Edward's such a loser, why are you so angry that he doesn't want you back?"

It's a good line, and it obviously isn't lost on Jane. She opens her mouth as if to say something, closes it again, and then starts to turn a deep red colour. It's a colour I've seen before — many times — and, aware of what's probably going to happen next, I move to step in between the two women. But before I can stop her, Jane picks up her wine glass from the table and aims the contents at Sam, who ducks just in time. Dan, unfortunately, doesn't.

As the three of us stand there in stunned silence, Jane pushes her chair back angrily and storms out. "Great," says Dan, fishing in his pocket and taking out a tissue, before dabbing at the white wine stains on his shirt. "I've spent the last few weeks having all manner of drinks thrown over me by my ex-girlfriends, and now yours are getting in on the act."

"Look on the bright side," I tell him, having finally worked out why he's always got a packet of Kleenex on him nowadays, and pleased that it's not for the reason I'd previously suspected. "At least I've only got the one."

"Thanks to me," he says. "You should have given her a slap."

"Dan! How can you say such a thing? I could never hit a girl."

Sam stares at the still-swinging front doors, wiping her arm where she's been splashed with Chardonnay. "But I could," she says, heading purposefully outside.

Dan and I watch her go, then look at each other for approximately a nanosecond before sprinting after her, knocking our stools over in the process.

"What's going on?" puffs Wendy, who's hot on our heels, even though she's left the bar unattended.

"Fight!" says Dan excitedly, nodding towards where Sam and Jane seem to be sizing each other up on the pavement outside the pub.

Wendy rubs her stomach anxiously. "Shouldn't you go and split them up?"

"Don't you dare!" orders Dan, grabbing my arm as I attempt to walk over and stop them. "My money's on Sam."

"Baby," says Wendy.

"Cut me some slack," he says. "It's not every day you get to see this. Apart from on the Internet, I mean."

"No," gasps Wendy, loudly enough for Sam and Jane to stop what they're doing. "Baby!"

As Dan and I stand there helplessly, Wendy leans heavily against his car, breathing noisily. "Quick," says Sam, rushing over and taking her by the hand. "Her waters have broken. We need to get her to hospital. And fast," she adds, eyeing the Porsche.

"Not in my car," wails Dan, a look of horror on his face at the thought of his pristine leather upholstery. "Please."

CHAPTER
TWENTY-THREE

I'm back at home, having taken Dan to get the Porsche valet-cleaned after his mercy rush to the hospital. Wendy's now the proud mother of a bouncing baby boy, whom she's said she's going to call Daniel, although I suspect that was the drugs talking, as on the way there, although grateful for Dan's breakneck driving, she'd rejected his suggestion that she call it Portia if it was a girl. As I'm wondering whether I'll be happy to say goodbye to this place, I hear a fumbling outside my front door.

I walk over and open it, expecting to find Mrs Barraclough doing her occasional trick of forgetting she's on the wrong floor and trying to unlock my door by mistake, but instead I see a face that a while ago I wasn't expecting ever to see again. In her left hand she's holding up a key ring, which she's regarding with suspicion.

We stare at each other awkwardly for what must be only a few seconds, but it seems like hours before Jane smiles at me and breaks the silence by jangling her set of keys. "Just thought I'd see if they still worked. The front door was fine, but I couldn't seem to get in here."

I know I should be angry that she still feels she can walk back in here again, but I just take a deep breath. It's been a long few days, and I don't want things to end on a bad note between us. Especially since the scene in the Admiral Jim. And, anyway, perhaps she's here to apologize for that. And if that's the case, maybe I should go first.

"Jane, I've changed . . ."

She reaches out and puts a finger on my lips. "I know. I can see that."

I pull away from her. "No, you don't understand. The locks. I've changed the locks. On the flat. After you left."

"Oh." Her face falls. "Right."

"Listen," I say, mindful of what Dan's been going through over the past few weeks. Even though I may not be on it, Slate YourDate has had me thinking too. "I wanted to say sorry."

"For changing the locks?"

"No, for . . ." I fold my arms to keep my hands from shaking as I try to remember the speech I've been rehearsing. "For the last few years. For letting myself go. For making it seem like I'd stopped caring about myself, for not caring about you, and more important for not caring about us. And for not realizing what that meant."

I pause for breath, thinking to myself that now would be a good time for Jane to apologize back — for leaving me in the lurch, for the manner of her departure, for what happened between her and that guy at her work, for sending the flowers, and even for trying to split Sam and me up. But perhaps not surprisingly, given what I've come to understand about her over the last few weeks, she doesn't.

"So, why did you change the locks?"

It's an innocent enough question. But the assumption behind it, the fact that she feels she can just march right back into my life the same way she just marched right out of it, and that I'd be here waiting, makes me angry, and I suddenly realize that I, to use Dan's phrase, have the power.

"Why do you think?"

Jane doesn't reply, even though I can tell that she's starting to work out what the answer might be.

"But I don't understand." She looks me up and down. "You did all this for me. After what I wrote." It's a statement, not a question. But it deserves an answer, nonetheless.

"Maybe at the beginning. But now it turns out I did it for me."

There's an even more awkward silence before she smiles again, but it's a much less confident smile this time. "I can't believe I lost."

For a moment, I think I can't have heard her right. Surely the word "you" should have been tagged on to the end of that sentence? And that one glaring omission makes any lingering compassion I might have had for her evaporate almost instantly.

"Jane, it was never a competition."

"Pardon?"

"You and Sam. It was never a competition. And if it was, you wouldn't even make the starting line-up." I swallow hard. Even after all this time, I still find it hard to argue with her. And yet, in a strange way, it feels good.

"What are you talking about?"

"You and me. We've had our time."

"Well," she says matter-of-factly, "you can't blame me for trying."

This stuns me a little. Is that it? All of her interference, all of the emotional turmoil she's put me — and Sam — through in her quest to get me back, and she simply dismisses it as if it was some exercise to see if she could. And, in actual fact, I do blame her for trying. She knew I was happy with Sam, and yet she couldn't help but put her happiness above mine. Again.

For the first time in a long, long while, I know exactly what to say to her.

"Goodbye, Jane."

"What?" She looks a little shocked. "Aren't you even going to invite me in?"

"For old times' sake?"

"Well . . . yes."

"I don't think I am, no."

Jane's face falls, and she tries to peer over my shoulder into the flat.

"Why not? Is this a bad time?"

I think about everything that's happened over the last few days, and in particular the recent developments with Sam. "Quite the opposite, actually."

"Is Sam here?" Jane asks nervously.

"No."

"Well then, why not?" she pleads.

"Because . . ." I don't even have to think about my answer, although I hesitate for a moment, wondering whether it'll come across as too harsh. And whether Jane will work out the obvious double meaning.

"Because what?"

"Because there's nothing of yours in here any more."

And the funny thing is, despite how hard it was coming to terms with how Jane left me, how tough the training seemed, and how difficult the dieting, not drinking, and giving up smoking were in order to try to win her back, shutting the door on Jane is surprisingly easy. And I know what the real reason for that is. Or rather, who it is.

That's how I achieve closure — quite literally, it seems. And although I don't feel particularly good about it, I don't feel especially bad about it either. And when I think about Dan's "when you don't give a shit" theory, I realize it's not a hundred per cent true. Because where Jane's concerned, I'll always give a shit — that's just the way I'm programmed. But I won't lose sleep over not knowing either. And surely that's what it's all about.

I wait until I hear the front door slam and I'm sure she's gone, then walk back through to the lounge, collapsing on the couch until my heart rate returns to normal, and I'm congratulating myself on my strength of will, while still feeling a little guilty, when there's a knock on the door. For a moment, I can't quite decide what to do. It's obviously Jane again, come back to try to talk me round, convince me of the error of my ways, or maybe just punch me in the face — and I'm contemplating not even answering it when there's the sound of a key in the lock. The door opens slowly, and I hear Sam's voice.

"Edward? Are you in there?"

With a sense of relief, I get up and walk into the hallway, where she looks at me quizzically, before leaning in and kissing me hello.

I inhale the cloud of perfume that's wafted in with her. "You smell nice."

Sam blushes with pleasure at the fact I've commented. "Thanks, it's . . ."

"Issey Miyake. I know."

"I saw Jane leaving. She didn't look too happy."

"I didn't let her in," I say, a little too quickly. "I mean, she wanted to come in, but I said no. I didn't think it would be a good idea. Not that anything would have happened, of course. I just thought that, well, it took her ten years to leave last time. And I didn't even want to give her ten minutes."

Sam lets me finish, then stands up on tiptoe to kiss me. "Don't think too badly about Jane," she says. "She just tried to do what she could to get you back. You did the same, after all."

"Yes, but I started going to the gym. I didn't try to sabotage her relationship."

"Take it as a compliment." Sam smiles. "There's not many of you blokes out there worth fighting for," she adds, stopping short of mentioning Dan by name. "Just promise me one thing, Edward."

"Anything," I say. And I mean it.

"You and her. It's over?"

"Sam, it was over the minute you walked — well, jogged — into my life. I just didn't know it at the time."

"So . . ."

"So?"

Sam takes both my hands. "Where do we go from here?"

"Well," I say, taking a long, lingering look around my front room. "I could do with a hand packing."

CHAPTER
TWENTY-FOUR

"I thought you were good. Great, in fact. We both did."

"Yeah?" As we stroll along the pavement, Dan can't keep the grin off his face. His first episode of *Close Encounters* was on yesterday, and there is no doubt about it, Dan was born to play the Wayne Kerr role.

"I'm sorry we didn't manage to get all your SlateYourDate stuff done in time."

Dan shrugs. "Doesn't seem to matter now."

"Why not?"

"Well, put it this way. Since the show went out yesterday afternoon, the offers have been flooding in, if you know what I mean?"

"Really?"

He nods. "That's the thing about dry spells. They're usually followed by a deluge. But the past few weeks have really got me thinking, you know? So I'm going to take my time. Be a bit more, well, choosey."

"You're kidding?"

Dan looks at me as if I'm stupid. "Of course I'm kidding, Edward. I haven't had sex in nearly two months."

"Which is why you're out for a drink with me this evening, rather than any of them." I can't keep the smile off my face. "And Polly?"

Dan met up with her for lunch today. And didn't get anything thrown over him, which I suppose was a result.

"Has a new boyfriend, so she tells me. And I'm not going to do anything to jeopardize that. After all, I want her to be happy. And who knows — we might even be friends one day?"

"And you're okay with that?"

Dan looks at me wistfully. "You win some, lose some. Serves me right, I suppose. But I'll get over it. I'm a big boy, after all."

I push him into the road. "That's not what Natasha tells me."

"Yes, well," says Dan. "Even a Jumbo Jet looks small if the hangar's that huge."

I shudder, then automatically turn the corner and head down the street towards the Admiral Jim, but after a few yards I notice that Dan's not with me. When I turn around, I see him walking along Western Road.

"Where are we going?" I say, hurrying over to catch him up.

"Keep up," says Dan. "There's something we need to do."

"We?" I say suspiciously. "Why is it always we? What's it got to do with me this time?"

"You'll see."

We walk silently through Hove until we reach the Coopers Arms. It's the kind of place that's managed to escape the recent modernization that's hit the rest of Brighton's pubs and bars, and by the look of the outside of the building, it missed a few before that as well.

"This must be the place," says Dan. "Keep your eyes peeled for a bloke with a small farmyard creature."

"What?"

"That's what she said. He's got a little goatee, apparently."

"Dan, that's a type of beard. Not an animal."

"It was a joke, Edward. I'm not completely stupid."

"No," I say. "You're not. And who's *she*? I thought you weren't doing any more of these SlateYourDate visits?"

"Polly," he says.

"Huh? But last time we looked, she hadn't written anything about you. On the site, I mean."

"She hasn't."

"So who are we looking for, exactly?"

"Polly's boyfriend. Steve. Who works here."

"Hold on," I say, putting a hand on Dan's arm. "What are you up to?"

"Well, I thought to myself, if you can't beat them" — Dan shrugs my hand off and cracks his knuckles — "beat them up."

"What?"

"Relax, Ed. I just want to talk to him."

"I thought you said you weren't going to interfere?"

"There's interfering," says Dan, "and there's helping. And I thought it was about time I started doing more of the second stuff. Particularly after it felt so good with you and Sam."

As we push the door open and head inside, I suddenly feel like I've walked into a scene from a bad sitcom. There's a couple of old men playing dominoes at a table in the corner, and a bored-looking barman leaning on the bar, flicking through a copy of the *Sun*. He's about our age, and wearing a Metallica T-shirt, and while the few tufts of hair sprouting from his chin could hardly be called a goatee, he still looks about forty years out of place.

"I guess that must be him," says Dan.

Seeing as he's the only other person in the place who's the right side of sixty, I'm not going to argue. "You're sure Polly's new boyfriend works *here*?"

"Yup. When he's not being a mature student, apparently."

"Well, that'll make a change."

"Huh?"

"Polly going out with someone who's mature."

As the door slams shut behind us, Steve looks up in surprise, as if anyone coming into the pub is a rare event. Judging by what looks like a thin layer of dust on the domino players in the corner, that might be true.

"What can I get you?" he says.

Dan stares at the old brass handpumps on the bar, and then looks nervously at the refrigerated shelf behind the bar, his eyes widening when he fails to spot any of his bottled lager.

"Have you got anything, er, fizzy?"

Steve searches down behind the bar, eventually surfacing with a bottle of what looks like Babycham. "Well . . . there's this," he says, peering at the sell-by date, which looks like it starts with the number "19". "Although I wouldn't want to risk it."

Dan makes a face. "Quite. Well, in that case, two bitters please," he says, pointing at the nearest of the brass pumps. "Halves."

As Steve fills two slightly dirty-looking half-pint glasses, Dan motions for me to pull up a stool, and I sit down next to him at the bar, automatically reaching for my wallet before he surprises me by waving my money away. "And one for yourself?" he asks.

Steve eyes the glasses of cloudy liquid he's just dispensed. "No. Thanks," he says, picking up his newspaper again.

Dan rolls his eyes at me, then turns his attention back to Steve. "Quiet night?"

He lowers his paper reluctantly, evidently irked that he might have to chat. "Pardon?"

"I said, 'quiet night?'" Dan peers into the gloomy pub interior. "When's the rush usually start?"

"You two are it."

"I'm Dan, by the way," says Dan, holding out a hand. Steve stares at it warily before giving it the briefest of shakes, then stuffs his hands in his pockets.

"Right."

Dan makes his 'this is hard work' face. "It's Steve, isn't it?"

"Er . . . That's right," says Steve suspiciously. "Do I know you?"

"No, not really. Though you might have seen me on . . . Ow."

"Sorry, mate," I say, as Dan rubs the spot on his shin where I've just kicked him. "My foot slipped off the stool. Steve, I'm Ed, by the way."

"We're friends of Polly," says Dan by way of an explanation.

"Polly? My Polly?"

To his credit, Dan doesn't wince at this. Instead, he takes a sip of his beer, then struggles manfully to swallow it. "That's right."

Steve scratches his head. "Really? She's never mentioned you. Either of you," he adds, turning his attention to me.

"Well, not friends, exactly," I explain.

"Acquaintances," adds Dan, sounding like someone from a 1960s East End gangster movie.

"So, how do you know her, exactly?" says Steve, backing away slightly from the bar.

"Ex-boyfriend," says Dan.

"What, both of you?"

"Nope," says Dan, laughing. "Just me, obviously."

I look across at him sharply but he just ignores me.

"What did you say your name was again?" says Steve.

"Dan. Dan Davis?"

"Dan Davis . . ." Steve thinks for a moment, then breaks into a grin. "I've got you. Wanker!"

"Well, it's pronounced 'Wayne Kerr', actually, but . . ." Dan suddenly stops talking and, as realization dawns, goes a rather scary shade of red.

"Yes, I remember now," says Steve, as I snort into my beer. "You're the guy from that stupid TV programme. 'Wanker Dan', she calls you. Broke her heart, apparently. She still can't watch any of that daytime antiques rubbish. Which is a blessing in disguise, I can tell you."

Dan's about to respond to that when we're interrupted by a gruff "The usual, Steve" from one of the domino-playing pensioners. *Which would be what? I wonder. Embalming fluid?*

"So, if it's not a personal question, what are you doing here?" asks Steve once he's refilled the old man's glass, and he's shuffled back to his game.

Dan manages to regain his composure. "We were just passing, so thought we'd stop in and have a drink. Nice place. Very . . . atmospheric."

"Yeah, right. It's a shithole. And I should know — I work here. Well, part-time."

"All right, Steve," says Dan. "I was just making conversation. I didn't want your life story. But I do want to talk to you about Polly."

Steve folds his arms defensively. "What about her?"

"Well, what are your, you know, intentions?"

"Who're you? Her father?"

"Steve," says Dan. "Don't take this the wrong way, but you're not very bright, are you? Polly's a great girl. I just want to make sure you're treating her OK. And that you know what you're doing."

I have to work hard to stop my jaw dropping open, and I'm obviously not the only one, as Steve stares at Dan incredulously. "If she's so great, why did you dump her then?"

"Well, if you must know . . ." Dan takes a deep breath. "She dumped me, actually."

"So you're here because you want her back?" says Steve nervously.

"God no," says Dan. "I mean, not that there's anything wrong with her. I just mean I'm not here for some pistols at dawn type thing. I'm here for you."

If Steve had started to visibly relax, he looks the opposite now. "How do you mean?" he says. "For me?"

"Well, you like her, don't you?"

"Of course I do."

"And she likes you?"

"I guess."

"So why is she thinking of dumping you then?"

Steve goes white and leans heavily against the bar. "She told you that?"

"Not in so many words, Stevie-boy. But talking to her, I'd say it's on the cards. Unless . . ."

"Unless?"

"Unless you pull your finger out and start treating her a bit better."

"Huh?" Steve walks around to our side of the bar, and I brace myself for the possibility of things turning nasty, but instead he just pulls up a stool and sits down. "How do you mean?"

As Dan starts explaining the finer points to him, I finish my drink, then glance at my watch, conscious that Sam will be home soon.

I get off my stool and tap him on the shoulder. "Do you still need me, Dan?"

He looks up from where he's drawing some sort of diagram on the back of a beer mat. "That's okay, mate. You get going. I'm all right on my own."

And as I walk back along the seafront towards Sam's — I mean *our* — flat, I realize that if Dan keeps on going like this, he probably won't be for much longer.

ISIS publish a wide range of books in large print, from fiction to biography. Any suggestions for books you would like to see in large print or audio are always welcome. Please send to the Editorial Department at:

ISIS Publishing Limited
7 Centremead
Osney Mead
Oxford OX2 0ES

A full list of titles is available free of charge from:

Ulverscroft Large Print Books Limited

(UK)
The Green
Bradgate Road, Anstey
Leicester LE7 7FU
Tel: (0116) 236 4325

(Australia)
P.O. Box 314
St Leonards
NSW 1590
Tel: (02) 9436 2622

(USA)
P.O. Box 1230
West Seneca
N.Y. 14224-1230
Tel: (716) 674 4270

(Canada)
P.O. Box 80038
Burlington
Ontario L7L 6B1
Tel: (905) 637 8734

(New Zealand)
P.O. Box 456
Feilding
Tel: (06) 323 6828

Details of ISIS complete and unabridged audio books are also available from these offices. Alternatively, contact your local library for details of their collection of ISIS large print and unabridged audio books.